LA PRESS 語研學院 Language Academy Press

秒懂老外
一句簡單英文就能通
GESTURE ENGLISH

U0079217

全書音檔QR碼

掃描後可點選各單元資料夾，直接點選音檔線上聆聽。

或是點選壓縮檔9786269724420.zip下載全書音檔。

iOS系統請升級至iOS13後再行下載，下載前請先安裝ZIP解壓縮程式或APP。

此為大型檔案，建議使用WiFi連線下載，以免占用流量，

並確認連線狀況，以利下載順暢。

Contents

8 使用説明

見面、道別

UNIT 1 ｜ 打招呼 10

12　情境 1　Waving Hand 揮手
13　情境 2　Greeting Hug 見面時的擁抱
14　情境 3　Loose Hug 鬆散的擁抱
15　情境 4　Shaking Hands 握手
16　情境 5　Kiss on the Cheeks
　　　　　　臉頰上親吻
17　情境 6　Welcome Kiss 歡迎的親吻
18　情境 7　Pinkie Wave 揮動小指
19　情境 8　Quick lowering of the head
　　　　　　one time 快速低頭一次
20　情境 9　Single upward nod
　　　　　　向上點頭一次
21　情境 10　Bumping a fist on top of
　　　　　　someone else fist
　　　　　　拳頭碰在別人的拳頭上方
22　情境 11　Hitting Chest With a
　　　　　　Clenched Fist 握拳打胸部

UNIT 2 ｜ 引導他人 23

24　情境 1　Outstretching Arm to a Door
　　　　　　將手臂伸向門
25　情境 2　Holding Hand on Lower
　　　　　　Back and Pushing Lightly
　　　　　　手放在下背部輕推
26　情境 3　Outstretching Hand with
　　　　　　Palm Facing up
　　　　　　伸出手，手掌朝上

UNIT 3 ｜ 道別 27

28　情境 1　Goodbye Hug 道別的擁抱

29　情境 2　Blowing a Kiss 飛吻
30　情境 3　Turning Shoulders Away
　　　　　　From Someone 轉開肩膀

情緒轉折

UNIT 4 ｜ 感到開心 31

33　情境 1　Bear Hug 熊抱
34　情境 2　Teammate Hug 隊友間的擁抱
35　情境 3　Big Smile 大笑
36　情境 4　Laughing Smile 帶著笑聲的微笑
37　情境 5　Showing Teeth in a Smile
　　　　　　露齒微笑
38　情境 6　Turned Up Lips 嘴角上揚
39　情境 7　Loud Voice 大聲
40　情境 8　Quickly Rubbing Palms
　　　　　　Together 快速摩擦手掌
41　情境 9　Bumping Fist with Someone
　　　　　　Else 與他人碰拳
42　情境 10　Excitedly Sweating 興奮地出汗
43　情境 11　Mouth Slightly Turned Up
　　　　　　嘴巴稍微上揚

UNIT 5 ｜ 感到放鬆 44

45　情境 1　Sitting with Legs Crossed at
　　　　　　Ankles 坐著、腳踝交叉
46　情境 2　Sitting with Legs Crossed at
　　　　　　Ankles 雙腿張開坐著
47　情境 3　Holding Palms Together
　　　　　　將手掌合十
48　情境 4　Closed Mouth 嘴巴閉著
49　情境 5　Leaning Shoulder Against
　　　　　　Wall 肩膀靠牆
50　情境 6　Putting Hands in Pants' Back
　　　　　　Pocket 把雙手放在後口袋

UNIT 6 感到自信 51

53	情境 1	Smug Smile 得意的微笑
54	情境 2	Arms Behind the Back 雙手背在後面
55	情境 3	Hands on Hips 手放屁股上
56	情境 4	Legs Apart While Standing 站著時雙腳大開
57	情境 5	Confident Voice 自信的語調
58	情境 6	Bearded Chin 有鬍子的下巴
59	情境 7	Hold Head Up High 昂著頭
60	情境 8	Flat Mouth 抿嘴
61	情境 9	Pushing Shoulder Back and Chest Out 肩膀後推、胸部挺出
62	情境 10	Body Standing Up Straight 身體站直

UNIT 7 嘲諷 63

64	情境 1	Half Smile 半個微笑
65	情境 2	Fake Smile 假笑
66	情境 3	Open Mouth Smile 咧嘴笑
67	情境 4	Sarcastic Voice 諷刺的語調

UNIT 8 感到害怕 68

69	情境 1	Hand on Chest 手放在胸口
70	情境 2	Scared Sweating 害怕的出汗
71	情境 3	Open Mouth and Breathing Fast 張開嘴喘氣
72	情境 4	Open Mouth and Gulping 倒抽一口氣
73	情境 5	Chewing Bottom Lips 咬著下唇
74	情境 6	Shaking Body 身體顫抖

UNIT 9 感到傷心 75

76	情境 1	Group Hug 群體擁抱
77	情境 2	Turned Down Lips 嘴角向下
78	情境 3	Mouth Slightly Turned Down 嘴角稍微向下

UNIT 10 感到緊張 79

81	情境 1	Sweaty, Clenched Fists 流汗、握緊的拳頭
82	情境 2	Wringing Hands 擰著手
83	情境 3	Fidgeting Body 身體坐立不安
84	情境 4	Sweating Nervously 緊張地出汗
85	情境 5	Biting Lips 咬嘴唇
86	情境 6	Grasping the Front of the Neck 握住脖子的前端
87	情境 7	Fidgeting Legs 坐立不安的腿
88	情境 8	Locked Ankles 腳踝扣一起
89	情境 9	Talking Fast 快速說話
90	情境 10	Flared Nostrils 撐開的鼻孔
91	情境 11	Raising shoulders and Lowering Head 提高肩膀、低頭
92	情境 12	Shaking Legs While Sitting 坐著的時候抖腿
93	情境 13	Red Ears 耳朵發紅
94	情境 14	Biting Fingernails 咬手指甲

UNIT 11 感到焦慮 95

97	情境 1	Furrowed Eyebrows 皺眉頭
98	情境 2	Rubbing the Back of the Neck 搓揉後頸
99	情境 3	Standing with Feet Together 雙腳併攏站立
100	情境 4	Running Tongue over Front Teeth 舌頭滑過前排牙齒
101	情境 5	Stressful Sweating 壓力大而出汗
102	情境 6	Rubbing Finger under Nose 手指在鼻子下摩擦
103	情境 7	Tense Body 身體緊繃
104	情境 8	Crossed Legs While Sitting 坐著時翹腳
105	情境 9	Rotating Head in Circle 頭部繞圈旋轉
106	情境 10	Itchy Palms 手掌發癢

107 情境 11 Circling Shoulders Forwards or Backwards 向前或向後繞肩

108 情境 12 Woman Leaning Back and Shaking Hair 女子往後靠、甩頭髮

109 情境 13 Massaging the Ears 按摩耳朵

UNIT 12 感到生氣 110

112 情境 1 Rolling Eyes 翻白眼

113 情境 2 Slamming Hands on the Table 雙手猛力拍桌

114 情境 3 Middle Finger 比中指

115 情境 4 Crossed Arms 手臂交叉

116 情境 5 Showing Teeth in a Snarl 秀出牙齒咆嘯

117 情境 6 Fisted Hands 雙手握拳

118 情境 7 Angry Voice 生氣的語調

119 情境 8 Body Too Closed to Somebody 身體太靠近他人

120 情境 9 Fisted Hand Hitting other Hand's Palm 握拳的手打另一隻手掌

121 情境 10 Shaking a Fist at Someone 對他人搖晃拳頭

122 情境 11 Grinding Back Teeth 緊咬後排牙齒

123 情境 12 Teeth Clenching 咬緊牙齒

UNIT 13 感到害羞 124

125 情境 1 Crossed Legs while Standing 站立時雙腿交叉

126 情境 2 Shy Smile 害羞的微笑

127 情境 3 Shy Voice 害羞的語調

UNIT 14 感到擔心 128

129 情境 1 Arm over Someone's Shoulder 手臂放在他人的肩膀上

130 情境 2 Touching Someone's Upper Arms 觸碰他人的上臂

131 情境 3 Putting a Hand on Someone's Upper Back 將手放在他人的上臂

UNIT 15 感到無聊、疲累 132

134 情境 1 Tilting Neck to One Side, and then the Otehr 脖子轉到一邊、再換另一邊

135 情境 2 Swinging Crossed Leg 擺動翹著的腿

136 情境 3 Leaning Cheek on Fist 臉頰靠在拳頭上

137 情境 4 Covered Mouth 遮住嘴巴

138 情境 5 Holding Shoulders Low 肩膀低垂

139 情境 6 Body Slouching on Chair 無精打采的坐在椅子上

140 情境 7 Crossing Your Leg and Shaking Foot Back and Forth 翹腳、腳前後搖晃

141 情境 8 Tugging on the Ears 拉耳朵

142 情境 9 Tapping Teeth with Fingernailes or Penciel, etc. 用手指甲或鉛筆等敲牙齒

UNIT 16 感到噁心 143

144 情境 1 Shaking Hands away from the Body 把手甩離身體

145 情境 2 Pulling the Chin in towards the Neck 下巴縮到脖子內

146 情境 3 Wrinkled Nose 皺鼻子

147 情境 4 Pinching Nose Closed 捏緊鼻子

和他人起衝突

UNIT 17 開玩笑或沒禮貌 148

149 情境 1 Wink 眨眼睛

150 情境 2　Sticking out the Toungue
吐出舌頭

151 情境 3　Pointing the Chin at Someone 用下巴指向某人

152 情境 4　Pulling Pants down and Showing Someone Your Naked Butt
拉下褲子，露出屁股

UNIT 18　警告他人 153

154 情境 1　Index Finger Pointing
用食指指著某人、某物

155 情境 2　Moving Index Finger Horizontally across Neck
食指水平滑過脖子

156 情境 3　Backside of Body Turned to Someone 身體背部面向他人

UNIT 19　表示抱歉和無辜 157

158 情境 1　Apologetic Hug 道歉的擁抱

159 情境 2　Both Arms up 雙臂舉高

160 情境 3　Both Hands up with Palms Facing out 抬起雙手、手掌向外

UNIT 20　不知道該怎麼做 161

162 情境 1　Throwing Hands in the Air
把手甩上空中

163 情境 2　Scratching Side of Neck with one Finger 用一根手指抓脖子

164 情境 3　Tucking Neck into Shoulders
把脖子縮進肩膀

165 情境 4　Tongue in Front of Teeth
舌頭放在牙齒前面

166 情境 5　Pressing Tongue againgst Cheek 把舌頭抵在臉頰上

167 情境 6　Nodding with Tilted Head
側著頭點頭

專注在某件事

UNIT 21　思考某件事 168

170 情境 1　Closed Eyes 閉上雙眼

171 情境 2　Upward Glance 眼睛向上瞥

172 情境 3　Furrowed Eyebrows 皺眉頭

173 情境 4　Tilting Head to Side
頭部傾向一側

174 情境 5　Index Finger Touching Chin
食指撫摸下巴

175 情境 6　Touching Side of the Mouth
觸摸嘴角

176 情境 7　Squeezing Bridge of Nose
捏鼻樑

177 情境 8　Slowly Nodding While Rubbing Chin
邊慢慢點頭，邊摸下巴

178 情境 9　Pulling on Earlobe and Shaking Head to the Side
拉耳垂、頭轉向一側

179 情境 10　Leaning Forehead against Fist 額頭靠在拳頭上

180 情境 11　Tapping Teeth together
牙齒碰在一起

UNIT 22　要他人安靜 181

182 情境 1　Putting Index Finger to Lips
食指放在嘴唇上

183 情境 2　Outstretching Arm with Palm Facing Someone
伸出手臂、手掌面向別人

184 情境 3　Plugging the Ears with Fingertips 用手指塞住耳朵

UNIT 23　同意某件事情 185

186 情境 1　Applauding Hands 鼓掌

187 情境 2　Thumbs Up 豎起大拇指

188 情境 3　Index Finger and Thumb Touching OK 手勢

189 情境 4 Nodding Head Up and Down 上下點頭

190 情境 5 Single Downwards Nod 單次向下點頭

191 情境 6 Nodding Quickly and Pointing at Someone 快速點頭、手指著他人

UNIT 24 不同意某件事 192

193 情境 1 Pursed Lips 噘嘴

194 情境 2 Flattened Lips 癟嘴

195 情境 3 Twitching Lips 嘴唇抽動

196 情境 4 Shaking Head Side to Side 左右搖頭

197 情境 5 Twisting Neck 轉脖子

198 情境 6 Rubbing Finger Alongside of Nose 手指摩擦鼻翼

UNIT 25 不知道別人在說甚麼 199

200 情境 1 Slowly Nodding Up and Down 慢慢上下點頭

201 情境 2 Shaking Head Side to Side Followed by Fast Nod 慢慢搖頭再快速點頭

202 情境 3 Shaking Shoulders 抖動肩膀

203 情境 4 Turning Ear towards Speaker 耳朵朝向說話者

204 情境 5 Turning Head Slightly to the Side 頭稍微轉到一邊

UNIT 26 引起注意 205

206 情境 1 Slowly Flexing and Extending Index Finger 慢慢伸縮食指

207 情境 2 Parted Lips 嘴唇微張

208 情境 3 Raising and Waving Arms 手臂舉高揮舞

209 情境 4 Jutting the Chin out 伸出下巴

210 情境 5 Body Facing Someone 身體面向他人

UNIT 27 在某些場合不自在 211

212 情境 1 Forced Smile 硬擠出的微笑

213 情境 2 Curving Shoulders Forward 肩膀向前彎曲

214 情境 3 Burning Ears 耳朵發燙

215 情境 4 Slowly Rubbing Palms Together 慢慢搓揉手掌

UNIT 28 說謊 216

217 情境 1 Downward Glance 向下瞥

218 情境 2 Biting the Tongue 咬住舌頭

219 情境 3 Rubbing End of Nose Back and Forth 來回摩擦鼻子後端

220 情境 4 Pulling Earlobe Downward 把耳垂往下拉

和朋友、家人相處

UNIT 29 關愛他人 221

222 情境 1 Soft Voice 輕柔的語調

223 情境 2 Eskimo Kiss 愛斯基摩式親吻

224 情境 3 Holding Someone's Hand 握住他人的手

225 情境 4 Wrapping Arm around Someone's Waist 手臂環在他人的腰上

226 情境 5 Patting Someone's Upper Back 輕拍他人的上背

UNIT 30 安慰他人 227

228 情境 1 Consolation Hug 安慰的擁抱

229 情境 2 Outstretched Arms 張開的雙臂

230　情境 3　Patting a Butt 輕拍屁股

和愛人在一起

UNIT
31　調情、約會 231

233　情境 1　Wide Eyes 睜大眼睛
234　情境 2　Puckered Lips 噘嘴
235　情境 3　Tongue between Lips Smile
　　　　　　舌頭在牙齒間的微笑
236　情境 4　Flirtatious Smile 調情的微笑
237　情境 5　Woman Playing with an
　　　　　　Earring 女子擺弄耳環
238　情境 6　Kissing on the Lips 接吻
239　情境 7　Kissing on Top of the Hand
　　　　　　親吻在手背上
240　情境 8　French Kiss
　　　　　　法式深吻（舌吻）
241　情境 9　Butterfly Kiss 蝴蝶之吻
242　情境 10　Touching someone's Cheek
　　　　　　觸摸他人的臉頰
243　情境 11　Leaning Body towards
　　　　　　Someone 身體靠向他人

UNIT
32　對他人有性趣 244

245　情境 1　Suggestive Smile
　　　　　　挑逗的微笑
246　情境 2　Tongue Licking Lips
　　　　　　舌頭舔嘴唇
247　情境 3　Shaking Butt Back and
　　　　　　Forth 屁股往前、後扭動
248　情境 4　Pushing Butt towards
　　　　　　Someone 屁股推向他人
249　情境 5　Slapping a Butt 打屁股
250　情境 6　Pinching a Butt 捏屁股

身體

UNIT
33　身體不太舒服 251

252　情境 1　Watering Eyes 眼睛濕潤
253　情境 2　Cupping Neck with two
　　　　　　Hands 雙手握住脖子
254　情境 3　Hand Touching someone's
　　　　　　Forehead 手觸摸他人的額頭
255　情境 4　Fever Sweating 發燒出汗
256　情境 5　Rubbing Knee or Ankle
　　　　　　揉膝蓋或腳踝
257　情境 6　Ringing Ears 耳鳴

UNIT
34　身體感覺熱或冷 258

259　情境 1　Excessive Heat Sweating
　　　　　　太熱而流汗
260　情境 2　Sweating from Movement
　　　　　　在運動中流汗
261　情境 3　Runny Nose 流鼻涕（水）
262　情境 4　Shoulders Pushed up and
　　　　　　Arms Closed
　　　　　　肩膀上推、雙臂交叉
263　情境 5　Shivering Body 身體顫抖
264　情境 6　Chattering Teeth 牙齒顫抖

UNIT
35　其他手勢 / 肢體 265

266　情境 1　Congratulatory Hug
　　　　　　祝賀的擁抱
267　情境 2　High Five Hands 擊掌
268　情境 3　Raised Eyebrows 眉毛上揚
269　情境 4　Index and Middle Fingers
　　　　　　Crossed 食指和中指交叉
270　情境 5　Kissing Fingertips 親吻手指頭
271　情境 6　Pointing Nose in the Air and
　　　　　　Sniffing
　　　　　　鼻子指向空氣、聞一下

☞ **分析英語母語人士在各種情境下的肢體動作！**

從 27 種身體部位分析出各個情境需要用到的手勢、肢體動作，並分類成 35 個情境單元，包括各種情緒表達，與認識的人見面、道別，和朋友互動的情況，到與情人曖昧、約會，甚至發展親密關係的情境。讓學習者能依照情境找出相對應的圖片、肢體動作的英語，並且看了圖片就可以了解怎麼比出這個肢體動作，並認識這些動作用英語該怎麼說。

手勢、肢體動作詳細解說

詳細說明每個手勢、肢體語言背後所代表的意義，這些說明包含了各個動作細節分析，以及背後所代表的意義，讓學習者在與外國人交流時更了解他們心裡的想法。

和外國人對話時會用到的英文對答

在每個情境下，都會有可能會用到的手勢、肢體動作、英語對話。透過閱讀這些對答例句，學習者可以看到在這些情境中外國人可能說的話是什麼，以及可以怎麼回答這些句子。

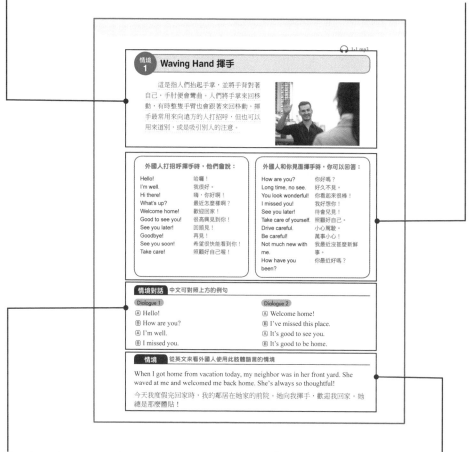

情境 1 **Waving Hand 揮手**

這是指人們抬起手掌，並將手背對著自己，手肘便會彎曲。人們將手掌來回移動，有時整隻手臂也會跟著來回移動。揮手最常用來向遠方的人打招呼，但也可以用來道別，或是吸引別人的注意。

外國人打招呼揮手時，他們會說：

Hello!	哈囉！
I'm well.	我很好。
Hi there!	嗨，你好啊！
What's up?	最近怎麼樣啊？
Welcome home!	歡迎回家！
Good to see you!	很高興見到你！
See you later!	回頭見！
Goodbye!	再見！
See you soon!	希望很快能看到你！
Take care!	照顧好自己喔！

外國人和你見面揮手時，你可以回答：

How are you?	你好嗎？
Long time, no see.	好久不見。
You look wonderful!	你看起來很棒！
I missed you!	我好想你！
See you later!	待會兒見！
Take care of yourself.	照顧好自己。
Drive careful.	小心駕駛。
Be careful!	萬事小心！
Not much new with me.	我最近沒甚麼新鮮事。
How have you been?	你最近好嗎？

情境對話 中文可對照上方的例句

Dialogue 1
Ⓐ Hello!
Ⓑ How are you?
Ⓐ I'm well.
Ⓑ I missed you.

Dialogue 2
Ⓐ Welcome home!
Ⓑ I've missed this place.
Ⓐ It's good to see you.
Ⓑ It's good to be home.

情境 從英文來看外國人使用此肢體語言的情境

When I got home from vacation today, my neighbor was in her front yard. She waved at me and welcomed me back home. She's always so thoughtful!

今天我度假完回家時，我的鄰居在她家的前院。她向我揮手，歡迎我回家。她總是那麼體貼！

實際情境下運用情境對話

看了這麼多例句，一定會想知道這些對答是如何運用的。本書還提供情境對話，讓學習者看完這些對答例句之後，能夠了解到真實情境會如何運用這些對答例句。

深入情境，體驗真實互動

提供真實的情境，讓學習者從英文來看外國人使用這些手勢、肢體動作的情形，往後遇到這些情況，就能夠大方、自然地與外國人互動了！

UNIT 1

Greeting 打招呼

☞ **打招呼時需要用到的動作，用英文要怎麼說呢？**

打招呼式見面時和認識的人所進行的交流，下列是打招呼會用到的手勢與肢體語言，請看圖片，並對照動作的英文和中文。

情境 1

Waving hands 揮手

情境 2

Greeting hug 見面時的擁抱

情境 3

Loose hug 鬆散的擁抱

情境 4

Shaking hands 握手

情境 5

kissing on the cheeks 臉頰上親吻

情境 6

Welcome kiss 歡迎的親吻

情境 **7**

Pinkie wave 揮小指頭

情境 **8**

Quickly lowering the
head once 快速低頭一次

情境 **9**

Single upward nod
向上點頭一次

情境 **10**

Bumping a fist on top of someone
else fist 拳頭碰在別人的拳頭上方

情境 **11**

Hitting chest with a clenched fist
握拳打胸部

情境 1 Waving Hand 揮手

這是指人們抬起手掌，並將手背對著自己，手肘便會彎曲。人們將手掌來回移動，有時整隻手臂也會跟著來回移動。揮手最常用來向遠方的人打招呼，但也可以用來道別，或是吸引別人的注意。

外國人打招呼揮手時，他們會說：

Hello!	哈囉！
I'm well.	我很好。
Hi there!	嗨，你好啊！
What's up?	最近怎麼樣啊？
Welcome home!	歡迎回家！
Good to see you!	很高興見到你！
See you later!	回頭見！
Goodbye!	再見！
See you soon!	希望很快能看到你！
Take care!	照顧好自己喔！

外國人和你見面揮手時，你可以回答：

How are you?	你好嗎？
Long time, no see.	好久不見。
You look wonderful!	你看起來很棒！
I missed you!	我好想你！
See you later!	待會兒見！
Take care of yourself.	照顧好自己。
Drive careful.	小心駕駛。
Be careful!	萬事小心！
Not much new with me.	我最近沒甚麼新鮮事。
How have you been?	你最近好嗎？

情境對話　中文可對照上方的例句

Dialogue 1

Ⓐ Hello!

Ⓑ How are you?

Ⓐ I'm well.

Ⓑ I missed you.

Dialogue 2

Ⓐ Welcome home!

Ⓑ I've missed this place.

Ⓐ It's good to see you.

Ⓑ It's good to be home.

情境　從英文來看外國人使用此肢體語言的情境

When I got home from vacation today, my neighbor was in her front yard. She waved at me and welcomed me back home. She's always so thoughtful!

今天我度假完回家時，我的鄰居在她家的前院。她向我揮手，歡迎我回家。她總是那麼體貼！

情境 2 Greeting Hug 見面時的擁抱

指兩位彼此熟識的人在見面時的擁抱，例如親密的朋友或家人之間。由其中一人或雙方開心地張開手臂招呼對方，並做出擁抱的邀請。接著，彼此以手臂圍繞對方，並微微收緊手臂。高度大約在上背部，偶爾伴隨在背上的輕拍或摩擦。

外國人打招呼擁抱時，他們會說：

How you been?	這段時間過得如何？
Long time, no see.	真的好久不見。
It's great to see you.	真高興見到你。
Hey, what's up?	嘿～過得好嗎？
You look great!	你看起來過得不錯！
Hi gorgeous!	嗨，美女／帥哥！
Where have you been?	你到哪兒去了？
You're a sight for sore eyes.	看到你真是太棒了。
I'm so glad you came.	我很高興你來了。
I'm so pleased to see you.	我很開心見到你。

外國人和你見面擁抱時，你可以回答：

I'm good!	我很好啊！
It's been too long.	真是好久不見。
I'm happy to see you, too.	見到你我也很開心。
Not much! What's up with you?	還不錯，你呢？
I've been around.	我就在這附近。
What's new with you?	你最近有新鮮事嗎？
I've been so busy lately.	我最近一直都忙。
You look wonderful!	你看起來很棒！
I'm happy I could make it.	我也很高興我能來。
I've missed you!	我好想你！

情境對話　中文可對照上方的例句

Dialogue 1

Ⓐ Hey there!
Ⓑ How you been?
Ⓐ I'm good.
Ⓑ I'm so glad you came.

Dialogue 2

Ⓐ It's great to see you.
Ⓑ I'm happy to see you, too.
Ⓐ Where have you been?
Ⓑ I've been around.

情境　從英文來看外國人使用此肢體語言的情境

My best friend lives in California. I went to visit him last year. When I got off the plane and saw him, he gave me a big hug and told me he had missed me.

我最好的朋友住在加州。去年我去那裡看他，當我下飛機看到他時，他就給了我一個大大的擁抱，並告訴我他很想我。

情境 3 Loose Hug 鬆散的擁抱

由不太願意擁抱的人,在不得不擁抱的情況下,所做出很勉強的擁抱。擁抱的人不會收緊手臂,而是將手臂鬆散地環繞在對方的肩膀上,輕而簡短地用手掌拍打對方的肩膀或後背,然後迅速後退。

外國人打招呼擁抱時,他們會說:

Good to see you.	見到你很高興。
It's been awhile.	有段時間沒見了。
Hey, there...	嘿,你好……
What was your name again?	再說一次你的名字好嗎?
When was the last time we saw each other?	我們上次見面是在甚麼時候?
Where do you live now?	你現在住在哪裡?
Now I remember where we met.	我現在想起我們在哪裡見過了。
How's your family?	你的家人好嗎?
Long time, no see.	好久不見。
How many years has it been?	有多少年沒見了?

外國人和你見面擁抱時,你可以回答:

Nice to see you, too.	我也很高興見到你。
I'm happy to see you.	很高興見到你。
I'm sorry, what's your name?	抱歉,你的名字是?
They're doing well.	他們都好。
I'm doing well.	我很好。
I haven't seen you in forever.	我超久沒見到你了。
It's been too long.	實在太久了。
I moved a few years ago.	我前幾年搬了家。
I'm working downtown now.	我現在在市中心工作。
I'm glad you could make it.	我很高興你趕來了。

情境對話 中文可對照上方的例句

Dialogue 1

Ⓐ Hey, there....
Ⓑ I'm happy to see you.
Ⓐ When was the last time we saw each other?
Ⓑ It's been too long.

Dialogue 2

Ⓐ Long time, no see.
Ⓑ I'm glad you could make it.
Ⓐ How's your family?
Ⓑ They're doing well.

情境 從英文來看外國人使用此肢體語言的情境

I ran into my ex-boyfriend at a party last night. We gave each other a quick hug and made small talk for a few minutes. It was so awkward!

我在昨晚的派對上遇到我的前男友。我們互相快速地擁抱了一下,小聊了幾分鐘,那實在太尷尬了!

情境 4 Shaking Hands 握手

指兩人握住彼此的右手，而雙手的手掌互相接觸，通常會加上手部的上下運動。人們在初次見面彼此介紹時、問候認識的人時、或敲定某些協議時會握手，而達成協議時的握手近似於承諾。

外國人打招呼握手時，他們會說：

Nice to meet you!	很高興見到你！
Welcome!	歡迎！
Congratulations!	恭喜你！
How are you?	你好嗎？
What's up?	你過得好嗎？
Hello!	哈囉！
Good to see you!	見到你真好！
It's a deal!	那就這麼說定了！
Thanks for coming.	感謝你的到來。
I'll see you later!	一會兒見！

外國人和你見面握手時，你可以回答：

Nice to meet you, too.	我也很高興認識你。
Good to meet you.	見到你真好。
I'm happy to finally meet you.	很高興終於見到你了。
Thank you!	謝謝！
Thanks for having me.	謝謝你們邀請我來。
I'm doing well.	我很好。
How have you been?	你最近好嗎？
Take care!	保重！
See ya!	再見！
I wouldn't miss it!	我不會錯過的！

情境對話 中文可對照上方的例句

Dialogue 1

Ⓐ Welcome!
Ⓑ Thank you!
Ⓐ I'm glad you came.
Ⓑ I wouldn't miss it!

Dialogue 2

Ⓐ Thanks for coming.
Ⓑ Take care!
Ⓐ I'll see you later.
Ⓑ See ya!

情境 從英文來看外國人使用此肢體語言的情境

I met my new boss today. His name is Michael and he seems really nice. After we were introduced and shook hands, he talked with me about my job and what I do for the company. I think we'll get along well.

今天我見到了我的新老闆。他叫 Michael，人似乎很親切。在我們互相介紹並握手後，他跟我說到我的工作，以及我為公司所做的事。我覺得我們會相處得不錯。

情境 5　Kiss on the Cheeks 臉頰上親吻

指一個人用嘴唇在另一個人的臉頰上快速地親吻。通常會伴隨一隻手放在對方手臂上，或是在擁抱過程中發生。在某些情況下，臉頰上的吻是打招呼或說再見的方式，而這也可能是愛意的表現。

外國人在臉頰親吻時，他們會說：

Hello!	你好！
How are you?	你好嗎？
It's good to see you!	很高興可以見面！
I missed you!	我很想念你！
How have you been?	你近來怎麼樣？
I'm glad you came to visit.	我很高興你來拜訪。
I'm happy you're here.	我很高興你在這裡。
Goodbye!	再見！
Take care!	保重！
See you soon!	下次再見！

外國人和你臉頰親吻時，你可以回答：

Hey there!	嘿，你好！
Nice to see you!	很高興看到你！
You look great.	你看起來很棒。
I can't believe it!	我真不敢相信！
I'm great!	我很好！
How have you been?	你最近好嗎？
Me too!	我也是！
What's new?	有甚麼新鮮事？
What's up?	你過得好嗎？
See you later!	待會兒見！

情境對話　中文可對照上方的例句

Dialogue 1

Ⓐ Hello!

Ⓑ Hey there!

Ⓐ It's good to see you!

Ⓑ You look great.

Dialogue 2

Ⓐ I'm glad you came to visit.

Ⓑ Me too!

Ⓐ Take care!

Ⓑ See you later!

情境　從英文來看外國人使用此肢體語言的情境

I had some family over for a cookout last night. My aunt and uncle came. I was so happy to see them! I gave them both a big kiss on the cheek when I saw them.

我邀請了一些家人昨晚來我家野炊。我的阿姨和叔叔都來了，我好高興看到他們！見到他們的時候，我在他們兩人的臉頰上留下大大的吻。

情境 6 Welcome Kiss 歡迎的親吻

兩人在嘴唇上快速地親吻。這種親吻是一種快速地向所愛的人問好的方式，可以發生於孩子與父母之間、對彼此有重要意義的人、或是好友之間。

外國人做歡迎的親吻時，他們會說：

Hello!	你好！
Welcome!	歡迎！
Come in!	進來吧！
I'm glad you're here!	我很高興你在這裡！
You made it!	你趕來了！
Welcome home!	歡迎回家！
How are you?	你好嗎？
It's good to see you!	很高興見到你！
I've missed you!	我很想你！
What's up?	怎麼啦？

外國人和你歡迎親吻時，你可以回答：

Hi there!	嗨，你好！
Good to see you.	見到你很高興。
I'm glad you're home.	很高興你回到家。
How was your day?	你今天過得怎麼樣？
Did you have a good day?	你今天過得愉快嗎？
I'm good!	我很好！
My day was good!	我過了很棒的一天！
I'm great!	我很棒！
I'm not so good.	我不是很好。
I'm sad.	我很難過。

情境對話 中文可對照上方的例句

Dialogue 1

Ⓐ Welcome!
Ⓑ Thanks!
Ⓐ How are you?
Ⓑ I'm great!

Dialogue 2

Ⓐ What's up?
Ⓑ I'm not so good.
Ⓐ Why?
Ⓑ I'm sad.

情境 從英文來看外國人使用此肢體語言的情境

When my daughter gets off the school bus, she always runs up to me and gives me a big hug and quick welcome kiss. She's always so excited to be home from school.

每當我的女兒從校車下來時，她總會跑向我，給我大大的擁抱和快速的歡迎之吻。放學回家總是讓她很興奮。

情境 7 Pinkie Wave 揮動小指

這是指除了小指以外的所有手指都握成拳、伸出手、伸展小指、手的前方朝向他人，並將小指上下移動，像是在揮手。在美國，這個動作是情侶或父母／孩子之間的甜蜜手勢，很多人用這個小手勢來表達「你好」或「我愛你」。

外國人在揮動小指時，他們會說：

I love you!	我愛你！
Hi!	嗨！
Hello!	哈囉！
I see you!	我看見你啦！
How are you?	你好嗎？
I haven't seen you in a while!	我好久沒見到你了！
It's good to see you.	見到你真好。
I missed you!	我很想念你！
You're special to me!	你對我來說很特別！
You mean a lot to me!	你對我來說很重要！

外國人和你揮動小指時，你可以回答：

I love you, too!	我也愛你！
Hey there.	嘿，你好啊。
I'm happy to see you.	我很高興見到你。
I've missed you!	我好想你！
I'm glad you're here.	很高興你在這裡。
I'm happy to see you.	很開心能見到你。
Good morning!	早上好！
I couldn't wait to see you.	我等不及要見你了。
Hi sweetie!	嗨，親愛的！
I feel the same way.	我也有同感。

情境對話　中文可對照上方的例句

Dialogue 1

Ⓐ Hi!
Ⓑ Hey there.
Ⓐ I haven't seen you in a while!
Ⓑ I've missed you!

Dialogue 2

Ⓐ I love you!
Ⓑ I love you, too!
Ⓐ You mean a lot to me!
Ⓑ I feel the same way.

情境　從英文來看外國人使用此肢體語言的情境

My son was getting ready to play in his band concert. He was very nervous. When he looked at me, I pinky waved at him from the audience and he got a big smile on his face.

我兒子在為他們樂團的音樂會做演奏準備。他很緊張，當他看著我時，我從觀眾席向他揮動小指，他的臉上露出燦爛的笑容。

情境 8 Quick lowering of the head one time 快速低頭一次

快速低頭一次便會點一次頭。這是對他人認可的動作，像是無聲的問候。許多人會這樣做，同時保持眼神交流，並微微地笑。

外國人快速低頭時，他們會說：

Hi!	嗨！
Hello!	哈囉！
What's up?	怎麼啦？
Good to see you!	很高興見到你！
I'm glad you're here!	我很高興你在這裡！
I didn't expect to see you.	我沒想到會見到你。
You look good!	你看起來挺好的！
I'm happy you came!	我很高興你來了！
I'm glad I ran into you.	我很高興遇到你。
I'm surprised to see you here!	我很驚訝在這裡見到你！

外國人和你快速低頭時，你可以回答：

Hey there!	嘿，你好！
How's it going?	進展如何？
How have you been?	你過得怎麼樣？
Nice to see you.	很高興見到你。
Good to see you.	很高興見到你。
I'm happy to see you.	很高興見到你。
What are you doing?	你在做甚麼？
What ya been up to?	你都在忙甚麼？
What's going on?	發生甚麼事？
Where are you headed?	你要去哪裡？

情境對話　中文可對照上方的例句

Dialogue 1

Ⓐ Welcome!
Ⓑ Thanks!
Ⓐ How are you?
Ⓑ I'm great!

Dialogue 2

Ⓐ I'm surprised to see you here!
Ⓑ Good to see you.
Ⓐ You look good!
Ⓑ What are you doing?

情境　從英文來看外國人使用此肢體語言的情境

I always see one of my old friends on the way to work. We walk by each other around 7:30 and he always give me a quick nod with his head and says hello. It's nice seeing him every morning.

上班的途中，我總會遇到我其中一位老朋友。我們會在七點三十分左右擦身而過，他總會向我快速地點頭問好。每天早上都能見到他真好。

情境 9　Single upward nod 向上點頭一次

當頭向後傾斜時，會將臉部朝上，而眼神則會與他人接觸。像這樣的向上點頭是表示問候，它可以是單一的動作，也可以搭配握手或說話。這是許多人在人行道或走廊上與他人擦身而過時所使用的一種快速動作。

外國人在向上點頭時，他們會說：

Hey!	嘿！
Hello!	哈囉！
Hi there!	嗨，你好！
Good to see you!	很高興見到你！
What's up?	怎麼啦？
Looking good!	看起來不錯！
How are you?	你好嗎？
Where have you been?	你去哪兒了？
I haven't seen you in forever!	我超久沒看到你了！
You look great!	你看起來很棒！

外國人和你向上點頭時，你可以回答：

How are you?	你好嗎？
What's new?	有甚麼新鮮事？
What's going on?	發生了甚麼事？
Hey there!	嘿，你好！
It has been a long time.	已經過好久了。
I'm happy to see you.	很高興見到你。
I've been around.	我都在這附近。
I've been gone.	我離開了一陣子。
Not much is new.	沒甚麼新鮮事。
Let's get together soon.	我們不久後見面吧。

情境對話　中文可對照上方的例句

Dialogue 1

Ⓐ Hello!

Ⓑ Hey there!

Ⓐ Good to see you!

Ⓑ It has been a long time.

Dialogue 2

Ⓐ Where have you been?

Ⓑ I've been around.

Ⓐ Looking good!

Ⓑ Let's get together soon.

情境　從英文來看外國人使用此肢體語言的情境

I ran into my coworker at the mall today. He gave me a nod and we talked for a few minutes. He's been doing well!

我今天在購物中心遇到我的同事，他對我點了點頭，我們聊了幾分鐘。他過得很好！

情境 10 Bumping a fist on top of someone else fist
拳頭碰在別人的拳頭上方

指兩個人握拳，一個人的拳頭往下移、另一個人的拳頭往上移，讓他們的拳頭碰在一起。這個手勢相似於拳頭正面碰拳，也可以用於打招呼或是認可的手勢（相似於擊掌）。

外國人在拳頭上碰拳時，他們會說：

What's up?	最近如何？
Good to see you!	很高興見到你！
I haven't seen you in a while!	我已經很久沒看到你了！
You look great!	你看起來很好！
What are you doing here?	你在這裡做甚麼？
Nice to see you.	很高興見到你。
How's it going?	最近如何？
What's new?	有甚麼新進展嗎？
How's life treating you?	你過得怎麼樣？
Are you doing well?	你最近好嗎？

外國人和你在拳頭上碰拳時，你可以回：

What's going on?	怎麼了？
What's happening?	發生甚麼事？
What are you up to?	你在做甚麼？
You look well!	你看起來很好！
I'm doing well.	我很好。
I'm having a hard time.	我過得很辛苦。
I've been better.	我有比較好了。
I'm great!	我很好！
Thank you!	謝謝你！
You're too kind.	你人太好了。

情境對話　中文可對照上方的例句

Dialogue 1

Ⓐ I haven't seen you in a while!
Ⓑ You look well!
Ⓐ How's life treating you?
Ⓑ I'm having a hard time.

Dialogue 2

Ⓐ What's up?
Ⓑ I'm doing well.
Ⓐ You look great!
Ⓑ You're too kind.

情境　從英文來看外國人使用此肢體語言的情境

I ran into Henry today. We bumped fists and talked for a while. He's been doing really well at his new job.

我今天碰到 Henry 了，我們碰拳又聊了一會兒，他在新工作真的表現得很好。

情境 11 Hitting Chest With a Clenched Fist 握拳打胸部

指人們把拳頭握住、彎曲手肘，所以拳頭置於胸前、手掌面向自己，接著他們打自己的胸口一兩下。這就像是在說「Here I am.」或是「It's me.」。

外國人握拳打胸部時，他們會說：

I'm here!	我在這。
It's me.	是我。
I did it.	我做到了。
It was me.	是我。
Check me out!	看看我！
I'm right here!	我在這裡。
I'm over here.	我就在這裡。
I was the one who did it.	是我做的。
I found it.	我找到了。
I helped out.	我幫忙解決的。

外國人握拳打胸部時，你可以回答：

I'm glad you made it!	我很高興你做到了！
Glad you're here.	很高興你在這裡。
There you are!	你來了！
I see you.	我看到你了。
Thanks for coming.	謝謝你來。
It's about time.	時間差不多了。
Who did this?	是誰做的？
I'm happy to help.	我很高興能幫忙。
Thanks for doing that.	謝謝你這麼做。
Thank you for coming.	謝謝你的到來。

情境對話 中文可對照上方的例句

Dialogue 1

Ⓐ I'm here!

Ⓑ Thank you for coming.

Ⓐ Of course!

Ⓑ I'm glad you made it.

Dialogue 2

Ⓐ Who did this?

Ⓑ It was me.

Ⓐ Thanks for doing that.

Ⓑ I was happy to help.

情境 從英文來看外國人使用此肢體語言的情境

I take attendance in my class each morning. When I call Jeremy's name, he always hits his fist on his chest to tell me he's there.

我每天早上都會在課堂上點名。當我叫到 Jeremy 的名字的時候，他總是用拳頭打自己的胸部，告訴我他在這裡。

Guide Someone
引導他人

☞ **引導他人時需要用到的動作，用英文要怎麼說呢？**

引導他人是見面時要請人們進門或是引導人們到別地方所進行的交流，下列
是引領他人會用到的肢體語言，請看圖片，並對照動作的英文和中文。

Outstretching arm to a door
將手臂伸向門

Holding hand on lower back and
pushing lightly
手放在下背部輕輕推動

Outstretching hand with palm
facing up 將手伸出，手掌朝上

情境 1 Outstretching Arm to a Door 將手臂伸向門

人們打開門並後退，同時扶著門讓門保持打開，並且將一隻手伸向門，手掌張開並朝上。這個手勢表示人們正在為他人扶著門，並以手臂引導他人通過開著的門。通常這個手勢是由男性為女性所做的。

外國人將手臂伸向門時，他們會說：

Go ahead.	來吧。
Lead the way.	請帶路。
You can go.	你可以走了。
I've got the door.	我扶著門了。
I've got it.	我扶著門了。
I'll hold the door.	我會扶著門。
You can head in.	你可以進去。
Why don't you go ahead?	你先走吧。
I'll follow you.	我會跟在你後面。
You go!	你先走！

外國人為你將手伸向門時，你可以回：

Thank you!	謝謝你！
Thanks!	謝謝！
Thanks for that.	謝謝幫忙。
Oh, thank you!	哦，謝謝你！
I'll lead the way.	我來帶路。
I'll go.	我來。
I'll go first.	我先走。
Are you sure?	你確定嗎？
That's so nice of you!	你人真好！
You have good manners.	你舉止真得體。

情境對話　中文可對照上方的例句

Dialogue 1

Ⓐ Go ahead!
Ⓑ Thanks!
Ⓐ I'll hold the door.
Ⓑ I'll go first.

Dialogue 2

Ⓐ Why don't you go ahead?
Ⓑ That's so nice of you!
Ⓐ I'll follow you.
Ⓑ Thanks for that.

情境　從英文來看外國人使用此肢體語言的情境

I went on a date with Josh last night. He was such a gentleman. He held the door open for me and motioned for me to go through first. He also pulled out my chair for me at the restaurant and helped me get my jacket on. It was a good first date!

昨晚我和 Josh 約會。他真是一位紳士，他為我扶開著的門，示意要我先通過。他還在餐廳幫我拉出椅子、又幫我穿上外套。真是美好的初次約會！

情境 2 Holding Hand on Lower Back and Pushing Lightly
手放在下背部輕推

人們將手掌放在另一個人的下背部，並輕輕將對方推向別處，這是一種引領他人到某個地點的方法。例如，男性可能會對女性這麼做，以引導對方穿過門口。這是男性經常為女性做的一種紳士行為。

外國人輕推你的背部時，他們會說：

Go ahead.	走吧。
This way.	往這裡走。
You can go.	你可以先走。
I'll show you the way.	我來為你指路。
Take this hallway.	走這個走廊。
Turn here.	在這裡轉彎。
You go first.	你先走吧。
You can go in first.	你先請進吧。
Lead the way!	帶路！
I'll walk in with you.	我陪你走進去。

外國人輕推你的背部時，你可以回答：

Thanks!	謝謝！
Are you sure?	你確定嗎？
I'll lead the way.	我會帶路。
Thank you.	謝謝你。
That's nice of you.	你們真好。
That would be great.	那太好了。
That's great.	太好了。
Will do!	會的！
Come with me.	跟我來。
You should come with me.	你應該跟我來。

情境對話 中文可對照上方的例句

Dialogue 1

Ⓐ Go ahead.
Ⓑ Thanks!
Ⓐ Take this hallway.
Ⓑ Are you sure?

Dialogue 2

Ⓐ I'll show you the way.
Ⓑ That would be great.
Ⓐ Turn here.
Ⓑ Thank you.

情境 從英文來看外國人使用此肢體語言的情境

When we got to the restaurant, Mike put his hand on my back and led me through the door. He showed me the way to the table he had reserved. It was a really nice dinner!

我們抵達餐廳時，Mike 把手放在我的背上，帶領我通過門口。他為我帶路到他之前預訂的位子。那頓晚餐非常美味！

情境 3
Outstretching Hand with Palm Facing up
伸出手，手掌朝上

伸出手臂，並且手掌張開並朝上時，這是給予方向的手勢。這個手勢是為他人指引他們應該走的路，引導他們走在自己前面或是帶路。許多人在為他人扶著打開的門時會這樣做。

外國人把手伸出來指路時，他們會說：

Go ahead.	走吧。
You can go!	你可以走了！
Lead the way.	帶路吧。
Through this door.	通過這扇門。
Follow me!	跟著我！
This way!	這條路！
Turn here.	在這裡轉彎。
You go on in.	你進去吧。
I'll be right there.	我馬上到。
I'll hold the door.	我會扶著門。

外國人把手伸出來指路時，你可以回：

Thank you!	謝謝你！
Thanks!	謝謝！
Thank you so much.	非常感謝你。
Thanks so much!	非常感謝！
I'll lead the way.	我會帶路。
I'll go that way.	我會走那條路。
Thanks for pointing to the right direction.	感謝你指出正確的方向。
You're so helpful.	你幫了大忙。
That was helpful!	這很有幫助！
You're too kind.	你太客氣了。

情境對話 中文可對照上方的例句

Dialogue 1

Ⓐ You can go!
Ⓑ Are you sure?

Ⓐ Go ahead.
Ⓑ Thank you!

Dialogue 2

Ⓐ Turn here.
Ⓑ Thanks for pointing to the right direction.

Ⓐ No problem!
Ⓑ You're so helpful.

情境 從英文來看外國人使用此肢體語言的情境

I wasn't sure where to go when I got to the restaurant. The host helped me find our group by pointing to the right direction with his palm facing up. He was so helpful!

我到餐廳時不確定該往哪裡走，東道主將手掌朝上，為我指出正確的方向，幫我找到我們的團隊。他幫了大忙！

Farewell 道別

☞ **道別時需要用到的動作，用英文要怎麼說呢？**

道別是要和家人、朋友分開時所進行的交流，下列是道別會用到的手勢與肢體語言，請看圖片，並對照動作的英文和中文。

Goodbye Hug 道別的擁抱

Blowing a Kiss 飛吻

Turning shoulders away
from someone 轉開肩膀

※ 補充說明：揮手、臉頰上親吻也是道別時會使用的肢體語言，可回去 Unit 1 p.12 及 p.16 複習。

情境 1 Goodbye Hug 道別的擁抱

道別時的擁抱，用以表達珍惜在一起的時光、同時也對離別表示遺憾。這種擁抱通常是由兩個有深厚情誼的人互相給予的，例如在親密的朋友或家人之間，之後有很長一段時間不能見面。由其中一人或雙方張開雙臂並做出擁抱的邀請，接著彼此以手臂圍繞對方，高度大約在上背部附近，偶爾會在背上輕拍或輕撫。

外國人做道別的擁抱時，他們會說：

Well, this is it.	那麼，就這樣了。
I'll miss you.	我會想念你的。
It's been great.	一切都很棒。
Take care of yourself.	好好照顧自己。
Until next time.	直到下次見面。
I'll write to you.	我會寫信給你。
Call me when you get there.	到那裡時給我個電話。
Drive carefully.	開車小心。
Don't be a stranger.	要常常聯絡。
Come back soon.	快點回來。

外國人和你道別的擁抱時，你可以回：

I'll see you soon.	我很快會再見到你。
Take care.	保重。
You be careful.	一切小心。
See you soon!	很快會再見面的！
See ya!	再見！
Don't forget me.	別忘了我。
Safe travels!	旅途平安！
Drive safe.	開車平安。
I'll be seeing you.	我會再見到你的。
I'll call you.	我會打給你的。

情境對話 中文可對照上方的例句

Dialogue 1

Ⓐ I'll miss you.
Ⓑ I'll miss you, too.
Ⓐ It's been great.
Ⓑ Don't forget me.

Dialogue 2

Ⓐ Good-bye!
Ⓑ See you soon!
Ⓐ Don't be a stranger.
Ⓑ I'll call you.

情境 從英文來看外國人使用此肢體語言的情境

I went out for dinner with a group of friends. As I was leaving, Jake hugged me goodbye and asked me to call him this week. He gave me his new phone number.

我和一群朋友出去吃飯。我正要離開時，Jack 擁抱我、說再見，並叫我在這個星期要打電話給他。他給了我他的新電話號碼。

情境 2　Blowing a Kiss 飛吻

飛吻是指手舉到唇邊，手掌對著自己的臉，在指尖親吻，然後將手掌放平，並朝著對方吹氣。這被認為是給遠方的人一個吻，許多父母和孩子在道別的場合下，慢慢走遠時會這樣做。

外國人飛吻時，他們會說：

I'll miss you!	我會想念你的！
Goodbye!	再見！
Take care!	照顧自己！
Talk to you soon!	以後再聊！
I hope to see you soon.	我希望很快能見到你。
Please come back soon!	請快點回來！
Don't go!	不要走！
I don't want to leave.	我不想離開。
I love you!	我愛你！
Have a good day!	祝你有美好的一天！

外國人和你飛吻時，你可以回：

Bye!	再見！
Bye-bye!	再見！
See you later!	待會兒見！
See ya!	掰啦！
I'll see you soon.	我們很快會再見。
Take care of yourself.	照顧好自己。
I'll visit soon!	我會很快會來看你！
I will!	我會的！
I have to go.	我得走了。
I can't stay.	我不能再待了。

情境對話　中文可對照上方的例句

Dialogue 1

Ⓐ I'll miss you!
Ⓑ I'll visit soon!
Ⓐ Goodbye!
Ⓑ Bye!

Dialogue 2

Ⓐ Please come back soon!
Ⓑ I will!
Ⓐ I love you!
Ⓑ I love you, too!

情境　從英文來看外國人使用此肢體語言的情境

I took my girlfriend back to college last week. I was really sad to leave her there. As I was driving away, I blew her a kiss and told her I loved her.

上週我送我的女朋友回到大學。我把她留在那裡，真的讓我很傷心。開車遠去時，我給了她一個飛吻，告訴她我愛她。

情境 3 Turning Shoulders Away From Someone 轉開肩膀

以雙肩正對著他人，意味著專注於對方身上。反之，在他人仍在說話或以眼神注視時，將雙肩從他身邊轉開，這個動作表示人們想要離開或是結束對話。

外國人轉開肩膀時，他們會說：

I should go.	我該走了。
It's getting late.	天色已晚。
I'm going to leave.	我要離開了。
I need to head home.	我要回家了。
I'm running late for the meeting.	我開會要遲到了。
I need to be somewhere.	我需要去某個地方。
I should get going.	我先走了。
It was good talking to you.	與你談話真好。
I'll talk to you later.	待會兒再和你聊。
Let's catch up later.	之後再聊。

外國人對你轉開肩膀時，你可以回：

So soon?	這麼快？
You're leaving already?	你已經走了嗎？
Are you sure?	你確定嗎？
We have time.	我們有時間。
Don't go yet!	先不要走！
I'm not done with my story.	我的故事還沒講完。
Where are you headed?	你要去哪裡？
We're on time.	我們準時。
We're not late.	我們沒遲到。
You're not running late!	你不會遲到！

情境對話　中文可對照上方的例句

Dialogue 1

Ⓐ I should go.
Ⓑ So soon?
Ⓐ I need to head home.
Ⓑ Are you sure?

Dialogue 2

Ⓐ I should get going.
Ⓑ Don't go yet!
Ⓐ I'm running late for the meeting.
Ⓑ We're on time.

情境　從英文來看外國人使用此肢體語言的情境

I got stuck talking to Linda at the party. She never shuts up! I finally turned away from her like I was leaving, and told her I needed to get going.

我在聚會上被 Linda 絆住了，她真是講個沒完沒了！最後我像要離開了一樣，從她那裡轉身，告訴她我得走了。

Feeling Happy 感到開心

☞ **感到開心時需要用到的動作，用英文要怎麼說呢？**

對某些事物感到開心就會產生各種手勢和肢體動作，下列是感到開心會用到的手勢與肢體語言，請看圖片，並對照動作的英文和中文。

情境 1

Bear hug 熊抱

情境 2

Teammate hug 隊友間的擁抱

情境 3

Big smile 大笑

情境 4

Laughing smile 帶著笑聲的微笑

情境 5

Showing teeth in a smile 露齒微笑

情境 6

Turned up lips 嘴角上揚

Loud voice 大聲

Quickly rubbing palms together
快速摩擦手掌

Bumping fist with someone else
與他人碰拳

Excitedly sweating 興奮地出汗

Mouth slightly turned up
嘴角稍微上揚

情境 1 Bear Hug 熊抱

這是一種單方面、用力擠壓的擁抱，強調擁抱者對接受者的情感。由擁抱者熱情地展開雙臂，表示他正在靠近，接著以手臂環繞被擁抱者，高度約在上背部，然後非常用力地收緊手臂。有時也會將被擁抱者抬離地面。

外國人熊抱時，他們會說：

Come here, buddy!	過來，兄弟！
You look like you need a bear hug.	你看起來像需要一個熊抱。
I'm going to squeeze the stuffing out of you.	我要把你的餡都擠出來。
Give me a hug!	給我一個擁抱！
It's great to see you!	很高興見到你！
Time for a bear hug!	熊抱的時間到了！
Growl! (growling noise)	喔喔喔喔！（嘶吼聲）
I won't squeeze too hard!	我不會擠太用力！
You're so huggable!	你太好抱了！
Come on, give me a big hug.	來吧，給我一個大大的擁抱。

外國人和你熊抱時，你可以回：

You're squishing me!	你要擠扁我了！
I can't breathe.	我無法呼吸了。
Let me go!	放手！
Let me loose.	鬆開我。
Loosen up a bit!	放鬆一點！
That's too tight!	太緊了！
You're squeezing me too hard.	你抱得太用力了。
Put me down!	放我下來！
Leave me alone.	不要煩我。
Set me down.	放我下來。

情境對話 中文可對照上方的例句

Dialogue 1

Ⓐ Come here, buddy!
Ⓑ You're squeezing me too hard.
Ⓐ You're so huggable!

Ⓑ Let me go!

Dialogue 2

Ⓐ You look like you need a bear hug.
Ⓑ Leave me alone.
Ⓐ I'm going to squeeze the stuffing out of you.
Ⓑ Let me loose.

情境 從英文來看外國人使用此肢體語言的情境

I saw a couple of my college friends tonight. My old roommate gave me a huge bear hug, when he saw me. I swear I couldn't breathe because he squeezed me so hard!

今晚我見到了幾個大學時的朋友，我的老室友看到我時，給了我一個超大的熊抱。我發誓我那時沒辦法呼吸，因為他超用力地抱緊我！

Teammate Hug 隊友間的擁抱

隊友的擁抱和祝賀的擁抱相同，但是這個擁抱是指兩名隊友分享勝利或成功，例如：運動、樂團或競賽。兩名隊友真誠、欣喜地擁抱時，他們會張開雙臂、做出擁抱的邀請，並將手臂環繞在對方的背部，熱情地緊抱對方。這種擁抱通常會加上在背部多次、有力的拍打，人們通常會在擁抱的時候跳躍、歡呼和舉起隊友。

外國人隊友間的擁抱時，他們會說：

Awesome!	太棒了！
We're number one!	我們是第一名！
We kicked butt!	我們超殺！
Yeah, we did it!	是的，我們做到了！
We're going to the finals!	我們進決賽了！
We're undefeated!	我們所向無敵！
We beat them!	我們擊敗他們了！
We're taking home the trophy!	我們把獎杯贏走了！
Can you believe it?	你能相信嗎？
Let's celebrate!	來慶祝吧！

外國人和你隊友間的擁抱時，你可以回：

I can't believe it.	我不敢相信。
You did great!	你做得很棒！
We did it!	我們做到了！
We were awesome.	我們好棒。
I can't believe this!	我真不敢相信！
We're the winners!	我們是贏家！
Let's have a party.	我們來開派對吧。
I'm so proud.	我很自豪。
I feel amazing.	我覺得好棒。
We did great!	我們做得很好！

情境對話 中文可對照上方的例句

Dialogue 1

Ⓐ We're going to the finals!

Ⓑ I can't believe this!

Ⓐ Let's celebrate!

Ⓑ Let's have a party.

Dialogue 2

Ⓐ We're taking home the trophy!

Ⓑ We're the winners!

Ⓐ We kicked butt!

Ⓑ I'm so proud!

情境 從英文來看外國人使用此肢體語言的情境

Our softball team made it to the state finals. We won our last game in overtime and won the state championship. After the game, our team ran on the field and jumped up and down and gave everyone hugs to celebrate.

我們的壘球隊打進了州區決賽。上一場比賽，我們在延長賽中獲勝，並贏得了州區冠軍。比賽結束後，我們的球隊在賽場奔跑、跳上跳下，並且擁抱了所有人來慶祝。

情境 3　Big Smile 大笑

這種笑容燦爛而真實。許多人說，大笑能點亮整個臉龐。大笑時會眼睛瞇起，嘴唇上揚，頭部輕微向後傾斜。這是真實的笑，並讓其他人知道這個人正感到高興和滿足。

外國人大笑時，他們會說：

It's good to see you!	很高興見到你！
I can't believe you're here!	我簡直不敢相信你在這裡！
I'm so happy!	我很開心！
I'm surprised.	我很驚喜。
This is amazing!	這真是太驚人了！
I love this!	我喜歡這個！
Thank you!	謝謝你！
You're the best!	你是最好的！
You shouldn't have!	你不用這樣的！
I'm amazed!	我很驚訝！

外國人對你大笑時，你可以回：

I'm so happy you're here!	我很高興你在這裡！
I'm glad you're here.	很高興你在這裡。
I'm thrilled to see you.	我很開心能見到你。
I'm glad I could come.	很高興我能來。
I'm happy to be here.	我很高興來到這裡。
We wanted to surprise you.	我們想給你一個驚喜。
I'm glad you like it.	很高興你喜歡它。
Of course!	當然！
You mean so much to us.	你對我們很重要。
You deserve it.	你應得的。

情境對話　中文可對照上方的例句

Dialogue 1

Ⓐ I can't believe you're here!
Ⓑ I'm glad I could come.
Ⓐ It's good to see you!
Ⓑ It's good to see you, too!

Dialogue 2

Ⓐ You shouldn't have!
Ⓑ You mean so much to us.
Ⓐ Thank you!
Ⓑ You deserve it.

情境　從英文來看外國人使用此肢體語言的情境

We threw a surprise party for my grandma's 90th birthday. She was so surprised when she walked in. Her whole face lit up and she had the biggest smile I've ever seen.

我們為奶奶的九十歲生日辦了一場驚喜派對。她走進來時超驚訝的，她整個臉都開朗了起來，臉上掛著我見過的最大的笑容。

情境 4 Laughing Smile 帶著笑聲的微笑

帶著笑聲的笑容與張開嘴的笑容類似，差別是這種笑會發出笑聲並將嘴張開，頭向後傾斜，眼睛可能合上。這種笑容意味著人們是真的開心，他們可能正在享受一個有趣的故事、在開玩笑、或是享受快樂的時光。

外國人大笑時，他們會說：

This is so funny!	這太有趣了！
What a funny story.	多麼有趣的故事。
I can't believe you did that!	我真不敢相信你這麼做！
I can't stop laughing!	我不能停止大笑！
Too funny!	太搞笑了！
Let's do this again.	讓我們再來一次吧。
I'm having a blast.	我玩得很盡興。
This is awesome!	這太棒了！
I think it's hilarious!	我覺得這很好笑！
You're crazy!	你瘋了！

外國人對你大笑時，你可以回：

That's hilarious!	這太好笑了！
It was hilarious!	太好笑了！
It was so funny!	真有趣！
I had such a good time.	我過得很開心。
It was so fun.	真有趣。
That's too funny!	太好笑了！
I laughed so hard.	我笑得很厲害。
My eyes are watering!	我都流眼淚了！
We need to do this more often.	我們得更常這樣做。
Let's do it tomorrow.	我們明天來做吧。

情境對話 中文可對照上方的例句

Dialogue 1

Ⓐ I can't believe you did that!
Ⓑ It was hilarious!
Ⓐ I can't stop laughing!
Ⓑ My eyes are watering!

Dialogue 2

Ⓐ I'm having a blast.
Ⓑ We need to do this more often.
Ⓐ I agree!
Ⓑ Let's do it tomorrow.

情境 從英文來看外國人使用此肢體語言的情境

I took my kids to the amusement park yesterday. We rode the new roller coaster. It was so fun! They laughed and had the biggest smiles. I'm glad we went there.

我昨天帶孩子去了遊樂園。我們坐了新的雲霄飛車，真是好玩！孩子們大笑，臉上掛著最大的笑容。我很高興我們去了那裡。

情境 5　Showing Teeth in a Smile 露齒微笑

露齒微笑會嘴唇彎曲並稍微分開，露出嘴巴內的牙齒。在笑的時候，牙齒可能會閉起來或張開，這展現出這個人很開心。

外國人露齒微笑時，他們會說：

This is awesome!	真的很棒！
It's so pretty!	這很漂亮！
You look wonderful!	你看起來很棒！
I love it!	我很喜歡！
This is for me?	這是給我的嗎？
You're the best!	你最棒了！
I love you!	我愛你！
You make me happy.	你讓我很快樂。
I feel great!	我覺得很棒！
It's amazing!	真好！

外國人對你露齒微笑時，你可以回：

Thank you!	謝謝你！
You're too sweet.	你太貼心了。
You're so kind.	你人真好。
What a nice thing to say!	真是太好了！
I appreciate that.	我很感謝。
It's for you!	這是給你的！
You deserve it.	你應得的。
That's so nice.	這真的很好。
Thanks!	謝謝！
I'm happy to hear that.	我很高興聽到這件事。

情境對話　中文可對照上方的例句

Dialogue 1

Ⓐ This is for me?
Ⓑ Yes, it is.
Ⓐ You're the best!
Ⓑ You deserve it.

Dialogue 2

Ⓐ You look wonderful!
Ⓑ You're too sweet.
Ⓐ You make me happy.
Ⓑ That's so nice.

情境　從英文來看外國人使用此肢體語言的情境

We threw a surprise party for my husband's birthday. When he walked in and everyone yelled surprise, he got a huge smile on his face! I'm so glad he enjoyed the party.

我們為我丈夫的生日辦了驚喜派對。當他走進來，大家大叫驚喜，他在臉上露出很大的笑容！我真的很高興他享受這個派對。

情境 6 Turned Up Lips 嘴角上揚

嘴角往上揚，可以是代表高興的微笑。微笑時，整個臉部都帶著笑意，牙齒露出或不露出都可以。而如果牙齒未露出，可能是表示噁心的假笑或怪表情。如果人們做怪表情、或對某事表現出厭惡，他們的臉部會比微笑更諂媚、更緊繃些。

外國人嘴角上揚時，他們會說：

It's great to see you!	很高興見到你！
I'm so happy!	我好開心！
That's funny!	那很好笑！
I love it!	我超愛這個！
It's beautiful!	那好美！
You're awesome!	你真棒！
Thank you!	謝謝你！
I can't believe it.	我真不敢相信！
That's horrible!	那太恐怖了！
It's awful!	太可怕了！

外國人對你嘴角上揚時，你可以回：

I'm glad you're here.	我很高興你在這裡。
You look wonderful!	你看起來真好！
You seem happy.	你似乎很高興。
You're really excited!	你真的很興奮！
It's perfect!	太完美了！
I'm glad!	我很高興！
I'm happy for you.	我為你感到高興。
I thought you'd like it.	我想你會喜歡。
I'm glad you like it.	很高興你喜歡它。
I'm so happy you made it.	我很高興你趕來了。

情境對話 中文可對照上方的例句

Dialogue 1

Ⓐ It's great to see you!

Ⓑ You look wonderful!

Ⓐ Thank you!

Ⓑ I'm glad you're here.

Dialogue 2

Ⓐ I love it!

Ⓑ I thought you'd like it.

Ⓐ Thank you!

Ⓑ You're welcome!

情境 從英文來看外國人使用此肢體語言的情境

I surprised my mom with a visit today. I could tell by her huge smile that she was happy to see me.

今天我去看我的母親，給她驚喜。從她燦爛的笑容，我可以看出她很高興能見到我。

情境 7 Loud Voice 大聲

這是一種非常大聲、震耳欲聾的音量，可以傳得很遠，並且被其他人聽到。人在玩得很開心、開玩笑或大笑時的時候，聲音會變得大聲。這種聲音與不高興時會使用的提高音量不同。

外國人大聲講話時，他們會說：

That's awesome!	棒極了！
You're too funny!	你太好笑了！
Tell the joke again!	再講一次這個笑話！
Tell me the story again!	再講一次這個故事！
I think you're hilarious.	我覺得你很搞笑。
Let's get another drink!	再喝一杯吧！
This is fun!	這好有趣！
I'm having a blast!	我玩得很盡興！
We're having a great time!	我們玩得很開心！
Let's do this again!	讓我們再來一次！

外國人對你大聲講話時，你可以回：

Thanks!	謝謝！
Thank you.	謝謝你。
You're too kind.	你太客氣了。
Are you serious?	你是認真的嗎？
I'm having a good time!	我玩得很開心！
I'll buy!	我買單！
This is great!	這太棒了！
We should do this again.	我們應該再做一次。
I'll take another round.	我要再來一輪。
This was a great idea.	這真是個好主意。

情境對話 中文可對照上方的例句

Dialogue 1

Ⓐ Let's get another drink!
Ⓑ I'll buy!
Ⓐ I'm having a blast!
Ⓑ We should do this again.

Dialogue 2

Ⓐ I think you're hilarious.
Ⓑ Thank you.
Ⓐ We're having a great time!
Ⓑ You're too kind.

情境 從英文來看外國人使用此肢體語言的情境

We went to a bar last night and it was so loud. They had a really good band playing. My throat hurts today because I had to talk in my loud voice all night.

昨晚我們去了一家酒吧，那裡很吵，他們有個很棒的樂團在演出。但今天我的喉嚨好痛，因為我必須整晚大聲說話。

情境 8

Quickly Rubbing Palms Together 快速摩擦手掌

這個手勢是將手掌合在一起，並快速摩擦。可能意味著人們非常興奮，或者他們期待著好事在他們身上發生。他們這麼做時通常會微笑。而這也可能意味著人們感到很冷，他們正在嘗試讓雙手溫暖起來。

外國人摩擦手掌時，他們會說：

I feel lucky!	我覺得很幸運！
Something good is going to happen!	有好事將會發生！
This is gonna be good!	這會很好的！
I'm excited!	我很興奮！
I can't wait!	我等不及了！
I feel great!	我感覺好極了！
I'm going to win!	我要贏了！
I know I'll win!	我知道我會贏！
I have a good feeling!	我有個好的感覺！
Something is about to happen!	有一些事即將發生！

外國人對你摩擦手掌時，你可以回：

What's going on?	發生了甚麼事？
I hope you're right.	我希望你是對的。
You look excited!	你看起來很興奮！
Me too!	我也是！
I'm excited too.	我也很興奮。
I'm nervous for you.	我為你感到緊張。
I feel happy for you!	我為你感到高興！
I'm excited for you!	我為你感到興奮！
Are you sure?	你確定嗎？
Don't get too excited.	不要太興奮。

情境對話 中文可對照上方的例句

Dialogue 1

Ⓐ Something good is going to happen!
Ⓑ Are you sure?
Ⓐ I have a good feeling!
Ⓑ I hope you're right!

Dialogue 2

Ⓐ I'm going to win!
Ⓑ I'm nervous for you.
Ⓐ I know I'll win!
Ⓑ Don't get too excited.

情境 從英文來看外國人使用此肢體語言的情境

My friend was playing poker last night. She had a good hand and was rubbing her palms together like she knew she was going to win. She bet all of her money and she ended up winning.

我的朋友昨晚在玩撲克牌，她的手氣很好。她將手掌合在一起摩擦，就像知道自己要贏了一樣。她押了所有的錢，結果最後她贏了。

情境 9 Bumping Fist with Someone Else 與他人碰拳

指兩個人的手握成一個拳頭,並輕輕「拳擊」另一個人的拳頭。這個手勢通常用於兩個人打招呼的時候,也可以是告訴他人,他們做得很好或是在運動上表現得很好的方式,類似擊掌。

外國人與他人碰拳時,他們會說:

Hey there!	嘿!
What's up?	最近好嗎?
Good to see you!	很高興看到你!
How are you?	你好嗎?
Welcome!	歡迎!
Good play!	打得真好!
Good game!	精采的比賽!
Nice hit!	好球!
You played well!	你打得真棒!
Good catch!	接得好!

外國人與你碰拳時,你可以回:

Hi there!	嗨!
It's been a while!	好久不見了!
You look good.	你真好看。
I'm happy to see you.	我很高興能見到你。
We did great!	我們做得很好!
The team did well.	團隊表現很好。
Thanks.	謝謝。
Thank you!	謝謝你!
That's nice of you to say!	你人真好!
It was awesome!	太棒了!

情境對話 中文可對照上方的例句

Dialogue 1

Ⓐ Hey there!
Ⓑ Hey!
Ⓐ Good to see you!
Ⓑ You look good.

Dialogue 2

Ⓐ Good game!
Ⓑ We did great!
Ⓐ You played well!
Ⓑ That's nice of you to say!

情境 從英文來看外國人使用此肢體語言的情境

John hit a homerun at the game tonight. Everyone on the team gave him a fist bump and pat on the back. He's a great player!

John 在今晚的比賽敲出一支全壘打,球隊的每個人都跟他碰拳並拍他的背,他真的是很棒的球員!

情境 10 **Excitedly Sweating 興奮地出汗**

興奮時出汗很常見，這可能是興奮的情緒所引起的，也可能是因為正在激動的人會靜不下來，而動得比平常更多。

外國人興奮地出汗時，他們會說：

I can't wait!	我等不及了！
I'm so excited!	我太激動了！
I can't contain myself.	我無法控制自己。
Are you excited?	你興奮嗎？
This is going to be awesome.	這太棒了。
It will be great.	這會非常棒。
I'm pumped up!	我好興奮！
I bet you're excited, too.	我打賭你也很興奮。
This will be awesome!	太棒了！
I'm ecstatic!	我欣喜若狂！

外國人興奮地出汗時，你可以回：

Me too!	我也是！
I'm excited, too!	我也很興奮！
It's so exciting!	太刺激了！
This is going to be fun.	這會很有趣。
It's going to be great!	這會很棒！
It will be awesome!	太棒了！
I can't wait either!	我也等不及了！
Let's go!	走吧！
I'm thrilled!	我好興奮！
It is going to be fun.	會很有趣的。

情境對話 中文可對照上方的例句

Dialogue 1

Ⓐ Are you excited?

Ⓑ It's so exciting!

Ⓐ This is going to be awesome.

Ⓑ It's going to be fun.

Dialogue 2

Ⓐ I'm pumped up!

Ⓑ It will be awesome.

Ⓐ I can't wait.

Ⓑ Let's go!

情境 從英文來看外國人使用此肢體語言的情境

I was so excited to ride the new roller coaster. The whole time we were in line, I was sweating from excitement. It was so fast! I can't wait to ride it again.

坐新的雲霄飛車讓我感到非常興奮。我們排隊的那整段時間，我都在因為興奮而流汗。車速超快的！我等不及要再搭一次了。

情境 11　Mouth Slightly Turned Up 嘴巴稍微上揚

嘴角稍微上揚表示微笑，通常發生於人對大部分的情況感到高興、正在享受某人的陪伴、或被某事逗樂之時。滿臉的笑容會使整個臉部都帶著笑意，而假笑則只有嘴巴有笑意。

外國人嘴巴稍微上揚時，他們會說：

That was funny!	真好笑！
What a good joke!	真是個好笑話！
It's good to see you!	很高興見到你！
I've missed you!	我很想你！
I'm glad you came.	我很高興你來了。
This is my favorite!	這是我最喜歡的！
I love this!	我喜歡這個！
You're too kind!	你太客氣了！
Thank you for coming.	謝謝你的到來。
Give me a hug!	給我一個擁抱！

外國人嘴巴稍微上揚時，你可以回：

Thanks!	謝謝！
I'm glad you liked it.	很高興你喜歡它。
I'm happy you're here!	很高興你在這裡！
I've missed you, too.	我也想念你。
It's so good to spend time with you.	花時間和你在一起真好。
I'm happy you could make it.	我很高興你能趕到。
Thank you for the invitation.	謝謝你的邀請。
I loved seeing you.	我很高興見到你。
Thank you!	謝謝！
You're too kind.	你太客氣了。

情境對話　中文可對照上方的例句

Dialogue 1
Ⓐ It's good to see you!
Ⓑ I'm happy you're here!
Ⓐ I've missed you!
Ⓑ I loved seeing you.

Dialogue 2
Ⓐ Thank you for coming.
Ⓑ Thank you for the invitation.
Ⓐ Give me a hug!
Ⓑ You're too kind.

情境　從英文來看外國人使用此肢體語言的情境

I had brunch with a group of my friends on Sunday. Everyone had smiles on their faces. I think we all enjoyed spending time with each other. We're going to do it again next month.

我星期天和一群朋友吃早午餐，每個人的臉上都掛著微笑，我認為我們所有人都喜歡和彼此一起度過的時光。我們將在下個月再聚一次。

Feeling Relax 感到放鬆

👉 **感到放鬆時需要用到的動作，用英文要怎麼說呢？**

對某些事物感到放鬆就會產生各種手勢和肢體動作，下列是感到放鬆會用到的手勢與肢體語言，請看圖片，並對照動作的英文和中文。

情境 1

Sitting with legs crossed at ankles
坐著、腳踝交叉

情境 2

Legs open while sitting
雙腳張開坐著

情境 3

Holding palms together 將手掌合十

情境 4

Closed mouth 嘴巴閉著

情境 5

Leaning shoulder against the wall
肩膀靠牆

情境 6

Putting hands in pants' back pockets
把雙手放在後口袋

情境 1 Sitting with Legs Crossed at Ankles 坐著、腳踝交叉

坐在椅子上，雙腿於腳踝處交叉上。
這個姿勢是指人們坐著，雙腿向前伸出，
身體向後傾斜。這是放鬆和舒適的表現，
如果此人的雙手放在頭後面，就是極為放
鬆的表現。

外國人坐著、腳踝交叉時，他們會說：

What's up?	過得如何？
How are you?	你好嗎？
I feel good!	我覺得很好！
I'm great.	我最近不錯。
I'm relaxing.	我正在放鬆。
I needed a break.	我需要休息一下。
How's it going?	怎麼樣了？
Good to see you!	很高興見到你！
I'm doing well.	我最近很好。
I ordered a drink.	我點了一杯酒。

外國人坐著、腳踝交叉時，你可以回：

Not much. You?	還好，你呢？
I'm great.	我很好。
I've been better.	我過得更好。
I'm doing well.	我過得不錯。
I'm happy to be here.	我很高興來到這裡。
Are you resting?	你在休息嗎？
I'm happy to see you.	很高興見到你。
You look great.	你看起來很不錯。
How are you?	你好嗎？
You look relaxed!	你看起來很放鬆！

情境對話 中文可對照上方的例句

Dialogue 1

Ⓐ What's up?
Ⓑ Not much. You?
Ⓐ I feel good!
Ⓑ You look great.

Dialogue 2

Ⓐ Hey there!
Ⓑ Are you resting?
Ⓐ I needed a break.
Ⓑ You look relaxed.

情境 從英文來看外國人使用此肢體語言的情境

By the time I got to the restaurant, my boyfriend was sitting at our table already. He was leaning back in his chair with his ankles crossed. I thought he was asleep, but he was just relaxing. I think he was happy to be done with work.

當我到達餐廳時，我男友已經坐在我們的位子上了。他的腳踝交叉，往後靠在椅子上。我還以為他睡著了，但他只是在放鬆。我覺得他因為能完成工作而開心。

情境 2 Sitting with Legs Crossed at Ankles 雙腿張開坐著

這是指坐下來時雙腿張開。以這種姿勢坐著時，其中一條腿或雙腿可能會以最大的幅度往一邊打開。這麼坐著是感到非常舒適和放鬆的表現。

外國人雙腿張開坐著時，他們會說：

I'm taking it easy.	我很放鬆。
I feel good!	我覺得很好！
I'm relaxing.	我在放鬆。
Let's watch TV!	看個電視吧！
What's on TV?	電視在播甚麼？
Can you grab me a drink?	你能給我杯飲料嗎？
Anything is fine.	都可以。
I'll get up soon.	我很快就起來了。
I'm reading a book.	我在讀一本書。
Grab me a blanket!	給我拿條毯子！

外國人雙腿張開坐著時，你可以回：

You look comfortable.	你看起來很舒服。
Are you comfortable?	你覺得舒服嗎？
What's going on?	怎麼了？
What are you watching?	你在看甚麼？
Is the game on?	比賽開始了嗎？
I haven't seen this show before.	我以前沒看過這個節目。
What can I get you?	我能拿甚麼給你？
Do you want a beer?	你要來杯啤酒嗎？
What book is that?	那是甚麼書？
How is that book?	那本書怎麼樣？

情境對話 中文可對照上方的例句

Dialogue 1

Ⓐ I'm taking it easy.
Ⓑ You look comfortable.
Ⓐ Let's watch TV!
Ⓑ Is the game on?

Dialogue 2

Ⓐ Can you grab me a drink?
Ⓑ What can I get you?
Ⓐ Anything is fine.
Ⓑ Do you want a beer?

情境 從英文來看外國人使用此肢體語言的情境

Joe takes up so much space when watching TV. He sits down and lets his legs flop all over. He says he's comfortable like that, but it takes up the whole couch!

Joe 看電視時佔了超大的位子。他坐下之後把他的雙腿整個往外張開。他說這樣子很舒服，但那樣坐著佔了整張沙發！

情境 3 Holding Palms Together 將手掌合十

將伸開手指的手掌併在一起是祈禱的手勢。許多人在冥想或祈禱時會像這樣握住自己的手,因為這樣可以幫助他們放鬆和專注。

外國人將手掌合十時,他們會說:

I'm relaxing.	我在放鬆。
I'm praying.	我在祈禱。
I'm meditating.	我在打坐。
I'm doing yoga.	我在做瑜伽。
I'm focusing.	我正在集中精力。
I need a few minutes.	我需要幾分鐘。
Give me a minute.	給我一點時間。
I want to be alone.	我想單獨待一會兒。
Leave me alone.	讓我獨處。
Let me be alone.	讓我一個人待著。

外國人雙腿張開坐著時,你可以回:

I'll be quiet.	我會安靜的。
Go ahead.	繼續。
Can I sit with you?	我可以和你一起坐嗎?
Can I pray with you?	我可以和你一起祈禱嗎?
Let me pray with you.	讓我和你一起禱告。
Sorry for interrupting!	對不起打擾到你了!
I didn't mean to interrupt.	我不是故意要打擾你。
I'll give you some time.	我會給你一些時間。
Take your time.	慢慢來。
Are you almost done?	你快好了嗎?

情境對話 中文可對照上方的例句

Dialogue 1
Ⓐ I'm meditating.
Ⓑ Can I sit with you?
Ⓐ Sure.
Ⓑ Are you almost done?

Dialogue 2
Ⓐ I'm praying.
Ⓑ I'll leave you alone.
Ⓐ Thanks.
Ⓑ Sorry for interrupting!

情境 從英文來看外國人使用此肢體語言的情境

I walked into my roommate's room and found her sitting on the floor with her hands together. It looked like she was praying, but she said she had just finished doing yoga and was meditating. She finds it relaxing.

我走進室友的房間,發現她合十雙手,坐在地板上。看起來她像是在祈禱,但她說她剛做完瑜伽,正在冥想。她發現這樣很放鬆。

情境 4 **Closed Mouth 嘴巴閉著**

嘴巴閉著通常意味著一個人正在放鬆，在那一刻甚麼也沒說。他們沒有消耗太多的能量，所以他們透過鼻子呼吸。

外國人將嘴巴閉著時，他們會說：

I'm okay.	我很好。
I'm just relaxing.	我只是在放鬆。
I feel alright.	我感覺還好。
I'm going to sit down.	我要坐下來。
I want to rest for a minute.	我想休息一分鐘。
I'm taking a breather.	我想喘口氣。
I'd like to enjoy the quiet.	我想享受安靜。
I don't have anything to add.	我沒甚麼要補充的。
I think you covered it.	我想你都說到了。
You said everything I would have.	我要說的你都說了。

外國人嘴巴閉著時，你可以回：

Are you sure?	你確定嗎？
Is something bothering you?	有甚麼事困擾你嗎？
You seem quiet.	你看起來很安靜。
Do you have anything to add?	你有甚麼要補充的嗎？
Do you have anything to say?	你有話要說嗎？
I'll leave you to your quiet.	我讓你靜一靜。
Sounds good.	聽起來不錯。
You don't have anything to add?	你沒有要補充的嗎？
What are your thoughts?	你有甚麼想法？
Enjoy your break!	去休息吧！

情境對話 中文可對照上方的例句

Dialogue 1

Ⓐ I'm going to sit down.
Ⓑ Is something bothering you?
Ⓐ I want to rest for a minute.
Ⓑ Enjoy your break.

Dialogue 2

Ⓐ I think you covered it.
Ⓑ You don't have anything to add?
Ⓐ You said everything I would have.
Ⓑ Sounds good.

情境 從英文來看外國人使用此肢體語言的情境

When I came inside, I found my dad sitting quietly in a chair. I was worried that something happened to him. He said he was just relaxing and enjoying the quiet.

當我走進屋子時，我發現我父親安靜地坐在椅子上，我擔心他出事了，他說他只是在放鬆和享受安靜。

情境 5　Leaning Shoulder Against Wall 肩膀靠牆

這是指雙腳踏穩並向後傾斜，把肩膀靠在牆上支撐自己。人們也會把後背靠著牆，或是把屁股靠在可以倚靠的東西上。這些是放鬆的姿勢，表示他們對身邊的人感到自在。

外國人將肩膀靠牆時，他們會說：

What's up?	怎麼啦？
It's good to see you!	很高興見到你！
It was nice talking to you!	跟你聊天很愉快！
You look great.	你看起來很棒。
It's been a while!	有一陣子了！
Grab a drink!	來喝一杯！
Hang out for a while!	出去玩一會兒吧！
Stick around!	待在這裡吧！
It was fun chatting with you!	和你聊天真有趣！
Let's get together again!	讓我們再聚一次！

外國人將肩膀靠牆時，你可以回：

How's your family?	你的家人好嗎？
Not much.	還可以。
Thank you!	謝謝！
Can I get you a drink?	我可以給你拿杯飲料嗎？
I can stay for a while.	我可以待一會兒。
It was really good seeing you.	很高興見到你。
I've missed you!	我很想你！
Let's do this again.	讓我們再來一次吧。
Are you busy tomorrow?	你明天忙嗎？
I'll see you soon.	我會很快再見到你的。

情境對話　中文可對照上方的例句

Dialogue 1

Ⓐ What's up?

Ⓑ Not much.

Ⓐ It's good to see you!

Ⓑ Can I get you a drink?

Dialogue 2

Ⓐ It was fun chatting with you!

Ⓑ I've missed you!

Ⓐ It's been a while!

Ⓑ Let's do this again.

情境　從英文來看外國人使用此肢體語言的情境

I ran into James in the hallway at work. We talked for quite a while. He leaned his shoulder against the wall and asked me about work and my family. He's so nice!

在工作時，我在走廊上遇到 James。我們聊了好一陣子，他將肩膀靠在牆上，問我有關工作和家人的事情。他人真親切！

情境 6

Putting Hands in Pants' Back Pocket
把雙手放在後口袋

這是指把手放在褲子屁股上的後口袋，手掌通常面向內側、貼住屁股。這個姿勢代表人們在這個情境下非常放鬆、舒適。

外國人把雙手放在後口袋時，他們會說：

What's going on?	怎麼了？
It's good to see you!	很高興見到你！
How have you been?	你最近如何？
I haven't seen you in a while.	我很久沒看到你了。
Wanna grab a beer?	要來喝杯啤酒嗎？
How's it going?	最近如何？
I've been busy lately.	我最近很忙碌。
You look great!	你看起來很好！
What's new?	有甚麼新鮮的嗎？
Take care!	保重！

外國人把雙手放在後口袋時，你可以回：

What else is new?	還有甚麼新奇的？
How's your family?	你的家人還好嗎？
I'm doing well.	我很好。
I'm great. You?	我很好，你呢？
It's been too long.	已經很久了。
Yes, let's go!	對啊，走吧！
I'd love to.	好啊！
Let's do it!	來吧！
I'm in!	我加入！／算我一份！
I'll see you soon!	下次見！

情境對話　中文可對照上方的例句

Dialogue 1

Ⓐ What's going on?
Ⓑ Hey there!
Ⓐ I haven't seen you in a while.
Ⓑ It's been too long.

Dialogue 2

Ⓐ How have you been?
Ⓑ I'm great. You?
Ⓐ Wanna grab a beer?
Ⓑ Let's do it!

情境　從英文來看外國人使用此肢體語言的情境

I ran into my old college roommate today. We stood and talked for quite a while. He stood there with his hands in his back pockets, and I leaned against the wall. We ended up meeting later to catch up and have a drink.

我今天遇到我之前的大學室友，我們站著聊天了一陣子。他站在那裡，把手插在褲子後口袋，我則是靠著牆。我們最後又見面去敘舊、喝一杯。

Feeling Confident
感到自信

☞ **感到自信時需要用到的動作，用英文要怎麼說呢？**

對某些事物感到自信就會產生各種手勢和肢體動作，下列是感到自信會用到的手勢與肢體語言，請看圖片，並對照動作的英文和中文。

情境
1

Smug smile 得意的微笑

情境
2

Arms behind the Back 雙手背在後面

情境
3

Hands on hips 手放屁股上

情境
4

Legs wide apart while standing
站著時雙腳大開

情境
5

Confident voice 自信的語調

情境
6

Bearded chin 有鬍鬚的下巴

情境 6
Holding head up high 昂著頭

情境 7
Flat mouth 抿嘴

情境 8
Pushing shoulders back and chest out 肩膀後推、胸部挺出

情境 9
Body standing up straight 身體站直

情境 1 Smug Smile 得意的微笑

臉上帶著得意的笑容時，嘴唇通常會抿在一起，嘴巴只有一側上彎，也可以稍微分開，上唇可能微微上揚，同時，瞇著眼睛以產生帶著懷疑的眼神。這個表情是自滿或自大的意思，也可以是有優越感的表現。如果上唇稍微上揚，則很可能是恐嚇和嘲笑的跡象。

外國人得意地微笑時，他們會說：

You're wrong.	你錯了。
I doubt you.	我懷疑你。
I won!	我贏了！
You lost!	你輸了！
I got the job!	我得到這份工作了！
You're being let go.	你被解雇了。
I'm dumping you.	我要把你甩了。
I'm breaking up with him.	我要跟他分手。
I'm over this.	我已經不在乎了。
I'm moving on.	我不在意了。

外國人得意地微笑時，你可以回：

I'm not wrong.	我沒有錯。
Why don't you believe me?	你為甚麼不相信我？
What's not to believe?	不該相信甚麼？
I'm being serious.	我是認真的。
Congratulations!	恭喜！
Way to go!	太棒了！
What do you mean?	你是甚麼意思？
You can't do that!	你不能那樣做！
How could you?	你怎麼能這樣？
I'm being serious.	我是認真的。

情境對話 中文可對照上方的例句

Dialogue 1

Ⓐ I doubt you.

Ⓑ Why don't you believe me?

Ⓐ You're wrong.

Ⓑ I'm being serious.

Dialogue 2

Ⓐ I got the job!

Ⓑ Congratulations!

Ⓐ I'm so excited!

Ⓑ Way to go!

情境 從英文來看外國人使用此肢體語言的情境

We lost the football championship game. One of the players from the other team came up to us with a smug smile and told us we didn't play very well and deserved to lose. I was so mad!

我們輸掉了足球冠軍賽。另一支球隊的一名球員臉上掛著沾沾自喜的笑容，跑來我們這裡，說我們表現不好，輸球是應該的。我好生氣！

情境 2　Arms Behind the Back 雙手背在後面

指雙臂繞在背部，雙手在後腰處交握。當手臂放在背後時，會產生一種脆弱感，表示人們在某種情況下，或與他人在一起時感到自在。這也可能意味著這個人在某種情況下感到充滿力量，並且知道自己是安全的。掌權者（例如老闆、老師和警察）經常將雙手放在背後站著。

外國人雙手背在後面時，他們會說：

What's up?	最近好嗎？
How's it going?	最近如何？
How have you been?	你近來怎麼樣？
What are you doing?	你在做甚麼？
I'm awesome!	我很好！
I feel great.	我感覺好極了。
I'm doing well.	我過得很好。
Let's hang out!	一起出去玩吧！
You're a good friend.	你真是個好朋友。
Let's grab a drink.	一起去喝一杯吧。

外國人雙手背在後面時，你可以回：

Not much.	沒甚麼。
Nothing new here.	沒甚麼新鮮事。
I'm doing well.	我過得很好。
I'm great!	我很好！
Good! How about you?	不錯！你呢？
I'm going to work.	我要去上班。
I'm just leaving.	我要走了。
You look great!	你看起來很棒！
You look nice today.	你今天看起來不錯。
I'm free tonight.	我今晚有空。

情境對話　中文可對照上方的例句

Dialogue 1

Ⓐ What's up?
Ⓑ Nothing new here.
Ⓐ How have you been?
Ⓑ I'm doing well.

Dialogue 2

Ⓐ How's it going?
Ⓑ Good! How about you?
Ⓐ I'm doing well.
Ⓑ You look great!

情境　從英文來看外國人使用此肢體語言的情境

We had a company meeting this morning. My boss always stands with his arms behind his back as we come in. He makes small talk with each of us and makes us feel welcome. He's a good person to work for.

今天早上我們公司開了會。我們進去時，我的老闆總會把雙手背在背後站著。他和我們每個人閒聊，讓我們感到被接納，他真是個值得為他工作的好人。

情境 3

Hands on Hips 手放屁股上

這是指將手肘彎曲，雙手放在臀部上，而腳略為分開。這個姿勢使人看起來比實際身材強壯，很多人利用這種站姿，讓自己看起來更堅定、自信，使他們看起來已經準備好採取行動。很多時候，超級英雄和警察都會以雙手叉腰的姿態出現，這個姿勢讓他們看起來像是「掌握情況」。

外國人把手放屁股上時，他們會說：

What's going on here?	這裡是怎麼回事？
What's this?	這是甚麼？
Be quiet!	安靜！
Who did this?	這是誰做的？
What happened?	發生了甚麼事？
I'm ready.	我準備好了。
I can handle it.	我能處理。
I'll take the lead.	我會帶頭。
I'm in charge.	我來負責。
I'll do it.	我會做的。

外國人把手放屁股上時，你可以回：

It wasn't me.	不是我。
I didn't do it.	我沒做。
Nothing!	沒事！
We didn't do anything.	我們甚麼也沒做。
It wasn't us.	不是我們弄的。
Nothing happened!	甚麼事都沒發生！
Don't look at me.	不要看我。
Why are you blaming me?	你為甚麼要怪我？
Don't worry about it.	別擔心這件事。
Fine, you do it.	好啊，那你來做吧。

情境對話 中文可對照上方的例句

Dialogue 1

Ⓐ What's going on here?
Ⓑ Nothing!
Ⓐ Who did this?
Ⓑ I didn't do it.

Dialogue 2

Ⓐ I can handle it.
Ⓑ Don't worry about it.
Ⓐ I'll do it.
Ⓑ Fine, you do it.

情境 從英文來看外國人使用此肢體語言的情境

I got home late last night. When I walked inside, my mom was so mad. She had her hands on her hips and was yelling at me about being in trouble for being late.

昨天晚上我很晚回到家，當我走進屋子時，我媽媽非常生氣。她的雙手叉著腰，大聲斥責我因為晚歸而麻煩大了。

情境 4 Legs Apart While Standing 站著時雙腳大開

指站著時將雙腿分開，這個姿勢為站著的人提供了穩固的立足點。雙腳間距越寬，站著的人就會顯得越大。這樣可以展現出優越的地位與力量。

外國人站著、雙腳大開時，他們會說：

What are you doing?	你在做甚麼？
Why are you here?	你為甚麼在這裡？
Who are you?	你是誰？
What do you want?	你想要甚麼？
You need to leave.	你得離開。
I asked you to leave.	我叫你離開。
Get out!	出去！
I'm in charge here.	這裡是我負責的。
I'll take the lead.	我會帶頭。
This is my space.	這是我的地盤。

外國人站著、雙腳大開時，你可以回：

I'm leaving.	我要離開了。
I was just leaving.	我剛離開。
I'm about to go.	我要走了。
I'll get out of here.	我會離開這裡。
Let me go.	讓我走。
I'm Sara.	我是Sara。
I have an appointment.	我有個預約。
I need to talk to your boss.	我得和你的老闆談談。
I'm not going anywhere.	我哪裡都不去。
Don't push me.	不要推我。

情境對話 中文可對照上方的例句

Dialogue 1

Ⓐ I asked you to leave.

Ⓑ I'm about to go.

Ⓐ Get out!

Ⓑ Don't push me.

Dialogue 2

Ⓐ Why are you here?

Ⓑ I have an appointment.

Ⓐ Who are you?

Ⓑ I'm Sara.

情境 從英文來看外國人使用此肢體語言的情境

When we went to the bar, the bouncer wasn't letting anyone in without a ticket. He stood at the door with his arms crossed and legs in a wide stance. He looked intimidating. I'm glad we had tickets and were able to get int.

我們去酒吧時，門口的保鏢不讓任何沒有門票的人進去。他站在門口，雙臂交叉、雙腿大開，看起來很嚇人。我很慶幸我們有門票，能夠入場。

情境 5 Confident Voice 自信的語調

有自信的人會以適當的語速和音量說話，他們結束對話時會用比開始對話時更高的語調。另外，聽起來自信的人會避免在句子中使用贅字（例如「嗯」、「啊」和「像是」等）。自信的聲音代表這個人對於在他人面前說話時會感到很自在。

外國人自信地說話時，他們會說：

Let me talk for a minute.	讓我先講一會兒。
I can lead the meeting.	我可以主持會議。
I'll take charge.	我會來負責。
Here's an example.	這裡有個例子。
Look at this chart.	請看這張圖表。
Let's talk about this.	讓我們談談這個。
I have an idea.	我有個主意。
Let me share my idea.	讓我分享我的想法。
I can give you my feedback.	我可以給你我的意見。
Here's my thoughts.	這是我的想法。

外國人自信地說話時，你可以回：

Go ahead.	繼續。
You can speak.	你可以說了。
You can take the lead.	你可以主持。
You can go first.	你可以先開始。
I see.	我明白了。
I understand.	我懂了。
That makes sense.	那很合理。
What's your idea?	你的想法是甚麼？
What do you think?	你怎麼想？
What's that?	那是甚麼？

情境對話　中文可對照上方的例句

Dialogue 1

Ⓐ I can lead the meeting.
Ⓑ Sure.
Ⓐ I have an idea.
Ⓑ What's your idea?

Dialogue 2

Ⓐ Let's talk about this.
Ⓑ What do you think?
Ⓐ Let me share my idea.
Ⓑ Go ahead.

情境　從英文來看外國人使用此肢體語言的情境

I was presenting our year-end report at the meeting. My boss cut in and took over the presentation. He has such a confident voice and did a really good job. I was bummed that I didn't get to do the whole presentation, but he did better than I would have.

我在會議上報告我們的年終報告。我的老闆插話並接手了簡報，他的語調非常自信，表現得非常出色。令我有點失望的是，結果我沒有機會自己簡報完，但他的表現確實比起我來做的話更好。

情境 6 Bearded Chin 有鬍子的下巴

如果鬍鬚修剪整齊且保養得當，就表示這個人特別在意自己的外表。蓬鬆散亂、如野草般的鬍鬚則可能表示這個人不修邊幅或是懶惰。用食指和拇指撫摸著有鬍鬚的下巴，代表這個人認為自己看起來不錯，好像在說「我很好看」。

外國人下巴留鬍子時，他們會說：

I feel hot!	我覺得性感！
I look good.	我看起來很好看。
I'm handsome.	我好帥。
Check me out!	看看我！
I'm on point today.	我今天很完美。
I just showered.	我剛洗完澡。
I feel good.	我覺得很好。
Do I look okay?	我看起來還好嗎？
Does this shirt look good?	這件襯衫好看嗎？
How do I look?	我看起來怎麼樣？

外國人下巴留鬍子時，你可以回：

That looks itchy.	那看起來很癢。
I don't like it.	我不喜歡。
I think you look nice.	我認為你看起來不錯。
It looks good!	看起來不錯！
You can pull it off.	你可以把它拉下來。
When are you going to shave?	你甚麼時候要刮鬍子？
You look scruffy.	你看起來很邋遢。
I think you look hot.	我認為你看起來很性感。
You look sexy.	你看起來很性感。
It makes you look tough!	它使你看起來強悍！

情境對話 中文可對照上方的例句

Dialogue 1

Ⓐ Check me out!
Ⓑ It looks good!
Ⓐ I'm handsome.
Ⓑ It makes you look tough!

Dialogue 2

Ⓐ Do I look okay?
Ⓑ I think you look nice.
Ⓐ I'm on point today.
Ⓑ You look sexy.

情境 從英文來看外國人使用此肢體語言的情境

My dad has a beard. Whenever I give him a kiss on his cheek, it scratches my face. I wish he would shave it off!

我爸爸留了鬍子。每當我親吻他的臉頰時，鬍子都會抓傷我的臉。我希望他能把鬍子剃掉！

情境 7　Hold Head Up High 昂著頭

　　將肩膀維持在正常位置，保持下巴往上抬，並稍微將頭向上仰，這個動作表示你感到驕傲或自信。有些人輸掉比賽或錯過某事後會昂著頭，這表示他們沒有對失敗感到難過，反之，他們為自己盡了全力而自豪。

外國人昂著頭時，他們會說：

Good game!	這是場好比賽！
I tried my best!	我已經盡力了！
Maybe I'll win next time.	也許下次我會贏。
I gave it my all.	我盡全力了。
I tried really hard.	我真的很努力。
It was a tough match.	這是一場艱難的比賽。
I had fun!	我玩得很開心！
It was a good time.	那曾是一段美好時光。
I'll do better next time.	下次我會做的更好。
I just missed it!	我剛剛錯過了！

外國人昂著頭時，你可以回：

Chin up!	抬起頭來！
You played well.	你打得很好。
You did a good job.	你做得很好。
Nice try!	不錯的嘗試！
It was a good game.	這是一個很棒的比賽。
They played well.	他們打得很好。
You gave it your all.	你全力以赴了。
You played your best.	你全力發揮了。
You did great!	你做得很棒！
Maybe next time!	也許下次會好的！

情境對話　中文可對照上方的例句

Dialogue 1

Ⓐ Good game!
Ⓑ You played well.
Ⓐ I tried really hard.
Ⓑ Maybe next time!

Dialogue 2

Ⓐ We lost!
Ⓑ It was a good game.
Ⓐ I'll do better next time.
Ⓑ You played your best.

情境　從英文來看外國人使用此肢體語言的情境

My son had his baseball tournament this weekend. They lost the championship game. The team they played with was really good. My son was bummed that they lost, but he held his head high.

我兒子這個週末參加了棒球比賽，結果他們輸掉了冠軍賽。和他們打的那支球隊真的很棒，我兒子因為輸了而感到沮喪，但他仍昂著頭。

情境 8　Flat Mouth 抿嘴

指嘴唇抿成一直線且嘴巴閉著。抿著嘴、瞇起眼而眉毛下垂的表情代表這個人感到擁有力量。例如，他們可能正在判斷他人或情況。

外國人抿嘴時，他們會說：

I dislike you.	我不喜歡你。
I wish you'd leave.	我希望你能離開。
I can't believe you're here.	我不敢相信你在這裡。
Who invited you?	誰邀請你來的？
Why did you come?	你為甚麼來？
Get lost.	走開。
His shirt is hideous.	他的襯衫很醜。
I can't stand her.	我受不了她。
Her dress is awful.	她的洋裝糟透了。
Ask them to leave.	請他們離開。

外國人抿嘴時，你可以回：

That's not nice!	這樣很差！
That's mean to say.	這麼說很苛薄。
I can't believe you said that.	我不敢相信你這麼說。
How could you be so mean?	你怎麼這麼苛薄？
Why did you say that?	你為甚麼這麼說？
I don't like it either.	我也不喜歡。
It's not that bad.	沒那麼糟糕。
It's hideous!	這太醜了！
I can't stand it either.	我也受不了。
I agree with you.	我同意你的看法。

情境對話　中文可對照上方的例句

Dialogue 1

Ⓐ I wish you'd leave.
Ⓑ Why?
Ⓐ I dislike you.
Ⓑ I can't believe you said that.

Dialogue 2

Ⓐ I can't stand her.
Ⓑ That's not nice!
Ⓐ Her dress is awful.
Ⓑ How could you be so mean?

情境　從英文來看外國人使用此肢體語言的情境

I could tell that something was bothering my mom because her mouth was flat. She gets that look when she doesn't like something. I asked her about it and she said she really didn't like the music that was playing. I turned it off.

我可以看得出來媽媽因為一些事煩心，因為她正抿著嘴。當她有不喜歡的事時，她臉上就會露出那種表情。我問她怎麼了，她說她真的不喜歡正在播放的音樂，我就把它關掉了。

情境 9 Pushing Shoulder Back and Chest Out
肩膀後推、胸部挺出

肩膀往後推時，會使胸部更為突出，並稍微向外擴展。這是一個顯示自信和力量的姿勢，擁有權力的人會做出這種姿勢。

外國人挺胸時，他們會說：

I'm in charge.	這裡由我負責。
I'll take the lead.	我來帶頭。
Follow me.	跟著我。
I'll lead the meeting.	我來主持會議。
Let me speak.	讓我發言。
I'll do the talking.	我會負責發言。
You won't be needed.	不需要你來。
I'm going to do it.	我會去做這件事。
I can handle it.	我能處理。
This will be easy.	這會很容易。

外國人挺胸時，你可以回：

Go ahead.	繼續吧。
You can go.	你可以去。
That's fine.	沒關係。
Lead the way.	帶路吧。
I'll follow you.	我會跟隨你。
Sounds good.	聽起來不錯。
That's great.	太好了。
Perfect!	完美！
I'll just listen.	我只會聽而已。
Let me know if I can help.	讓我知道是否有我可以幫忙的地方。

情境對話 中文可對照上方的例句

Dialogue 1

Ⓐ I'll do the talking.
Ⓑ Go ahead.
Ⓐ You won't be needed.
Ⓑ I'll just listen.

Dialogue 2

Ⓐ I'll lead the meeting.
Ⓑ That's fine.
Ⓐ This will be easy.
Ⓑ Let me know if I can add anything.

情境 從英文來看外國人使用此肢體語言的情境

When we walked into the courtroom, I could tell my attorney was going to do well. He had his chest puffed out and his shoulders back. He told me to just sit quietly and he would do the talking.

當我們走進法庭時，我可以看得出來說我的律師會做得很好。他挺胸、肩膀往後。他告訴我安靜地坐著就好，他會負責講話。

情境 10 **Body Standing Up Straight 身體站直**

當一個人的身體以正確的姿勢站直，腳與肩膀同寬，手臂自然垂放在身體兩側、後背打直、肩膀向後拉，這使得他看起來有自信也更有威嚴。

外國人身體站直時，他們會說：

I'm in charge.	這由我來負責。
I'll take the lead.	我會領頭。
I've got it.	我已經懂了。
Let me hold the door.	讓我來扶這扇門。
This way, please.	這邊請。
Follow me.	跟我走。
I'll talk about it.	我會談論這個議題。
Let me interrupt.	容我打斷一下。
I'll handle it.	我會處理這件事。
Let me do the talking.	讓我來發言。

外國人身體站直時，你可以回：

Go ahead.	請繼續。
Sounds good.	聽起來不錯。
Go for it!	加油！
I'll follow you.	我會跟著你。
After you.	你先走。
Take the lead.	請你領頭。
That works for me.	這對我來說可行。
You can go first.	就讓你先來吧。
Go right ahead.	開始吧
That's fine with me.	我沒關係。

情境對話 中文可對照上方的例句

Dialogue 1

Ⓐ Let me do the talking.
Ⓑ Go right ahead.
Ⓐ I'll take the lead.
Ⓑ That works for me.

Dialogue 2

Ⓐ Let me hold the door.
Ⓑ You can go first.
Ⓐ Follow me.
Ⓑ Thank you.

情境 從英文來看外國人使用此肢體語言的情境

My manager and I were firing someone today. He told me to let him do the talking and I could just listen. He stood nice and straight and talked really formal when he fired the guy. I was impressed.

我的經理和我今天把一個人開除了，他告訴我讓他來說話，我只要聽就好。經理把那位職員開除時，他站得直挺、用非常正式的語氣說話。讓我印象深刻。

UNIT 7

Cynicism 嘲諷

👉 **嘲諷、假裝時需要用到的動作，用英文要怎麼說呢？**

對某些事物嘲諷就會產生各種手勢和肢體動作，下列是嘲諷會用到的手勢與
肢體語言，請看圖片，並對照動作的英文和中文。

情境 1

Half smile 半個微笑

情境 2

Fake smile 假笑

情境 3

Open mouth smile 咧嘴笑

情境 4

Sarcastic voice 諷刺的語調

※Mouth slightly turn up 嘴角稍微上揚也可以是代表假裝的臉部表情，可以看到
Unit 4 的 p.38。

情境 1 # Half Smile 半個微笑

這表示只用半邊臉微笑，半邊的嘴唇向上彎，並且語氣幾乎咆哮著，眼睛／臉部的其他部分沒有笑意。這個表情代表這個人在諷刺，或者不太確定情況。這也可能意味著他們並不同意他人所說的話。

外國人微笑一半時，他們會說：

I don't buy it.	我不買帳。
You're lying.	你在撒謊。
I'm joking.	我在開玩笑。
It was a joke.	這是個玩笑。
I'm teasing you.	我在逗你。
They're lying.	他們在說謊。
I don't believe them.	我不相信他們。
I think he's lying.	我認為他在說謊。
He's making it up.	他在編故事。
It can't be true.	這不可能是真的。

外國人微笑一半時，你可以回：

I'm not lying.	我沒有說謊。
I'm telling you the truth.	我在告訴你事實。
I'm being serious.	我是認真的。
I wouldn't lie to you.	我不會對你說謊。
I wouldn't lie about this!	這種事我不會撒謊！
I'm not making it up.	我沒有編故事。
I thought you were serious.	我以為你是認真的。
Don't tease me!	別逗我！
I didn't know you were joking.	我不知道你在開玩笑。
I didn't find it funny.	我不覺得好笑。

情境對話 中文可對照上方的例句

Dialogue 1

Ⓐ You're lying.
Ⓑ I'm not lying.
Ⓐ I don't buy it.
Ⓑ I'm being serious.

Dialogue 2

Ⓐ It was a joke.
Ⓑ I didn't know you were joking.
Ⓐ I was.
Ⓑ I thought you were serious.

情境 從英文來看外國人使用此肢體語言的情境

Larry told me about his date last night. He was bragging about how hot his new girlfriend is. I just listened with a half-smile on my face. I think he knows I don't believe him.

Larry 跟我談到他昨晚的約會，他在吹噓自己的新女友有多辣。我只是聽著，臉上掛著半個微笑，我想他知道我不相信他所說的。

Fake Smile 假笑

假笑是指嘴唇的四周往上彎，而面部其他部分卻沒有笑意。假笑時，可能不會露出牙齒，眼睛也沒有笑意。一般來說，假笑意味著這個人想表達他很愉悅或認同，但他的真實感受卻不是愉悅／認同。

外國人假笑時，他們會說：

I'm glad you came!	非常高興你來了！
I'm happy to see you!	我很開心見到你！
You look amazing!	你看起來好美！
Your presentation rocked!	你的簡報太強了！
You did great!	你做得很好！
I'd love to join you!	我很想加入你！
I'll meet you there!	我們那裡見！
That sounds awesome.	這聽起來很棒。
You're so funny!	你太搞笑了！
That joke was great!	那個笑話真棒！

外國人假笑時，你可以回：

Thank you!	謝謝你！
You're so sweet.	你真貼心。
You're being nice.	你人真好。
Are you being serious?	你是認真的嗎？
That's sweet.	太貼心了。
Seriously?	真的嗎？
Are you kidding?	你在開玩笑嗎？
What are you saying?	你在說甚麼？
You're being rude.	你這樣很粗魯。
I think you're lying.	我認為你在說謊。

情境對話　中文可對照上方的例句

Dialogue 1

Ⓐ I'm glad you came!

Ⓑ Me, too.

Ⓐ You look amazing!

Ⓑ You're so sweet.

Dialogue 2

Ⓐ Your presentation rocked!

Ⓑ Seriously?

Ⓐ You did great!

Ⓑ Thank you!

情境　從英文來看外國人使用此肢體語言的情境

I have a coworker that I don't get along with. She's always rude to me. After my presentation, she told me that I did a good job in front of everyone. She had a very obvious fake smile, and everyone knew she was being sarcastic. I can't stand her!

我有一個處得不太好的同事，她總是對我很無禮。在我的簡報之後，她在大家面前告訴我，我表現得很好。她的假笑非常明顯，所有人都知道她在諷刺，我真受不了她！

情境 3　Open Mouth Smile 咧嘴笑

這種微笑會使嘴巴張開，牙齒露出，卻沒有發出笑聲。人們很少咧嘴笑卻不發出笑聲，因此這種笑容被認為是假笑。儘管是假笑，卻比閉著嘴的微笑更容易讓人相信。這種微笑使得其他人認為你也對此感到滿意，或者使他們認為你很開心。

外國人咧嘴笑時，他們會說：	
This is great!	這很棒！
It's awesome!	這超棒的！
I'm having a blast!	我玩得很盡興。
Let's do it again!	讓我們再來一次！
I love it!	我喜歡！
I really like this.	我真的很喜歡。
Thank you!	謝謝你！
This is the best!	這是最好的！
You shouldn't have!	你不應該這麼做的！
I'm so surprised!	我好驚訝喔！

外國人咧嘴笑時，你可以回：	
I'm glad you're having fun.	我很高興你玩得開心。
I think so, too!	我也這麼認為！
I'm happy you like it!	我很高興你喜歡！
Isn't it great?	這不是很棒嗎？
Me too!	我也是！
You're welcome.	不客氣。
I'm happy you had a good time.	我很高興你過得開心。
You deserve it.	你應得的。
Were you really surprised?	你真的很驚訝嗎？
Did we surprise you?	我們有讓你驚喜嗎？

情境對話　中文可對照上方的例句

Dialogue 1

Ⓐ I really like this.
Ⓑ Isn't it great?
Ⓐ I love it!
Ⓑ I'm glad you're having fun.

Dialogue 2

Ⓐ I'm so surprised!
Ⓑ Were you really surprised?
Ⓐ I really like this.
Ⓑ I'm so happy you like it.

情境　從英文來看外國人使用此肢體語言的情境

We surprised our parents with an anniversary party. My dad was thrilled, and we think my mom liked it. She had a huge, open smile. I couldn't tell if she was faking or if she was really surprised.

我們為爸媽舉行了週年派對讓他們驚喜，我爸爸很興奮，我們覺得我媽媽也喜歡，她的嘴巴張開，露出燦爛的笑容。我不知道她是在假裝還是真的很驚訝。

情境 4 · Sarcastic Voice 諷刺的語調

諷刺時，人們會拉長字句的音節，用比正常語調更高的音調開始說話，然後再逐漸降低語調。通常諷刺的語調會與諷刺的臉部表情搭配，例如翻白眼。這意味著說話的人希望對方覺得自己不好、或是質疑對方剛才所說的話。

外國人諷刺時，他們會說：

Really?	是嗎？
Do you mean that?	你是那個意思嗎？
Are you being serious?	你是認真的嗎？
Of course you think that.	你當然會這麼想。
I think you're funny.	我覺得你真有趣。
That's a great story.	這真是個好故事。
Let's talk about it again.	讓我們再說一次。
Obviously you're right.	你顯然是對的。
I hope that's true.	我希望那是真的。
You should keep talking.	你應該繼續講話。

外國人諷刺時，你可以回：

Why do you say that?	你為甚麼這麼說？
What's the matter?	怎麼了？
What does that mean?	這是甚麼意思？
Do you think I'm lying?	你覺得我在說謊嗎？
I didn't make that up.	不是我編出來的。
You're being rude!	你這樣很無禮！
That bothers me.	這讓我不開心。
Don't be sarcastic.	不要挖苦我。
I don't like when you talk like that.	我不喜歡你這樣說話。
Knock it off.	住口。
I didn't find it funny.	我不覺得好笑。

情境對話　中文可對照上方的例句

Dialogue 1
Ⓐ You should keep talking.
Ⓑ Are you being serious?
Ⓐ No.
Ⓑ Don't be sarcastic.

Dialogue 2
Ⓐ That's a great story.
Ⓑ What does that mean?
Ⓐ I don't believe you.
Ⓑ I didn't make that up.

情境　從英文來看外國人使用此肢體語言的情境

I was telling a story at lunch, and my friend kept saying sarcastic comments. She acted like she didn't believe what I was saying. I asked her about it later, and she told me she thought I was lying. I can't believe she doesn't believe me!

我在午餐時講了一個故事，我的朋友一直在說諷刺的評論。她表現得好像不相信我所說的話。後來我去問她，她說她以為我在撒謊。我簡直不敢相信她不相信我！

UNIT 8
Feeling Scared
感到害怕

☞ **感到害怕時需要用到的動作，用英文要怎麼說呢？**

感到害怕就會產生各種手勢和肢體動作，下列是感到害怕會用到的手勢與肢體語言，請看圖片，並對照動作的英文和中文。

情境 1

Hand on chest 手放在胸口

情境 2

Scared sweating 害怕的出汗

情境 3

Open mouth and breathing fast
張開嘴喘氣

情境 4

Open mouth and gulping
倒抽一口氣

情境 5

Chewing bottom lips 咬著下唇

情境 6

Shaking Body 身體顫抖

Hand on Chest 手放在胸口

這個姿勢是將張開的手掌放在上胸部，並覆蓋在心臟的位置上，這是代表驚喜的意思。很多時候，人們做出這個手勢時會倒抽一口氣，也有很多人吃驚時會做出這個動作。

外國人手放胸口時，他們會說：

Oh my!	我的天啊！
I can't believe it!	我簡直不敢相信！
This is amazing!	這真是太了不起了！
Look at that!	看看那個！
Wow!	哇！
You scared me!	你嚇到我了！
Don't scare me!	別嚇我！
The snake scared me!	那條蛇嚇到我了！
It's scary!	好嚇人！
I'm afraid!	我好害怕！

外國人手放胸口時，你可以回：

It's for you.	這是給你的。
We did it for you.	這是我們為你做的。
I made it for you.	這是我為你做的。
Isn't it amazing?	這不是很驚人嗎？
That's awesome!	這太棒了！
I wanted to surprise you.	我想要給你驚喜。
Don't be scared!	不要害怕！
I'll get rid of it.	我會把它弄走的。
I'll take care of you.	我會照顧你的。
You're okay.	你沒事的。

情境對話 中文可對照上方的例句

Dialogue 1
Ⓐ Oh my!
Ⓑ Don't be scared!
Ⓐ You scared me!
Ⓑ I didn't mean to.

Dialogue 2
Ⓐ Look at that!
Ⓑ Isn't it amazing?
Ⓐ It's beautiful.
Ⓑ It's for you.

情境 從英文來看外國人使用此肢體語言的情境

I asked my girlfriend to marry me last night. We were outside near a lake and I got down on one knee. She was so surprised! She put her hand over her heart and gasped. She said yes!

昨晚我跟女友求婚了。我們來到戶外靠近湖邊，然後我單膝跪下，我的女友超級驚訝！她把手按在胸口上，倒抽了一口氣，然後說了「Yes！」。

情境 2　Scared Sweating 害怕的出汗

與壓力的出汗（p. 101）類似，當人害怕時就會出汗，呼吸和心跳加快，導致體溫升高。這樣會使人在害怕時感到發熱，並開始流汗。

外國人害怕而流汗時，他們會說：

I'm afraid.	我很怕。
I'm scared.	我嚇壞了。
The haunted house is scary.	那棟鬼屋很恐怖。
I don't like it here.	我不喜歡它在這裡。
I think we're in danger.	我認為我們有危險。
I want to leave.	我想離開。
I need to get out of here.	我要離開這裡。
I can't stay here.	我不能待在這裡。
I hate this.	我討厭這個。
I don't want to be here.	我不想在這裡。

外國人害怕而流汗時，你可以回：

You're okay.	你沒事。
You're fine!	你很好！
Don't be afraid!	不要害怕。
You'll be fine.	你會沒事的。
It's no big deal.	沒甚麼大不了的。
We're not leaving.	我們沒有要離開。
Calm down.	冷靜下來。
Relax!	放鬆點！
We can't go anywhere.	我們不能去任何地方。
I'll hold your hand.	我會握住你的手。

情境對話　中文可對照上方的例句

Dialogue 1

Ⓐ I'm afraid.
Ⓑ Don't be afraid!
Ⓐ I don't like it here.
Ⓑ You'll be fine.

Dialogue 2

Ⓐ I need to get out of here.
Ⓑ We can't go anywhere.
Ⓐ The haunted house is scary.
Ⓑ I'll hold your hand.

情境　從英文來看外國人使用此肢體語言的情境

We went to a haunted house over the weekend. It was scary! There were clowns and scary guys with chainsaws. I was sweating so bad by the time we got out of it. I'll never go to one of those again.

週末我們去了一棟鬼屋。那真是太可怕了！那裡有一些小丑和拿著電鋸的可怕傢伙，當我們逃出去時，我滿身大汗。我永遠不會再去任何鬼屋了。

Open Mouth and Breathing Fast 張開嘴喘氣

張開嘴喘氣可能表示一個人感到恐懼或生氣。如果有人感到壓力過大,他們也會張大嘴巴,沉重地呼吸。最後,消耗了大量精力(例如:爬樓梯或鍛煉)的人,也可能會張著嘴喘氣。

外國人張開嘴喘氣時,他們會說:

I'm really nervous.	我真的好緊張。
I'm afraid!	我好害怕!
I feel anxious.	我很焦慮。
I'm stressing out!	我壓力好大!
I'm freaking out!	我嚇壞了!
I can't breathe.	我無法呼吸。
I just ran up the stairs.	我剛才跑上樓梯。
I was mowing the grass.	我剛才在割草。
I was running.	我剛才在跑步。
I was hurrying!	我很著急!

外國人張開嘴喘氣時,你可以回:

Don't panic!	不要驚慌!
Calm down.	冷靜下來。
Take a deep breath.	深呼吸。
You can do this.	你可以的。
You got this.	你明白了。
You'll be just fine.	你會好起來的。
It will be alright.	會沒事的。
Are you okay?	你還好嗎?
Do you need some water?	你需要水嗎?
You're going to be okay.	你會沒事的。

情境對話 中文可對照上方的例句

Dialogue 1

Ⓐ I'm really nervous.
Ⓑ Take a deep breath.
Ⓐ I'm freaking out!
Ⓑ Don't panic!

Dialogue 2

Ⓐ I can't breathe.
Ⓑ Are you okay?
Ⓐ I was running.
Ⓑ Do you need some water?

情境 從英文來看外國人使用此肢體語言的情境

Jacob called me yesterday. I had just gotten home from a long run and was breathing heavily and fast and I could hardly talk. He asked me if I was okay, so I told him I had just gotten home from running. He ended up asking me to dinner this weekend.

Jacob 昨天打電話給我。那時我才剛去長跑完回到家,我的呼吸沉重而急促,我幾乎無法說話。他問我還好嗎,所以我告訴他我才剛從跑完步回來。他最後邀我這個週末一起吃晚飯。

情境 4 **Open Mouth and Gulping 倒抽一口氣**

張開嘴並吸入一大口氣時，這被稱為倒抽一口氣。遇到疼痛、突然被嚇到或感到驚訝的情況時，這種反應就很常見。

外國人倒抽一口氣時，他們會說：

You scared me!	你嚇到我了！
I didn't know you were here!	我不知道你在這裡！
He startled me.	他嚇了我一跳。
I hurt myself.	我弄傷了我自己。
I stubbed my toe!	我撞到腳趾了！
I hit my elbow!	我的手肘撞到了！
I twisted my ankle.	我的腳踝扭到了。
You surprised me!	你讓我驚喜！
I can't believe this!	我真不敢相信！
It's amazing!	太奇妙了！

外國人倒抽一口氣時，你可以回：

Sorry about that!	對不起！
I'm so sorry!	我很抱歉！
I didn't mean to scare you.	我不是故意要嚇你的。
Are you okay?	你還好嗎？
How did you do that?	你是如何做到的？
Don't be scared!	不要害怕！
Did we startle you?	我們嚇了你一跳嗎？
Did you like it?	你喜歡嗎？
You're okay!	你沒事的！
Did you like your surprise?	你喜歡你的驚喜嗎？

情境對話 中文可對照上方的例句

Dialogue 1

Ⓐ I hurt myself.
Ⓑ Are you okay?
Ⓐ I twisted my ankle.
Ⓑ I'm sorry.

Dialogue 2

Ⓐ I didn't know you were here!
Ⓑ Did we startle you?
Ⓐ You scared me!
Ⓑ Sorry about that!

情境 從英文來看外國人使用此肢體語言的情境

I came home from work today and didn't expect anyone to be there. When I walked in, my husband was home already. He startled me! I let out a big gasp and grabbed my heart. He thought it was funny.

我今天下班回到家，沒料到家裡已經有人了。當我走進門時，我先生已經在家。他嚇了我一跳！我倒抽一口氣，抓住我的胸口。他認為這樣很有趣。

情境 5 Chewing Bottom Lips 咬著下唇

人們咬下唇會反覆地咬或咀嚼下唇，這通常表示恐懼和焦慮。這也可能意味著人們在某種情況下感到不舒服，或是在擔心某事。

外國人咬著下唇時，他們會說：

I worry about him.	我擔心他。
I feel anxious today.	我今天很焦慮。
I can't settle down.	我不能安定下來。
I'm nervous!	我很緊張！
I hope everything is okay.	我希望一切都很好。
I just want it to be done.	我只是希望可以完成。
I feel uncomfortable here.	我在這裡不自在。
I'd like to leave.	我想離開了。
I'm going to go.	我要走了。
I'll see you later.	一會兒見。

外國人咬著下唇時，你可以回：

I'm sure he'll be fine.	我確定他會沒事的。
It will be okay.	會沒事的。
Everything will work out.	一切都會解決。
Don't be nervous.	不要緊張。
Calm down.	冷靜下來。
Relax!	放輕鬆！
Everything will be alright.	一切都會好起來的。
You can leave if you want.	你想走的話就走吧。
Go ahead and leave.	你就離開吧。
Just relax for a bit.	放鬆一下。

情境對話　中文可對照上方的例句

Dialogue 1

Ⓐ I feel uncomfortable here.
Ⓑ Just relax for a bit.
Ⓐ I'd like to leave.
Ⓑ You can leave if you want.

Dialogue 2

Ⓐ I hope everything is okay.
Ⓑ It will be okay.
Ⓐ I worry about him.
Ⓑ I'm sure he'll be fine.

情境　從英文來看外國人使用此肢體語言的情境

I'm getting ready to present at our yearly conference. I'm so nervous! My hands are sweating and I can't stop biting my lip. I'll be relax when this is over.

我正準備在我們的年度會議上發言。我好緊張！我的雙手都在流汗，而我一直在咬嘴唇。會議結束時我一定會很放鬆。

情境 6 Shaking Body 身體顫抖

當身體顫抖時，整個身體經歷肌肉細微的抽動、抖動，這代表人們對某件事真的很緊張或害怕。

外國人身體顫抖時，他們會說：

I'm so scared.	我真的很害怕。
I'm afraid.	我很害怕。
I can't do it.	我做不到。
Please don't make me do it.	請不要讓我做這件事。
I want it to be over.	我想要這件事快點結束。
I hate this!	我討厭這件事！
It's awful!	真糟糕！
I'm afraid of heights.	我害怕很高的地方。
I can't stay here.	我不能待在這裡。
I have to get out of here.	我要離開這裡。

外國人身體顫抖時，你可以回：

You're going to be okay.	你會好好的。
Don't be scared.	別害怕。
You'll be fine.	你會沒事的。
I'm here!	我在這裡！
It's almost over.	快結束了。
We can leave.	我們可以離開了。
Take a deep breath.	深呼吸。
We have to do it.	我們必須要這樣做。
Let's go.	走吧。
It's going to be alright.	會沒事的。

情境對話 中文可對照上方的例句

Dialogue 1

Ⓐ I'm so scared.
Ⓑ It's almost over.
Ⓐ I have to get out of here.
Ⓑ You'll be fine.

Dialogue 2

Ⓐ I hate this!
Ⓑ You're going to be okay.
Ⓐ I'm afraid of heights.
Ⓑ Take a deep breath.

情境 從英文來看外國人使用此肢體語言的情境

I had to have a tooth pulled yesterday. I was so scared that my hands were sweating and my whole body was shaking. It wasn't too bad, but I'm glad it's over.

我昨天必須要去拔牙，我太害怕，以致於我的手冒汗、整個身體發抖。結果沒有太糟，但我很高興這已經結束了。

Feeling Sad 感到傷心

☞ **感到傷心時需要用到的動作，用英文要怎麼說呢？**

對某些事物感到傷心就會產生各種手勢和肢體動作，下列是感到傷心會用到的手勢與肢體語言，請看圖片，並對照動作的英文和中文。

情境
1

Group hug 群體擁抱

情境
2

Turned down lips 嘴角向下

情境
3

Mouth slightly turned down
嘴唇稍微向下

情境 1 Group Hug 群體擁抱

群體擁抱在美國是比較新的流行（最近 15 年），是一種一起經歷在艱難的時光／事件中（情緒上、身體上、悲傷或創傷）的多人擁抱。有點像是橄欖球隊圍成一圈，一群人聚集在一起，並將手臂同時伸展開來，放在其他人的背上。

外國人群體擁抱時，他們會說：

Group hug!	群體擁抱！
Everybody come together.	大家都聚在一起。
We have each other.	我們還有彼此。
We made it through the crisis.	我們度過了危機。
Let's move on.	讓我們繼續前進。
We can't give up now.	我們現在不能放棄。
You guys are the best.	你們是最棒的。
There's strength in numbers.	人多力量大。
To better times!	為了更好的時光！
We did it together.	我們一起做到了。

外國人群體擁抱時，你可以回：

We made it.	我們做到了。
I needed you guys.	我需要你們。
Get in here.	過來這裡吧。
You're the greatest.	你是最棒的。
We'll get through this.	我們會通過難關的。
We were there for each other.	我們彼此扶持。
We had each other's back.	我們有彼此的後盾。
I'm glad I have you guys.	很高興有你們在我身邊。
I'm happy we did it together.	很高興我們一起完成了。
I'm glad we did it.	我很高興我們做到了。

情境對話 中文可對照上方的例句

Dialogue 1

Ⓐ Group hug!
Ⓑ Get in here.
Ⓐ Everybody come together.
Ⓑ I'm glad we did it.

Dialogue 2

Ⓐ We can't give up now.
Ⓑ We'll get through this.
Ⓐ We have each other.
Ⓑ I needed you guys.

情境 從英文來看外國人使用此肢體語言的情境

We had a horrible storm come through last night. After it passed, my family and friends all hugged each other. It was a scary time and we were happy to make it through together.

昨晚我們經歷了一場可怕的暴風雨。風暴過去之後，我的家人和朋友都互相擁抱。那真是段可怕的時光，我們很高興能一起度過。

情境 2　Turned Down Lips 嘴角向下

這是指皺著眉頭，嘴角往下。這通常表示人們感到難過，或對某事表達不滿意。當人皺眉時，他們的頭會朝向地面，眼睛則會往下看。

外國人嘴角向下時，他們會說：

I feel sad.	我很難過。
I did something wrong.	我做錯事情了。
I don't feel well.	我覺得不舒服。
Something is wrong.	有事情出錯了。
I'm worried.	我很擔心。
I'm scared.	我很害怕。
I'm so upset.	我好難過。
I'm hurt.	我很傷心。
I messed up.	我搞砸了。
I failed my class.	我這堂課被當了。

外國人嘴角向下時，你可以回：

What's wrong?	怎麼了？
You don't look good.	你看起來不太好。
Are you sick?	你生病了嗎？
What's the matter?	怎麼了嗎？
What are you worried about?	你在擔心甚麼？
Don't freak out.	不要慌張。
You're okay.	你沒事的。
It will work out.	會順利的。
Don't get upset.	不要不開心。
You'll do better next time.	下次你會做得更好。

情境對話　中文可對照上方的例句

Dialogue 1
- Ⓐ I'm so upset.
- Ⓑ What's wrong?
- Ⓐ I failed my class.
- Ⓑ Everything will be fine.

Dialogue 2
- Ⓐ Something is wrong.
- Ⓑ What's the matter?
- Ⓐ I don't feel well.
- Ⓑ I hope you feel better soon.

情境　從英文來看外國人使用此肢體語言的情境

I could tell something was wrong when I saw Mike's face. He was frowning and looked pale. He told us he wasn't feeling well, so we made him go home and rest. I hope he feels better tomorrow.

當我看到 Mike 的表情時，我就知道有事情不太對勁了。他皺著眉頭，臉色蒼白。他告訴我們他覺得不太舒服，所以我們叫他回家休息。我希望他明天會好些。

情境 3　Mouth Slightly Turned Down 嘴角稍微向下

嘴角向下表示不開心，在人們對某事感到不滿時就會發生。他們可能對所發生的事情感到悲傷、壓力或不安。

外國人嘴角稍微向下時，他們會說：

I'm upset.	我很失望。
I'm mad at him.	我在生他的氣。
He's a jerk.	他是個混蛋。
I can't stand her.	我受不了她。
I miss him.	我很想念他。
I wish he was here.	我希望他在這裡。
I'm worrying about work.	我很擔心工作。
I have a big test tomorrow.	我明天有個大考。
I'm panicking about my job.	我對我的工作感到恐慌。
I don't feel well.	我覺得不舒服。

外國人嘴角稍微向下時，你可以回：

What's wrong?	怎麼了？
Why are you mad?	你為甚麼生氣？
Did something happen?	發生甚麼事了嗎？
Tell me what's wrong.	告訴我怎麼了。
Tell me about it.	跟我說說。
Call him!	打電話給他！
Can I help?	我可以幫忙嗎？
How can I help you?	我該如何幫助你？
Is there something I can do?	有甚麼我可以做的嗎？
What do you need?	你需要甚麼？

情境對話　中文可對照上方的例句

Dialogue 1

Ⓐ I'm mad at him.
Ⓑ Why are you mad?
Ⓐ He's a jerk.
Ⓑ Did something happen?

Dialogue 2

Ⓐ I miss him.
Ⓑ Tell me what's wrong?
Ⓐ I wish he was here.
Ⓑ Call him!

情境　從英文來看外國人使用此肢體語言的情境

Jackie had a frown on her face most of the day today. I finally asked her what was wrong, and she said she wasn't feeling well. I think she's getting sick.

Jackie 今天大部分的時間都皺著眉頭。我最終還是問她出了甚麼問題，她說她不舒服。我覺得她生病了。

Feeling Nervous
感到緊張

☞ **感到緊張時需要用到的動作，用英文要怎麼說呢？**

對某些事物感到緊張就會產生各種手勢和肢體動作，下列是感到緊張會用到的手勢與肢體語言，請看圖片，並對照動作的英文和中文。

情境
1

Sweaty, clenched fists
流汗、握緊的拳頭

情境
2

Wringing hands 擰著手

情境
3

Fidgeting body 身體坐立不安

情境
4

Sweating Nervously 緊張地出汗

情境
5

Biting lips 咬嘴唇

情境
6

Grasping the front of the neck
握住脖子的前端

情境 **7**

Fidgeting legs 坐立不安的腿

情境 **8**

Locked ankles 腳踝扣在一起

情境 **9**

Talking fast 快速地說話

情境 **10**

Flared nostrils 撐開的鼻孔

情境 **11**

Raising shoulders and lowering head 提高肩膀、低頭

情境 **12**

Shaking legs while sitting 坐著抖腿

情境 **13**

Red ears 耳朵發紅

情境 **14**

Biting fingernails 咬手指甲

Sweaty, Clenched Fists 流汗、握緊的拳頭

指拳頭成球狀握緊,這可能是有壓力或緊張的表現。當人們緊張時,他們的體溫會上升,導致他們流汗。

外國人的拳頭流汗、握緊時,他們會說:

I'm so upset!	我好沮喪!
I'm never going to finish this.	我永遠完成不了這件事。
I can't do it.	我做不到。
I'm so nervous.	我好緊張。
I have to speak next.	我必須下一個發言。
I'm going to an interview.	我要去一場面試。
I have to talk to the boss soon.	我必須馬上跟老闆談話。
I'm late.	我遲到了。
Can you help me?	你可以幫我嗎?
I can't calm down!	我無法冷靜!

外國人的拳頭流汗、握緊時,你可以回:

What's the matter?	怎麼了?
Is something wrong?	有甚麼不對勁的嗎?
Don't be nervous!	別緊張!
You can do it!	你做得到的!
You'll do great.	你會做得很好的!
You're just fine.	你沒事的。
It's going to be fine.	會沒事的。
I can't help you.	我沒辦法幫你。
I'll help you.	我會幫你的。
What do you need?	你需要甚麼?

情境對話 中文可對照上方的例句

Dialogue 1

Ⓐ I'm so nervous.

Ⓑ What's the matter?

Ⓐ I have to speak next.

Ⓑ You can do it.

Dialogue 2

Ⓐ Can you help me?

Ⓑ What do you need?

Ⓐ I'm never going to finish this.

Ⓑ I'll help you.

情境 從英文來看外國人使用此肢體語言的情境

We have a huge project due in biology class. Jason called me and told me he was having a hard time with it. I went to his house to help him. When I got there, his fists were clenched and sweaty, and he was really nervous. I helped him get it finished on time.

我們的生物課有一個很大的報告期限要到了。Jason 打給我並跟我說他在做這個報告有困難,我就去他家幫他。當我到的時候,他的拳頭緊握、流汗,而且他真的很緊張。我幫忙他把報告及時完成。

情境 2 Wringing Hands 擰著手

擰手是極度緊張的手勢。人們擰自己的雙手時會將手緊握、揉捏雙手、並且把手搓在一起。他們可能還會不停地撥弄手指，或是按壓指關節以發出響聲。這些通常發生在壓力大的情況下，並且伴隨其他緊張時的習慣動作，例如踱步、用腳反覆輕拍地面、或是出汗。

外國人擰著手時，他們會說：

I can't wait.	我真等不及了。
I'm so nervous.	我好緊張。
I feel anxious.	我很焦慮。
I can't relax!	我無法放鬆！
I can't sit still.	我沒辦法坐著。
I'm very upset.	我很沮喪。
I'm distracted.	我無法專注。
I can't focus.	我無法集中精神。
I'm confused.	我很困惑。
I'm scared!	我很害怕！

外國人擰著手時，你可以回：

Calm down!	冷靜點！
Don't be nervous.	不要緊張。
Why are you nervous?	你為甚麼緊張呢？
What's wrong?	怎麼了嗎？
Stop freaking out.	別慌。
You're making me nervous!	你讓我好緊張！
Don't panic!	不要驚慌！
I need you to focus.	我需要你集中精神。
Don't be nervous about this.	不要為這件事緊張。
I've got it under control.	我已經控制住情況了。

情境對話 中文可對照上方的例句

Dialogue 1

Ⓐ I'm so nervous.
Ⓑ Calm down!
Ⓐ I can't relax!
Ⓑ What's wrong?

Dialogue 2

Ⓐ I'm very upset.
Ⓑ I need you to focus.
Ⓐ I can't focus.
Ⓑ Don't be nervous about it.

情境 從英文來看外國人使用此肢體語言的情境

I had to present at a work conference today. I was so nervous! I was sweating and wringing my hands. I'm so glad it's over!

我今天必須在一個工作會議上做簡報。我好緊張！我滿頭大汗，還一直擰著我的手。我很高興一切都結束了！

情境 3 **Fidgeting Body 身體坐立不安**

當一個人一直不斷地做小動作就代表他坐不住，可能包含玩頭髮、凹手指的關節發出劈啪的聲音、抖腳或是擰手。這通常代表這個人對某件事很激動、緊張或是很不耐煩。

外國人身體坐立不安時，他們會說：

I can't wait.	我等不及了。
I'm getting excited.	我好興奮。
I'm freaking out!	我好慌張！
It's so exciting!	真令人興奮！
This is awesome!	太棒了！
I'm so nervous.	我好緊張。
I have to present next.	我必須下一個簡報。
I feel sick.	我覺得不舒服。
I can't do it.	我做不到。
I'm worried I'll mess up.	我擔心我會搞砸。

外國人身體坐立不安時，你可以回：

Calm down!	冷靜！
You're freaking out!	你太驚慌了！
It will be okay!	會沒事的！
You'll do great!	你會做得很好！
Don't be nervous.	別緊張。
You got this!	你會成功的。
You're going to do great.	你會做得很棒的。
You'll be alright.	你會順利的。
Yes, you can!	沒錯，你可以的！
You'll do just fine.	你會做得很好的。

情境對話 中文可對照上方的例句

Dialogue 1

Ⓐ I'm getting excited.
Ⓑ You're freaking out!
Ⓐ I can't wait.
Ⓑ Calm down!

Dialogue 2

Ⓐ I have to present next.
Ⓑ Don't be nervous.
Ⓐ I'm worried I'll mess up.
Ⓑ You'll do just fine.

情境 從英文來看外國人使用此肢體語言的情境

My sister's band was playing at a festival in town. It was their first big concert. I saw my sister before they started, and she was really nervous. She kept fidgeting and cracking her knuckles. They ended up doing great!

我妹妹的樂團要在小鎮的一個慶典上表演，這是他們第一場大型演唱會。我在他們開始前看到我妹妹，她真的很緊張，一直坐立不安、折她的手指關節。最後他們表現得很好！

情境 4 Sweating Nervously 緊張地出汗

人們在非常緊張時可能會擰扭自己的手、踱步、大動作移動手腳、並且大量出汗，或是腋下也在出汗。

外國人緊張地出汗時，他們會說：

I'm so nervous!	我好緊張！
I'm worried.	我很擔心。
I'm nervous about today.	我很緊張今天的事。
This is nerve-wracking.	這真是令人不安。
I'm a bundle of nerves!	我好緊張！
I hope this ends well.	我希望這一切順利。
I'm worried.	我很擔心。
Are you nervous, too?	你也緊張嗎？
Do you think it'll be okay?	你覺得會順利嗎？
I hope it's okay!	我希望這會順利！

外國人緊張地出汗時，你可以回：

Don't be!	別緊張！
You'll be fine.	你會沒事的。
You'll do great.	你會做得很棒。
It's going to be fine.	會沒事的。
I think you'll be fine.	我想你會沒事的。
There's nothing to worry about.	甚麼都別擔心。
Not at all.	一點也不。
Take a deep breath!	深呼吸！
It will work out.	這件事會解決的。
Let's wait and see.	讓我們拭目以待。

情境對話　中文可對照上方的例句

Dialogue 1

Ⓐ I'm nervous about today.
Ⓑ It will work out.
Ⓐ Are you nervous, too?
Ⓑ Not at all.

Dialogue 2

Ⓐ Do you think it'll be okay?
Ⓑ It's going to be fine.
Ⓐ I'm a bundle of nerves!
Ⓑ There's nothing to worry about.

情境　從英文來看外國人使用此肢體語言的情境

I was at the doctor with my husband. He was sweating nervously and kept telling me he was worried about the appointment. I told him it was going to be fine, and it was. The doctor said he was very healthy.

我和我先生一起去看醫生，他緊張地流汗，一直跟我說他很擔心看診。我告訴他，一切都會沒事的，而他真的沒事，醫生說他很健康。

情境 5　Biting Lips 咬嘴唇

指用前排牙齒咬嘴唇，可能是嘴唇的側面或中間。通常是咬住下唇，但也有咬住上唇的情況。這是焦慮或緊張的動作，很多人會習慣咬嘴唇，在壓力大的情況下這麼做會令人感到慰藉。這也可能是表示人們試圖忍住不說想說的話。

外國人咬嘴唇時，他們會說：

I'm nervous!	我很緊張！
I'm excited!	我很興奮！
I'm stressing out!	我壓力好大！
I'm freaking out!	我好慌張！
I feel antsy!	我好焦慮！
I'm so worried.	我好擔心。
I'm unprepared.	我沒有準備。
I disagree.	我不同意。
I'm biting my tongue.	我忍著沒說出來。
I feel differently.	我的感覺不太一樣。

外國人咬嘴唇時，你可以回：

Don't freak out!	不要慌張！
You're fine.	你會沒事的。
Everything will be fine.	一切都會沒事的。
It will be okay.	事情會好的。
It'll work out.	這會解決的。
You're going to do great.	你會做得很棒的。
You'll do awesome.	你會做得很好。
You're okay.	你很好啊！
You don't agree with me?	你不同意我的看法嗎？
Tell me your thoughts.	告訴我你的想法。

情境對話　中文可對照上方的例句

Dialogue 1
Ⓐ I'm nervous.
Ⓑ You'll be fine.
Ⓐ I'm so worried.
Ⓑ You're going to do great.

Dialogue 2
Ⓐ I'm freaking out!
Ⓑ Don't freak out!
Ⓐ I'm unprepared.
Ⓑ Everything will be fine.

情境　從英文來看外國人使用此肢體語言的情境

My husband had a job interview this morning. He bites his lips when he gets nervous, so I could tell he was worried about it. I told him I'm sure he'll do fine.

我先生今天早上有一場工作面試。他緊張時就會咬住嘴唇，因此我看得出來他對這件事感到擔心。我告訴他，我確定他會表現得不錯。

情境 6 Grasping the Front of the Neck 握住脖子的前端

這是指拱起手掌握住脖子的前端，並且摩擦。通常做這個動作時，人會將頭往後傾斜，仰起頭並吐氣。人們會在他們感到不適時做這個動作，來幫助自己定定神。除了握住脖子，打著領帶的男性也可能會調整領帶；若是戴著項鍊的女性則可能會擺弄項鍊。

外國人握住脖子的前端時，他們會說：

I feel overwhelmed.	我感到不知所措。
I'm getting tired.	我累了。
I'm stressing out.	我壓力好大。
I'm freaking out.	我嚇壞了。
I'm nervous.	我很緊張。
I don't know what to do.	我不知道該怎麼辦。
I'm at a loss.	我很茫然。
What should I do?	我該怎麼辦？
What do you think?	你是怎麼想的？
Tell me what to do!	告訴我該怎麼做！

外國人握住脖子的前端時，你可以回：

Take a deep breath.	深呼吸。
You're doing great.	你做得很好。
You'll be fine.	你會沒事的。
Don't freak out.	不要慌張。
Take a break.	休息一下。
Don't be nervous.	不要緊張。
We'll figure it out.	我們會解決的。
You need to calm down.	你需要冷靜下來。
It's not a big deal.	這沒甚麼大不了的。
I can help.	我可以幫忙。

情境對話　中文可對照上方的例句

Dialogue 1

Ⓐ I feel overwhelmed.
Ⓑ Take a deep breath.
Ⓐ I don't know what to do.
Ⓑ You'll be fine.

Dialogue 2

Ⓐ I'm at a loss.
Ⓑ Don't panic.
Ⓐ What should I do?
Ⓑ We'll figure it out.

情境　從英文來看外國人使用此肢體語言的情境

I have a habit of grabbing the front of my neck when I'm worried about something. I just did it yesterday at work. I couldn't get my computer to work and I started to freak out. A coworker ended up helping me.

我有個習慣，當我擔心某件事時，我就會握住脖子前端。我昨天上班時就這麼做了，我沒辦法讓我的電腦正常運作，我就開始慌亂，後來有位同事來幫我了。

情境 7 Fidgeting Legs 坐立不安的腿

人們在坐立不安時，有幾種不同的方法來擺弄雙腿。如果是雙腿交叉坐著，坐著的人可以反覆把腳趾彎起再伸開、搖晃腳掌、或是抖腿；如果雙腿沒有交叉，坐著的人可能會用腳趾輕拍地面，或是反覆地讓腿在地面輕微彈起。這些動作都可能是緊張或不耐煩的表現。

外國人的腿坐立不安時，他們會說：

What time is it?	現在幾點了？
We're late.	我們遲到了。
We're going to be late.	我們要遲到了。
They are late.	他們遲到了。
The meeting is running long.	會議開了很久。
I don't get this.	我不明白這件事。
I think we're lost.	我覺得我們迷路了。
You took a wrong turn.	你轉錯方向了。
This isn't working.	這沒有用。
I should leave.	我得走了。

外國人的腿坐立不安時，你可以回：

It's almost noon.	快中午了。
We'll be right on time.	我們會準時到達的。
We're not late!	我們沒遲到！
You're making me nervous.	你讓我很緊張。
We have enough time.	我們時間很夠。
We have a lot of time.	我們有很多時間。
We're not lost.	我們沒有迷路。
I have the directions.	我知道怎麼去。
It will work!	會有用的！
We're fine on time.	我們絕對可以準時。

情境對話 中文可對照上方的例句

Dialogue 1

Ⓐ What time is it?

Ⓑ 7:00

Ⓐ We're late.

Ⓑ We'll be right on time.

Dialogue 2

Ⓐ I think we're lost.

Ⓑ We're not lost.

Ⓐ You took the wrong turn.

Ⓑ I have the directions.

情境 從英文來看外國人使用此肢體語言的情境

I got stuck in a long meeting at work today. I had a doctor's appointment at 5, and I was so worried I was going to be late. My friend was in the meeting with me and she told me to stop fidgeting and tapping my toes. I guess she could tell that I was nervous.

我今天都在開在一場很長的會議，而且我 5 點有個醫生的門診，我很擔心會遲到。我的朋友和我一起參加了同一場會議，她叫我不要再坐立不安，用我的腳趾點地板。我猜她看得出我很緊張。

情境 8 **Locked Ankles 腳踝扣在一起**

這是指坐著時將雙腿在腳踝處交叉，並且將腿置於椅子下，這個姿勢就是腳踝扣在一起。一般來說，這個姿勢下的雙腿非常緊繃，雙腳也彎曲。這可能意味著你在退縮、感到不確定或是恐懼。這也是在會議或面試中的常見姿勢。

外國人的腳踝扣一起時，他們會說：

Tell me about yourself.	向我介紹你自己吧。
What do you know about the job?	你對這項工作了解多少？
Are you qualified?	你有符合資格嗎？
I have a question.	我有個問題。
Here is my resume.	這是我的簡歷。
Can you repeat that?	你可以再説一遍嗎？
I'll present next.	接下來我會做簡報。
I have the details.	我有些細節要説明。
The information is right here.	資訊都在這裡。
I wrote the report.	我寫了這份報告。

外國人的腳踝扣一起時，你可以回：

I can tell you about myself.	我可以告訴你關於自己的事。
I'm familiar with the company.	我很熟悉這間公司。
I can answer that question.	我可以回答那個問題。
I'm very qualified.	我非常符合資格。
I'm excited about the job.	我對這工作很興奮。
It sounds interesting.	聽起來很有趣。
I have some questions.	我有一些問題。
I have a lot of experience.	我有很多經驗。
Here is the report.	報告在這裡。
I just finished the report.	我剛完成報告。

情境對話　中文可對照上方的例句

Dialogue 1
Ⓐ Tell me about yourself.
Ⓑ I'm very qualified.
Ⓐ What do you know about the job?
Ⓑ I'm familiar with the company.

Dialogue 2
Ⓐ Here's my resume.
Ⓑ Thank you.
Ⓐ I have a lot of experience.
Ⓑ I have some questions.

情境　從英文來看外國人使用此肢體語言的情境

I just finished up my job interview. I was nervous at first and sat with my ankles crossed really tightly under my chair. The person doing the interview was so nice, and I quickly relaxed. The job sounds interesting and I hope they offer it to me.

我剛結束我的工作面試。起先我很緊張，坐著的時候，我的腳踝真的緊緊在椅子下面交叉著。負責面試的人很親切，所以我很快就放鬆了。這份工作聽起來很有趣，我希望他們能給我這個職位。

10-9.mp3

情境 9 Talking Fast 快速地說話

這是指很快地說話，並且在單字和句子之間沒有適當的停頓。這是緊張與不信任的表現，說話很快的人通常與交談對象缺乏目光交流，可能會很難理解他們的想法。

外國人快速說話時，他們會說：

I'll go next.	接下來換我。
I'm up next.	我下一個。
I have to go.	我得走了。
I'm going to grab another drink.	我要再來一杯飲料。
I feel really uncomfortable.	我真的很不舒服。
I should go.	我該走了。
Let me repeat that.	讓我重複一遍。
I'll go over it again.	我會再說一次。
Let me try again.	讓我再試一次。
I'm having a hard time.	我現在處境困難。

外國人快速說話時，你可以回：

Go ahead.	去吧。
I think it was my turn.	我認為該輪到我了。
You skipped me.	你跳過我了。
Can you say that again?	你能再說一遍嗎？
What's wrong?	怎麼了？
Don't be nervous.	不要緊張。
Say it again.	再說一次。
Relax.	放輕鬆。
Take your time.	慢慢來。
We can take a break.	我們可以休息一下。

情境對話　中文可對照上方的例句

Dialogue 1

Ⓐ I feel really uncomfortable.
Ⓑ Don't be nervous.
Ⓐ I'm up next.
Ⓑ Relax.

Dialogue 2

Ⓐ I'm having a hard time.
Ⓑ We can take a break.
Ⓐ Thank you.
Ⓑ Take your time.

情境　從英文來看外國人使用此肢體語言的情境

I had to present in my class today. I was so nervous about talking in front of everyone. I talked really fast and the professor asked me to repeat myself several times. I'll probably get a bad grade.

今天我必須在課堂上做簡報。要在大家面前講話讓我非常緊張，我講得超級快，於是教授要求我再重新講幾次。我可能會得到很差的成績。

UNIT10 Feeling Nervous 感到緊張　89

情境 10　Flared Nostrils 撐開的鼻孔

這是指鼻孔變寬，使鼻孔看起來比原來的樣子還大。這麼做能讓更多的空氣被吸入和排出，並幫助一個人為更大的事情做準備，可能會是一場戰鬥、或是他們所擔心的事情等等。這也可能意味著這個人非常不滿。

外國人快速說話時，他們會說：

I'm getting worried.	我很擔心。
I'm starting to feel nervous.	我開始感到緊張。
I'm trying to calm down.	我試著讓自己冷靜。
I can't calm down!	我不能冷靜下來！
I'm mad!	我很生氣！
I'm going to punch him!	我要去揍他！
I'll feel better when it's over.	結束的時候我會感覺好一點。
It's about to happen.	這將要發生了。
I'm going to lose it.	我要失控了。
I'm really pissed off!	我真的很生氣！

外國人快速說話時，你可以回：

What's wrong?	怎麼了？
Don't be nervous.	不要緊張。
Why not?	為甚麼不呢？
Don't do it.	不要這麼做。
You'll regret it.	你會後悔的。
I wouldn't do it if I were you.	如果我是你，我不會這樣做。
Calm down!	冷靜點！
You need to calm down.	你需要冷靜下來。
Stop it!	停下來！
Walk away from him.	離他遠一點。

情境對話　中文可對照上方的例句

Dialogue 1

Ⓐ I'm starting to feel nervous.
Ⓑ Don't be nervous.
Ⓐ I'm trying to calm down.
Ⓑ Relax!

Dialogue 2

Ⓐ I'm mad!
Ⓑ You need to calm down.
Ⓐ I'm going to lose it.
Ⓑ Just relax.

情境　從英文來看外國人使用此肢體語言的情境

I ran into Michael right before he was going to give his speech. He seemed nervous. He was sweating and his nostrils were flared. I wished him luck and told him he'd do great.

就在 Michael 要發表演講之前，我遇到了他。他似乎很緊張，他在出汗，鼻孔張大。我祝他好運，並且跟他說他會做得很好。

Raising shoulders and Lowering Head
情境 11 提高肩膀、低頭

將肩膀保持在提高的位置，並低著頭，這個動作意味著這個人擔心會發生一些事情。他們擔心有人會在身體上或語言上攻擊他們。

外國人提高肩膀、低頭時，他們會說：

I feel uncomfortable.	我覺得不舒服。
I don't like it here.	我不喜歡它在這裡。
I feel out of place.	我感覺不自在。
I'd like to leave.	我想離開。
I'm going to go.	我要走了。
I don't want to stay here.	我不想留在這裡。
Something bad is going to happen.	有不好的事情要發生了。
I have a bad feeling.	我有不好的感覺。
I want to go.	我想要走了。
I'm not happy here.	我在這裡不開心。

外國人提高肩膀、低頭時，你可以回：

What's the matter?	怎麼了？
What's your problem?	你怎麼了？
Don't feel that way.	不要那樣想。
Don't leave yet!	先不要離開！
You're going to be fine.	你會沒事的。
What are you worried about?	你擔心甚麼？
Nothing will happen.	甚麼事都不會發生。
It's just a feeling.	這只是一種感覺。
You'll be fine.	你會沒事的。
You can leave.	你可以離開。

情境對話 中文可對照上方的例句

Dialogue 1
Ⓐ I feel uncomfortable.
Ⓑ What's the matter?
Ⓐ I feel out of place.
Ⓑ You can leave.

Dialogue 2
Ⓐ I don't want to stay here.
Ⓑ What's your problem?
Ⓐ I have a bad feeling.
Ⓑ It's just a feeling.

情境 從英文來看外國人使用此肢體語言的情境

I knew something was wrong with Jake when I saw him. He was looking down and had his shoulders pushed up. He told me he didn't want to stay at the party because there were some guys there that he was afraid of. We left and he felt much better.

當我看到 Jack 時，我就知道事情有點不對勁。他的眼睛往下看，肩膀往上抬。他告訴我他不想待在派對上，因為那裡有些讓他害怕的傢伙。我們離開後，他感覺好多了。

情境 12 Shaking Legs While Sitting 坐著的時候抖腿

這是指在坐著的時候，腳指頭放在地板上而腳跟往上提，而人們會快速提起腿、同時足部維持在地面上。這也是坐不住的一種表現，代表這個人很緊張、壓力大，或很無聊。

外國人坐著抖腿時，他們會說：

I'm freaking out!	我好驚慌！
I'm worried.	我很擔心。
I'm panicking.	我好害怕。
I lost something important.	我弄丟很重要的東西。
I'm starting to panic.	我開始感到害怕。
I'm really nervous.	我真的很緊張。
I have to finish this.	我必須完成這件事。
I'm running out of time.	我快沒時間了。
I'm so late!	我太晚了。
I'm in big trouble.	我有大麻煩了。

外國人坐著抖腿時，你可以回：

Don't panic!	別害怕！
Don't worry.	別擔心！
Don't freak out.	別慌張！
You need to calm down.	你需要冷靜一下。
Take a deep breath.	深呼吸。
You'll be fine.	你會沒事的。
What's wrong?	怎麼了？
Everything will be alright.	一切都會好的。
You'll get there on time.	你會準時到的。
Do you need help?	你需要幫忙嗎？

情境對話　中文可對照上方的例句

Dialogue 1

Ⓐ I'm freaking out!
Ⓑ Everything will be alright.
Ⓐ I lost something important.
Ⓑ Do you need help?

Dialogue 2

Ⓐ I'm so late!
Ⓑ Don't freak out.
Ⓐ I'm in big trouble.
Ⓑ You'll be fine.

情境　從英文來看外國人使用此肢體語言的情境

When I saw Sophia, she was sitting at her desk with her legs shaking. I knew something was wrong. She said she was nervous about presenting at the meeting this afternoon.

當我看到 Sophia 時，她坐在桌子前、抖腿，我知道一定有事情不對勁，她說她對今天下午的會議要上台簡報感到很緊張。

情境 13 Red Ears 耳朵發紅

這是指耳朵會發紅（或是臉紅）、發熱。這通常發生於人們對某件事很緊張，這可能也暗示出他們在說謊，或是他們覺得慌張或害羞。

外國人耳朵發紅時，他們會說：

I feel uncomfortable.	我覺得不舒服。
I'm feeling out of place.	我覺得不自在。
I'm nervous.	我很緊張。
I feel awkward.	我覺得很怪。
Am I overdressed?	我會穿得太正式嗎？
Does this look okay?	這樣看起來還好嗎？
I don't know what to say.	我不知道要講甚麼。
I'm feeling shy.	我覺得很害羞。
Stop looking at me!	不要再看我了！
I'm embarrassed.	我很尷尬。

外國人耳朵發紅時，你可以回：

Why?	為甚麼？
Don't be!	別緊張！
You're fine!	你很好啊。
It's going to be okay.	會沒事的。
You'll do great.	你會做得很好的。
You can do it.	你做得到的。
What's bothering you?	你在煩惱甚麼？
You look great.	你看起來很好。
I can't!	我沒辦法！
Don't be nervous!	別緊張！

情境對話 中文可對照上方的例句

Dialogue 1

Ⓐ Am I overdressed?
Ⓑ You're fine!
Ⓐ I'm feeling out of place.
Ⓑ You look great.

Dialogue 2

Ⓐ I'm feeling shy.
Ⓑ Why?
Ⓐ I don't know what to say.
Ⓑ It's going to be fine.

情境 從英文來看外國人使用此肢體語言的情境

When I got to the party, everyone turned and looked at me. My ears got red and I felt nervous. Mike came up to me and told me I looked beautiful. He was really nice to me the whole night.

我去派對的時候，每個人都轉頭、看著我。我耳朵發紅、覺得很緊張。Mike 走向我，告訴我今天我看起來很美。他整晚都對我非常貼心。

情境 14 Biting Fingernails 咬手指甲

這是指手舉在嘴巴前、手掌鬆鬆的握拳、面向下巴，用牙齒咬指甲。這是緊張的習慣，有些人會在他們覺得對某些事情不自在或緊張的時候這麼做。

外國人用牙齒咬手指甲時，他們會說：

I'm freaking out!	我好慌張！
I'm nervous!	我很緊張！
I can't do it.	我做不到。
I'm going to lose.	我會輸的。
I'm scared.	我很害怕。
I'm worried.	我很擔心。
I think I'm lost.	我想我很迷惘。
He's mad at me.	他對我很生氣。
I think we're breaking up.	我想我們會分手。
I'm very frustrated.	我非常挫折。

外國人用牙齒咬手指甲時，你可以回：

Don't do that.	別這樣做。
That's gross!	真噁心！
What's the matter?	怎麼了？
It's going to be okay.	會沒事的。
You'll do great!	你會做得很好的。
Don't be nervous.	不要緊張！
What are you scared of?	你在害怕甚麼？
I'll help you.	我會幫你的。
Did you talk to him?	你有跟他談談嗎？
You're freaking out!	你太慌張了！

情境對話 中文可對照上方的例句

Dialogue 1

Ⓐ I'm freaking out!
Ⓑ What's the matter?
Ⓐ I think I'm lost.
Ⓑ It's going to be okay.

Dialogue 2

Ⓐ He's mad at me.
Ⓑ It's going to be okay.
Ⓐ I think we're breaking up.
Ⓑ Did you talk to him?

情境 從英文來看外國人使用此肢體語言的情境

Jessica was really upset today. She was biting her nails and crying at that time. She told me that her and her boyfriend had a big fight and she was worried he was going to break up with her. I told her to call him and talk about it.

Jessica 今天非常沮喪。她那時候一邊咬她的指甲、一邊哭。她告訴我她跟她男朋友大吵一架，而且她擔心男友會跟她分手。我告訴她打給她男朋友並談談這件事。

Feeling Anxious
感到焦慮

☞ **感到焦慮時需要用到的動作，用英文要怎麼說呢？**

對某些事物感到焦慮就會產生各種手勢和肢體動作，下列是感到焦慮會用到的手勢與肢體語言，請看圖片，並對照動作的英文和中文。

情境 1

Furrowed eyebrows 皺眉頭

情境 2

Rubbing the back of the neck
搓揉後頸

情境 3

Standing with feet together
雙腳併攏站立

情境 4
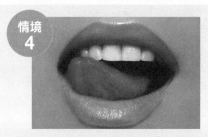
Running tongue over front teeth
舌頭滑過前排牙齒

情境 5

Stressful sweating 壓力大而出汗

情境 6

Rubbing finger under nose
手指在鼻子下方摩擦

情境
7

Tense Body 身體緊繃

情境
8

Crossed legs while sitting
坐著時翹腳

情境
9

Rotating head in circle 頭部繞圈旋轉

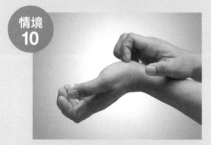

情境
10

Itchy palms 手掌發癢

情境
11

Circling shoulders forwards or
backwards 向前或向後繞肩

情境
12

Woman leaning back and
shaking hair 女子往後靠、甩頭髮

情境
13

Massaging the ears 按摩耳朵

情境 1 Furrowed Eyebrows 皺眉頭

這是指將兩道眉毛擠在一起,並在額頭中間產生皺紋。皺眉頭使眼睛看起來是往上看。皺眉頭可能表示人們感到焦慮或壓力,也可能表示人們感到困惑,或是不明白發生了甚麼。許多人在思考問題或試圖找出答案時,都會皺起眉頭。

外國人皺眉頭時,他們會說:

What's that?	那是甚麼?
I don't get it.	我不懂。
I'm not understanding.	我不明白。
What's going on?	這是怎麼回事?
I can't get it!	我搞不懂!
I'm not sure.	我不太確定。
I don't understand!	我想不通!
I'm trying!	我在努力!
This doesn't make sense.	這沒道理啊。
I'm lost.	我很迷惘。

外國人皺眉頭時,你可以回:

I'll show you.	我來解釋給你聽。
I'll help you.	我會幫助你的。
Let me help.	讓我來幫忙。
This should help.	這應該會有所幫助。
I can explain it to you.	我可以為你說明。
I'll show you how to do it.	我給你看該怎麼做。
I can do it.	我可以做得到。
Let me do it.	讓我來吧。
Can I do it for you?	讓我來好嗎?
Can I help you?	我可以幫忙嗎?

情境對話　中文可對照上方的例句

Dialogue 1
- A I can't get it!
- B Let me help.
- A This doesn't make sense.
- B I can explain it to you.

Dialogue 2
- A What's that?
- B Our homework assignment.
- A I don't get it.
- B I'll do it for you.

情境　從英文來看外國人使用此肢體語言的情境

One of my students was struggling with their math homework. She had a confused look on her face and was feeling frustrated because she didn't understand. We worked on the homework together until she had a better understanding.

我有一個學生正在為數學作業苦苦掙扎。她一臉困惑,因為無法理解而感到沮喪。我們一起做作業,直到她比較能理解為止。

情境 2 Rubbing the Back of the Neck 搓揉後頸

這是指用手搓揉或按摩自己的後頸。人們會在感到緊張、或感到焦慮不安時出現這麼做。摩擦後頸可以使精神平靜，並且有助於集中注意力。有些人在長時間處理某件事之後，可能會搓揉後頸，使自己平靜下來。

外國人搓揉脖子的後面時，他們會說：

I don't get it!	我不明白！
I'm lost.	我很迷惘。
I broke it!	我把它弄壞了！
I'm confused.	我很困惑。
I'm nervous!	我很緊張！
I can't understand.	我搞不懂。
I need help!	我需要幫助！
I'm scared!	我很害怕！
I messed up.	我搞砸了。
I'm struggling.	我在掙扎。

外國人搓揉脖子的後面時，你可以回：

I'll help you.	我會幫助你的。
What's wrong?	怎麼了？
Let me take a look.	讓我來看看。
Let me look at it.	讓我看一下。
We'll fix it.	我們會修理它。
I'll help.	我會幫忙。
I can help.	我可以幫忙。
Don't be scared!	不要害怕！
What's the matter?	怎麼了嗎？
What's the problem?	問題是甚麼？

情境對話　中文可對照上方的例句

Dialogue 1

Ⓐ I don't get it.
Ⓑ Let me look at it.
Ⓐ Here you go.
Ⓑ I can help.

Dialogue 2

Ⓐ I'm confused.
Ⓑ What can I do to help?
Ⓐ I can't understand.
Ⓑ Let me take a look.

情境　從英文來看外國人使用此肢體語言的情境

I knew something was wrong, when I saw Jason rubbing the back of his neck. He looked tired and confused. He couldn't figure out the new computer program, so I helped him with it.

一看到 Jason 搓著脖子，我就知道事情不太妙了。他看起來又累又困惑，他搞不懂新的電腦程式，所以我就幫他理解這個軟體。

情境 3 Standing with Feet Together 雙腳併攏站立

雙腳併攏站著（距離小於肩寬）時，可能表示人們很焦慮。當人們的雙腳完全併攏，連膝蓋也彼此觸碰時，暗示他們正試著保護自己免受某些傷害，有可能是身體或心理上的威脅。如果雙腿完全貼合，也可能表示人們覺得很冷，並試著使自己溫暖。

外國人雙腳併攏站立時，他們會說：

I'd like to leave.	我想離開。
I feel out of place.	我覺得格格不入。
This is strange.	這很奇怪。
I feel weird.	我覺得怪怪的。
I'm uncomfortable here.	我在這裡不舒服。
I'm going to leave.	我要走了。
I'm freezing!	我要凍僵了！
Can you turn the heat on?	你可以把暖氣打開嗎？
Get me a blanket!	給我一條毯子吧！
I need a sweater.	我需要一件毛衣。

外國人雙腳併攏站立時，你可以回：

Just relax!	放鬆一點！
Take it easy.	輕鬆點。
Don't be weird.	不要那麼奇怪。
You're doing fine.	你表現很好。
We'll leave soon.	我們很快就要走了。
I want to stay.	我想留下。
Just be yourself.	做你自己吧。
I'll turn on the heater.	我會打開暖氣。
Here's a blanket.	這裡有條毯子。
Take my sweater.	穿我的毛衣吧。

情境對話 中文可對照上方的例句

Dialogue 1

Ⓐ I'd like to leave.
Ⓑ We'll leave soon.
Ⓐ I'm uncomfortable here.
Ⓑ Relax!

Dialogue 2

Ⓐ I'm freezing!
Ⓑ I'll turn on the heater.
Ⓐ Thank you.
Ⓑ Here's a blanket.

情境 從英文來看外國人使用此肢體語言的情境

We went to a friend's house last night and hung out outside for a bit. I could tell John was anxious. He had his arms crossed and was standing with his legs close together. I asked if he wanted to sit by my side since he felt relax beside me.

昨晚我們去了一個朋友家，在室外待了一會兒。我看得出 John 覺得焦慮，他的雙臂交叉，雙腿併攏站著。我問他要不要來坐我旁邊，因為他在我旁邊感到自在。

Running Tongue over Front Teeth 舌頭滑過前排牙齒

情境 4

指舌頭置於嘴巴前端，滑過前排的牙齒。這可能是一次滑過牙齒，或是前後滑過很多次。這個動作是壓力大的表現，舌頭滑過牙齒可以幫助舒緩或使人平靜。

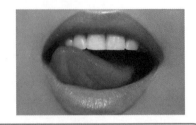

外國人的舌頭滑過前排牙齒時，他們會說：

I'm trying to calm down.	我試著要冷靜。
Give me a minute.	給我一分鐘。
I'm taking a break.	我在休息。
I feel overwhelmed.	我覺得難以承受。
I'm stressing out.	我壓力很大。
This has been difficult.	這非常困難。
It's a stressful time.	這是有壓力的時間。
I'm trying to focus.	我試著要專注。
I need a few minutes.	我需要一點時間。
I'm trying my best.	我試著盡力做好。

外國人的舌頭滑過前排牙齒時，你可以回：

How can I help?	我要如何幫忙呢？
I'll help you!	我會幫你的！
Let me do something.	讓我做點事情吧。
I wish I could help.	我希望我可以幫忙。
I don't know what to say.	我不知道該說甚麼。
Let's talk about it.	讓我們談談這件事吧。
You're going to be fine.	你會沒事的。
It will work out.	事情會順利的。
Let's take a break.	讓我們休息一下吧。
Want to get a drink?	想要喝點飲料嗎？

情境對話　中文可對照上方的例句

Dialogue 1

Ⓐ I'm trying to calm down.
Ⓑ Let's talk about it.
Ⓐ I need a few minutes.
Ⓑ It will work out.

Dialogue 2

Ⓐ I'm stressing out.
Ⓑ You're going to be fine.
Ⓐ I feel overwhelmed.
Ⓑ How can I help?

情境　從英文來看外國人使用此肢體語言的情境

I'm feeling really overwhelmed at work right now. I feel like I'm constantly stressed. Today I was working on a project and I was deep in thought. I was running my tongue over my teeth to help me focus. My boss interrupted me, and I yelled at him. I apologized right away, but I think I made him mad.

我現在對工作真的難以承受。我覺得我好像一直都壓力很大。今天我正在做一份專案，而我沉浸在思緒中。我當時正在用我的舌頭滑過我的牙齒，來幫助我專心。結果我的老闆打斷我，而我對他大吼。我馬上道歉，但我覺得我讓他生氣了。

情境 5 Stressful Sweating 壓力大而出汗

人們感到壓力大時，會大量出汗。當身體感到壓力時，呼吸和心跳會加快，從而導致體溫升高。這會使人感到身體發燙，同時開始冒汗。

外國人壓力大而出汗時，他們會說：

I'm stressing out!	我很慌張！
I'm working on a project.	我正在做一個專案。
I'm studying for a test.	我正在讀一個考試。
I'm doing my homework.	我正在做我的作業。
I'm writing a paper.	我正在寫一份論文。
I'm finishing the report.	我正在完成報告。
I have a deadline to meet.	我有個期限要趕。
I have to work late.	我必須工作到很晚。
I'm getting fired.	我要被解雇了。
I can't finish it in time.	我不能及時完成。

外國人壓力大而出汗時，你可以回：

Don't freak out.	不要慌張。
Calm down.	冷靜下來。
Take a deep breath.	深呼吸。
Do you need help?	你需要幫助嗎？
How's it going?	最近怎麼樣？
How are you doing?	你好嗎？
It will be alright.	會沒事的。
It will all work out.	一切都會解決的。
Are you sure?	你確定嗎？
You're going to be fine.	你會沒事的。

情境對話 中文可對照上方的例句

Dialogue 1

Ⓐ I'm stressing out!
Ⓑ Take a deep breath.
Ⓐ I'm working on a project.
Ⓑ Do you need help?

Dialogue 2

Ⓐ I'm writing a paper.
Ⓑ How's it going?
Ⓐ I can't finish it in time.
Ⓑ It will be alright!

情境 從英文來看外國人使用此肢體語言的情境

I could tell something was wrong when I walked into Jerry's office. He was mumbling and really sweaty. He told me he was working on a year-end report and today was the deadline. I offered to help him, but he said he didn't need any help.

當我走進 Jerry 的辦公室時，我可以看出情況不太對勁。Jerry 喃喃自語、滿身大汗。他告訴我他正在寫年終報告，而今天是截止日期。我要提供他協助，但他說他不需要任何幫忙。

情境 6 Rubbing Finger under Nose 手指在鼻子下摩擦

這是指手握拳、手掌朝下，食指以水平方向伸出，並在鼻孔處來回摩擦，這個手勢表示人們正在嘗試減輕他們可能感受到的壓力。做出這個手勢的人正感到緊張與壓力，甚至可能是害怕讓別人知道他們的真正想法。

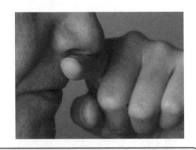

外國人手指在鼻子下摩擦時，他們會說：

I'm stressing out.	我很慌張。
My neck is tense.	我的脖子很緊繃。
I feel stressed.	我感到壓力很大。
I have a lot going on right now.	我現在有很多事情要做。
I'm really busy.	我真的很忙。
I don't have anything to add.	我沒甚麼要補充的。
I'm worried about work.	我在擔心工作。
I have a big project going on.	我有個大型專案在進行。
I need to meet a deadline.	我有個截止日要趕。
I'm getting nervous.	我很緊張。

外國人手指在鼻子下摩擦時，你可以回：

What's wrong?	怎麼了？
Can I rub it for you?	我可以幫你捏捏嗎？
Why?	為甚麼？
What's going on?	發生了甚麼事？
What are you busy with?	你在忙甚麼呢？
Try not to worry about it.	盡量不要擔心。
Take a deep breath.	深呼吸。
When is your deadline?	你的截止日是甚麼時候？
Don't be anxious.	不要焦慮。
What's bothering you?	有甚麼事困擾著你嗎？

情境對話 中文可對照上方的例句

Dialogue 1
Ⓐ My neck is tense.
Ⓑ What's wrong?
Ⓐ I have a lot going on right now.
Ⓑ Don't be anxious.

Dialogue 2
Ⓐ I'm getting nervous.
Ⓑ Why?
Ⓐ I have a big project going on.
Ⓑ When is your deadline?

情境 從英文來看外國人使用此肢體語言的情境

When I got to work, John was already at his desk working. He looked tired and nervous, and he kept rubbing under his nose. He said he was worried about a deadline for a report.

我到公司時，John 已經在他的辦公桌前工作了。他看起來既疲憊又緊張，而且一直在摩擦鼻子下方，他說他擔心一份報告的截止日期。

情境 7　Tense Body 身體緊繃

當身體變得僵硬、挺直時，肩膀會往上、手臂和雙腿打直。這可能代表這個人很心煩或壓力大，也可能代表他在這個場合不太自在，所以還沒放鬆。

外國人身體緊繃時，他們會說：

I'm worrying about it.	我非常擔心這件事。
I won't finish it in time.	我不會在時間內完成。
I can't do it.	我做不到。
I feel overwhelmed.	我感到不知所措。
I'm upset.	我覺得很心煩。
I don't feel good.	我不太舒服。
I feel uncomfortable.	我覺得很不安。
I'm out of place.	我覺得不自在。
Do I look awkward?	我看起來很奇怪嗎？
I can't be myself yet.	我還沒辦法做自己。

外國人身體緊繃時，你可以回：

Don't worry about it.	不要擔心。
You'll get it done.	你會完成的。
You can do it.	你做得到。
You're doing great.	你做得很好。
Keep it up!	繼續下去吧！
What's wrong?	怎麼了？
What's going on?	發生甚麼事了？
Why do you feel that way?	為甚麼你有這種感受？
You look great.	你看起來很棒。
You're doing alright.	你做得很好。

情境對話　中文可對照上方的例句

Dialogue 1

Ⓐ I feel overwhelmed.
Ⓑ What's wrong?
Ⓐ I won't finish it in time.
Ⓑ You'll get it done.

Dialogue 2

Ⓐ Do I look awkward?
Ⓑ You look great.
Ⓐ I feel uncomfortable.
Ⓑ Don't worry about it.

情境　從英文來看外國人使用此肢體語言的情境

The baseball game came down to the last inning. I was up to bat and had to get a good hit, so we could score. My body was tense and I felt really nervous. I ended up hitting a homerun!

棒球比賽來到最後一局，我準備上場打擊，而且必須要打出安打才可以得分。我的身體很緊繃，而我真的覺得很緊張。最後，我打出一支全壘打！

情境 8 **Crossed Legs While Sitting 坐著時翹腳**

這是指坐著時，將一條腿跨在另一條腿的膝蓋上方。這個動作可能表示焦慮，特別是當雙腿緊繃或是緊緊地靠在一起的時候。

外國人坐著並翹腳時，他們會說：

I'm busy.	我很忙。
I'm working.	我在工作。
I can't help you right now.	我現在不能幫你。
I'm swamped.	我忙死了。
I need to focus.	我需要集中精神。
Can you close my door?	你能把我的門關上嗎？
Don't interrupt me.	別打擾我。
I can't take the call.	我沒辦法接電話。
I'm behind.	我的進度落後。
I'm trying to catch up.	我正在努力趕上。

外國人坐著並翹腳時，你可以回：

Are you okay?	你還好嗎？
Is everything alright?	一切都還好嗎？
Why not?	為甚麼不行呢？
What's the problem?	有甚麼問題嗎？
I'll let you be.	那我不打擾你了。
Can I help you?	我可以幫你嗎？
I'll leave you alone.	那你先一個人忙吧。
Do you need help?	你需要幫助嗎？
I was trying to help.	我只是想要幫忙。
I'll leave you to it.	你先忙吧。

情境對話　中文可對照上方的例句

Dialogue 1

Ⓐ I'm swamped.
Ⓑ What's the problem?
Ⓐ I'm trying to catch up.
Ⓑ I'll leave you to it.

Dialogue 2

Ⓐ I can't take the call.
Ⓑ Is everything alright?
Ⓐ I need to focus.
Ⓑ I'll leave you alone.

情境　從英文來看外國人使用此肢體語言的情境

I can always tell when my wife is upset about work. She sits at her desk, staring at her laptop with her legs and arms crossed. She's been having a hard time with work lately.

我總是能看出我太太甚麼時候對工作不開心。她坐在書桌前盯著筆電，翹著腳和雙臂交叉。最近她的工作一直都很辛苦。

情境 9 Rotating Head in Circle 頭部繞圈旋轉

以頭繞圈旋轉整個頭部，這表示脖子僵硬，旋轉可以幫助放鬆緊繃的肌肉。也可以將頭部從一側傾斜到另一側，這表示這個人感到疲倦，或是壓力很大。

外國人頭部繞圈旋轉時，他們會說：

I have a headache.	我頭疼。
I need to move around.	我需要動一動。
My neck hurts.	我的脖子痛。
My back is stiff.	我的背部僵硬。
My head hurts.	我頭疼。
I'm getting tired.	我累了。
I'm getting stiff.	我越來越僵硬了。
I need to stand up.	我得站起來。
I need to sit down.	我得坐下。
I need a pain killer.	我需要來顆止痛藥。

外國人頭部繞圈旋轉時，你可以回：

Are you okay?	你還好嗎？
Do you need something?	你需要甚麼嗎？
Can I help?	我可以幫忙嗎？
Maybe you need a break.	也許你需要休息一下。
I'll get you some water.	我去給你拿點水。
Here's some medicine!	這裡有一些藥！
Let me rub it.	讓我揉一揉。
Stretch out.	伸展一下。
Relax for a bit!	放鬆一下！
Take it easy.	放輕鬆。

情境對話 中文可對照上方的例句

Dialogue 1

Ⓐ I have a headache.
Ⓑ Do you need something?
Ⓐ I need a pain killer.
Ⓑ That should help.

Dialogue 2

Ⓐ I need to move around.
Ⓑ Are you okay?
Ⓐ My back is stiff.
Ⓑ Let me rub it.

情境 從英文來看外國人使用此肢體語言的情境

We stayed up late working on the project last night. I could tell Sara was getting tired when she started rotating her head to stretch her neck and back. She said she was really sore and tired from working so late.

昨晚我們為了一個專案熬夜。當 Sara 開始旋轉頭部，以伸展脖子和背部時，我可以看出她很疲倦。她說工作到這麼晚，真的很痠又很累。

情境 10 Itchy Palms 手掌發癢

手掌發癢是指為人們即將發生的事感到坐立難安或焦慮。手掌可能實際上沒有發癢，但人們可能以看起來像是手掌發癢的方式搓手。

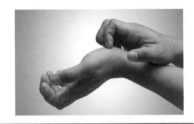

外國人手掌發癢時，他們會說：

I can't wait!	我等不及了！
I feel lucky!	我覺得很幸運！
Something is about to happen.	有事情要發生了。
I feel a change coming.	我感覺到改變要來了。
I'm excited!	我很興奮！
I can't hold still!	我無法不動！
I'm anxious!	我很焦慮！
I feel excited!	我覺得很興奮！
I'm really happy!	我真的很開心！
I know something good will happen!	我知道會發生好事！

外國人手掌發癢時，你可以回：

What do you mean?	你是甚麼意思？
What's going on?	發生了甚麼事？
That's awesome!	太棒了！
I can't wait either!	我也等不及了！
I'm happy for you.	我為你感到高興。
That would be great!	那太好了！
What's happening?	發生了甚麼事？
Don't get your hopes up.	不要抱太多期待。
Let's wait and see.	讓我們拭目以待。
Me too!	我也是！

情境對話 中文可對照上方的例句

Dialogue 1

Ⓐ Something is about to happen.
Ⓑ What do you mean?
Ⓐ I feel lucky!
Ⓑ That would be great!

Dialogue 2

Ⓐ I feel excited!
Ⓑ What's going on?
Ⓐ I know something good will happen!
Ⓑ That's awesome!

情境 從英文來看外國人使用此肢體語言的情境

We entered our names in the drawing for the new car. Sue kept telling me her palms were itchy and she knew she would win. I thought she was crazy. When they read the winner, she did win! I couldn't believe it!

我們在新車抽獎活動投入了我們的名字，Sue 一直告訴我她的手掌很癢，而且她知道自己會贏，我以為她瘋了。而當他們宣布得獎者時，她真的抽中了！我簡直不敢相信！

情境 11 Circling Shoulders Forwards or Backwards
向前或向後繞肩

這是指一邊或兩邊的肩膀向前或向後繞，通常這樣做是為了運動和伸展緊繃的肌肉。這個動作表示人們可能感到壓力或焦慮，這也可能出現在正在準備重要事情（例如比賽或大型演講）的人身上，這麼做可以幫助他們放鬆心情，並做好心理準備。

外國人向前或向後繞肩時，他們會說：

I feel tired.	我累了。
I'm overwhelmed.	我不知所措。
I need to finish this.	我得完成這個。
My neck is sore.	我脖子好痠。
I have a headache.	我頭疼。
I need to stretch out.	我需要伸展。
I'm almost finished.	我幾乎要做完了。
I've been working for a long time.	我已經工作了很長時間。
I'll give it my all!	我會全力以赴！
I'm going to try my best.	我會盡力而為。

外國人向前或向後繞肩時，你可以回：

Are you okay?	你還好嗎？
What's up?	怎麼了？
Need anything?	需要甚麼嗎？
Can I rub it?	我可以幫你揉揉嗎？
Here's a pain reliever.	這裡有止痛藥。
I can help you.	我可以幫助你。
What can I do to help?	我該怎麼幫忙？
You should rest.	你應該休息。
Let's take a break.	讓我們休息一下。
You'll do great.	你會做得很棒。

情境對話 中文可對照上方的例句

Dialogue 1
Ⓐ I feel tired.
Ⓑ What's going on?
Ⓐ I've been working for a long time.
Ⓑ Let's take a break.

Dialogue 2
Ⓐ I have a headache.
Ⓑ Are you okay?
Ⓐ I need to stretch out.
Ⓑ Here's a pain reliever.

情境 從英文來看外國人使用此肢體語言的情境

My dad is helping me build a new deck on my house. He worked all day on it. I could tell he was tired because he kept rolling his shoulders, but he wouldn't take a break. We ended up getting it finished up.

我父親正在幫我的房子蓋新的露台，他整天都在工作。我可以看出來他累了，因為他不停地轉動肩膀，但他不願意停下來休息。我們最後把它完成了。

情境 12

Woman Leaning Back and Shaking Hair
女子往後靠、甩頭髮

這是指長頭髮的女子靠在她的座位上，頭往後傾斜並把臉往上看，把頭髮往外甩。通常她也會用手去摸頭髮、按摩頭皮，這是舒緩壓力的一種方式，也可能幫助人們放鬆、更專注。

外國女子往後靠、甩頭髮時，他們會說：

I need to focus.	我需要專注。
I'm almost done.	我快做完了。
The day is almost over.	今天就快結束了。
I'm getting tired.	我好累。
I'll get it finished.	我會把它完成。
I just need a break.	我只需要休息一下。
I'm taking a quick break.	我先休息一下下。
I'm thinking about it.	我思考一下。
Let me clear my head.	讓我清理一下我的思緒。
I'm taking five!	我休息五分鐘！

外國女子往後靠、甩頭髮時，你可以回：

Are you okay?	你還好嗎？
Are you doing alright?	你做得還行嗎？
Are you stressing out?	你壓力很大嗎？
You'll be okay!	你會好好的！
You'll get it done.	你會完成這件事的。
Go take some time off.	去休息一下吧！
Let me help.	讓我幫你吧！
Grab some coffee.	喝杯咖啡吧！
Let's take a break.	我們來休息一下。
We're almost finished.	我們幾乎要完成了。

情境對話 中文可對照上方的例句

Dialogue 1

Ⓐ I'll get it finished.
Ⓑ Are you doing alright?
Ⓐ I'm taking a quick break.
Ⓑ Grab some coffee.

Dialogue 2

Ⓐ We're almost finished.
Ⓑ I'm taking five!
Ⓐ Are you okay?
Ⓑ I'm tired.

情境 從英文來看外國人使用此肢體語言的情境

My wife shakes her hair out when she gets tired. After a long day, she likes to sit in a chair and lean back and shake her hair while running her hands through it. I think it helps relieve some stress and tension.

我太太在她累的時候會甩頭髮，在疲累的一天後，她喜歡坐在一張椅子上，往後靠、甩她的頭髮並用手梳頭。我想這能有助於舒緩一些壓力和緊繃。

情境 13 Massaging the Ears 按摩耳朵

當人們在揉整個耳朵時，可能包含用食指和中指上下搓揉耳朵的不同部位，或是用手指頭繞圓圈從左到右按摩耳道的洞口。這代表人們覺得很壓力大，按摩耳朵可以幫助減緩壓力感。

外國人按摩耳朵時，他們會說：

I feel overwhelmed.	我感到不知所措。
I'm stressing out.	我覺得壓力大。
I'm panicking!	我很害怕！
I need to get this done!	我需要搞定這件事！
I'm running late.	我要來不及了。
I'm behind.	我進度落後。
I need to catch up.	我需要趕上進度。
I have to work late.	我要工作到很晚了。
I'm trying to meet a deadline.	我試著要趕上截止日。
I'm going to miss the deadline.	我要錯過截止日了。

外國人按摩耳朵時，你可以回：

Why do you feel that way?	為甚麼你有這種感覺？
Relax!	放輕鬆！
Don't panic.	別慌張。
Take a break.	休息一下。
Take a breather.	來休息一會兒。
Take a deep breath.	深呼吸。
It's going to be fine.	會沒事的。
I can help you.	我可以幫你。
You're doing great!	你做得很好。
You'll get it done.	你會完成的。
Why don't I help?	何不讓我幫忙吧？
What's wrong?	怎麼了？

情境對話 中文可對照上方的例句

Dialogue 1
Ⓐ I have to work late.
Ⓑ What's wrong?
Ⓐ I'm behind.
Ⓑ Why don't I help?

Dialogue 2
Ⓐ I feel overwhelmed.
Ⓑ Why do you feel that way?
Ⓐ I'm going to miss the deadline.
Ⓑ Don't panic.

情境 從英文來看外國人使用此肢體語言的情境

Larry seemed really stressed out at work today. He was rushing around and sweating. I even saw him rubbing his ears. When I asked him what was wrong, he told me he was running behind on a project.

Larry 今天工作似乎真的壓力很大。他四處奔波，又流很多汗。我甚至看到他在揉耳朵。我問他發生甚麼事的時候，他跟我說他有個專案進度落後。

Feeling Angry 感到生氣

☞ **感到生氣時需要用到的動作，用英文要怎麼說呢？**

對某些事物感到生氣就會產生各種手勢和肢體動作，下列是感到生氣時會用
到的手勢與肢體語言，請看圖片，並對照動作的英文和中文。

情境 1

Rolling eyes 翻白眼

情境 2

Slamming hands on the table
雙手猛力拍桌

情境 3

Middle finger 比中指

情境 4

Crossed arms 手臂交叉

情境 5

Showing teeth in a snarl
秀出牙齒咆嘯

情境 6

Fisted hands 雙手握拳

情境 7

Angry voice 生氣的語調

情境 8

Body too closed to someone else
身體靠他人太近

情境 9

Fisted hand hitting other
hand's palm 拳頭打另一隻手的手掌

情境 10

Shaking a fist at someone
對他人搖晃拳頭

情境 11

Grinding back teeth 緊咬後排牙齒

情境 12

Teeth clenching 咬緊牙齒

情境 1 Rolling Eyes 翻白眼

翻白眼是指眼珠在眼窩中繞圈轉動。當有人說了奇怪或愚蠢的話時,其他人就會翻白眼。此外,當有人對他人不滿、或是不同意對方所說的話時,他們也可能會翻白眼。青少年經常在父母管教他們、或是說出令他們尷尬的話時翻白眼。

外國人翻白眼時,他們會說:

Don't listen to him.	不要聽他的。
That doesn't make sense.	那根本沒道理。
I can't believe you said that.	我真不敢相信你這麼說。
You're impossible!	你太扯了!
I'm mad at you.	我對你很生氣。
I can't stand you!	我受不了你!
I'm not listening.	我沒在聽。
That's annoying!	那真煩人!
You're bothering me.	你在打擾我。
I disagree.	我不同意。

外國人翻白眼時,你可以回:

I don't care.	我不在乎。
Do whatever you want.	隨你高興怎麼做。
You never listen to me.	你從來都不聽我的。
You don't have to agree with me.	你不必贊同我的看法。
I can do what I want.	我可以照我的意思做。
I'm so mad at you.	我很生你的氣。
You're so annoying!	你真的很煩人!
I'm frustrated with you.	我對你很失望。
I'm so mad.	我很生氣。
I think it makes sense.	我覺得這很合理。

情境對話 中文可對照上方的例句

Dialogue 1

Ⓐ That doesn't make sense.
Ⓑ I'm frustrated with you.
Ⓐ I'm not listening.
Ⓑ You never listen to me.

Dialogue 2

Ⓐ That's annoying!
Ⓑ I can do what I want.
Ⓐ I disagree.
Ⓑ I think it make sense.

情境 從英文來看外國人使用此肢體語言的情境

I had an awful day at school today. My best friend and I got into a fight and she told me she didn't agree with my choices. I rolled my eyes at her and told her I couldn't stand her.

今天我在學校過得很糟。我和我最好的朋友吵架了,她跟我說她不同意我的選擇,我就對她翻了個白眼,跟她說我很受不了她。

情境 2 Slamming Hands on the Table 雙手猛力拍桌

這是指張開的手掌在餐桌上、書桌上、或是任何平坦表面上猛擊，以發出巨大的拍打聲。這意味著人們對某事感到非常不高興或生氣，而在某些情況下，這麼做則是為了引起所有人的注意。很多時候，當有人用雙手大力拍桌時，房間中所有人都會安靜下來，並看著或聽著發出聲響的人。

外國人雙手拍桌時，他們會說：

This is wrong!	這是錯誤的！
I can't believe it.	我無法相信。
This isn't right!	這不對！
I'm furious!	我很火大！
This can't be!	這不可能！
Listen to me!	聽我說！
Pay attention!	注意！
Look at me!	看著我！
I'm talking!	我在說話！
Stop interrupting!	別打斷我！

外國人雙手拍桌時，你可以回：

It will be fine.	會沒事的。
Get over it.	熬過去吧。
I'm listening.	我在聽。
Calm down.	冷靜下來。
I'm mad, too.	我也很生氣。
It will be okay.	會沒事的。
Move on.	繼續前進。
Stop dwelling on it.	別一直想著這件事了。
I was talking first!	我先說的！
I'm paying attention.	我正在專心。

情境對話　中文可對照上方的例句

Dialogue 1

Ⓐ This is wrong!

Ⓑ It will be okay.

Ⓐ We need to fix it.

Ⓑ Stop dwelling on it.

Dialogue 2

Ⓐ Listen to me!

Ⓑ I'm listening.

Ⓐ This isn't right.

Ⓑ Get over it.

情境　從英文來看外國人使用此肢體語言的情境

I tried to give my ideas at the meeting, but my boss slammed his hands on the table and told me to stop interrupting. I just kept my mouth shut after that.

我試圖在會議上提出自己的想法，但我老闆用雙手大力拍桌，叫我不要再打斷他了。那之後我就閉上嘴，甚麼也沒說。

情境 3　Middle Finger 比中指

這個手勢是舉起手，伸出中指，以手背對著人，可以用「flip sb. off」、「flip sb. the bird」表示。這是一個極為粗俗的手勢，代表「screw you」或是「up yours」，意思是「去你的」。有些人會在與朋友開玩笑時比中指，但是大多數人對這個手勢很反感，並且非常不禮貌。

外國人比中指時，他們會說：

I hate you.	我討厭你。
Go to hell.	下地獄吧。
Screw you!	去你的！
This is what I think of you.	我就是這樣看你的。
You don't matter to me.	你對我而言不重要。
You're an asshole.	你真是個混蛋。
You're a jerk!	你是個笨蛋！
I can't stand them!	我受不了他們！
I'm so pissed!	我超火大！
They are awful!	他們爛透了！

外國人比中指時，你可以回：

I hate you, too!	我也恨你！
You're a liar.	你是個騙子。
Get over it.	克服它吧。
It wasn't me.	又不是我。
Don't get upset with me.	不要對我不高興。
You're just mad.	你只是在生氣罷了。
Calm down!	冷靜點！
Don't start a fight.	不要起衝突。
You need to relax.	你需要放鬆一下。
Chill out.	放鬆點吧。

情境對話　中文可對照上方的例句

Dialogue 1

Ⓐ I hate you!

Ⓑ Chill out.

Ⓐ Go to hell.

Ⓑ You're just mad.

Dialogue 2

Ⓐ I can't stand them!

Ⓑ Don't start a fight.

Ⓐ I'm so pissed!

Ⓑ Calm down!

情境　從英文來看外國人使用此肢體語言的情境

I was walking down the sidewalk and a man ran right into me. I dropped all my things. He didn't even stop to see if I was alright. I yelled at him and when he turned around, I flipped him off.

我走在人行道上，一名男子突然朝著我衝過來，我的東西掉了一地，他甚至完全沒有停下來，看看我有沒有怎麼樣。我對他大吼，當他轉身時，我對他比了中指。

情境 4 Crossed Arms 手臂交叉

這是指手肘彎折，並繞過身體，雙手握住另一隻手的上臂。雙臂交叉可能表示人們感到焦慮或不舒服，如果雙臂交叉而雙手緊握成拳，這可能表示他們正在生氣，或是不同意正在發生的某件事。此外，若是雙臂交叉並稍微彎曲身體，則可能表示他們感到寒冷，試著使自己暖和。

外國人手臂交叉時，他們會說：

I'm not impressed.	我沒有印象深刻。
I'm bored.	我覺得無聊了。
This is lame.	這好爛。
I'm really upset.	我真的不太開心。
I'm angry.	我很生氣。
I hate you!	我討厭你！
You made me mad.	你讓我火大。
You're a jerk!	你是個混蛋！
I'm freezing!	我要凍僵了！
Turn the heat on!	把暖氣打開！

外國人手臂交叉時，你可以回：

Why?	為甚麼？
I like it.	我喜歡。
I think it's good.	我認為這很好。
It's cool.	那很酷。
I'm mad, too.	我也很生氣。
You need to calm down.	你得冷靜下來。
You're uptight!	你太焦慮了！
I didn't do anything.	我甚麼也沒做。
Here's a blanket.	這裡有條毯子。
It feels nice in here.	在這裡面很舒服。

情境對話 中文可對照上方的例句

Dialogue 1

Ⓐ I'm angry.
Ⓑ Why?
Ⓐ This is lame.
Ⓑ I like it.

Dialogue 2

Ⓐ Turn the heat on.
Ⓑ It feels nice in here.
Ⓐ I'm freezing!
Ⓑ Here's a blanket.

情境 從英文來看外國人使用此肢體語言的情境

My dad likes to keep the house cool in the winter. I went to his house last night and was freezing! I was really mad. He saw me shivering with my arms crossed and got me a blanket.

我父親喜歡在冬天使房子保持涼爽。昨晚我去了他家，我快凍僵了！我真的很生氣。他看到我雙臂交叉地發著抖，於是給了我一條毯子。

情境 5 Showing Teeth in a Snarl 秀出牙齒咆嘯

指嘴唇向下彎曲並微微打開的時候，通常牙齒會緊緊咬在一起、鼻子稍微皺在一起，並發出咆嘯聲。這代表這個人對某件事很生氣或感到噁心。

外國人秀出牙齒咆嘯時，他們會說：

That's disgusting!	這真噁心！
I can't believe you ate that.	我不相信你會吃這種東西。
It's gross!	這好噁心喔！
Ewwww!	噁！
Yuck!	呸！
I'm so irritated.	我好生氣。
I'm really angry with you.	我真的對你很生氣。
I hate them.	我討厭他們。
It's nasty!	這真的很討厭！
It's gross outside.	外面好噁心。

外國人秀出牙齒咆嘯時，你可以回：

I agree!	我同意！
What is that?	那是甚麼？
Don't touch it!	不要碰那個！
It tasted good.	這很好吃。
It wasn't bad.	這沒有很糟。
What's the matter?	怎麼回事？
Don't taste it!	不要吃這個！
Is something bothering you?	你在困擾甚麼事嗎？
You don't seem like yourself	你似乎不太像自己。
You look mad!	你看起來很生氣！

情境對話 中文可對照上方的例句

Dialogue 1

Ⓐ I can't believe you ate that.

Ⓑ It tasted good.

Ⓐ Yuck!

Ⓑ You should try it!

Dialogue 2

Ⓐ I'm so irritated.

Ⓑ You don't seem like yourself.

Ⓐ I'm really angry with you.

Ⓑ What's the matter?

情境 從英文來看外國人使用此肢體語言的情境

I tried alligator for the first time. Everyone at the table was disgusted. Robert even showed his teeth in a snarl. He told me he would never eat it. It wasn't too bad!

我今天第一次吃鱷魚，在餐桌的每個人都覺得很噁心。Robert 甚至秀出他的牙齒咆嘯，他告訴我他不會再吃這道料理，但沒那麼糟啊！

情境 6 Fisted Hands 雙手握拳

這個手勢是將雙手緊緊地握成拳頭，放在身體的側面。雙手握拳最常表示人們極為不開心或是生氣。他們壓抑著怒氣，以握緊雙拳釋放一些他們所感到的壓力。此外，也有些人在做一些具有挑戰性或困難的事情之前會雙手握拳，例如發表重要談話或是搬舉重物的時候。

外國人雙手握拳時，他們會說：

I'm so mad!	我好生氣！
I'm pissed off!	我超火大！
I'm angry!	我很憤怒！
I can't stand him!	我受不了他了！
I'm furious.	我氣炸了。
I can't believe this!	我真不敢相信！
I can do this!	我可以做到的！
I'm going to win.	我會贏的。
I'm upset!	我很不開心！
This isn't fair!	這不公平！

外國人雙手握拳時，你可以回：

Relax!	放輕鬆！
Get over it.	熬過去吧。
Take a deep breath.	深呼吸。
You need to move on.	你必須往前走。
Don't freak out.	不要慌張。
You're freaking out.	你嚇壞了。
I'm mad, too!	我也很生氣了！
Life isn't fair.	人生真不公平。
Nothing is fair.	沒有甚麼是公平的。
You can't do anything about it.	你對此無能為力。

情境對話 中文可對照上方的例句

Dialogue 1

Ⓐ I'm pissed off!
Ⓑ What's wrong?
Ⓐ This isn't fair!
Ⓑ Life isn't fair.

Dialogue 2

Ⓐ I'm angry.
Ⓑ Take a deep breath.
Ⓐ I can't believe this!
Ⓑ You can't do anything about it.

情境 從英文來看外國人使用此肢體語言的情境

I almost got into a fight at the bar last night. A jerk kept pushing me. I wanted to punch him in the face. I had my hands fisted and was ready to fight, but my friends kept me from hitting him.

昨晚在酒吧，我差點和人打起來了。有個混蛋一直推我，我想往他的臉上揍一拳，我握緊了拳頭，準備動手，但是我的朋友們阻止我揍他。

情境 7 Angry Voice 生氣的語調

生氣的語調是大吼的聲音。不高興的人說話很快而且非常大聲,通常會比平常說話時更常揮動手臂,他們也可能在談話時咆哮或冷笑。

外國人用生氣的聲音時,他們會說:

I'm so upset with you!	我對你很不滿!
You lied to me!	你騙了我!
You cheated on me!	你背叛了我!
You're drunk!	你喝醉了!
I'm leaving you.	我要離開你。
You need to leave.	你得走了。
Get out of my house!	滾出我的房子!
I hate you!	我恨你!
You're a jerk!	你是個混蛋!
I can't believe you did that!	我無法相信你這麼做了!

外國人用生氣的聲音時,你可以回:

Don't be mad!	不要生氣!
I didn't mean to.	我不是故意的。
I'll explain it to you.	我會跟你解釋。
I'm not drunk!	我沒有喝醉!
It didn't happen.	那根本沒發生。
I'm not leaving.	我不會離開。
You can't kick me out.	你不能把我趕走。
That didn't happen.	那沒有發生。
I'm not going anywhere.	我哪裡都不去。
I didn't do it.	我沒有這麼做。

情境對話 中文可對照上方的例句

Dialogue 1

Ⓐ I'm so upset with you!

Ⓑ Don't be mad.

Ⓐ You cheated on me!

Ⓑ I'll explain it to you.

Dialogue 2

Ⓐ Get out of my house!

Ⓑ I'm not leaving.

Ⓐ You need to leave.

Ⓑ You can't kick me out.

情境 從英文來看外國人使用此肢體語言的情境

My neighbors were having a big fight last night. It sounds like the guy cheated on his wife. She was throwing things and screaming at him. The cops ended up coming there and breaking up the fight.

昨晚我的鄰居大吵一架。聽起來那個傢伙背著他的太太亂來,他的太太對他扔東西,並對著他尖叫。警察之後來了,並阻止了他們的大吵。

情境 8 Body Too Closed to Somebody 身體太靠近他人

當人們的身體太靠近其他人，這暗示出靠很近的人不是很需要別人的關懷並想和你親近（例如缺乏安全感的女朋友），就是指他們對你很生氣，而這是一種侵略的動作。

外國人的身體太靠近他人時，他們會說：

Pay attention to me!	注意我這裡！
I want to be close to you.	我想要靠近你。
I want to spend time with you.	我想要和你共處。
Will you look at me?	你會看著我嗎？
What's wrong with you?	你是怎麼回事？
I'm very upset with you.	我對你很失望。
You make me mad!	你讓我很生氣！
I can't stand you!	我真受不了你！
I want to kill you!	我想要殺了你！
You're an idiot!	你這個白癡！

外國人的身體太靠近他人時，你可以回：

You're too close.	你靠太近了。
Back up.	後退。
You're close enough.	你靠得夠近了。
Can you get off me?	你可以起來嗎？
Go away!	走開！
What's wrong?	怎麼了？
I didn't do anything!	我沒有做任何事！
You're being mean!	你真苛薄！
What's bothering you?	你在煩惱甚麼？
Why do you say that?	為甚麼你這樣說？

情境對話 中文可對照上方的例句

Dialogue 1

Ⓐ I can't stand you!

Ⓑ What's wrong?

Ⓐ You're an idiot!

Ⓑ Why do you say that?

Dialogue 2

Ⓐ I'm very upset with you.

Ⓑ I didn't do anything!

Ⓐ You make me mad!

Ⓑ You're being mean!

情境 從英文來看外國人使用此肢體語言的情境

I started dating a new girl last week. We went to a Christmas party and she was so clingy. She kept hanging on me and stood too close the whole time. I ended up breaking up with her that night.

我上禮拜開始和一個新認識的女孩約會，我們去一場聖誕派對，她真的非常黏人，她一直緊緊抓著我又靠得太近了，最後我在那晚直接跟她分手了。

情境 9

Fisted Hand Hitting other Hand's Palm
握拳的手打另一隻手掌

指一個人的一隻手緊緊握拳，並用拳頭捶另一隻手張開的手掌。這個手勢通常是在人們對其他人生氣的時候，想要打他們或是向他們表達憤怒的表現。

外國人用拳頭打手掌時，他們會說：

He's going to pay!	他要付出代價！
I'm going to get him.	我要去逮他。
I'll kill him!	我要殺了他！
He's dead!	他死定了！
I hate him!	我討厭他！
She's going to suffer.	她要付出代價。
I'll make him regret it.	我會讓他後悔。
She's going down!	她要被捧了！
I'm going to take him down.	我要去把他捧扁。
I'll punch him for you.	我幫你去捧他。

外國人用拳頭打手掌時，你可以回：

What happened?	怎麼了？
Why?	為甚麼？
What's going on?	發生甚麼事了？
What is wrong?	怎麼了嗎？
What did he do?	他做了甚麼？
Why are you upset?	你為甚麼難過？
What are you going to do?	你要做甚麼？
That's harsh!	太嚴厲了！
Don't do anything stupid.	不要做任何愚蠢的事。
Let's take a walk.	我們去走走。

情境對話　中文可對照上方的例句

Dialogue 1

Ⓐ He's going to pay!

Ⓑ Why?

Ⓐ I hate him!

Ⓑ What did he do?

Dialogue 2

Ⓐ I'll make him regret it.

Ⓑ Don't do anything stupid.

Ⓐ I'll punch him for you.

Ⓑ That's harsh!

情境　從英文來看外國人使用此肢體語言的情境

I had to tell Ryan that his girlfriend cheated on him. He was so upset at first, and then he got really angry. He kept punching his palm, telling me she was going to pay for what she did. I finally got him to calm down a little bit.

我必須告訴 Ryan，他的女朋友劈腿。他剛開始很難過，之後他變得很生氣。Ryan 一直用拳頭捶他的手掌，告訴我他女友要為劈腿付出代價，我最後才讓他冷靜一點。

情境 10 **Shaking a Fist at Someone 對他人搖晃拳頭**

這是指人們把拳頭握緊、並放到他人面前，他們和其他人有眼神接觸、對他們搖拳頭。這顯示出他們對其他人很生氣、並無言以對。駕駛通常會對另一位惹怒他們的駕駛做這個動作。

外國人對你搖拳頭時，他們會說：

You're an idiot!	你這個白癡！
What a moron!	真是個笨蛋！
I can't believe you did that.	我不相信你做這件事。
You hit my car!	你撞到我的車子！
You're the one that hit me!	你才是撞我的人！
You turned in front of me!	你在我前面轉彎！
You're such a jerk!	你真是個渾蛋！
I can't stand you!	我受不了你！
How could you do that?	你怎麼可以做這種事？
You're unbelievable.	你真是不可理喻。

外國人對你搖拳頭時，你可以回：

Why did you say that?	為甚麼你這樣說？
How dare you?	你怎麼敢？
I didn't mean to!	我不是故意的！
It was an accident!	這是個意外！
I'm so sorry.	我很抱歉。
Please don't be mad.	請不要生氣。
Don't be mad at me!	不要對我生氣！
Why?	為甚麼？
What did I do?	我做了甚麼？
I didn't do anything!	我沒有做任何事！

情境對話 中文可對照上方的例句

Dialogue 1

Ⓐ I can't believe you did that.
Ⓑ I didn't mean to!
Ⓐ You're an idiot!
Ⓑ It was an accident!

Dialogue 2

Ⓐ How could you do that?
Ⓑ You're the one that hit me!
Ⓐ You're unbelievable!
Ⓑ I didn't do anything!

情境 從英文來看外國人使用此肢體語言的情境

I accidentally backed into someone's car in the parking lot today. He got out of his car and was so mad at me! He was yelling and shaking his fist at me. I apologized over and over, but he was so rude.

我今天在停車場不小心倒車撞到某個人的車子，他走到車外、對我非常生氣！他還對我大吼、搖晃拳頭。我一直道歉，但他非常無禮。

情境 11 **Grinding Back Teeth 緊咬後排牙齒**

這是指把下顎閉得非常緊，牙齒咬緊。後排牙齒往前、後摩擦，變成咬牙切齒的動作。這個通常是指一個人很挫折、焦慮或非常生氣。

外國人緊咬後排牙齒時，他們會說：	
I'm so mad!	我很生氣！
I'm really upset.	我真的很沮喪。
I broke my computer.	我把我的電腦用壞了。
I can't believe it!	我不相信！
That's so dumb!	這太蠢了！
Why are you here?	你為甚麼在這裡？
I can't stand him.	我受不了他。
Look at this!	看這個！
It's all messed up.	全都搞砸了。
I have to fix this.	我必須修理這個。

外國人緊咬後排牙齒時，你可以回：	
Relax!	放鬆
What happened?	發生甚麼事了？
What's the matter?	怎麼了？
What's the problem?	有甚麼問題嗎？
What can I do to help?	有甚麼我可以幫忙的嗎？
I think it will be okay.	我覺得會沒事的。
It'll be alright.	會沒事的。
Calm down.	冷靜。
I'll help you.	我會幫助你。
We can fix it.	我們可以修理它。

情境對話 中文可對照上方的例句

Dialogue 1
Ⓐ I'm so mad!
Ⓑ What happened?
Ⓐ I broke my computer.
Ⓑ We can fix it!

Dialogue 2
Ⓐ Look at this!
Ⓑ What's the matter?
Ⓐ It's all messed up.
Ⓑ I'll help you.

情境 從英文來看外國人使用此肢體語言的情境

My roommate's computer wasn't working last night. He was trying to finish a project that was due today. He was sweating and grinding his teeth while working on the computer. I was able to help him get it working again.

我室友的電腦昨天當機了。他那時試著要完成一份今天要交的報告。他一直流汗、咬牙切齒，同時又在修理電腦。而我能幫他把電腦修好再次運作。

情境 12　Teeth Clenching 咬緊牙齒

這是指嘴巴緊閉，下巴閉得非常緊。這與咬牙切齒相似，但牙齒咬住的時候沒有其他動作，只是把牙齒咬得非常緊。這個是對某件事沮喪、生氣或焦慮的徵兆。

外國人咬緊牙齒時，他們會說：

I'm pissed off.	我很火大。
I want to hit something.	我想要打某個東西。
I'm so angry.	我非常生氣。
This makes me upset.	這讓我很沮喪。
It's so frustrating!	真的很挫折！
Now we have to start over.	現在我們必須重新開始。
I can't believe this.	我無法相信這件事。
It's unbelievable.	真不敢相信。
How could you do this?	你怎麼能做這件事？
This is awful!	這真的很糟糕。

外國人咬緊牙齒時，你可以回：

Why?	為甚麼？
What happened?	發生甚麼事了？
Whoa! Chill out!	哇！冷靜！
What's the matter?	怎麼了？
Let's talk about it.	我們來談談這件事。
How are you feeling?	你感覺如何？
Don't freak out.	別慌張。
Why are you yelling?	你為甚麼要大吼大叫？
I didn't do anything!	我沒有做任何事！
It will be alright.	會沒事的。

情境對話　中文可對照上方的例句

Dialogue 1

Ⓐ I'm so angry!
Ⓑ Whoa! Chill out!
Ⓐ I want to hit something.
Ⓑ Let's talk about it.

Dialogue 2

Ⓐ How could you do this?
Ⓑ I didn't do anything!
Ⓐ I'm pissed off!
Ⓑ What is wrong?

情境　從英文來看外國人使用此肢體語言的情境

I knew something was wrong right away when I saw John. His teeth were clenched and he looked really upset. I found out that he was fired from his job.

我一看到 John 的時候，我就知道事情不對勁了。他的牙齒咬緊，而且看起來非常沮喪。我發現他被解雇了。

Feeling Shy 感到害羞

☞ **感到害羞時需要用到的動作，用英文要怎麼說呢？**

對某些事物感到害怕就會產生各種手勢和肢體動作，下列是感到害怕時會用到的手勢與肢體語言，請看圖片，並對照動作的英文和中文。

情境 1
Crossed legs while standing
站立時雙腿交叉

情境 2
Shy smile 害羞的微笑

情境 3
Shy voice 害羞的語調

※ 補充說明：耳朵發紅也是害羞時會使用的肢體語言，可回去 Unit 9 p.93 複習。

Crosssed Legs while Standing 站立時雙腿交叉

情境 1

指站著時，將一條腿在另一條腿前方交叉。這個姿勢表示人們很害羞，還可能伴隨著雙手在背後交握，並且低著頭的情況。由於這種姿勢不穩定，站著的人可能看起來坐立難安，或是身體輕微搖晃。

外國人站立、雙腿交叉時，他們會說：

I feel nervous.	我覺得緊張。
I'm out of place.	我感覺不自在。
I'm unsure of myself.	我對自己不確定。
I don't know what to say.	我不知道該說甚麼。
I feel lost.	我感到迷惘。
I'm shy.	我很害羞。
I feel awkward.	我覺得很尷尬。
I don't fit in.	我格格不入。
I feel funny.	我覺得不舒服。
This is awkward.	這真是尷尬。

外國人站立、雙腿交叉時，你可以回：

Don't be nervous.	不要緊張。
You're fine.	你很好。
You're doing great.	你做得很好。
You're okay!	你不錯啊！
Just be yourself.	做你自己就好。
Everyone loves you!	大家都愛你！
You fit in with us.	你很融入我們。
Take a seat.	請坐。
Why are you nervous?	你為甚麼緊張？
Be yourself!	做你自己吧！

情境對話 中文可對照上方的例句

Dialogue 1

Ⓐ I feel nervous.
Ⓑ You're doing great.
Ⓐ I'm out of place.
Ⓑ Just be yourself.

Dialogue 2

Ⓐ I feel funny.
Ⓑ Why?
Ⓐ I don't know what to say.
Ⓑ Everyone loves you!

情境 從英文來看外國人使用此肢體語言的情境

I had to go to a company dinner with my husband and his coworkers. There was a new employee there that looked nervous. He was standing with his legs crossed and seemed out of place. We stood by him to help him relax a little bit.

我必須和先生和他的同事去他公司的聚餐。那裡有個新員工看起來很緊張。他站著雙腿交叉站立，似乎很不自在。我們站在他身邊，以幫助他放鬆一點。

情境 2　Shy Smile 害羞的微笑

害羞的微笑與調情的微笑非常相似，這種通常會把嘴張開一半，下巴會向下傾斜。這個人不會與他人進行眼神交流，而是迅速地環視整個房間，或是看著地板。這些行為表明這個人在某種情況下並不自在，並且感到害羞或格格不入。

外國人害羞地微笑時，他們會說：

I feel awkward.	我覺得尷尬。
This is awkward.	這好尷尬。
I should probably go.	我可能應該得走了。
I feel out of place.	我覺得格格不入。
I'm uncomfortable.	我覺得不太舒服。
I feel funny.	我覺得很奇怪。
I shouldn't be here.	我不應該在這裡。
I don't know anyone.	我不認識任何人。
I'm at a loss.	我很茫然。
Everyone is looking at me.	大家都在看我。

外國人害羞地微笑時，你可以回：

You're fine.	你很好。
You look great.	你看起來很棒。
Don't leave.	不要離開。
Don't go!	不要走！
I understand.	我明白。
Don't go anywhere.	不要去任何地方。
It's still early.	現在還早。
Stay a little longer.	再多留一會兒。
You fit right in.	你很融入。
No one is looking!	沒有人在看！

情境對話　中文可對照上方的例句

Dialogue 1

Ⓐ I should probably go.
Ⓑ Stay a little longer.
Ⓐ I feel awkward.
Ⓑ Don't go anywhere.

Dialogue 2

Ⓐ I shouldn't be here.
Ⓑ Don't leave.
Ⓐ I don't know anyone.
Ⓑ You fit right in.

情境　從英文來看外國人使用此肢體語言的情境

My friend came with me to the Christmas party tonight. I could tell she was nervous when we first got there because of her shy smile. I talked her into staying, and she ended up having a blast.

我的朋友今晚和我一起參加了聖誕派對。我可以從她害羞的微笑看出來，她剛到那裡時很緊張。我說服她留下來，而她最終玩得很盡興了。

情境 3 Shy Voice 害羞的語調

這是一種小聲、難以聽見的聲音。有時候用害羞的語調說話的人，說話速度會變慢，並且有點拖長句子。當人們的語調很害羞時，會很難和很多人說話或與大群人交談，因為他們的聲音很小聲。害羞的人說話時會避免目光接觸，他們可能會看著地板。

外國人用害羞的語調說話時，他們會說：

I feel out of place.	我覺得格格不入。
This is awkward.	這好尷尬。
Can you hear me now?	你現在聽到我說的嗎？
Let me speak up.	讓我大聲點。
I'm trying to speak louder.	我試著大聲說話。
This is hard for me.	這對我來說很難。
I feel uncomfortable.	我覺得不太舒服。
Does this sound better?	這樣聽起來好點嗎？
Did you hear me?	你聽得到我嗎？
Can I have a minute?	可以等我一下嗎？

外國人用害羞的語調說話時，你可以回：

You're fine.	你沒事的。
You're doing great.	你做得很好。
Yes, that's better.	嗯，這樣好點了。
That's good!	很好！
I can hear you.	我可以聽到你的聲音。
Keep it up!	繼續保持！
You're doing a good job.	你做得很好。
Can you talk louder?	你能大聲點嗎？
I didn't hear you.	我沒聽到你說話。
What did you say?	你剛才說甚麼？

情境對話　中文可對照上方的例句

Dialogue 1

Ⓐ I feel out of place.
Ⓑ You're fine.
Ⓐ This is hard for me.
Ⓑ You're doing great.

Dialogue 2

Ⓐ Did you hear me?
Ⓑ What did you say?
Ⓐ Let me speak up.
Ⓑ Yes, that's better.

情境　從英文來看外國人使用此肢體語言的情境

We had to take a class at work for the new computer program we'll be using. The presenter had a shy voice, and I could hardly hear her talking. I had to keep asking her to speak up.

我們的工作需要參加我們即將使用的新電腦程式課程。講者有個害羞的語調，我幾乎聽不到她講話，我得要一直請她說大聲點。

Feeling Concerned
感到擔心

☞ **感到擔心時需要用到的動作，用英文要怎麼說呢？**

對某些事物感到擔心就會產生各種手勢和肢體動作，下列是感到擔心時會用到的手勢與肢體語言，請看圖片，並對照動作的英文和中文。

情境 1

Arm over someone's shoulder
手臂放在他人的肩膀上

情境 2

Touching someone's upper arms
觸碰他人的上臂

情境 3

Putting a hand on someone's
upper back 將手放在他人的上背

情境 1
Arm over Someone's Shoulder
手臂放在他人的肩膀上

將手臂繞過另一人的脖子,並放在對方的肩膀或上背部,這表示人們在乎他們所擁抱的人,而這是令人感到安全的保護動作,也可以是在乎或擔心對方的表現。以手臂搭在他人的肩膀上不如用手臂環繞在腰上來得親密,這通常是朋友間的動作,而不是其他意義重大的人。

外國人的手臂放在他人肩膀時,他們會說:

Are you okay?	你還好嗎?
You seem upset.	你好像不開心。
What's up?	怎麼了嗎?
What's bothering you?	你有甚麼煩惱嗎?
How can I help?	我可以怎麼幫忙呢?
Do you feel alright?	你感覺還好嗎?
You look tired.	你看起來很累。
What can I do?	我能做甚麼呢?
You're okay!	你沒事的!
You'll be okay.	你會沒事的。

外國人的手臂放在他人肩膀時,你可以回:

I'm okay.	我很好。
I'm alright.	我沒事。
I've been better.	我已經好多了。
I'm not the greatest.	我不是最好的。
I'm upset.	我不太開心。
I'm bummed.	我很惱怒。
I don't feel well.	我覺得不太舒服。
I don't know.	我不知道。
I'm tired.	我累了。
I hope so.	我希望如此。

情境對話 中文可對照上方的例句

Dialogue 1

Ⓐ Are you okay?

Ⓑ I'm okay.

Ⓐ You seem upset.

Ⓑ I'm bummed.

Dialogue 2

Ⓐ Do you feel alright?

Ⓑ I don't feel well.

Ⓐ How can I help?

Ⓑ I don't know.

情境 從英文來看外國人使用此肢體語言的情境

Mary asked me how I was doing yesterday. She put her arm around my shoulders and asked if I was okay. I think she knows I'm having a hard time right now. I told her how I was feeling and that I've been upset lately. It felt good to talk to her.

Mary 問我昨天過得怎麼樣。她將手臂環繞在我的肩膀上,問我是否還好。我想她知道我現在過得不好,我告訴她我的感覺,以及最近我覺得不太開心。和她說話感覺很好。

情境 2　Touching Someone's Upper Arms 觸碰他人的上臂

指人們將手掌放在他人的上臂，這是一種代表支持的手勢，表現出他們很關心他們所接觸的人。

外國人觸碰他人的上臂時，他們會說：

Do you need help?	你需要幫助嗎？
Are you okay?	你還好嗎？
What's wrong?	怎麼了？
What's bothering you?	你有甚麼煩惱？
I'm here for you.	我在這裡陪你。
I'll sit with you.	我坐你旁邊。
I can go with you.	我可以和你一起去。
Don't worry.	不用擔心。
I'll take care of it.	我會處理的。
You're okay!	你會沒事的！

外國人觸碰他人的上臂時，你可以回：

Yes, I need help.	是的，我需要幫助。
I'm fine.	我很好。
Thanks for checking on me.	感謝你來看我。
I'm worried about work.	我擔心工作。
I'll be okay!	我會沒事的！
I'm upset.	我很沮喪。
I don't feel well.	我感覺不舒服。
I don't know what's wrong.	我不知道怎麼了。
I don't feel right.	我感覺不對勁。
Thank you.	謝謝你。

情境對話　中文可對照上方的例句

Dialogue 1

Ⓐ Are you okay?

Ⓑ I don't feel well.

Ⓐ Do you need help?

Ⓑ Yes, I need help.

Dialogue 2

Ⓐ What's wrong?

Ⓑ I'm upset.

Ⓐ What's bothering you?

Ⓑ I'm worried about work.

情境　從英文來看外國人使用此肢體語言的情境

On my way home from work, I saw my neighbor sitting on her front porch crying. She looked very upset, so I stopped to check on her. I put my hand on her arm and sat by her. She said she wasn't feeling well and was resting. I helped her get inside and got her some water.

下班回家的路上，我看到我的鄰居坐在她家前廊哭泣。她看起來非常沮喪，所以我停下來看看她。我把手放在她的手臂上，並坐在她旁邊。她說她覺得不舒服，正在休息。我幫忙扶她進到屋裡，給她倒了杯水。

情境 3

Putting a Hand on Someone's Upper Back
將手放在他人的上背

　　將手掌放在另一人的上背，這個動作非常類似於將手放在他人的上臂上、或是將手臂環繞在他人的肩膀上。這是兩人之間相互支持和關懷的表現。

外國人觸碰他人的上臂時，他們會說：

What's going on?	怎麼回事？
Are you okay?	你還好嗎？
What can I do to help?	我該怎麼幫忙？
Do you need help?	你需要幫助嗎？
What do you need?	你需要甚麼嗎？
How can I help?	有甚麼我可以幫忙的嗎？
I'm here for you.	我在這裡陪你。
I can help you.	我能幫你。
I'm sorry.	對不起。
I know you're upset.	我知道你很沮喪。

外國人觸碰他人的上臂時，你可以回：

I'll be just fine.	我會沒事的。
I'm alright.	我很好。
It's nothing.	沒事。
Don't worry about it.	不用擔心。
I need to see a doctor.	我得去看醫生。
I'll be okay.	我會沒事的。
I don't need help.	我不需要幫助。
I need help.	我需要幫助。
I'm worried about work.	我在擔心工作。
I'm not feeling well.	我感覺不舒服。

情境對話 中文可對照上方的例句

Dialogue 1

Ⓐ What's going on?
Ⓑ It's nothing.
Ⓐ I know you're upset.
Ⓑ Don't worry about it.

Dialogue 2

Ⓐ What do you need?
Ⓑ I don't need help.
Ⓐ Are you sure?
Ⓑ I'll be okay.

情境 從英文來看外國人使用此肢體語言的情境

Mary was sitting alone in the break room yesterday. I put my hand on her back and asked if she was alright. She said she thought she was getting sick. She ended up staying home for the rest of the day. I hope she's feeling better!

Mary 昨天獨自坐在休息室。我把手放在她的背上，問她是否還好。她說她覺得自己生病了，之後她在那天剩下的時間都在家裡。我希望她感覺好些了！

Feeling Bored or Exhausted
感到無聊、疲累

☞ **感到無聊、疲累時需要用到的動作，用英文要怎麼說呢？**

對某些事物感到無聊、疲累就會產生各種手勢和肢體動作，下列是感到無聊、疲累時會用到的手勢與肢體語言，請看圖片，並對照動作的英文和中文。

情境 1

Tilting neck to one side, and then the other 脖子轉到一邊、再換另一邊

情境 2

Swinging crossed leg 擺動翹著的腿

情境 3

Leaning cheek on fist
臉頰靠在拳頭上

情境 4

Covered mouth 遮住嘴巴

情境 5

Holding shoulders low 肩膀低垂

情境 6

Body slouching in chair
無精打采地坐在椅子上

Crossing your leg and shaking foot
back and forth 翹腳、腳前後搖動

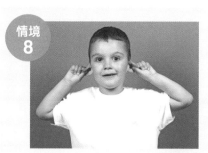

Tugging on ears 拉耳朵

Tapping teeth with fingernails or
pencils, etc.
用手指甲或鉛筆等敲牙齒

※ 補充說明：頭部繞圈也是無聊、疲累時會使用的肢體語言，可回去 Unit 11
p.105 複習。

情境 1

Tilting Neck to One Side, and then the Otehr
脖子轉到一邊、再換另一邊

將頭部從一邊往另一邊傾斜，像是試著要讓耳朵碰到肩膀一樣，這是疲累的表現，人們會試著傾斜頭部來放鬆脖子的肌肉。這個動作表示人們一直在努力工作，他們開始覺得疲倦或耗盡體力。

外國人把脖子轉到一側、再換另一邊時，他們會說：	
I'm almost done.	我快弄完了。
I need a break.	我需要休息一下。
I'm getting tired.	我累了。
I'm exhausted!	我精疲力盡了！
I think it's finished.	我覺得已經完成了。
I need to sit down.	我得坐一下。
My head hurts.	我頭好痛。
Let's take a break.	我們休息一下吧。
I need a drink!	我要喝一杯！
I'm worn out!	我累斃了！

外國人把脖子轉到一側、再換另一邊時，你可以回：	
You'll be done soon.	你很快就會弄完的。
It looks good.	看起來不錯。
You're doing great.	你做得很好。
It's almost done.	幾乎要做好了。
You're getting close.	你快做完了。
Take a break.	休息一下吧。
Let's take a break.	讓我們休息一下。
Rest for a minute.	休息一分鐘。
Here's some water.	這裡有水。
Do you need help?	你需要幫助嗎？

情境對話　中文可對照上方的例句

Dialogue 1

Ⓐ I need a break.
Ⓑ Let's take a break.
Ⓐ I'm exhausted!
Ⓑ Here's some water.

Dialogue 2

Ⓐ I think it's finished.
Ⓑ It looks good.
Ⓐ I'm worn out!
Ⓑ You did great!

情境　從英文來看外國人使用此肢體語言的情境

I just spent fifteen hours at work finishing a project. My neck is so stiff, and I keep tilting it back and forth to help loosen the muscles. I'm happy to be done with that project!

我才剛花了 15 個小時來完成一項企畫案。我的脖子非常僵硬，我得不斷來回歪頭，來幫助放鬆肌肉。我很高興那個企畫案已經完成了！

情境 2　Swinging Crossed Leg 擺動翹著的腿

指坐著時將一條腿翹在另一條腿的膝蓋上，並且來回擺動翹著的腿。這是無聊或煩悶的表現。除了擺動腿部以外，人們還可能歪著身子或用手托住頭。

外國人擺動翹著的腿時，他們會說：

Can we go?	我們可以走了嗎？
What time is it?	現在是幾點？
This is taking forever.	這會花很久的時間。
I'm bored.	我很無聊。
When can we leave?	我們甚麼時候可以走？
Who is this?	那是誰？
I can't stand this.	我受不了這件事。
They're bothering me.	他們在打擾我。
I'm so annoyed.	我覺得很煩。
Are you bored?	你很無聊嗎？

外國人擺動翹著的腿時，你可以回：

Not yet.	還沒有。
I'm not ready.	我還沒準備好。
We're not leaving.	我們不會離開。
We're not going anywhere.	我們不會去任何地方。
Just a few more minutes.	再過幾分鐘就好。
You're being rude.	你很沒禮貌。
We'll leave later.	我們一會兒就離開。
I'll leave soon.	我很快就要離開了。
You can go.	你可以走了。
I'm not going yet.	我還沒要走。

情境對話　中文可對照上方的例句

Dialogue 1

Ⓐ Can we go?
Ⓑ Not yet.
Ⓐ This is taking forever.
Ⓑ Just a few more minutes.

Dialogue 2

Ⓐ What time is it?
Ⓑ 10:00.
Ⓐ When can we leave?
Ⓑ We'll leave later.

情境　從英文來看外國人使用此肢體語言的情境

I took my son shopping with me yesterday. I made him sit while I tried on a few dresses at the mall. He was so bored! He sat in a chair and swung his crossed leg the whole time asking if we could leave. I was really mad at him.

我昨天帶兒子去逛街。我在購物中心試穿幾件洋裝時，我讓他坐著。他覺得很無聊！他坐在椅子上一直晃翹著的腿，問我們是否可以走了。我真的很生他的氣。

情境 3 Leaning Cheek on Fist 臉頰靠在拳頭上

指一個人手握拳並把他們的臉頰靠在拳頭上。手掌面向臉頰而頭稍微傾斜。這代表這個人很疲憊或無聊。類似的手勢也有把臉靠在手掌上，或是把下巴托在拳頭上。

外國人把臉頰靠在拳頭上時，他們會說：

I'm so bored.	我好無聊。
I'm tired.	我累了。
I find it boring.	我覺得這很無聊。
This isn't exciting.	這一點都不刺激。
It's lame.	真爛。
I don't find it interesting.	我不覺得這很有趣。
I'm bored to tears.	我無聊到流眼淚。
	（指打哈欠的流淚）
How boring!	真無聊！
This is so dull.	這真令人乏味。
I'd like to leave.	我想要離開了。

外國人把臉頰靠在拳頭上時，你可以回：

Pay attention.	專心。
Don't ignore me.	不要忽略我。
You don't like it?	你不喜歡這個嗎？
It's so interesting!	這很有趣啊！
I love it!	我喜歡！
You can leave.	你可以離開。
Can you sit up?	你可以坐直嗎？
Don't be rude.	不要沒禮貌。
I agree/disagree!	我同意／不同意！
Let's leave!	我們走吧！

情境對話　中文可對照上方的例句

Dialogue 1

Ⓐ This isn't exciting.
Ⓑ Pay attention.
Ⓐ I'm so bored.
Ⓑ You can leave.

Dialogue 2

Ⓐ This is so dull.
Ⓑ I agree.
Ⓐ I'd like to leave.
Ⓑ Let's leave.

情境　從英文來看外國人使用此肢體語言的情境

My best friend and I went to the new comedy club in town. We were so bored! The comedian wasn't funny and we just sat there leaning on the table. Sara actually fell asleep with her cheek leaning on her fist. We didn't stay long.

我和我最好的朋友去了市區新開的喜劇俱樂部，我們很無聊！那個喜劇演員一點都不好笑，我們就坐在那裡靠在桌子上。結果 Sara 其實睡著了、臉頰靠在她的拳頭上。我們沒有待很久。

情境 4 Covered Mouth 遮住嘴巴

一般而言，露出口腔內部被認為是不禮貌的，因此張開嘴時，有些人會用手遮住嘴巴，例如打哈欠、咯咯笑時，或是會在一邊吃東西一邊說話時用手摀嘴巴。

外國人遮住嘴巴時，他們會說：

I'm tired!	我累了！
I feel sleepy.	我睏了。
I'm ready for bed.	我準備睡覺了。
It's so early.	太早了。
I want to go back to bed.	我想回去睡覺。
That was funny!	真好笑！
I can't help but laugh.	我忍不住笑了。
Tell me another joke!	再跟我說一個笑話！
I have a funny story.	我有個有趣的故事。
Stop tickling me!	別再搔我癢了！

外國人遮住嘴巴時，你可以回：

Go to bed.	上床睡覺。
Take a nap.	小睡一下。
Are you feeling okay?	你還好嗎？
What's wrong?	怎麼了？
You can go to bed.	你可以上床睡覺了。
I'll tell you one more.	我再跟你說一個。
That's hilarious!	太好笑了！
You're too funny!	你好好笑了！
I'm laughing so hard.	我笑得很厲害。
I can't stop laughing.	我笑到停不下來。

情境對話　中文可對照上方的例句

Dialogue 1

Ⓐ I feel sleepy.
Ⓑ You can go to bed.
Ⓐ It's so early.
Ⓑ It's okay!

Dialogue 2

Ⓐ That was funny!
Ⓑ I can't stop laughing.
Ⓐ Tell me another joke!
Ⓑ I'll tell you one more.

情境　從英文來看外國人使用此肢體語言的情境

I didn't sleep well last night, so I'm really tired today. I can't stop yawning! I keep covering my mouth, but I think my coworker is noticing how sleepy I am.

昨晚我沒有睡好，所以今天真的很累。我不能止住哈欠！我一直摀著嘴，但我想我的同事有注意到我很想睡。

情境 5　Holding Shoulders Low 肩膀低垂

感到疲倦或精疲力竭時，肩膀就會垂下，像是要垂到地面一樣。消耗大量精力（身體疲倦）或撐完漫長而糟糕的一天（精神疲倦）後，人們的肩膀就可能會低垂著。

外國人肩膀低垂時，他們會說：

I'm exhausted.	我精疲力盡了。
That was tough.	那很棘手。
It was hard.	這個很難。
I'm tired!	我累了！
I'm beat!	我被打倒了！
I feel beat up.	我覺得被打倒了。
I need some sleep.	我需要睡一下。
I'm going to rest.	我要休息了。
I'm done!	我受夠了！
I'm over it.	我不在乎了。

外國人肩膀低垂時，你可以回：

What's wrong?	怎麼了？
Are you okay?	你還好嗎？
Do you feel okay?	你覺得還好嗎？
Get some rest.	休息一下。
Let's take five.	讓我們休息五分鐘。
Let's call it a day.	今天就到此為止吧。
Is everything okay?	一切還好嗎？
That was a big job.	那真是個大工程。
Here's some water.	這裡有水。
Have a seat!	請坐下！

情境對話　中文可對照上方的例句

Dialogue 1

Ⓐ I'm exhausted.

Ⓑ Do you feel okay?

Ⓐ I need some sleep.

Ⓑ Get some rest.

Dialogue 2

Ⓐ I'm beat!

Ⓑ That was a big job.

Ⓐ It was hard.

Ⓑ Let's call it a day.

情境　從英文來看外國人使用此肢體語言的情境

Leah and I ran the Chicago marathon yesterday. We crossed the finish line together! I felt okay, but Leah looked awful. Her shoulders hung really low and she looked pale. She said she felt beat up. I'm sure she'll feel better today.

Leah 和我昨天參加了芝加哥馬拉松。我們一起越過終點線！我感覺還好，但是 Leah 看起來很糟糕。她的肩膀垂得非常低、臉色蒼白。她說她覺得像是被痛打了一樣，我確定她今天會覺得好多了。

情境 6 **Body Slouching on Chair 無精打采的坐在椅子上**

當肩膀向前拱著、身體彎取、頭往前垂下時，身體會呈現沒精打采的樣子。坐在椅子上時，人們可能會滑下椅子或把背拱著，這讓他們表現出沒安全感或無聊的樣子。

外國人無精打采的坐在椅子上時，他們會說：

This is boring.	這好無聊。
I'm bored.	我好無聊。
I don't get it.	我不太了解。
I feel uncomfortable.	我覺得不舒服。
I'd like to leave.	我想離開了。
I wish I could go home.	真希望我能回家。
I'm going to go.	我要走了。
I don't need to be here.	我不需要在這裡。
This doesn't interest me.	這不會讓我感到有趣。
I find it boring.	我覺得這很無聊。

外國人無精打采的坐在椅子上時，你可以回：

I think it's interesting!	我覺得這很有趣！
Can I help you?	你要我幫忙嗎？
I'll explain it again.	我會再解釋一次。
What's wrong?	怎麼了？
We're almost done.	我們快做完了。
Leave, then.	那你走吧。
Sit up.	坐直。
We'll leave soon.	我們快要走了。
It's not boring!	這不會無聊！
I like it.	我喜歡這個點子。

情境對話 中文可對照上方的例句

Dialogue 1

Ⓐ This is boring.
Ⓑ It's not boring!
Ⓐ I wish I could go home.
Ⓑ Leave, then.

Dialogue 2

Ⓐ I don't get it.
Ⓑ I'll explain it again.
Ⓐ Thanks!
Ⓑ Sit up.

情境 從英文來看外國人使用此肢體語言的情境

My boyfriend and I went to a movie theater last night. He sat slouched in the chair and didn't even watch the movie. He told me he was bored and didn't like the movie. I thought it was good.

我男朋友和我昨晚去電影院看電影，他無精打采地坐在椅子上，甚至沒在看電影。他跟我說他很無聊，而且不喜歡這部片，但我覺得這部片很不錯。

情境 7 Crossing Your Leg and Shaking Foot Back and Forth 翹腳、腳前後搖晃

當人坐著的時候把腿翹在另一條腿的膝蓋上，把懸著的腿往前後搖擺，同時把腳掌往前後搖晃，這是無聊或煩躁的一種表現。人們除了會搖晃他們的腿，也會把身體往前傾，或是用手撐住他們的頭。

外國人翹腳、腳往前後搖動時，他們會說：

What time is it?	幾點了？
Can we go?	我們可以走了嗎？
This is taking forever.	這根本沒完沒了。
I'm bored.	我好無聊。
When can we leave?	我們甚麼時候可以走？
Who is this?	這是誰？
I can't stand this.	我受不了這件事。
They're bothering me.	他們在打擾我。
I'm so annoyed.	我覺得好煩。
Are you bored?	你很無聊嗎？

外國人翹腳、腳往前後搖動時，你可以回：

Stop it!	不要再說了！
What's wrong?	怎麼了？
It's still early.	現在還早。
Why?	為甚麼？
It's almost done.	快完成了。
I don't know!	我不知道！
Stop talking.	別再說了。
Let's leave.	我們走吧。
We'll leave soon.	我們很快就要走了。
It's getting late.	時間不早了。

情境對話 中文可對照上方的例句

Dialogue 1

Ⓐ When can we leave?
Ⓑ Why?
Ⓐ I'm bored.
Ⓑ It's still early.

Dialogue 2

Ⓐ This is taking forever.
Ⓑ Stop it!
Ⓐ Can we go?
Ⓑ We'll leave soon.

情境 從英文來看外國人使用此肢體語言的情境

A group of my friends and I went to brunch on Sunday. I had to take my little sister. She was so bored. She sat slumped in her chair while shaking her crossed leg. I was really mad at her.

我和一群朋友在週日去吃早午餐，我必須帶著我的妹妹。她很無聊，坐在椅子上把頭低著並晃著她翹著的腳。我真的對她很生氣。

情境 8 Tugging on the Ears 拉耳朵

當人們用食指和拇指把耳朵往下拉時，這個是無聊或興趣缺缺的表現。人們這樣做的時候，他們可能也會避開眼神接觸，不看說話的人。

外國人拉耳朵時，他們會說：

I'm bored!	我好無聊！
This is boring.	這真無聊。
Can we go?	我們可以走了嗎？
I should go.	我該走了。
I need to leave.	我要離開了。
I'm going to head out.	我要出去了。
See you later!	等會兒見！
I'm getting bored.	我感到很厭倦。
I can't stand this.	我受不了了。
It's so boring!	真無趣！

外國人拉耳朵時，你可以回：

We're not leaving.	我們還沒要走。
We're staying.	我們還要待著。
No, we can't.	不，我們不行。
We have to stay.	我們必須要待在這。
Pay attention.	專心。
You're being rude.	你很沒禮貌。
Don't leave!	別走！
It's almost over.	快結束了。
It will be done soon.	很快就會完成了。
Don't say that.	不要這樣說。

情境對話　中文可對照上方的例句

Dialogue 1

Ⓐ This is boring.
Ⓑ It's almost over.
Ⓐ Can we go?
Ⓑ No, we can't.

Dialogue 2

Ⓐ I'm going to head out.
Ⓑ Don't leave!
Ⓐ I can't stand this.
Ⓑ Don't say that.

情境　從英文來看外國人使用此肢體語言的情境

My friend and I are in the same art history class. I think it's really interesting, but she hates it. She never pays attention. She's always looking around the room and tugging on her ears. She's going to get a bad grade.

我和我的朋友上同一門藝術史課程。我覺得課程很有趣，但她很討厭這門課，她從來都不專心聽課。她總是環顧教室四周、拉耳朵。她之後會得到很差的成績。

Tapping Teeth with Fingernailes or Penciel, etc.
用手指甲或鉛筆等敲牙齒

情境 9

這是指一個人用某個物品（一枝鉛筆、原子筆、手指甲等）去敲前排的牙齒，這會從嘴巴發出聲音。這是無聊的表現，但也可能代表一個人正在努力想某件事。

外國人用指甲或鉛筆敲牙齒時，他們會說：

I'm bored.	我好無聊。
This is boring.	這好無聊。
I'm really tired.	我真的好累。
I can't stand this.	我受不了這個。
I'm focusing on this.	我正專心在這件事上。
I need to focus on my project.	我需要專注在我的專案上。
I can't have any interruptions.	我不能有任何打擾。
I'm thinking through this.	我正在想這件事。
It's a tough project.	這是一份很難的專案。
Let me work on this.	讓我處理這件事。

外國人用指甲或鉛筆敲牙齒時，你可以回：

I think you'll like it.	我覺得你會喜歡的。
It will get better.	事情會好轉的。
What's the matter?	怎麼了？
Don't do that!	別這麼做！
Can I help you?	我可以幫你嗎？
I'll shut your door.	我會幫你關門。
You're almost done!	你幾乎要完成了。
I'll leave you to it.	我不打擾你。
I'll stop by later.	我等等再來。
I'll give you some space.	我會給你一些空間。

情境對話　中文可對照上方的例句

Dialogue 1

Ⓐ I'm really tired.
Ⓑ What's the matter?
Ⓐ This is boring.
Ⓑ You're almost done!

Dialogue 2

Ⓐ I can't have any interruptions.
Ⓑ What's the matter?
Ⓐ I need to focus on my project.
Ⓑ I'll leave you to it.

情境　從英文來看外國人使用此肢體語言的情境

I stopped by Mark's office today. He was tapping his teeth and squinting at his computer. I knew he was deep in thought, so I didn't interrupt him. I'll stop by later to ask my question.

我今天經過 Mark 的辦公室。他敲著他的牙齒，瞇著眼看著他的電腦。我知道他沉浸在思緒中，所以我沒有打擾他。我之後才要進去問我的問題。

Feeling Disgusted
感到噁心

UNIT 16

☞ **感到噁心時需要用到的動作，用英文要怎麼說呢？**

對某些事物感到噁心就會產生各種手勢和肢體動作，下列是感到噁心時會用到的手勢與肢體語言，請看圖片，並對照動作的英文和中文。

Shaking hands away from the body
把手甩離身體

Pulling the chin in towards the neck
下巴縮到脖子內

Wrinkled nose 皺鼻子

Pinching nose closed 捏緊鼻子

※ 補充說明：秀出牙齒咆嘯也是感到噁心時會使用的肢體語言，可回去 Unit 12 p.116 複習。

情境 1　**Shaking Hands away from the Body 把手甩離身體**

這是指手掌攤平面向地板，手腕往前後移動使得手網前後甩動，上手臂緊貼身體而手肘彎曲。這代表人們試著把某些東西甩離手部。這是很普遍的手勢，代表他們手上有很噁心的東西讓他們想要甩掉。

外國人把手甩離身體時，他們會說：

Yuck!	呸！
Ewwww!	噁！
Gross!	好噁喔！
Get it off!	拿走！
This is sticky!	這個好黏！
I need to wash my hands.	我需要去洗手。
Do you have any soap?	你有肥皂嗎？
I have to dry my hands.	我要去把手用乾。
I got it on my hands.	我沾到手上了。
That's disgusting!	太噁心了！

外國人把手甩離身體時，你可以回：

What's wrong?	怎麼了？
What is it?	那是甚麼？
Wipe them off!	把它擦掉！
Get away from me!	離我遠一點！
Here's a towel.	這裡有條毛巾。
Wash your hands!	去洗手！
Here's some soap.	這裡有肥皂。
I'll get some.	我去拿一些來。
What was it?	剛剛那是甚麼？
Don't touch it!	不要摸！

情境對話　中文可對照上方的例句

Dialogue 1

Ⓐ Yuck!
Ⓑ What is it?
Ⓐ This is sticky!
Ⓑ Wash your hands!

Dialogue 2

Ⓐ I need to wash my hands.
Ⓑ What's wrong?
Ⓐ I got it on my hands.
Ⓑ Here's some soap.

情境　從英文來看外國人使用此肢體語言的情境

After lunch, Jane got up and shook her hands around. She was upset because they were sticky. I showed her where the bathroom was, so she could wash her hands.

午餐後，Jane 起身並把手甩一甩，她很心煩因為她的雙手很黏，我跟她說廁所在哪裡，所以她可以去把手洗乾淨。

情境 2 Pulling the Chin in towards the Neck 下巴縮到脖子內

這是指頭部稍微向後移動，並往脖子的方向縮下巴。這個動作是人在擔心自己會受到身體傷害時，所採取的保護措施。當人們擔心自己會在情感上受到傷害時，也會做這個動作。若是伴隨嘬起嘴唇和皺眉的表情，就是感到噁心的樣子。

外國人的下巴縮到脖子內時，他們會說：

I'm worried!	我很擔心！
I'm scared.	我很害怕。
I don't want to get hurt.	我不想受傷。
Please don't hurt me.	請不要傷害我。
Yuck!	噁！
That's disgusting!	真噁心！
Ewwww! Gross!	嘔！真噁心！
Snakes are disgusting!	蛇好噁心！
Don't put dirt on me!	不要把灰塵弄到我身上！
I hate worms!	我討厭蠕蟲！

外國人的下巴縮到脖子內時，你可以回：

Don't be!	不要擔心！
Don't worry about it.	不用擔心這件事。
It will be fine.	會沒事的。
I'm not going to hurt you.	我不會傷害你。
It's not gross!	這又不噁心！
Just try it!	試試吧！
Hold it.	握住它。
It's okay.	沒事的
I do not!	我沒有！
I do, too.	我也是。

情境對話 中文可對照上方的例句

Dialogue 1

Ⓐ I don't want to get hurt.
Ⓑ You'll be fine.
Ⓐ I'm scared.
Ⓑ It's okay!

Dialogue 2

Ⓐ Ewwww! Gross!
Ⓑ Just try it!
Ⓐ That's disgusting!
Ⓑ It will be fine.

情境 從英文來看外國人使用此肢體語言的情境

We went to the zoo and were looking at the different animals. My son put his face up to a display case and a snake slithered towards him. He pulled his chin in and started to cry because it scared him. He thought snake is disgusting.

我們去動物園看不同的動物。我兒子把臉貼在一個展示櫃上，一條蛇向著他溜過去。他把下巴往內縮、開始哭泣，因為蛇嚇到他了。他覺得蛇很噁心。

情境 3 Wrinkled Nose 皺鼻子

這是透過向上努嘴、雙頰向外推、鼻子從頂端拉動，就能皺起鼻子。有些人在皺鼻子時會露出嘴唇。皺鼻子通常意味著人聞到難聞的氣味，而當人想到難聞的氣味、或不好的經歷時，也會出現這種表情。例如，打牌的人手氣不好時，就可能會皺起鼻子。

外國人皺鼻子時，他們會說：

Do you smell that?	你聞到了嗎？
What is that?	那是甚麼？
That stinks!	好臭！
It's awful!	太糟糕了！
I need fresh air!	我需要新鮮空氣！
I can't stand it.	我受不了了。
It's a really bad smell!	聞起來真臭！
These cards are awful.	這些牌太爛了。
I got the worst hand!	我手氣太差了！
I'm going to lose.	我要輸了。

外國人皺鼻子時，你可以回：

It's really bad.	真的很糟糕。
That's disgusting.	那太噁心了。
That's not good.	這不太好。
What's wrong?	怎麼了？
Maybe not!	也許不是！
You can't be sure.	你不能確定。
You might not.	你可能不會。
It's not that bad.	沒那麼糟糕。
I don't see the problem.	我沒看到問題。
That's the worst!	那是最糟糕的！

情境對話 中文可對照上方的例句

Dialogue 1

Ⓐ Do you smell that?

Ⓑ That's awful!

Ⓐ I need fresh air!

Ⓑ That's the worst!

Dialogue 2

Ⓐ These cards are awful.

Ⓑ What's wrong?

Ⓐ I got the worst hand!

Ⓑ I don't see the problem.

情境 從英文來看外國人使用此肢體語言的情境

We were at a party, and Lisa looked at me with a wrinkled nose. I asked her what was wrong, and she said someone by her passed gas and she could smell it.

我們在一個聚會上，Lisa 皺著鼻子看著我。我問她怎麼了，她說有人在她旁邊放屁，她可以聞到那股臭味。

🎧 16-4.mp3

情境 4 Pinching Nose Closed 捏緊鼻子

這是指用拇指和食指捏住鼻子的末端，這樣會緊閉鼻孔，使空氣無法進入鼻子，並迫使人用嘴呼吸。這個手勢意味著人們聞到了非常難聞的氣味，並且不想吸進這個氣味。

外國人捏緊鼻子時，他們會說：

Do you smell that?	你聞到了嗎？
Did you fart?	你放屁了嗎？
Who did that?	誰放的？
What's that smell?	那是甚麼味道？
It's awful!	太可怕了！
I can't breathe!	我無法呼吸了！
I need to go outside for some air.	我需要出去呼吸一下。
It stinks!	太臭了！
I can't stand it!	我受不了了！
I'm going to throw up!	我要吐了！

外國人捏鼻子時，你可以回：

That's disgusting!	太噁心了！
It wasn't me.	不是我。
Did you do that?	是你做的嗎？
I don't smell anything.	我甚麼都沒聞到。
Yes, I smell it.	對，我聞到了。
I can't smell it.	我聞不到。
It's horrible!	太可怕了！
I need fresh air.	我需要新鮮空氣。
Let's go outside.	我們出去吧。
I think someone farted.	我認為有人放屁。

情境對話 中文可對照上方的例句

Dialogue 1

Ⓐ Do you smell that?
Ⓑ Yes, I smell it.
Ⓐ Did you fart?
Ⓑ It wasn't me.

Dialogue 2

Ⓐ What's that smell?
Ⓑ I can't smell it.
Ⓐ I need to go outside for some air.
Ⓑ I don't smell anything.

情境 從英文來看外國人使用此肢體語言的情境

When I walked into the living room, it smelled awful! I pinched my nose and asked my husband what that smell was. He was embarrassed and told me he farted right before I walked in.

當我走進客廳時，那裡聞起來很臭！我捏起鼻子問我先生那是甚麼味道，他不好意思地告訴我，他在我走進去之前放屁了。

Joking or Being Impolite
開玩笑或沒禮貌

☞ **開玩笑或沒禮貌時需要用到的動作，用英文要怎麼說呢？**

對其他人開玩笑或沒禮貌就會產生各種手勢和肢體動作，下列是開玩笑、沒禮貌時會用到的手勢與肢體語言，請看圖片，並對照動作的英文和中文。

情境 1

Wink 眨眼睛

情境 2

Sticking out the tongue 吐出舌頭

情境 3

Pointing the chin at someone
用下巴指向某人

情境 4

Pulling pants down and
showing someone your naked butt
拉下褲子，露出屁股

情境 1　Wink 眨眼睛

這是指快速閉起來再睜開一隻眼睛，而另一隻眼睛同時保持張開。眨眼可以用來向他人表達確認，或者表示人們正在開玩笑，或是逗弄著他人。很多時候，當有人開另一個人的玩笑時，他們會向對方眨眼，好讓對方知道自己在逗弄他們。通常一個人眨眼時會對著某個對象。

外國人眨眼睛時，他們會說：

How are you doing?	你好嗎？
What's up?	怎麼了？
It's good to see you!	很高興見到你！
Got ya!	你上當了！
I'm joking around.	我在開玩笑。
I'm teasing you.	我鬧你的。
It's a joke!	開個玩笑啦！
I'm kidding!	我在說笑的！
I'm giving you a hard time.	我是在整你啊。
I'm playing around!	我只是鬧著玩！

外國人眨眼睛時，你可以回：

I'm great.	我很好。
Are you joking around?	你是在開玩笑嗎？
You're kidding, right?	你在開玩笑，對吧？
Is that a joke?	那是個玩笑嗎？
Are you teasing me?	你在鬧我嗎？
I thought you were kidding.	我認為你在開玩笑。
You're funny!	你真好笑！
You're such a joker.	你真是個逗趣的人。
You're a funny guy.	你是個有趣的傢伙。
Stop messing around.	別鬧了。

情境對話　中文可對照上方的例句

Dialogue 1

Ⓐ How are you doing?

Ⓑ I'm great.

Ⓐ It's good to see you!

Ⓑ You, too!

Dialogue 2

Ⓐ I'm teasing you.

Ⓑ Stop messing around.

Ⓐ It's a joke.

Ⓑ You're such a joker.

情境　從英文來看外國人使用此肢體語言的情境

When I got to work, my coworker told me I was late for a meeting. I got really worried, and he laughed and winked at me and told me he was kidding around. He's always joking around like that.

我到公司時，我同事跟我說我開會遲到了。我那時真的很擔心，結果他笑著對我眨了眨眼，告訴我他在開玩笑。他老是那樣鬧著玩。

情境 2 Sticking out the Toungue 吐出舌頭

指將舌頭從嘴裡吐出並對著他人，這個舉止非常不禮貌，通常被視為非常幼稚。如果一個人漫不經心地取笑別人，這個人可能會開玩笑地向對方吐出舌頭，這是一種逗弄他人的表現。最後，有些人在努力做某事時，會微微吐出舌頭，他們會將舌頭稍微伸出嘴邊，並可能會瞇起眼睛。

外國人吐出舌頭時，他們會說：

I don't like you!	我不喜歡你！
You're mean!	你很壞心！
I think you're annoying!	我覺得你很煩！
You bother me!	你在打擾我！
Go away!	走開！
Leave me alone!	別煩我！
Get away from me!	離我遠點！
You're irritating!	你真煩人！
I'm trying to focus.	我正在努力集中精神。
I can't figure this out.	我搞不懂這個。

外國人吐出舌頭時，你可以回：

I don't like you either!	我也不喜歡你！
No one likes you.	沒有人喜歡你。
You're rude!	你很沒禮貌！
I was here first.	我先來這裡的。
I'm not mean!	我沒有很苛薄！
Don't be a jerk.	不要當個混蛋。
I'm not leaving.	我不會走。
I'm not listening to you.	我沒在聽你的話。
What's wrong?	怎麼了？
Need help?	需要幫助嗎？

情境對話 中文可對照上方的例句

Dialogue 1

Ⓐ I don't like you!

Ⓑ I don't like you either!

Ⓐ Leave me alone!

Ⓑ I was here first.

Dialogue 2

Ⓐ Get away from me!

Ⓑ What's wrong?

Ⓐ You're irritating!

Ⓑ Don't be a jerk.

情境 從英文來看外國人使用此肢體語言的情境

My little brother was mad at me yesterday. He wanted me to change the TV channel, but I was there first. He finally left me alone. As he was leaving the room, he stuck his tongue out at me because he was mad.

我的小弟昨天在生我的氣。他要我轉到別的電視頻道，但是我是先到的。最後他留下我一個人在那裡，當他離開房間時，因為他很生氣，他向我吐了舌頭。

情境 3 Pointing the Chin at Someone 用下巴指向某人

以下巴指向某人時，脖子會拉長，頭部稍微向後傾斜。快速地將下巴指向另一個人是一種侮辱他人的行為。

外國人用下巴指向某人時，他們會說：

What did you say to me?	你對我說了甚麼？
Are you talking about me?	你是在說我嗎？
You're bothering me.	你打擾到我了。
I wish you'd leave.	我希望你能離開。
I don't like you very much.	我非常不喜歡你。
I'm trying to be nice.	我試著對你親切。
I'm not happy with you.	我對你很不開心。
You're very frustrating.	你真令人沮喪。
I'm upset with you.	我對你不高興。
You made me angry.	你讓我生氣。

外國人用下巴指向某人時，你可以回：

I didn't say anything.	我甚麼也沒說。
I said to shup up.	我叫你閉嘴。
I didn't mean it.	我不是那個意思。
I wouldn't do that.	我不會那樣做。
I'd never do that!	我永遠不會那樣做！
I can't believe you think that.	我無法相信你這麼想。
That's so rude!	太無禮了！
I'm not trying to be rude.	我不是想要沒禮貌。
You're being mean!	你這樣很苛薄！
I didn't mean to make you mad.	我不是故意要讓你生氣。

情境對話　中文可對照上方的例句

Dialogue 1

Ⓐ What did you say to me?

Ⓑ I said to shut up.

Ⓐ I'm trying to be nice.

Ⓑ I'm not trying to be rude.

Dialogue 2

Ⓐ You're bothering me.

Ⓑ That's so rude!

Ⓐ I wish you'd leave.

Ⓑ You're being mean!

情境　從英文來看外國人使用此肢體語言的情境

I was talking with a group of friends. I said that I didn't like Jackie's new haircut very much. Mary pointed her chin at me and told me I was being mean. I didn't mean to be rude, I was just talking.

我在和一群朋友聊天。我說我不太喜歡 Jackie 的新髮型，Mary 將下巴對著我，並跟我說我很苛薄。我不是故意要無禮，我只是說說罷了。

情境 4　Pulling Pants down and Showing Someone Your Naked Butt 拉下褲子，露出屁股

指彎腰的時候把褲子和內褲拉下來、露出屁股，而且屁股面向他人。這稱為「mooning（亮出光屁股）」，是一種熟人之間很普遍開玩笑的羞辱。在年輕人和青少年之間最普遍。類似的動作也有親吻自己的手、並拍在自己的屁股上。

外國人拉下褲子，露出屁股時，他們會說：

Take this!	接招！
Kiss my butt!	親我屁屁！
This is what we think of you!	這就是我怎麼看你的！
Go to hell!	下地獄吧！
You're a jerk!	你這混蛋！
We don't like you.	我們不喜歡你。
Screw you!	去你的！
Kiss this!	親這個！
Check it out!	看這個！
Look at me!	看我！

外國人拉下褲子，露出屁股時，你可以回：

Don't do that!	不要這樣！
That's gross.	太噁了！
You're an asshole!	你這渾球！
I hate you!	我討厭你！
Why would you do that?	你為甚麼這樣做？
You're immature!	你真的很不成熟！
I don't like you, either.	我也不喜歡你。
The feeling goes both ways.	我也是這樣看你的。
Loser!	魯蛇！
Pull up your pants.	把褲子拉起來。
Don't do it again.	不要再這樣了。

情境對話　中文可對照上方的例句

Dialogue 1

Ⓐ This is what we think of you!
Ⓑ Don't do that!
Ⓐ Kiss my butt!
Ⓑ That's gross.

Dialogue 2

Ⓐ Check it out!
Ⓑ Why would you do that?
Ⓐ You're a jerk!
Ⓑ The feeling goes both ways.

情境　從英文來看外國人使用此肢體語言的情境

After our football game, one of the other team's players stood by our bus. When we were all on the bus, he yelled to get our attention. When everyone was looking, he turned around and mooned us. I guess he was upset that they lost.

我們的橄欖球賽結束後，其他球隊的一名球員站在我們的巴士旁邊，當我們都上車時，他大叫來吸引我們的注意，結果大家看著的時候，他轉過去、秀出光屁股對著我們，我猜他一定很難過他們輸球。

UNIT 18

Warning someone
警告他人

☞ **警告他人時需要用到的動作，用英文要怎麼說呢？**

警告他人就會產生各種手勢和肢體動作，下列是警告他人時會用到的手勢與肢體語言，請看圖片，並對照動作的英文和中文。

情境 1

Index finger pointing
用食指指著某人、某物

情境 2

Moving index finger horizontally across neck 脖子水平滑過脖子

情境 3

Backside of body turned to someone
身體背部面向他人

情境 1 Index Finger Pointing 用食指指著某人、某物

指手掌握拳，僅伸出食指，並且伸出手指的人會將手臂向前伸展。通常，這個手勢意味著人們希望其他人將注意放在他所指向的人事物上。如果有人在與他人的對話中，將手指指向另一個人，則可能意味著他們正在指責對方或是威脅他們。

外國人用食指指著某人、某事時，他們會說：

Look!	看！
Look over there.	看那邊。
I'm watching this.	我正在看這個。
Do you see that?	你看到了嗎？
Look at that!	看那個！
Watch this!	看這個！
I'm looking at them.	我正看著他們。
It was her!	就是她！
It's his fault!	這是他的錯！
I think it was you.	我認為是你。

外國人用食指指著某人、某事時，你可以回：

What do you see?	你看到甚麼？
What is that?	那是甚麼？
I see it!	我看到了！
Awesome!	太棒了！
Neat!	漂亮！
Stop pointing at people.	不要指著別人。
Don't point.	不要指指點點的。
How do you know it was her?	你怎麼知道就是她？
Pointing isn't nice!	用手指別人不好！
Stop blaming me.	不要怪我了。

情境對話 中文可對照上方的例句

Dialogue 1

Ⓐ Look!

Ⓑ What do you see?

Ⓐ Look at that bird.

Ⓑ Awesome!

Dialogue 2

Ⓐ It was her!

Ⓑ Stop pointing at people.

Ⓐ It's her fault.

Ⓑ Pointing isn't nice.

情境 從英文來看外國人使用此肢體語言的情境

Someone in our house broke my mom's vase. She was really upset and asked who broke it. My sister pointed at me! I didn't break it, but she blamed me. I got in trouble for it.

在我們家有人打破了媽媽的花瓶。她真的很不高興，問是誰打破的，我妹妹指著我！我沒有打破花瓶，但她怪到我身上，因此我麻煩大了。

情境 2 Moving Index Finger Horizontally across Neck 食指水平滑過脖子

這是指手握成拳並伸出食指，手掌朝著地面，伸向脖子，用伸出的食指滑過脖子。這個手勢意味著「把嘴閉上，甚麼也不要說」、或是「你死定了，因為你麻煩大了」。

外國人的食指滑過脖子時，他們會說：

Don't say anything.	甚麼都不要說。
Be quiet!	安靜！
You better not!	你最好沒有！
Don't say another word.	不要再說了。
No talking!	不准說話！
You're in trouble.	你有麻煩了。
You're dead!	你死定了！
Pipe down!	安靜點！
Shut up!	閉嘴！
Zip it!	把嘴閉上！

外國人的食指滑過脖子時，你可以回：

My lips are sealed.	我的口風很緊的。
I'm not talking.	我沒在說話。
I'll keep my mouth shut.	我會把嘴閉著。
I didn't do anything.	我甚麼也沒做。
I didn't say anything.	我甚麼也沒說。
I won't!	我不會的！
I'm not!	我沒有！
I didn't talk to anyone.	我沒有告訴任何人。
I'll keep it a secret.	我會保守秘密。
I'm staying quiet.	我會保持安靜的。

情境對話 中文可對照上方的例句

Dialogue 1

Ⓐ Be quiet!
Ⓑ I'm not talking.
Ⓐ Don't say another word.
Ⓑ I'll keep my mouth shut.

Dialogue 2

Ⓐ You're in trouble.
Ⓑ I didn't talk to anyone.
Ⓐ You better not!
Ⓑ I'm staying quiet.

情境 從英文來看外國人使用此肢體語言的情境

Jessica told me she's pregnant, but it's still pretty early and she wants to keep it a secret. We ran into a bunch of our friends, and I almost told them. She looked at me and slide her finger across her neck to remind me to be quiet.

Jessica 跟我說她懷孕了，但這還是懷孕初期，她想要保守秘密。我們遇到一群朋友，我差點就要告訴他們了。她看著我，手指滑過脖子，來提醒我安靜。

情境 3 Backside of Body Turned to Someone
身體背部面向他人

身體轉向、只有背部面向他人是非常明顯的肢體動作，代表人們不想和那個人說話，這也代表人們希望他可以走開。

外國人身體背部面向他人時，他們會說：

I don't want to speak to you.	我不想跟你說話。
I'm not talking to you.	我不是在跟你說話。
I don't want to look at you.	我不想看著你。
I'm not listening to you.	我沒有在聽你說話。
I can't stand you.	我真受不了你。
You bother me.	你打擾到我了。
I find you irritating.	我覺得你很討人厭。
I can't listen to you anymore.	我不能再聽你說話。
I need to get away from you.	我要離你遠一點。
You're annoying.	你真的很煩。

外國人身體背部面向他人時，你可以回：

I don't care.	我不在乎。
I'm not talking to you, either.	我也不是在跟你說話。
That's fine with me.	我無所謂。
The feeling is mutual.	我也對你有這種感覺。
Go to hell!	下地獄吧！
Screw you!	去你的！
You're not listening.	你根本沒在聽。
I hate you!	我討厭你！
You're a jerk!	你這混蛋！
Shut your mouth.	閉上你的嘴。

情境對話 中文可對照上方的例句

Dialogue 1

Ⓐ I'm not talking to you.
Ⓑ I don't care.
Ⓐ You're annoying.
Ⓑ Screw you!

Dialogue 2

Ⓐ I can't listen to you anymore.
Ⓑ That's fine with me.
Ⓐ I find you irritating.
Ⓑ You're a jerk!

情境 從英文來看外國人使用此肢體語言的情境

I heard that Mary started the rumors about me cheating on David. She tried talking to me yesterday, and I told her I was never going to talk to her again. Then, I turned my back to her. I think she knows how mad I am.

我聽說 Mary 開始了我背叛 David 的謠言，她昨天試著跟我說話，而我告訴她我不要再跟她說話了，接著把背對著她，我想她知道我有多生氣了。

156

Showing Apology and Innocence
表示抱歉和無辜

☞ **表示抱歉、無辜需要用到的動作，用英文要怎麼說呢？**

表示抱歉、無辜就會產生各種手勢和肢體動作，下列是表示抱歉、無辜時會用到的手勢與肢體語言，請看圖片，並對照動作的英文和中文。

Apologetic hug 道歉的擁抱

Both arms up 雙臂舉高

Both Hands up with palms facing out
抬起雙手、手掌向外

情境 1 Apologetic Hug 道歉的擁抱

這種擁抱是為了向熟人表示：「很抱歉我誤會了你」、或是「很抱歉我羞辱了你」，這有可能是單方或雙方的擁抱。人們會伸出雙臂要求擁抱，接著雙方的手臂彼此環繞，大概在背部附近，並輕輕地收緊手臂。如果是在朋友、商業夥伴或家人之間，擁抱通常很簡短，但是如果在戀人之間，通常會更親密。

外國人做道歉的擁抱時，他們會說：

I'm sorry I hurt your feelings.	對不起，我傷了你的感受。
I'll make it up to you.	我會補償你的。
I won't do it again.	我不會再這樣了。
Can you forgive me?	你能原諒我嗎？
I didn't mean to do it.	我不是故意的。
Are we still friends?	我們還是朋友嗎？
You know how much I value our friendship.	你知道我有多珍惜我們的友誼。
Let's start over.	讓我們重新開始。
I don't want to hurt you.	我不想傷害你。
Let's forget this happened.	讓我們忘了這件事發生過吧。

外國人做道歉的擁抱時，你可以回：

It's alright.	不要緊。
You're okay.	你沒事的。
You're forgiven.	我原諒你了。
It's not a big deal.	沒甚麼大不了的。
I understand.	我明白。
I know you didn't mean it.	我知道你不是這個意思。
Yes, we're still friends.	是的，我們還是朋友。
You really hurt my feelings.	你真的傷了我的感受。
I'm still upset.	我還是很難過。
I'm still angry with you.	我還在生你的氣。

情境對話 中文可對照上方的例句

Dialogue 1

Ⓐ I didn't mean to do it.
Ⓑ You really hurt my feelings.
Ⓐ I won't do it again.
Ⓑ I know you didn't mean it.

Dialogue 2

Ⓐ I'm sorry I hurt your feelings.
Ⓑ It's alright.
Ⓐ Are we still friends?
Ⓑ Yes, we're still friends.

情境 從英文來看外國人使用此肢體語言的情境

My brother borrowed my car last week and got into an accident. I was so mad at him! Last night he apologized and gave me a hug. I feel a little bit better, but I'm still mad.

我哥哥上星期借走了我的車，結果出了車禍。我很氣他！昨晚他向我道歉，並給了我一個擁抱。我覺得好一點了，但我還在生氣。

情境 2 Both Arms up 雙臂舉高

指雙臂舉高、伸向天空，手掌朝前方。這個姿勢表達沒有做某件事，好像在說自己是無辜的。這個動作也可以用來表示沒有持有任何武器，在危險情況下，人們會舉起雙臂，好讓其他人知道他們不會構成危險。警察會要求嫌犯把手舉起來，好讓警察知道他們手中沒有任何武器。

外國人把雙臂舉高時，他們會說：

I didn't do it.	我沒有做。
I don't have it.	我沒有那個東西。
I didn't take it.	我沒有拿那個。
It wasn't me.	不是我。
Don't look at me.	不要看我。
Don't blame me.	不要責怪我。
Stop blaming me.	別再責怪我了。
I'm innocent.	我是無辜的。
I'm not to blame.	這不該責怪我。
I didn't mean to.	我不是故意的。

外國人把雙臂舉高時，你可以回：

It was you!	就是你！
Liar!	騙子！
Stop lying!	不要再說謊了！
I think you did it.	我認為是你做的。
You're to blame.	這該責怪你。
I don't think so.	我不這麼認為。
You look guilty!	你看起來有過錯！
You're lying.	你在說謊。
I saw you do it.	我看到是你做的。
I blame you!	我就責怪你！

情境對話 中文可對照上方的例句

Dialogue 1

Ⓐ I didn't do it.
Ⓑ Liar!
Ⓐ It wasn't me.
Ⓑ I saw you do it.

Dialogue 2

Ⓐ Stop blaming me.
Ⓑ You're to blame.
Ⓐ I didn't take it.
Ⓑ Stop lying!

情境 從英文來看外國人使用此肢體語言的情境

Mark was at the bank when it was robbed the other day. When the robbers came in, he put his hands up, so they knew he didn't have any weapons. He was really scared, but he's doing okay now.

前天那間銀行被搶的時候，Mark 就在那裡。搶匪進來時，他舉起手，讓他們知道他沒有任何武器。那時他真的很害怕，但他現在已經沒事了。

Both Hands up with Palms Facing out
抬起雙手、手掌向外

情境 3

這是指彎曲肘部並抬起雙手，手掌朝外。這個手勢是在說「不是我」或者「我是無辜的」。這也可能意味著他們並沒有被要求提供的東西（例如錢）。

外國人抬起雙手、向外時，他們會說：

It wasn't me.	不是我。
I didn't do it.	我沒做這件事。
I don't have it.	我沒有這個東西。
I don't have anything.	我甚麼都沒有。
My hands are empty.	我的手都是空的。
Don't look at me.	不要看著我。
I'm innocent.	我是無辜的。
I didn't take it.	我沒有拿。
It must have been someone else.	一定是其他人。
Don't blame me!	不要責怪我！

外國人抬起雙手、向外時，你可以回：

Are you sure?	你確定嗎？
You did it!	你做的！
Show me your hands!	讓我看到你的手！
Where did you put it?	你放在哪裡了？
Sit down!	坐下！
Don't move.	不要動。
Stay put.	留在原地。
Who did it?	誰做的？
Who would do this?	誰會這樣做？
I can't believe someone did this.	我不敢相信有人這樣做。

情境對話　中文可對照上方的例句

Dialogue 1

Ⓐ It wasn't me.
Ⓑ Are you sure?
Ⓐ It must have been someone else.
Ⓑ Who did it?

Dialogue 2

Ⓐ You did it!
Ⓑ I didn't take it.
Ⓐ Show me your hands!
Ⓑ My hands are empty.

情境　從英文來看外國人使用此肢體語言的情境

I walked into my house last night, and it was a disaster. Lots of things were everywhere and a few things were missing. My wife was home and threw her hands up and told me it wasn't her, like I was going to blame her. It looks like someone must have broke in and robbed us.

昨晚我走進我家，那真是一場災難。家裡的很多東西四散各地，有幾樣東西不見了。我太太在家裡，她把手舉起來，告訴我不是她弄的，好像我要責怪她一樣。看來是有人闖入我們家，洗劫了我們。

Not Knowing what to Do 不知道該怎麼做

☞ **不知道該怎麼做要用到的動作，用英文要怎麼說呢？**

人們不知道該怎麼做某件事就會產生各種手勢和肢體動作，下列是不知道該怎麼做時會用到的手勢與肢體語言，請看圖片，並對照動作的英文和中文。

情境
1

Throwing hands in the air
把手甩上空中

情境
2

Scratching side of neck with one finger 用一根手指抓脖子

情境
3

Tucking neck into shoulders
把脖子縮進肩膀

情境
4

Tongue in front of teeth
舌頭放在牙齒前

情境
5

Pressing tongue against cheek
把舌頭抵在臉頰上

情境
6

Nodding with tilted head 側著頭點頭

情境 1 Throwing Hands in the Air 把手甩上空中

指迅速地將雙臂向上抬起，甩動鬆軟無力的雙手。當人感到不知所措或生氣時時，便會出現這種手勢。經常發生於人們打算放棄某件事的時候。攤開兩隻手臂也有類似的意思，這個手勢也代表這個人可能沒有帶足夠的錢出去。

外國人把手甩上空中時，他們會說：

I can't!	我沒辦法！
I don't know!	我不知道！
I'm unsure.	我不確定。
I can't figure it out.	我搞不懂。
I'm upset!	我很沮喪！
I'm angry!	我很生氣！
I don't get it.	我想不通。
I don't understand.	我不明白。
I'm lost!	我很迷惘！
I'm confused.	我很困惑。

外國人把手甩上空中時，你可以回：

You can do this.	你可以做得到這件事。
What's wrong?	怎麼了嗎？
You're okay.	你沒事的。
You can do it.	你做得到的。
You got this!	你可以的！
Let's take a walk.	我們去散個步吧。
Take a break.	休息一下吧。
Let's do it together.	我們一起做吧。
Let me explain it to you.	讓我來跟你説明。
I'll help you with it.	我會幫你的。

情境對話 中文可對照上方的例句

Dialogue 1

Ⓐ I don't understand.
Ⓑ Let me explain it to you.
Ⓐ I can't figure it out.
Ⓑ I'll help you with it.

Dialogue 2

Ⓐ I'm confused.
Ⓑ What's wrong?
Ⓐ I don't get it.
Ⓑ Let's do it together.

情境 從英文來看外國人使用此肢體語言的情境

We've been working on a group project for our class. It hasn't been going very well. Mike got so frustrated during one of our meetings that he threw his hands in the air and walked out.

我們一直在做我們班的小組專題，而事情進行得不太順利，Mike 在我們其中一次的會議中非常沮喪，他向空中甩手，接著就走了出去。

情境 2 Scratching Side of Neck with one Finger 用一根手指抓脖子

用食指抓脖子的一側，可能意味著人們對某件事不太確定。這可能表示他們在某個情況下，不知道下一步該怎麼做、對問題的答案不確定、或是對自己不確定。通常一個人在做出這個動作時會往下看，或是將視線從所有人身上移開。

外國人用一根手指抓脖子時，他們會說：

I'm not sure.	我不確定。
I don't know.	我不知道。
Who knows!	誰知道啊！
I can't do it.	我做不到。
I'm not able to.	我沒辦法。
I can't make it.	我做不到。
Let me check.	讓我看看吧。
I'm unsure.	我不確定。
I have no idea.	我甚麼都不知道。
How should I know?	我怎麼會知道？

外國人用一根手指抓脖子時，你可以回：

What's wrong?	怎麼了嗎？
Is there a problem?	有問題嗎？
We can figure it out.	我們可以一起弄清楚。
Why not?	為甚麼不行？
You can do it.	你做得到。
What do you mean?	你的意思是甚麼？
You should know this.	你應該知道這一點。
Get back to me.	你再回覆我吧。
Let me know.	讓我知道。
I'll do it for you.	我會為你做的。

情境對話 中文可對照上方的例句

Dialogue 1

Ⓐ I can't do it.
Ⓑ Why not?
Ⓐ I have no idea.
Ⓑ We can figure it out.

Dialogue 2

Ⓐ Is there a problem?
Ⓑ Let me check.
Ⓐ Get back to me.
Ⓑ I will.

情境 從英文來看外國人使用此肢體語言的情境

I asked a coworker a question today. I knew she didn't know the answer because she kept scratching her neck and wouldn't look at me. She should have known the answer, so I told her she needs to figure it out and let me know.

我今天問了同事一個問題，我知道她不曉得答案，因為她一直搔著脖子，而且不看著我。她之前就應該要知道答案的，所以我告訴她，她得把這個搞清楚，並且讓我知道。

情境 3 **Tucking Neck into Shoulders 把脖子縮進肩膀**

這是指聳肩並把頭往下縮在雙肩之間，像是要藏住脖子一樣。這個動作表示人們感覺自己不適任，正試著讓自己顯得更小。這個姿勢也表示人們正試著「躲藏起來」，他們不想被別人注意到。

外國人把脖子縮進肩膀時，他們會說：

I don't know.	我不知道。
I'm confused.	我很困惑。
I'm at a loss.	我很茫然。
I can't answer that.	我無法回答。
I didn't do it.	我沒有做這件事。
I'm feeling overwhelmed.	我感到不知所措。
I need to leave.	我得走了。
I'm going home.	我要回家了。
I can't stay here.	我不能留在這裡。
I feel out of place.	我覺得格格不入。

外國人把脖子縮進肩膀時，你可以回：

You did it.	你做到了。
I think it was you.	我想就是你。
Why?	為甚麼？
What's wrong?	怎麼了嗎？
Why are you confused?	你為甚麼感到困惑？
Let me help you.	讓我來幫助你。
What can I do to help you?	我能做甚麼來幫你呢？
Why are you leaving?	你為甚麼要離開？
Where are you going?	你要去哪裡？
What's the matter?	怎麼了？

情境對話 中文可對照上方的例句

Dialogue 1

Ⓐ I'm feeling overwhelmed.
Ⓑ Why?
Ⓐ I don't know.
Ⓑ What can I do to help you?

Dialogue 2

Ⓐ I can't stay here.
Ⓑ What's wrong?
Ⓐ I feel out of place.
Ⓑ Where are you going?

情境 從英文來看外國人使用此肢體語言的情境

My sister hates big crowds, so I knew she wouldn't have fun at my party. Shortly after she got there, she came up to me with her shoulders up and her head hung down and said she had to leave. I tried to talk her into staying, but she wouldn't.

我姐姐很討厭人潮，所以我知道她在我的派對上不會玩得很開心。她抵達派對後不久，她就肩膀提高、向我走來，垂著頭說她得走了。我試著說服她留下來，但她不肯。

情境 4 Tongue in Front of Teeth 舌頭放在牙齒前面

這是指舌頭捲起並蓋住上排的門牙。
這個動作會將上唇向外推,這是不太確定
的表現,人在不確定在某個情況下該說甚
麼時會這樣做。

外國人把舌頭放在牙齒前面時,他們會說:

I'm not sure.	我不確定。
I don't know.	我不知道。
What should we get?	我們應該得到甚麼?
I'm not positive.	我不是很確定。
Who knows!	誰會知道啊!
I have no idea!	我沒有想法!
I haven't got a clue.	我沒有頭緒啊!
How should I know?	我怎麼會知道?
Not as far as I know.	據我所知沒有。
Your guess is as good as mine!	我跟你一樣也不知道!

外國人把舌頭放在牙齒前面時,你可以回:

That's okay.	沒關係。
Figure it out!	去搞清楚!
No problem.	沒問題。
It's alright.	沒關係。
No worries.	沒問題。
I'll find out.	我會找出答案的。
Let me do it.	讓我去做。
I'll figure it out.	我會想出來的。
We should find out.	我們應該找出答案。
I'm at a loss.	我很茫然。

情境對話 中文可對照上方的例句

Dialogue 1

Ⓐ What should we get?
Ⓑ I have no idea!
Ⓐ It's alright.
Ⓑ We should find out.

Dialogue 2

Ⓐ I don't know.
Ⓑ I'll figure it out.
Ⓐ I'm sorry.
Ⓑ That's okay.

情境 從英文來看外國人使用此肢體語言的情境

I asked my son where is homework was. He gave me a blank look with his tongue wrapped around his teeth and finally said he didn't know. I made him go back to school to get it.

我問我兒子他的作業到在哪裡。他用舌頭裹住牙齒,給了我一個茫然的表情,最後他終於說不知道。我迫使他回到學校把作業帶回來。

情境 5 **Pressing Tongue againgst Cheek 把舌頭抵在臉頰上**

指將舌頭推向臉頰，並保持嘴巴閉合，這麼做會使臉頰略為突出。這個表情可能意味著人們不確定某些情形，這也可能表示人們在開始講話之前思考他們要說甚麼。

外國人把舌頭抵在臉頰上時，他們會說：

Let me think.	讓我想想。
I'm thinking.	我在想。
Let me gather my thoughts.	讓我整理一下我的想法。
I'm thinking about it.	我正在考慮。
I'm unsure.	我不確定。
I'm not sure.	我不太確定。
They all look good.	全部看起來很好。
I can't choose.	我無法選擇。
There's too many options.	有太多選擇了。
I'll think about the options.	我會考慮這些選項。

外國人把舌頭抵在臉頰上時，你可以回：

What are you thinking about?	你在想甚麼？
What'd you decide?	你會決定甚麼？
I'll give you some time.	我會給你一些時間。
Think about it.	考慮一下。
Need me to choose?	需要我來選嗎？
Do you need help?	你需要幫助嗎？
I can help.	我可以幫忙。
What are the choices?	有甚麼選擇呢？
Which is better?	哪個比較好？
Do you like one more?	你想要再來一個嗎？

情境對話 中文可對照上方的例句

Dialogue 1

Ⓐ There's too many options.
Ⓑ What'd you decide?
Ⓐ I don't know which to choose.
Ⓑ Need me to choose?

Dialogue 2

Ⓐ I'm thinking.
Ⓑ What are you thinking about?
Ⓐ Work.
Ⓑ Do you need help?

情境 從英文來看外國人使用此肢體語言的情境

We were picking out a gift for my mom. We found a couple of bracelets, and I let my sister choose which to buy. She stared at them with her tongue againgst her cheek, so I knew she couldn't make a decision. We ended up deciding on one together.

我們在為我媽挑選禮物。我們看到一些手鍊，我讓我姐姐決定要買哪一條。她用舌頭抵住臉頰，凝視著它們，因此我知道她正在努力下決定。我們最後一起選了一條。

情境 6 **Nodding with Tilted Head 側著頭點頭**

側著頭點頭是指將耳朵靠近肩膀，由左向右反覆傾斜，變成傾斜的點頭。這個動作通常同時還會噘嘴，在美國，這種動作表示人們不確定某件事，或是他們無法為某件事做選擇。

外國人斜著頭點頭時，他們會說：

I can't decide.	我無法決定。
I can't make a choice.	我不能選擇。
I can't choose.	我沒辦法選。
There's too many choices!	選擇太多了！
Which would you choose?	你會選擇哪一個？
I can't pick!	我選擇不了！
You make the decision!	你來決定！
I can't decide.	我不能決定。
I would choose the first one.	我會選第一個。
I like that one.	我喜歡那個。

外國人斜著頭點頭時，你可以回：

Need help?	需要幫助嗎？
What are the options?	有甚麼選擇？
Why not?	為甚麼不呢？
I like them all.	我全部都喜歡。
Make a choice.	做出選擇吧。
You're taking forever.	你想太久了。
You could pick any of them.	你可以選其中任何一個。
They all look good.	全部看起來很好。
I'd choose that.	我會選那個。
Just pick one.	就選一個吧。

情境對話 中文可對照上方的例句

Dialogue 1

Ⓐ There's too many choices!
Ⓑ Just pick one.
Ⓐ I can't pick!
Ⓑ You're taking forever.

Dialogue 2

Ⓐ I can't make a decision!
Ⓑ They all look good.
Ⓐ Which would you choose?
Ⓑ I'd choose that.

情境 從英文來看外國人使用此肢體語言的情境

We went out for ice cream. I asked John what kind he was going to get and he tilted his head back and forth. He couldn't decide, so I talked him into getting a strawberry sundae.

我們出去吃冰淇淋。我問 John 他要吃哪一種，他來回歪了歪頭。他無法決定，所以我說服他點了一份草莓聖代。

UNIT 21

Thinking about Something
思考某件事

☞ **思考某件事時需要用到的動作，用英文要怎麼說呢？**

思考某件事時就會產生各種手勢和肢體動作，下列是思考某件事時會用到的手勢與肢體語言，請看圖片，並對照動作的英文和中文。

情境 1

Closed eyes 閉上雙眼

情境 2

Upward glance 眼睛向上瞥

情境 3

Furrowed eyebrows 皺眉頭

情境 4

Tilting head to side 頭部傾向一側

情境 5

Index finger touching chin
食指撫摸下巴

情境 6

Touching side of the mouth 觸摸嘴角

Squeezing bridge of nose 捏鼻樑

Slowly nodding while rubbing chin
邊慢慢點頭，邊摸下巴

Pulling on earlobe and shaking head
to the side 拉耳垂、頭轉向一側

Leaning forehead against fist
額頭靠在拳頭上

Tapping teeth together 牙齒碰在一起

21-1.mp3

情境 1 Closed Eyes 閉上雙眼

這可能表示人們正在試著拒絕看到眼前的事物。若是不願意看到或想到眼前發生的事，人們常常會閉上雙眼。此外，也有人藉著閉上眼睛來幫助自己整理思緒。在交談時閉上眼睛，對於在說話之前先整理出要說的話有幫助。而瞇眼則代表正在思考不確定的事。

外國人閉上雙眼時，他們會說：

I can't look!	我看不到！
I don't want to see it.	我不想看到它。
I'm afraid!	我很害怕！
It hurts my eyes!	這會傷害我的眼睛！
It's awful!	太可怕了！
I can't believe it.	我真不敢相信。
Let me think.	讓我想想。
Let me get my thoughts together.	讓我整理一下思緒。
Let me think about it.	讓我思考一下。
It might take a while.	可能要一點時間。

外國人閉上雙眼時，你可以回：

Keep your eyes closed!	閉上眼睛！
Don't look!	別看！
Shut your eyes!	把眼睛閉上！
Take your time.	慢慢來。
Take all the time you need.	你可以慢慢來。
Let me know when you're ready.	準備好了就告訴我。
What are you thinking about?	你在想甚麼？
What did you come up with?	你想到了甚麼嗎？
Did you figure it out?	你想通了嗎？
About what?	關於甚麼？

情境對話 中文可對照上方的例句

Dialogue 1

Ⓐ I can't believe it.
Ⓑ Shut your eyes!
Ⓐ It's awful!
Ⓑ Don't look!

Dialogue 2

Ⓐ Let me think.
Ⓑ Take your time.
Ⓐ It might take a while.
Ⓑ Take all the time you need.

情境 從英文來看外國人使用此肢體語言的情境

When I got to the office, my coworker had her eyes closed at her desk. I thought she fell asleep, but it turned out she was just thinking really hard about something.

我進辦公室時，我的同事正閉著雙眼坐在位子上。我還以為她睡著了，結果她只是很認真地在思考某件事。

情境 2 Upward Glance 眼睛向上瞥

這是指一個人的雙眼都往上看。如果一個人的頭擺正，向上看就表示他正在思考某件事。而當一個人正在說話，如果他停下來並向上看，代表他正在思考接下來該說甚麼，或者正在找適當的話語。如果有人低下頭並向上看，則可能意味著他在猶豫或隱瞞某些事情。

外國人眼睛向上瞥時，他們會說：

Let me think.	讓我想想。
What's the word I'm looking for?	我要說的是哪個字？
I think I remember that.	我想我記得那件事。
I'm trying to remember.	我試著記起來。
I don't remember.	我不記得了。
I'm trying to picture it.	我試著想像看看。
I'm not sure.	我不確定。
I have a secret.	我有個秘密。
I have a crush on you.	我對你一見鍾情。
I'm not telling you.	我不要告訴你。

外國人眼睛向上瞥時，你可以回：

What are you thinking about?	你在想甚麼？
What don't you remember?	你不記得甚麼？
I can help you.	我可以幫你。
Let's talk through it.	我們完整討論一下。
Me, too.	我也是。
I don't feel the same way.	我的感覺不一樣。
I feel the same way.	我也有同感。
Why won't you tell me?	為甚麼你不告訴我？
Just tell me!	就告訴我吧！
Be honest with me.	老實跟我說。

情境對話　中文可對照上方的例句

Dialogue 1

Ⓐ Let me think.
Ⓑ What are you thinking about?
Ⓐ I'm not telling you.
Ⓑ Why won't you tell me?

Dialogue 2

Ⓐ I'm trying to remember.
Ⓑ What don't you remember?
Ⓐ The directions to her house.
Ⓑ I can help you.

情境　從英文來看外國人使用此肢體語言的情境

Steve asked me what the girl at the party looked like. I had to think really hard to remember her. I glanced upward to think about it, and then shared some details with him. Steve said he knows her.

Steve 問我那個派對上的女孩長甚麼樣子，我得要很努力地回想，我往上看並思考這個女生，接著我跟他說了這些細節，而 Steve 說他認識她。

情境 3　Furrowed Eyebrows 皺眉頭

指將兩道眉毛擠在一起，並在額頭中間產生皺紋。皺眉頭使眼睛看起來像往上看。當人皺眉頭時，可能表示他感到焦慮或壓力，也可能表示他感到困惑，或是不明白發生了甚麼事。許多人在思考問題或試圖找出答案時，也會皺起眉頭。

外國人皺眉頭時，他們會說：

What's that?	那是甚麼？
I don't get it.	我不懂這個。
I'm not understanding.	我不明白。
What's going on?	這是怎麼回事？
I can't get it!	我搞不懂！
I'm not sure.	我不太確定。
I don't understand!	我想不通！
I'm trying!	我在努力！
This doesn't make sense.	這沒道理啊。
I'm lost.	我很迷惘。

外國人皺眉頭時，你可以回：

I can explain it.	我可以解釋。
Let me help.	讓我來幫忙。
This should help.	這應該會有所幫助。
I'll explain it.	我會說明這個。
Let me explain it.	讓我說明一下。
I'll show you how to do it.	我會示範給你看怎麼做。
I can do it.	我做得到。
I'll do it for you.	我來幫你做吧。
Can I do it for you?	讓我來好嗎？
Can I help you?	我可以幫你嗎？

情境對話　中文可對照上方的例句

Dialogue 1

Ⓐ I can't get it!
Ⓑ Let me help.
Ⓐ This doesn't make sense.
Ⓑ I can explain it.

Dialogue 2

Ⓐ What's that?
Ⓑ Our homework.
Ⓐ I don't get it.
Ⓑ I'll do it for you.

情境　從英文來看外國人使用此肢體語言的情境

One of my students was struggling with her math homework. She had a confused look on her face and was feeling frustrated because she didn't understand. We worked on the homework together until she had a better understanding.

我其中一個學生正在為她的數學作業苦苦掙扎。她一臉迷惘，因為無法理解而感到沮喪。我們一起做那份作業，直到她比較能理解為止。

情境 4 Tilting Head to Side 頭部傾向一側

將頭部向左或向右傾斜，並保持在那個位置。通常，完成這個動作後，眼睛會略為瞇起。這個動作表示人們感到困惑，或是正試著理解某些東西。

外國人的頭部傾向一側時，他們會說：

I'm thinking.	我正在思考。
I'm contemplating.	我正在考慮中。
The report.	這份報告。
It doesn't make sense to me.	對我來說這不合理。
I'm not following you.	我沒聽懂你說的。
I don't get it.	我不明白。
Can you explain again?	你能再解釋一次嗎？
Say that again!	再說一次！
What was that?	那是甚麼？

外國人的頭部傾向一側時，你可以回：

What are you thinking about?	你在想甚麼？
Okay.	好的。
I'll leave you to it.	你繼續想吧。
What doesn't make sense?	甚麼不合理？
Can I help?	我可以幫忙嗎？
I can help you.	我可以幫助你。
Sure.	當然好啊。
I'll show you again.	我會再給你看一次。
I can repeat it.	我可以重複一遍。
Do you need me to repeat it?	你要我再講一次嗎？

情境對話 中文可對照上方的例句

Dialogue 1

Ⓐ I'm thinking.
Ⓑ What are you thinking about?
Ⓐ The report.
Ⓑ I can help you.

Dialogue 2

Ⓐ I don't get it.
Ⓑ I'll show you again.
Ⓐ Let me think about it.
Ⓑ Sure.

情境 從英文來看外國人使用此肢體語言的情境

I was teaching a math class and noticed some students were tilting their heads to one side. I asked if they were struggling, and they were. I repeated what I was teaching and they caught it the second time.

我在教一堂數學課，並注意到一些學生將頭向一邊傾斜。我問他們是不是不太懂，結果他們真的不懂。我重複再教了一次，到了第二次他們才聽懂。

情境 5 **Index Finger Touching Chin 食指撫摸下巴**

這是指拇指墊在下巴下方，支撐著頭部，而食指在下巴附近彎曲，其他手指握成鬆散的拳頭。食指可能在下唇正下方，並來回摩擦下巴。這個手勢表示這個人正在思考剛才說到的事情，而他正要做決定。

外國人用食指撫摸下巴時，他們會說：

That's interesting.	那很有意思。
I can't decide.	我沒辦法決定。
I' thinking about it.	我正在考慮。
I'm torn on the options.	我很難決定這些選擇。
I don't understand.	我不明白。
Can you repeat yourself?	你能重複一遍嗎？
Let me think.	讓我想想。
I can't choose!	我無法選擇！
I'm making a decision.	我正在做決定。
Give me a minute!	給我一點時間！

外國人用食指撫摸下巴時，你可以回：

What did you decide?	你決定了甚麼？
What's your choice?	你的選擇是甚麼？
Let me know what you decide.	讓我知道你的決定。
I can explain it again.	我可以再說明一次。
Do you need help?	你需要幫助嗎？
Let me choose.	讓我來選。
I'll make the decision.	我會做出決定。
I can give you some time.	我可以給你一些時間。
Take a few minutes.	花幾分鐘考慮吧。
Give it some time.	花點時間決定吧。

情境對話 中文可對照上方的例句

Dialogue 1

Ⓐ What did you decide?
Ⓑ I can't choose!
Ⓐ Give it some time.
Ⓑ Let me think.

Dialogue 2

Ⓐ I'm thinking about it.
Ⓑ Let me know what you decide.
Ⓐ I'm torn on the options.
Ⓑ I can give you some time.

情境 從英文來看外國人使用此肢體語言的情境

I had to ask my boss about the project. I could tell that he was thinking about my question because he was resting his chin on his hand and looked confused. I'm going to give him some time to think through my question.

我必須向老闆詢問這個企畫，我能看得出來他在思考我的問題，因為他用手撐著下巴，一臉困惑，我會給他一些時間來思考我的問題。

情境 6 Touching Side of the Mouth 觸摸嘴角

指將手舉到嘴邊，鬆鬆地握拳，並把食指伸到嘴角。這是表示某人正在思考，或是對某種情況感到納悶的動作。通常視線也會往上看，並稍微瞇起眼睛。

外國人觸摸嘴角時，他們會說：

Hmm....	嗯……
I wonder what that is.	我想知道那是甚麼。
I wonder what happened.	我想知道發生了甚麼事。
What was the noise?	那是甚麼聲響？
Let me think about it.	讓我想想。
I'm thinking.	我正在想。
I'll give it some thought.	我會考慮一下。
I try to think through it.	我試著想通這件事。
I can't picture it.	我無法想像。
Tell me again.	再跟我說一遍。

外國人觸摸嘴角時，你可以回：

What are you thinking about?	你在想甚麼？
What are your thoughts?	你有甚麼想法？
I can tell you what happened.	我可以告訴你發生了甚麼事。
Let me help you.	讓我來幫助你。
Let's talk through it.	我們徹底討論一下。
We can work on it together.	我們可以一起做這件事。
Do you need help?	你需要幫助嗎？
I'll repeat it.	我會重複一遍。
I'll tell you again.	我會再告訴你一次。
I'll give you a hand with it.	我會幫你這件事。

情境對話 中文可對照上方的例句

Dialogue 1

Ⓐ Hmm...
Ⓑ What are you thinking about?
Ⓐ I wonder what that is.
Ⓑ I'll repeat it.

Dialogue 2

Ⓐ I can't picture it.
Ⓑ Let me help you.
Ⓐ Tell me again.
Ⓑ We can work on it together.

情境 從英文來看外國人使用此肢體語言的情境

I was working with a partner on this project, and he couldn't understand. He kept putting his finger to his mouth and squinting at me like he was confused. I finally asked him what he didn't understand and we finished it together.

我當時正在與一個夥伴一起做這份專案，而他搞不懂。他一直把手指放在嘴邊，瞇起眼睛看著我。最後我問他哪裡不懂，然後我們一起完成那個專案。

Squeezing Bridge of Nose 捏鼻樑

這是指以食指和拇指擠壓在兩眼之間的部位，也就是鼻樑。這個手勢可能意味著人們正在評估某件他們認為令人心煩的事物，可能是發生在會議上或對話中。

外國人捏鼻樑時，他們會說：

Let me think.	讓我想想。
I'm thinking about it.	我正在考慮。
I need to think on it.	我需要考慮一下。
Let me do some research.	讓我做一些調查。
I'll look into it.	我會調查這件事。
I don't think it will work.	我不認為這會有用。
I disagree with the plan.	我不同意這個計畫。
I'm opposed.	我反對。
I don't like the idea.	我不喜歡這個主意。
I think it's a bad idea.	我認為這是個壞主意。

外國人捏鼻樑時，你可以回：

What did you come up with?	你想出了甚麼？
What did you decide?	你決定了甚麼？
About what?	關於甚麼？
Take your time.	慢慢來。
I already decided.	我已經決定了。
Why not?	為甚麼不行？
I think it's a good idea.	我認為這是個好主意。
Let me know what you decide.	讓我知道你的決定。
Do you need help?	你需要幫助嗎？
What's wrong with it?	這怎麼了嗎？

情境對話 中文可對照上方的例句

Dialogue 1

Ⓐ I don't like the idea.
Ⓑ Why not?
Ⓐ I don't think it will work.
Ⓑ What's wrong with it?

Dialogue 2

Ⓐ I need to think on it.
Ⓑ Let me know what you decide.
Ⓐ Let me do some research.
Ⓑ Take your time.

情境 從英文來看外國人使用此肢體語言的情境

I told my boss about my new idea for marketing. He seemed to like it. He thought about it for a while and pinched the bridge of his nose. He said he'll think about it and get back to me.

我告訴老闆我新的行銷想法，他似乎很喜歡。他想了一會兒，捏了一下鼻樑。他說他會考慮一下，再回答我。

情境 8 Slowly Nodding While Rubbing Chin
邊慢慢點頭，邊摸下巴

指用手握住下巴並且一邊撫摸，同時慢慢上下點頭。這個動作表示人們正在思考某件事，並覺得它可能行得通，或是覺得這個想法不錯。然而向左右點頭則代表人們正在思考某事，但不覺得是好主意。

外國人慢慢點頭摸下巴時，他們會說：

I'm thinking about it.	我正在考慮這件事。
It seems like a good idea.	似乎是個好主意。
I'll think it through.	我會仔細考慮的。
Let me think about it.	讓我想想吧。
I'm thinking!	我正在想！
I'm considering it.	我正在考慮。
I'm giving it some thought.	我正在思考。
It looks like the right choice.	看起來是正確的選擇。
I think it's a good idea.	我認為這是個好主意。
I think I like it.	我想我喜歡這個。

外國人慢慢點頭摸下巴時，你可以回：

I think it's the right choice.	我認為這是正確的選擇。
I like it.	我喜歡這個。
Take your time.	慢慢來。
Think through it.	仔細考慮吧。
Give it some thought.	考慮一下。
I'll give you some time.	我會給你時間。
Do you have any questions?	你有任何問題嗎？
I think it will work.	我認為它會行得通。
It should work.	它應該有用。
Should we go with it?	我們要做這件事嗎？
What's your decision?	你的決定是甚麼？

情境對話　中文可對照上方的例句

Dialogue 1

Ⓐ I'm thinking about it.
Ⓑ Take your time.
Ⓐ It looks like the right choice.
Ⓑ Think through it.

Dialogue 2

Ⓐ I'm considering it.
Ⓑ I think it's a good choice.
Ⓐ I think I like it.
Ⓑ Me, too.

情境　從英文來看外國人使用此肢體語言的情境

I work for a car dealership. I was trying to sell a car to a man, and he wasn't sure if he wanted to buy it. I was explaining the options to him, and he started to nod slowly and rub his chin. Then, I persuaded him to buy it!

我在一間汽車經銷商工作。之前我試著賣車給一個客人，而他不確定他是否要買車。我向他解釋了各種選項，他開始慢慢地點點頭並摩擦下巴。之後我成功說服他買車了！

情境 9 Pulling on Earlobe and Shaking Head to the Side
拉耳垂、頭轉向一側

指人們用拇指和食指抓著耳垂、往下拉，而他們也會把頭偏向兩側，把耳朵拉向一側的肩膀，接著另一隻耳朵再靠向另一側的肩膀。這個動作代表他們正在思考某件事情。

外國人拉耳垂、頭轉向一側時，他們會說：

Let me think about it.	讓我想一下。
It makes sense.	有道理。
I'm contemplating it.	我正在思考這件事。
I'm thinking about it.	我正在想這件事。
Let me think.	讓我想想。
I'll ponder it.	我會仔細考慮。
I wonder if it would work.	我想知道這是否可行。
Do you think it's a good idea?	你覺得這是好點子嗎？
I can't decide.	我沒辦法決定。
I can't choose!	我沒辦法選擇！

外國人拉耳垂、頭轉向一側時，你可以回：

Sounds good.	聽起來不錯。
Take your time.	你慢慢想。
Do you need anything else?	你還需要其他東西嗎？
It's a good choice.	這是個好選擇。
I think it would work.	我覺得這會可行。
What do you think?	你怎麼想呢？
Do you need any help?	你需要任何幫助嗎？
Let me see it.	讓我看看。
I can choose for you.	我可以幫你選。
Let me decide.	讓我來決定。
I can make the decision.	我可以做決定。

情境對話 中文可對照上方的例句

Dialogue 1

Ⓐ I wonder if it would work.
Ⓑ What do you think?
Ⓐ I'll ponder it.
Ⓑ I think it would work.

Dialogue 2

Ⓐ I can't choose!
Ⓑ I can choose for you.
Ⓐ Sounds good.
Ⓑ Do you need anything else?

情境 從英文來看外國人使用此肢體語言的情境

I was trying to find the perfect dress for the Christmas party. Finally, I tried on a pretty green dress that I loved. My best friend looked unsure. She tilted her head and tugged on her earlobe. She told me that it looked okay.

我試著要找出最完美的耶誕派對裝扮，最後，我試了一件我很喜歡的一件漂亮綠色洋裝。我最好的朋友卻不確定。她歪著頭並拉她的耳垂，之後她告訴我這件看起來還行。

情境 10 Leaning Forehead against Fist 額頭靠在拳頭上

指一個人手握拳並放在自己面前，手掌朝向自己、額頭倚靠在握著的拳頭上。通常，有些人做這個動作是在往下看他們正在處理的事物上，例如專注在企畫案或報告上。這表示他們正在努力思考某件事，或是正在困擾的事情。

外國人把額頭靠在拳頭上時，他們會說：

I'm thinking about it.	我正在思考這件事。
I need to read this.	我需要閱讀這個文件。
I'm reading through it.	我正在讀這整本書。
I'm working on it now.	我正在處理這件事。
I'm almost done with it.	我幾乎要完成了。
I'm taking a test.	我正在考試。
I'm writing a paper.	我正在寫一份論文。
I'm finishing the report.	我正在完成這份報告。
I'm focusing on this.	我正專注在這件事。
I need to focus.	我需要專注。

外國人把額頭靠在拳頭上時，你可以回：

What are you working on?	你正在做甚麼？
What is it?	那是甚麼？
How's it going?	情況如何？
How are you doing?	你還好嗎？
Do you need help?	你需要幫忙嗎？
Can I read it?	我可以讀這個嗎？
It's a good book!	這是一本好書！
I'll leave you alone.	我不打擾你。
I'll let you be.	你繼續。
I'll come back.	我等等再回來。

情境對話　中文可對照上方的例句

Dialogue 1

Ⓐ I'm reading through it.
Ⓑ What is it?
Ⓐ I'm finishing the report.
Ⓑ Can I read it?

Dialogue 2

Ⓐ What are you working on?
Ⓑ I'm focusing on this.
Ⓐ What is it?
Ⓑ I'm writing a paper.

情境　從英文來看外國人使用此肢體語言的情境

I saw Luke at the library. He was leaning his head on his fist and looked really confused. I stopped to say hi and he told me he was proof-reading his paper for literature class.

我看到 Luke 在圖書館裡，他把頭靠在拳頭上、看起來很困惑。我靠近他跟他打招呼，他跟我說他在校對他文學課的論文。

情境 11　Tapping Teeth together 牙齒碰在一起

指一個人稍微慢慢地上下移動他們的下顎，讓牙齒碰在一起，這會發出輕輕碰撞的聲音。這個動作通常是由在思考某件事或沉浸在思緒中的人所做的。

外國人把牙齒碰在一起時，他們會說：

I'm thinking.	我正在思考。
I need to think.	我需要思考。
Let me think.	讓我想想。
Give me a minute.	給我一分鐘。
I need a few minutes.	我需要一點時間。
I'm thinking about it.	我正在思考這件事。
I'll make a decision.	我會做決定。
Let me think through it.	讓我想想這件事。
I'll think on it.	我會想這件事。
I'll give it some thought.	我會考慮一下的。

外國人把牙齒碰在一起時，你可以回：

About what?	思考甚麼？
What are you thinking about?	你在想甚麼？
I'll give you some time.	我會給你一些時間。
I'll come back.	我等等再回來。
Let me know when you're done.	你做好的時候跟我說。
Anything I can do?	有任何我可以做的嗎？
Can I help you?	我可以幫你嗎？
I'll give you some space.	我會給你一些空間。
I'll let you be.	我不打擾你。
I'll stop by later.	我等等再過來這裡。

情境對話　中文可對照上方的例句

Dialogue 1

Ⓐ Give me a minute.
Ⓑ I'll give you some space.
Ⓐ I need to think.
Ⓑ Can I help you?

Dialogue 2

Ⓐ Let me think through it.
Ⓑ I'll let you be.
Ⓐ Thanks.
Ⓑ I'll stop by later.

情境　從英文來看外國人使用此肢體語言的情境

I sat next to Jacob in the meeting today. When he was concentrating on something, he tapped his teeth together. He didn't even know he was doing it. It drove me crazy!

我在今天開會時坐在 Jacob 的旁邊。當他專注在某件事的時候，他會把牙齒碰在一起。他甚至不知道自己這樣做，這讓我很惱怒！

Asking Someone to Stop Talking
要他人安靜

☞ **要他人安靜時需要用到的動作，用英文要怎麼說呢？**

要他人安靜時就會產生各種手勢和肢體動作，下列是要他人安靜時會用到的手勢與肢體語言，請看圖片，並對照動作的英文和中文。

情境
1

Putting index finger to lips
食指放在嘴唇上

情境
2

Outstretching arm with palm facing someone 伸出手臂、手掌面向別人

情境
3

Plugging the ears with fingertips
用手指塞住耳朵

情境 1 Putting Index Finger to Lips 食指放在嘴唇上

指手握成拳，只有食指伸出，食指的一側抵在嘴唇上，而食指指尖幾乎要觸碰到鼻子，握拳那隻手的大拇指則抵在下巴。這個手勢通常伴隨著「噓」的聲音，這樣做是為了小聲地告訴他人保持安靜。老師會在學生面前做這件事，告訴他們該安靜下來注意聽了。

外國人把食指放在嘴唇上時，他們會說：

Be quiet!	安靜！
Shhhhh!	噓！
Hush!	噓！
No talking!	不准說話！
Please whisper!	請用耳語！
You're too loud!	你太大聲了！
You need to be quiet.	你得安靜。
Quiet down.	安靜下來。
Listen to me.	聽我說。
Close your mouth!	閉上你的嘴！

外國人把食指放在嘴唇上時，你可以回：

I'm sorry!	對不起！
I'll quiet down.	我會安靜下來。
I'll shut up.	我會閉嘴。
I'm not being loud.	我沒有很大聲。
It wasn't me!	不是我！
It was them.	是他們。
They're being loud.	他們很大聲。
I'm trying to be quiet.	我會試著安靜。
I'm listening!	我在聽啊！
I am whispering.	我在低聲說。

情境對話 中文可對照上方的例句

Dialogue 1

Ⓐ Shhhhh!

Ⓑ I'm not being loud.

Ⓐ No talking!

Ⓑ I'll shut up.

Dialogue 2

Ⓐ Be quiet!

Ⓑ I'm sorry!

Ⓐ You're too loud.

Ⓑ I'm trying to be quiet.

情境 從英文來看外國人使用此肢體語言的情境

We were at the library, and I was telling a friend about a book I had just read. The librarian put her finger to her lips and told me to be quiet. I apologized and told her I'd whisper.

我們在圖書館，而我正在跟一位朋友談論我剛才讀過的書。圖書管員把她的手指放在嘴唇上，告訴我要安靜。我道歉，並告訴她我會低聲說話。

情境 2　Outstretching Arm with Palm Facing Someone
伸出手臂、手掌面向別人

指伸出手臂並將手對著他人，手掌朝
向對方。這個手勢意味著他們希望對方停
止正在做的事。就好像舉起停止標誌，使
某人立即停車。類似的手勢也有將手掌張
開、朝向下方。

外國人手掌面向別人時，他們會說：

Stop!	停止！
Stop talking!	別說話了！
I asked you to stop.	我叫你停下來。
Be quiet.	安靜。
Hush!	噓！
Shut up!	閉嘴！
Don't talk again.	不要再說話了。
Listen to me!	聽我說！
Keep quiet.	保持安靜。
Hold your tongue!	別說話！

外國人手掌面向別人時，你可以回：

Why did you do that?	為甚麼要那樣做？
Don't do that to me!	不要那樣對我！
I'll be quiet.	我會安靜的。
I'm sorry.	對不起。
I'm not going to shut up.	我不會閉嘴的。
You can't make me!	你不能逼我！
I don't want to.	我不想。
I'm listening.	我正在聽。
I can say what I want.	我可以說我想說的。
Don't tell me what to do.	你不能告訴我要怎麼做。

情境對話　中文可對照上方的例句

Dialogue 1

Ⓐ Stop!

Ⓑ I can say what I want.

Ⓐ Be quiet.

Ⓑ You can't make me!

Dialogue 2

Ⓐ Hush!

Ⓑ I'm sorry.

Ⓐ Keep quiet.

Ⓑ I'll be quiet.

情境　從英文來看外國人使用此肢體語言的情境

I was telling a friend about my plans this weekend, but she cut me off. She put her palm right in my face and told me to shut up because she had something to tell me. At first, I thought it was really rude, but then I realized she really needed to talk to me about something.

我想告訴我朋友這個週末的計畫，但她打斷了我。她把手掌對著我的臉上，要
我閉上嘴，因為她有話跟我說。一開始我覺得這很粗魯，但後來我才了解到她
真的需要跟我聊聊某件事。

Plugging the Ears with Fingertips 用手指塞住耳朵

指用食指放在耳道裡堵住耳道，把聲音阻隔在耳朵外。這可能代表空間中的音量太大聲，讓他人的耳朵難受。也可能代表他們不想聽到其他人說的話。

外國人用手指塞住耳朵時，他們會說：

It's too loud!	太大聲了！
Turn the music down!	把音樂關小聲點！
My ears hurt!	我耳朵好痛！
I can't hear anything!	我聽不到任何聲音！
Turn down the volume.	把音量調小聲點。
The speakers are loud!	喇叭太大聲了！
I have to cover my ears!	我必須把耳朵摀住！
I should have brought ear plugs!	我應該要戴耳塞的。
I don't want to hear this.	我不想聽這個。
I'm not listening!	我沒在聽！

外國人用手指塞住耳朵時，你可以回：

I'll turn it down.	我會調小聲點。
I'll turn it off.	我來關掉。
I'll speak up!	我會講大聲點！
I agree!	我也同意！
I will!	我會的！
Listen to me!	聽我說！
Unplug your ears!	不要摀耳朵！
I can't hear anything.	我聽不到任何聲音。
I have ear plugs.	我有耳塞。
Is that better?	這樣比較好嗎？

情境對話 中文可對照上方的例句

Dialogue 1

Ⓐ Turn the music down!

Ⓑ Is that better?

Ⓐ It's too loud!

Ⓑ I'll turn it off.

Dialogue 2

Ⓐ I should have brought ear plugs!

Ⓑ I have ear plugs.

Ⓐ My ears hurt!

Ⓑ Is that better?

情境 從英文來看外國人使用此肢體語言的情境

The music at the concert was so loud! It hurt my ears so bad that I needed to plug them. I wish I had taken ear plugs.

演唱會的音樂太大聲了！讓我的耳朵難受到我需要把耳朵塞住。我真希望我有戴耳塞。

Agree Something
同意某件事情

☞ **同意某件事情時需要用到的動作，用英文要怎麼說呢？**

同意某件事情時就會產生各種手勢和肢體動作，下列是同意某件事情時會用到的手勢與肢體語言，請看圖片，並對照動作的英文和中文。

情境 1

Applauding hands 鼓掌

情境 2

Thumbs up 豎起大拇指

情境 3

Index finger and thumb touching
OK 手勢

情境 4

Nodding head up and down
上下點頭

情境 5

Single downwards nod 單次向下點頭

情境 6

Nodding quickly and pointing at
someone 快速點頭、手指著他人

情境 1 Applauding Hands 鼓掌

這是指持續拍手以發出響亮的「掌聲」。這通常是愉快或是認可的表現，在演講、音樂會、表演或體育比賽期間，觀眾便會鼓掌。當許多人鼓掌時，會產生持續的掌聲，這種反應方式讓表演者知道他們表現得很好。

外國人鼓掌時，他們會說：

That was great!	那太棒了！
I loved it!	我好愛它！
This is awesome!	這超棒！
It's amazing!	太美妙了！
They did a good job!	他們做得很好！
What a great speech!	多麼好的演講！
I liked the play.	我喜歡這齣戲。
The concert was awesome!	音樂會很棒！
It's over.	結束了。
We won!	我們贏了！

外國人鼓掌時，你可以回：

It was amazing!	太神奇了！
They did great.	他們做得很好。
I enjoyed that!	我很喜歡！
That was a blast!	那太讚了！
They did wonderfully.	他們做得很棒。
Did you like it?	你喜歡嗎？
What did you think?	你覺得呢？
He nailed it!	他做得真好！
I wasn't impressed.	我沒甚麼深刻的印象。
It wasn't my favorite.	那不是我最喜歡的。

情境對話　中文可對照上方的例句

Dialogue 1

Ⓐ That was great!
Ⓑ Did you like it?
Ⓐ The concert was awesome!
Ⓑ It wasn't my favorite.

Dialogue 2

Ⓐ What a great speech.
Ⓑ I enjoyed that!
Ⓐ I loved it!
Ⓑ He nailed it!

情境　從英文來看外國人使用此肢體語言的情境

We went to a Garth Brooks concert last weekend. When he sang the last song, everyone sang along and applauded the whole time. It was awesome!

上週末我們去了一場 Garth Brooks 的演唱會。當他唱到最後一首歌時，所有人都一起跟著唱，並且一直在鼓掌。真是太棒了！

情境 2 Thumbs Up 豎起大拇指

這是指伸出手臂，手掌握拳，所有手指都彎曲，只有拇指豎起來，而拳頭會稍微轉向，以使拇指朝向天空。這個手勢是認可或滿意的意思，指同意某人、對某個情況或想法感到滿意、或是表達一切都好的訊息。有些人在自己受傷（例如在運動比賽中）之後會豎起大拇指，好讓大家知道自己沒事。

外國人豎起大拇指時，他們會說：

I like it!	我喜歡！
That looks great!	那看起來很棒！
I feel good!	我覺得很好！
I agree!	我同意！
That's a good idea!	這是個好主意！
I'm in!	算我一份！
I'm okay!	我很好！
You did great!	你做得很好！
I'm happy with it!	我很滿意！
You're okay!	你很好！

外國人豎起大拇指時，你可以回：

Awesome!	太棒了！
I'm glad you like it.	我很高興你喜歡。
It looks good!	看起來不錯！
You did great!	你做得很棒！
We did it!	我們做到了！
We made it.	我們辦到了。
It's perfect.	太完美了。
Good job!	幹得好！
You look great.	你看起來很棒。
I'm glad you're okay.	我很高興你沒事。

情境對話　中文可對照上方的例句

Dialogue 1

Ⓐ I like it!

Ⓑ It looks good!

Ⓐ I agree.

Ⓑ It's perfect.

Dialogue 2

Ⓐ I'm happy with it!

Ⓑ I'm glad you like it.

Ⓐ What do you think?

Ⓑ You look great.

情境　從英文來看外國人使用此肢體語言的情境

Mike took a hard hit at the football game. I was worried he would got hurt. When he stood up, he gave me a thumbs up to let me know he was alright.

Mike 在足球比賽中吃了一記猛擊。我擔心他會受傷，當他站起來時，他對著我豎起大拇指，讓我知道他沒事。

情境 3 # Index Finger and Thumb Touching OK 手勢

在他人面前伸出手臂，將拇指和食指相連，以比出「O」的字形，同時將其他手指伸直，手掌面對做出手勢的人。這個手勢有點類似豎起拇指，意味著一切都好，或是這個人對情況感到滿意。這也可能表示他們認可他人的觀點、或是同意他人所說的話。

外國人比 OK 手勢時，他們會說：

Sounds good!	聽起來不錯！
I'm in!	算我一份！
Okay!	好的！
I'm good with it!	我覺得沒問題！
I think it's great.	我覺得那很好。
It's perfect!	太完美了！
It went well!	進展很順利！
I'm okay.	我很好。
He's alright!	他沒事！
I'll be fine.	我會沒事的。

外國人比 OK 手勢時，你可以回：

Great!	太好了！
I'm glad you're okay.	我很高興你沒事。
Cool!	酷！
Awesome!	太棒了！
I'm glad you agree.	我很高興你同意。
I'm happy you could make it.	我很高興你能做到。
That's awesome!	那太棒了！
Perfect!	太完美了！
He looks fine.	他看起來不錯。
I'm happy you're alright.	我很高興你沒事。

情境對話 中文可對照上方的例句

Dialogue 1
Ⓐ It's perfect!
Ⓑ Awesome!
Ⓐ I think it's great.
Ⓑ I'm glad you agree.

Dialogue 2
Ⓐ I'm okay.
Ⓑ I'm happy you're alright.
Ⓐ I'll be fine.
Ⓑ Cool!

情境 從英文來看外國人使用此肢體語言的情境

After we lost the game, my teammate looked really upset. I asked if she was alright, and she gave me the okay gesture. I think she was bummed that we lost, but I'm glad she's okay.

在我們輸掉比賽之後，我的隊友看起來真的很沮喪。我問她還好嗎，她對我比了一個 OK 的手勢。我想她因為我們落敗而感到難過，但我還是很高興她沒事。

情境 4 Nodding Head Up and Down 上下點頭

這是指保持頭部筆直，並反覆把頭抬起和放下。像這樣點頭的意思是「是的」，或是同意某件已完成的事或已說過的話。此外，點頭的動作也有可能會持續。

外國人上下點頭時，他們會說：

Yes!	是！
Sure!	當然！
That sounds good!	聽起來不錯！
That's perfect!	那很完美！
I think that will work.	我認為那行得通。
That's a good idea.	好主意。
I like it!	我喜歡這個！
That looks great!	看起來很棒！
I'm happy with that.	我對此感到滿意。
It's what I wanted!	這就是我想要的！

外國人上下點頭時，你可以回：

Awesome!	太棒了！
Great!	太好了！
I'm happy we agree.	我很高興我們同意。
I'm glad you like it!	很高興你喜歡它！
Perfect!	完美！
I agree with you.	我同意你的看法。
I did, too.	我也是。
I wanted that one, too!	我也想要那個！
It looks good.	這看起來不錯。
I'm glad you're happy with it!	很高興你對此感到滿意！

情境對話　中文可對照上方的例句

Dialogue 1
Ⓐ I'm happy with that.
Ⓑ I'm glad you like it!
Ⓐ That's perfect!
Ⓑ Great!

Dialogue 2
Ⓐ I think that will work.
Ⓑ I agree with you.
Ⓐ It's what I wanted!
Ⓑ I did, too.

情境　從英文來看外國人使用此肢體語言的情境

My friend asked me to paint her living room for her. I went there yesterday and finished it up. When she walked in, I asked if she liked it and she nodded her head and said she loved it.

我的朋友找我幫她油漆客廳。昨天我去她家，完成了粉刷工作。當她走進去時，我問她是否有喜歡，她點了點頭，說她很喜歡。

情境 5 Single Downwards Nod 單次向下點頭

指單次向地面點頭，人們做這個動作時，眼神會與他人保持接觸。這個動作意味著人們理解他們所聽到的內容，或是表達某事對他們來說是合理的。

外國人單次向下點頭時，他們會說：

Understood!	明白了！
I understand.	我明白。
I get it.	我知道了。
I know what you mean.	我知道你的意思。
I see what you mean.	我明白你的意思了。
I see where you're coming from.	我知道你為甚麼會這麼說。
That's a good point.	那是個很好的觀點。
That makes sense to me.	我覺得很合理。
I hear what you're saying.	我有了解你說的。
I hear you.	我了解你。

外國人單次向下點頭時，你可以回：

I'm glad you get it.	很高興你了解了。
That's great.	太好了。
I'm happy you understand.	很高興你能理解。
That's true.	沒錯。
I'm glad it makes sense.	我很高興這很合理。
Do you have any questions?	你有任何問題嗎？
Awesome!	太棒了！
Glad you understand!	很高興你理解！
I'm happy you see my point.	很高興你明白我的觀點。
I'm glad you agree.	很高興你同意。

情境對話 中文可對照上方的例句

Dialogue 1

Ⓐ I know what you mean.
Ⓑ I'm happy you understand.
Ⓐ I see where you're coming from.
Ⓑ Thanks.

Dialogue 2

Ⓐ I get it.
Ⓑ Do you have any questions?
Ⓐ No, I don't.
Ⓑ Glad you understand!

情境 從英文來看外國人使用此肢體語言的情境

After my lesson, I asked the class if anyone had any questions. No one raised their hand, so I asked if everyone understood. Several people told me that they did understand, and a few people gave me a nod to let me know it made sense.

上完我的課後，我問全班是否有任何人有問題，沒有人舉手，所以我問大家是否都理解。有幾個人告訴我他們確實理解，也有幾個人點頭，讓我知道他們聽得懂。

🎧 23-6.mp3

情境 6 Nodding Quickly and Pointing at Someone 快速點頭、手指著他人

人們會用手指指著正在說話或剛說完話的人，同時反覆地上下點頭。這個手勢表示同意他們的意見，並且認為那些想法很好。

外國人快速點頭、手指著他人時，他們會說：

You're right!	你是對的！
I think you're right!	我覺得你是對的！
That makes sense to me.	我覺得這很合理。
Good plan!	好計畫！
I like it!	我喜歡！
You have good ideas!	你有很棒的想法！
I like that idea.	我喜歡這個點子。
I'm on board!	我加入！
I get it!	我懂了！
That's a good idea!	好主意！

外國人快速點頭、手指著他人時，你可以回：

Thank you.	謝謝你。
Glad you agree.	很高興你同意了。
I'm glad that makes sense.	我很高興這很合理。
I'm happy to hear that.	我很高興聽到這個。
That makes me happy.	那讓我很高興。
Awesome!	太棒了！
That's great!	太好了！
You're too kind.	你太客氣了。
That's nice of you to say.	你這樣說真好。
I appreciate it!	我很感激！

情境對話 中文可對照上方的例句

Dialogue 1
Ⓐ That makes sense to me.
Ⓑ I'm happy to hear that.
Ⓐ Good plan!
Ⓑ Glad you agree.

Dialogue 2
Ⓐ I like that idea.
Ⓑ Thank you.
Ⓐ I'm on board!
Ⓑ I appreciate it!

情境 從英文來看外國人使用此肢體語言的情境

I saw the president of the company speak at our annual meeting. I agreed with a lot of the things he was saying, so I nodded and pointed at him a few times. I wanted him to know that I agreed.

我看到公司總裁在我們的年度會議上講話。我同意他說的很多事情，所以我好幾次點頭並指向他。我想讓他知道我同意他所說的。

UNIT 24

Disagree Something
不同意某件事

☞ **不同意某件事情時需要用到的動作，用英文要怎麼說呢？**

不同意某件事情時就會產生各種手勢和肢體動作，下列是不同意某件事情時會用到的手勢與肢體語言，請看圖片，並對照動作的英文和中文。

情境 1

Pursed lips 噘嘴

情境 2

Flattened lips 癟嘴

情境 3

Twitching lips 嘴唇抽動

情境 4

Shaking head side to side 左右搖頭

情境 5

Twisting neck 轉脖子

情境 6

Rubbing finger alongside of nose
手指摩擦鼻翼

※ 補充說明：半個微笑也是不同意時會使用的肢體語言，可回去 Unit 7 p.64 複習。

情境 1 Pursed Lips 噘嘴

指將嘴唇的四周往內縮，使嘴唇向前突出並顯得更窄小。這個表情代表著緊張，也可能表示人們正感到挫折、或是並不贊成某種情況。一般認為人們噘嘴是為了把嘴閉緊，以免說出負面的話。噘嘴也可能表示人們正在思考，或正試圖針對某事做出決定。而當人們試圖做出決定時，他們的眼睛也會稍微閉上。

外國人噘嘴時，他們會說：

I disagree.	我不同意。
I feel differently.	我的感覺不一樣。
I'm upset.	我不太開心。
I don't like them.	我不喜歡他們。
I'm unhappy.	我不快樂。
I feel frustrated.	我感到挫折。
That's not my opinion.	那不是我的意見。
I'm thinking.	我在思考。
Let me think.	讓我想想。
Let me choose.	讓我選擇。

外國人噘嘴時，你可以回：

Why?	為甚麼？
What's wrong?	怎麼了嗎？
What's your opinion?	你的看法是甚麼？
Which would you choose?	你會選擇哪一個？
What's the problem?	有甚麼問題嗎？
What's the issue?	有甚麼問題呢？
Fine!	好吧！
What would you pick?	你會選擇甚麼？
Don't you like it?	你不喜歡嗎？
Get over it!	克服它吧！

情境對話　中文可對照上方的例句

Dialogue 1

Ⓐ I'm unhappy.
Ⓑ Why?
Ⓐ I don't like them.
Ⓑ Why not?

Dialogue 2

Ⓐ I'm upset.
Ⓑ What's wrong?
Ⓐ I feel frustrated.
Ⓑ Get over it!

情境　從英文來看外國人使用此肢體語言的情境

My best friend and I went shopping. I tried on a really pretty dress. I could tell by my friend's pursed lips that she didn't like it.

我和我最好的朋友去逛街，我試穿了一件非常漂亮的洋裝，但我可以從我朋友噘嘴的反應看出她並不喜歡這件洋裝。

情境 2 Flattened Lips 癟嘴

指嘴唇保持水平，但緊緊擠壓閉上，形成扁平線條。這可能代表人們不同意某件事，但他們忍住不說負面的意見，也可能表示人們努力不哭、不悲傷。在少數情況下，這個表情是指拒絕進食，並且常見於非常討厭某些食物，並拒絕進食的孩子上。

外國人癟嘴時，他們會說：

I disagree.	我不同意。
I think you're wrong.	我認為你錯了。
It's ugly.	這很醜。
You made a bad choice.	你做了很糟的選擇。
I don't like it.	我不喜歡這個。
I'm not upset.	我沒有不開心。
I'm not crying.	我沒有在哭。
I don't feel bad.	我沒有不高興。
I hate eggs!	我討厭吃蛋！
I don't want anymore!	我再也不要了！

外國人癟嘴時，你可以回：

With what?	不同意甚麼？
What don't you agree with?	你不同意甚麼？
I think it's a good choice.	我認為這是一個不錯的選擇。
I'm not wrong!	我沒有錯！
I think we made the right choice.	我認為我們做出了正確的選擇。
You look upset.	你看起來很沮喪。
What's the problem?	出了甚麼問題？
You look irritated.	你看起來很惱怒。
You're being rude.	你這樣很沒禮貌。
I don't care what you think.	我不在乎你怎麼想。

情境對話 中文可對照上方的例句

Dialogue 1

Ⓐ I disagree.
Ⓑ With what?
Ⓐ You made a bad choice.
Ⓑ I think we made the right choice.

Dialogue 2

Ⓐ I don't like it.
Ⓑ What's the problem?
Ⓐ It's ugly.
Ⓑ I don't care what you think.

情境 從英文來看外國人使用此肢體語言的情境

Jackie kept looking at me with a funny face. Her lips were in a straight line and she just looked funny. I finally asked her what was wrong, and she told me she didn't like my dress. She told me it was ugly. I can't believe she would say that!

Jackie 一直用古怪的表情看著我。她把嘴唇抿成一直線，看起來很奇怪。最後我問她到底怎麼了，她告訴我她不喜歡我的洋裝。她說我的洋裝很醜，我簡直不敢相信她會這麼說！

情境 3　Twitching Lips 嘴唇抽動

抽動是非常細微、快速的動作，當嘴唇抽動時，可以顯示人們內心的想法。嘴唇抽動可能代表人們不同意剛才聽到的話或是不相信某件事。這個表情是不認同的表現。

外國人嘴唇抽動時，他們會說：

I don't believe you.	我不相信你。
You're lying.	你在撒謊。
Stop lying!	不要再說謊了！
I can't stand you.	我受不了你。
I don't want to listen.	我不想要聽。
You're frustrating.	你真是令人沮喪。
I'm doubting you.	我懷疑你。
You aren't making sense.	你說的根本不合理。
I think you're wrong.	我覺得你是錯的。
I disagree.	我不同意。

外國人嘴唇抽動時，你可以回：

Why not?	為甚麼不相信？
Why?	為甚麼？
I didn't lie.	我沒說謊！
You don't believe me?	你不相信我嗎？
Why don't you believe me?	你為甚麼不相信我？
I'm telling the truth.	我說的是實話。
I'm not wrong.	我沒有錯。
Maybe you're wrong.	也許是你搞錯了。
I'm being honest.	我很誠實。
Don't call me a liar!	不要叫我騙子！

情境對話　中文可對照上方的例句

Dialogue 1

Ⓐ I don't believe you.
Ⓑ Why?
Ⓐ You're lying.
Ⓑ I don't lie.

Dialogue 2

Ⓐ I'm doubting you.
Ⓑ I'm being honest.
Ⓐ You aren't making sense.
Ⓑ I'm telling the truth.

情境　從英文來看外國人使用此肢體語言的情境

Steve was telling me about his new car and how nice it is. I felt like he was bragging. His lips kept twitching when I'd ask him questions about it. I think he's lying about how nice it is.

Steve 和我談到他的新車還有這台車有多好，我覺得他在吹牛。當我問他有關車子的問題時，他的嘴唇一直抽動。我認為他說那台車有多好都是在說謊。

Shaking Head Side to Side 左右搖頭

指保持頭部筆直，並由左向右反覆地水平移動。人們像這樣搖著頭是表示「不」，或是並不認同所發生的事或他人剛才說的話。

外國人左右搖頭時，他們會說：	
No!	沒有！
No way!	門都沒有！
Nope!	不！
I'm not doing it.	我不會做的。
I'm not going.	我不去。
I can't make it.	我趕不上。
It's a no for me.	對我來說這不行。
I have to say no.	我得說不。
I don't want it.	我不想要。
I don't want any.	我甚麼都不想要。

外國人左右搖頭時，你可以回：	
What do you mean?	你是甚麼意思？
Why not?	為甚麼不要？
You promised!	你答應過的！
What's the problem?	有甚麼問題嗎？
Why can't you come?	你為甚麼不能來？
Fine!	好吧！
That's a bummer.	真是令人討厭。
Are you sure?	你確定嗎？
What a shame.	真可惜。
You should try it.	你應該嘗試一下。

情境對話　中文可對照上方的例句

Dialogue 1

Ⓐ I'm not doing it.
Ⓑ Why not?
Ⓐ I don't want it.
Ⓑ You promised!

Dialogue 2

Ⓐ I can't make it.
Ⓑ Why can't you come?
Ⓐ I have to work.
Ⓑ That's a bummer.

情境　從英文來看外國人使用此肢體語言的情境

I asked Robert if he would go see the new Tom Cruise movie with me. He just shook his head side to side. I told him I'd go without him.

我問 Robert 是否要和我一起去看 Tom Cruise 的新電影。他只是向左右搖了搖頭，我告訴他那我就自己去看了。

情境 5 Twisting Neck 轉脖子

這是指水平地由左往右反覆旋轉脖子，是一種表示否定的點頭，類似於拒絕某件事或某個人，表明不喜歡某件事物，或是暗示某事不好／不正面。如果有人像這樣搖了頭卻不說話，意思就是「不要」。

外國人轉脖子時，他們會說：

No.	不。
I can't.	我沒辦法。
I won't do it.	我不會這麼做的。
I didn't finish it.	我沒有把它完成。
It's not here.	它不在這裡。
I don't like it.	我不喜歡這個。
It's gross.	那好噁心。
I don't know.	我不知道。
I hate it!	我討厭它！
I'm not going to.	我沒這麼打算。

外國人轉脖子時，你可以回：

Why not?	為甚麼不呢？
What's wrong?	怎麼了？
Is there a problem?	有問題嗎？
Do you have a problem?	你有甚麼問題嗎？
Where is it?	那個在哪裡？
Is it lost?	那個不見了嗎？
Is it bad?	那不好嗎？
Don't say that!	不要這樣說！
You should try it.	你應該嘗試一下。
Give it another try.	再試試吧。

情境對話 中文可對照上方的例句

Dialogue 1

Ⓐ No.
Ⓑ Why not?
Ⓐ I won't do it.
Ⓑ Don't say that!

Dialogue 2

Ⓐ It's not here.
Ⓑ Where is it?
Ⓐ I don't know.
Ⓑ Is it lost?

情境 從英文來看外國人使用此肢體語言的情境

I asked everyone to go on the hike. Jack just shook his head back and forth when I asked him. He told me he hates hiking. I guess he isn't going to come with us.

我邀請大家一起去健行，當我去問 Jack 時，他只是來回搖著頭。他告訴我他討厭健行，我猜他不會和我們一起去了。

Rubbing Finger Alongside of Nose 手指摩擦鼻翼

指伸出食指，其他手指握成拳頭，食指在眼睛下方、沿鼻子和臉頰相交的鼻翼部分摩擦。這個手勢通常是指人們不同意某件事，但也可能代表他們在某件事上撒謊。

外國人用手指摩擦鼻翼時，他們會說：

I don't like it.	我不喜歡這個。
I think it's wrong.	我認為這是錯的。
I have a different idea.	我有不同的想法。
Can I share my idea?	我可以分享我的想法嗎？
I don't want to do this.	我不想做這件事。
Can we go somewhere else?	我們可以去別的地方嗎？
I don't think you should do that.	我不認為你應該那樣做。
You shouldn't do that!	你不應該那樣做！
I disagree.	我不同意。
I don't like the idea.	我不喜歡這個主意。

外國人用手指摩擦鼻翼時，你可以回：

Why wouldn't you?	為甚麼不呢？
What do you mean?	你是甚麼意思？
What's wrong with it?	這怎麼了嗎？
What's your idea?	你的想法是甚麼？
What's your thought?	你是怎麼想的呢？
Go ahead!	繼續吧！
Tell us what you think.	告訴我們你的想法。
Tell me why.	告訴我為甚麼。
It's not wrong!	這沒有錯！
I think it's a good idea.	我認為這是一個好主意。

情境對話 中文可對照上方的例句

Dialogue 1

Ⓐ I don't like it.
Ⓑ What do you mean?
Ⓐ I don't think you should do that.
Ⓑ Tell me why.

Dialogue 2

Ⓐ I don't like the idea.
Ⓑ What's wrong with it?
Ⓐ Can I share my idea?
Ⓑ Tell us what you think.

情境 從英文來看外國人使用此肢體語言的情境

Jane was telling all of my friends and me about her new boyfriend. She was talking about how sweet he is. My other friend kept rubbing her nose and under her eyes. My friend thought Jane was lying about it.

Jane 跟我和我所有的朋友說到她的新男友，她告訴我們他有多貼心，而我的另一個朋友一直揉著她的鼻子和眼睛下方。我朋友認為 Jane 在撒謊。

UNIT 25

Not Knowing What other's Talking about
不知道別人在說甚麼

☞ **不知道別人在說甚麼時需要用到的動作，用英文要怎麼說呢？**

不知道別人在說甚麼時就會產生各種手勢和肢體動作，下列是不知道別人在說甚麼時會用到的手勢與肢體語言，請看圖片，並對照動作的英文和中文。

情境 1

Slowly nodding up and down
慢慢上下點頭

情境 2

Shaking head side to side followed by fast nod 慢慢搖頭再快速點頭

情境 3

Shaking shoulders 抖動肩膀

情境 4

Turning ear towards speaker
耳朵朝向說話者

情境 5

Turning head slightly to the side
頭稍微轉到一邊

情境 1 Slowly Nodding Up and Down 慢慢上下點頭

在做這個動作時，有時人們可能會稍微轉頭，並把眼睛瞇起來。這樣點頭是指人們認為正在說明某件事的人說得不太合理，或是覺得很難理解他們在說甚麼。

外國人慢慢上下點頭時，他們會說：

I don't follow.	我沒跟上。
I don't get it.	我不明白。
I'm not following.	我聽不懂。
It doesn't make sense to me.	我覺得這不合理。
You're not making sense.	你說的沒有道理。
Can you repeat that?	你可以再說一遍嗎？
I don't understand.	我不明白。
I don't understand what you're saying.	我不明白你在說甚麼。
What are you trying to say?	你想要說甚麼？
This confuses me.	這使我感到困惑。

外國人慢慢上下點頭時，你可以回：

What don't you get?	你哪裡聽不懂？
Can I explain it again?	我能再解釋一次嗎？
I'll explain it again.	我會再解釋一次。
Let me go over it again.	讓我再重複一遍。
I'll help you understand.	我會幫助你理解的。
We can discuss it later.	我們能晚點再討論。
Let me try again.	讓我再試一次。
What don't you understand?	你不明白甚麼？
What doesn't make sense?	甚麼事不合理呢？
What are you confused about?	你對甚麼感到困惑？

情境對話 中文可對照上方的例句

Dialogue 1

Ⓐ I'm not following.
Ⓑ What don't you understand?
Ⓐ It doesn't make sense to me.
Ⓑ I'll explain it again.

Dialogue 2

Ⓐ I don't understand what you're saying.
Ⓑ Let me go over it again.
Ⓐ This confuses me.
Ⓑ I'll help you understand.

情境 從英文來看外國人使用此肢體語言的情境

After I explained the graph in the meeting, my coworker seemed confused. She was nodding slowly and squinting at the graph. I asked if she had any questions, and she asked if I could explain it again. I explained it the second time, and she understood it afterward. 在會議上，我說明完這張圖表後，我的同事似乎很困惑。她慢慢地點了頭，瞇眼看著圖表。我問她有沒有甚麼問題，她問我是否可以再解釋一次。於是我又說明了一次，後來她就聽懂了。

情境 2 **Shaking Head Side to Side Followed by Fast Nod 慢慢搖頭再快速點頭**

指由左向右慢慢搖頭，通常是眼睛會向上看或向下看（以避免眼神接觸），接著又迅速轉換為上下快速點頭。這個動作表示人們並不記得他人正在討論的內容，後來又想起來了。

外國人慢慢搖頭再快速點頭時，他們會說：

I remember now!	我想起來了！
Yes, I remember!	是的，我記得！
I do remember!	我記得了！
I just now remembered!	我剛才想起來了！
It just came back to me.	我剛剛才想起來。
I can see it now!	現在我知道了！
I get it!	我知道了！
I remember!	我記得了！
Thanks for reminding me.	謝謝你的提醒。
You helped me remember!	你幫助我記起來了！

外國人慢慢搖頭再快速點頭時，你可以回：

Good!	很好！
I'm glad you remember.	很高興你能記得。
It's about time!	是時候了！
Thank goodness.	謝天謝地。
Awesome.	太棒了。
I'm happy you remembered.	很高興你記得。
I was happy to help!	很高興我能幫助你！
That's great.	太好了。
No problem!	沒問題！
Anytime!	隨時！

情境對話 中文可對照上方的例句

Dialogue 1
Ⓐ I remember now!
Ⓑ It's about time!
Ⓐ It just came back to me.
Ⓑ I'm happy you remembered.

Dialogue 2
Ⓐ Yes, I remember!
Ⓑ I'm glad you remember.
Ⓐ Thanks for reminding me.
Ⓑ No problem!

情境 從英文來看外國人使用此肢體語言的情境

I was telling my roommate about Luke, and she said she didn't remember him. I was trying to describe him to her. She was shaking slowly side to side like she didn't remember, and then nodded yes right away when she did remember him.

我正在跟我的室友說有關 Luke 的事，她說她不記得他了。我試著描述他這個人給她聽。她像是不記得了一樣，慢慢地搖頭，接著當她想起來這個人時，馬上點頭說是。

情境 3 **Shaking Shoulders 抖動肩膀**

這個動作是肩膀小幅度、快速的聳肩,雙肩往上提至耳朵、接著往下呈現一般休息的姿勢。當人們做這個動作時,可能也會把頭轉到兩側。這代表他們不知道某件事情的答案,或是不知道對方在說甚麼。

外國人抖動肩膀時,他們會說:

What are you saying?	你說甚麼?
I don't know!	我不知道!
I can't figure it out.	我無法理解。
It beats me!	我不明白!
I haven't got a clue.	我還沒有頭緒。
Who knows?	誰知道呢?
I'm not sure.	我不確定。
I couldn't tell you.	我不能告訴你。
Tell me what you mean!	告訴我你的意思!
What were you talking about?	你說了甚麼?

外國人抖動肩膀時,你可以回:

Let me repeat it.	讓我再重複一次。
Come on!	拜託!
Figure it out.	把它想清楚。
Are you sure?	你確定嗎?
Who would know?	誰會知道呢?
You should know.	你應該知道的。
Let me ask someone else.	我去問其他人吧。
What should I do?	我應該要怎麼做?
Let me explain it.	讓我解釋這件事。
Let me think about it.	讓我想想看。

情境對話 中文可對照上方的例句

Dialogue 1

Ⓐ I can't figure it out.

Ⓑ Who would know?

Ⓐ It beats me!

Ⓑ Let me ask someone else.

Dialogue 2

Ⓐ What were you talking about?

Ⓑ Let me repeat it.

Ⓐ Thanks.

Ⓑ No problem.

情境 從英文來看外國人使用此肢體語言的情境

I asked one of the salesmen about the new products. He just shrugged his shoulders and told me he didn't know. I told him it was his job to know, and he better figure it out.

我要求了其中一個銷售員介紹這些新產品,他只是聳肩跟我說他不知道,我跟他說這是了解新產品是他的工作,他最好把這些產品搞懂。

情境 4 Turning Ear towards Speaker 耳朵朝向說話者

指人們把他們整個頭轉到一側，因此耳朵會面向前面。這可能暗示出他們聽不清楚和無法了解你說的話，也可能代表他們需要你重複他們聽不清楚的事情。

外國人的耳朵朝向說話者時，他們會說：

What was that?	那是甚麼？
Can you speak up?	你可以大聲點嗎？
I didn't hear you.	我聽不到你的聲音。
I can't hear well.	我沒辦法聽清楚。
I'm hard of hearing.	我聽不太到。
Can you repeat that?	你可以再說一遍嗎？
What did you say?	你說甚麼？
Were you talking to me?	你在跟我說話嗎？
Say it again!	再說一遍！
What?	甚麼？

外國人的耳朵朝向說話者時，你可以回：

I'll repeat myself.	我再重複一次。
I can speak up.	我可以說大聲一點。
I can talk louder.	我可以說大聲一點。
Let me say it again.	我再說一次。
Did you get that?	你聽得懂嗎？
Do you need me to repeat it?	你要我再說一次嗎？
I was talking to someone else.	我在跟別人說話。
No, I wasn't.	不，我沒有。
I'll say it again.	我會再說一次。
I'll go over it again.	我會再重新講一次。

情境對話 中文可對照上方的例句

Dialogue 1

Ⓐ Can you speak up?
Ⓑ I'll repeat myself.
Ⓐ I'm hard of hearing.
Ⓑ I can talk louder.

Dialogue 2

Ⓐ What did you say?
Ⓑ I'll go over it again.
Ⓐ I didn't hear you.
Ⓑ I can speak up.

情境 從英文來看外國人使用此肢體語言的情境

When Sara asked me a question, I couldn't understand her because she was talking too quiet. I turned my ear towards her and asked her to repeat it.

當 Sara 問我一個問題時，我聽不太懂她在說甚麼，因為她太小聲了。所以我把耳朵朝向她，並請她再說一遍。

情境 5 **Turning Head Slightly to the Side 頭稍微轉到一邊**

指將頭部稍微靠近他人。有些人在聽不清對方的說話內容時會這樣做，這個動作使耳朵更靠近說話的人，並引導對方再說一次。若是人們在保持目光接觸的同時稍微將頭轉開，則可能表示他們認為自己比對方好，或者懷疑對方所說的。

外國人把頭稍微轉向一邊時，他們會說：

What was that?	你說甚麼？
Can you repeat it?	你能重複一遍嗎？
I didn't hear you.	我沒聽見你說的。
I have a hard time hearing.	我很難聽清楚。
Can you say it again?	你能再說一遍嗎？
What did they say?	他們說了甚麼？
I disagree with you.	我不同意你說的。
I don't believe that.	我不相信那件事。
I think you're lying.	我認為你在說謊。
I didn't see you there.	我在那沒見到你。

外國人把頭稍微轉向一邊時，你可以回：

Let me repeat myself.	讓我重複一遍。
I can repeat it.	我可以重複一遍。
I'll speak up.	我會大聲點。
Should I speak up?	要我說大聲點嗎？
Yes, I will.	好的，我會的。
I'll say it again.	我會再說一遍。
Why don't you agree?	你為甚麼不同意？
Why don't you believe me?	你為甚麼不相信我？
I'm not lying!	我沒有說謊！
I wouldn't make it up.	我不會編出這些事。

情境對話 中文可對照上方的例句

Dialogue 1

Ⓐ Can you repeat it?
Ⓑ Yes, I will.
Ⓐ I have a hard time hearing.
Ⓑ I'll speak up.

Dialogue 2

Ⓐ I disagree with you.
Ⓑ Why don't you believe me?
Ⓐ I think you're lying.
Ⓑ I'm not lying!

情境 從英文來看外國人使用此肢體語言的情境

I work as a waitress. Tonight I was taking an older man's order and after I introduced myself, he turned his head to the side and asked me to repeat myself. I made sure to speak loud enough so he could hear me.

我從事服務生的工作。今晚我幫一位長輩點餐，在我自我介紹之後，他將頭轉向旁邊，請我再說一次。我得用夠大聲的音量說話，這樣他才聽得到。

Seeking for Attention
引起注意

👉 **引起注意時需要用到的動作，用英文要怎麼說呢？**

引起注意時就會產生各種手勢和肢體動作，下列是引起注意時會用到的手勢與肢體語言，請看圖片，並對照動作的英文和中文。

情境 **1**

Slowly flexing and extending index finger 慢慢伸縮食指

情境 **2**

Parted lips 嘴唇微張

情境 **3**

Raising and waving arms 手臂舉高揮舞

情境 **4**

Jutting the chin out 伸出下巴

情境 **5**

Body facing someone 身體面向他人

※ 補充說明：用食指指著某人、某物也是引起注意時會使用的肢體語言，可回去 Unit 18 p.154 複習。

情境 1 Slowly Flexing and Extending Index Finger 慢慢伸縮食指

對著他人伸出手臂、手掌朝上、伸出食指，其他的手指都握成拳，接著食指慢慢收起，再馬上伸直，將此動作重複數次，並告訴他人「come here.」或「come to me.」。

外國人慢慢伸縮食指時，他們會說：

Come here!	過來！
Get over here.	到這裡來。
I need to talk to you.	我要跟你說話。
I like you.	我喜歡你。
Come to me.	到我這裡來。
I want to talk to you.	我想跟你說話。
Come over here.	過來這裡。
We need to talk.	我們得談談。
I'd like a minute.	我需要一點時間。
I see you!	我看見你了！

外國人慢慢伸縮食指時，你可以回：

I'm coming.	我過來了。
I'm on my way.	我在路上了。
I'm getting there.	我正要到那裡去。
I'll be right there.	我馬上過去。
Just a minute.	馬上到。
Hold your horses!	稍等一下！
I don't have time right now.	我現在沒時間。
We can talk later.	我們可以稍後再談。
Not now!	現在不方便！
I'm not coming over there.	我不會過去那裡。

情境對話 中文可對照上方的例句

Dialogue 1

Ⓐ Come here!

Ⓑ I'm coming.

Ⓐ I want to talk to you.

Ⓑ I'll be right there.

Dialogue 2

Ⓐ I'd like a minute.

Ⓑ We can talk later.

Ⓐ Get over here.

Ⓑ Hold your horses!

情境 從英文來看外國人使用此肢體語言的情境

When I was little, I always knew I was in big trouble, when my mom would use her pointer finger to call me over to her. She used to crouch down and look right at me when she did it, and I knew she needed to talk to me about something I did wrong.

我還小的時候，每當我媽媽用她的食指叫我過去她那裡時，我總是知道我的麻煩大了。每當她這麼做時，她習慣會彎下腰看著我，我就知道她想要和我談談我做錯了甚麼事情。

情境 2　Parted Lips 嘴唇微張

指嘴唇微微張開。通常嘴唇微張時，人們會用嘴巴呼吸。這個表情表示人們正要說話、或是正想要說些甚麼。這個表情也可以當作調情的表現，特別是當人用舌頭舔張開的嘴唇時。當作調情的表現時，人們通常做這個動作，同時會凝視著他們感興趣的對象。

外國人的嘴唇微張時，他們會說：

I have something to say.	我有話要說。
Let me add something.	讓我補充一些事。
Can I speak?	我可以說話嗎？
I have a question.	我有個問題。
Can I ask a question?	我能問個問題嗎？
Can I talk to you?	我能和你說個話嗎？
I have some news.	我有些消息。
I'd like to get to know you.	我想多了解你。
I think you're pretty.	我覺得你很漂亮。
You're hot!	你好性感！

外國人的嘴唇微張時，你可以回：

What's that?	甚麼事？
Yes?	嗯？
Go ahead.	說吧。
What are you thinking?	你在想甚麼？
Of course.	當然
What's going on?	怎麼了嗎？
What's your news?	你有甚麼消息？
I think you're cute!	我覺得你很可愛！
I'm not interested.	我沒興趣。
Let's get together some time.	讓我們找時間再聚吧。

情境對話　中文可對照上方的例句

Dialogue 1

Ⓐ I have something to say.
Ⓑ Go ahead.
Ⓐ I'd like to get to know you.
Ⓑ Let's get together some time.

Dialogue 2

Ⓐ I have some news.
Ⓑ What's going on?
Ⓐ I think you're pretty.
Ⓑ Seriously?

情境　從英文來看外國人使用此肢體語言的情境

I was at a dinner party last night, and I could tell that Sara wanted to say something. Her lips were parted, and she kept trying to speak, but would get cut off. I finally asked her what she wanted to say, and she told us she was moving. She seems really excited about it.

昨晚我參加了一場晚宴，我看得出來 Sara 那時有些話想說。她的嘴唇微張，一直試圖說話，但都被打斷。最後我問她想說甚麼，她告訴我們她要搬家了。她似乎對這件事感到非常興奮。

情境 3　Raising and Waving Arms 手臂舉高揮舞

指兩隻手臂向上伸展，手掌面向前方、手臂和手掌來回揮動。人們會用這個手勢來吸引某人的注意。在人群中，這個手勢可以使自己更容易被看見、被發現。需要幫助的人也可能使用這個手勢，例如：迷路的健行者，或是在危險處境無法脫身的人。

外國人把手臂舉高揮舞時，他們會說：

Look at me!	看這裡！
Do you see me?	你看得到我嗎？
Did you see me?	你看見我了嗎？
Watch for me!	等等我！
I need help!	我需要幫助！
Please help me!	請幫助我！
I'm lost!	我迷路了！
I'm stuck!	我被卡住了！
Send me help!	請找人來幫我！
Call for help!	去找人救援！

外國人把手臂舉高揮舞時，你可以回：

I see you!	我看到你了！
I'm coming!	我來了！
Yes, I saw you.	是的，我看到你了。
I'll send help.	我會派人去救援。
I found them.	我找到他們了。
They're safe.	他們很安全。
We'll get you out.	我們會把你救出來。
I'm here to help.	我來這裡幫你了。
You're going to be fine.	你會沒事的。
Are you okay?	你還好嗎？

情境對話　中文可對照上方的例句

Dialogue 1

Ⓐ Do you see me?
Ⓑ I see you!
Ⓐ I'm stuck!
Ⓑ You're going to be fine.

Dialogue 2

Ⓐ Please help me!
Ⓑ We'll get you out.
Ⓐ Send me help!
Ⓑ I'll send help.

情境　從英文來看外國人使用此肢體語言的情境

There were a few hikers that got lost in Hawaii last week. A search helicopter spotted them waving their arms. They got lost because they went off the trail and ended up getting stuck deep in a ravine. They're lucky to be alive.

上個星期，有些健行者在夏威夷迷路了，一架搜救直升機發現他們揮舞著手臂。他們迷路是因為離開了路徑，結果陷入了深谷。他們很幸運還活著。

情境 4 Jutting the Chin out 伸出下巴

指輕輕將頭向後傾斜，可以使下巴迅速地朝某個方向伸出。這個動作可以包括眼睛注視著下巴所對著的方向。這可能是向他人做出一個小指示，讓對方去看你的下巴所指向的事物，也可能是威脅或大膽的動作。在與他人保持眼神交流的同時快速地突出下巴，可能是威脅或反抗的行為。

外國人伸出下巴時，他們會說：

Look at that!	看那個！
Did you see that?	你看見了嗎？
What was that?	那是甚麼？
Did you look at her?	你有看到她嗎？
What was she wearing?	她穿的是甚麼啊？
She looked awful!	她看起來很糟！
I felt bad for her.	我為她感到難過。
He's over there.	他在那邊。
What are you looking at?	你在看甚麼？
Stop looking at me.	別看著我。

外國人伸出下巴時，你可以回：

What are you looking at?	你在看甚麼？
See what?	看甚麼？
I don't know!	我不知道！
I didn't see her.	我沒看到她。
I missed it.	我錯過了。
I disagree.	我不同意。
I thought she looked nice.	我覺得她看起來不錯。
I'm watching them.	我在看他們。
I'm looking at that.	我在看那個。
Look over there.	看那邊。

情境對話 中文可對照上方的例句

Dialogue 1

Ⓐ Did you look at her?
Ⓑ I didn't see her.
Ⓐ She looked awful!
Ⓑ I missed it.

Dialogue 2

Ⓐ What are you looking at?
Ⓑ Look over there.
Ⓐ What was she wearing?
Ⓑ I thought she looked nice.

情境 從英文來看外國人使用此肢體語言的情境

We were walking along the beach, and my husband jutted his chin at the ocean and told me to look quickly. There were a bunch of dolphins swimming in the water. We watched them for a few minutes.

我們正沿著海灘散步，我先生用下巴指向海邊，告訴我快看，有一群海豚在水中游泳。我們觀賞牠們幾分鐘。

情境5 Body Facing Someone 身體面向他人

指人們把身體面向他人時，胸部和軀幹會朝向那個人的方向，這代表人們把注意力放在他的身上，要準備聽他說話。

外國人將身體面向他人時，他們會說：

I'm listening.	我正在聽。
I hear you.	我聽到你的話了。
I'm paying attention.	我正在專心聽。
I understand.	我了解。
I see what you're saying.	我了解你說的話。
You've got my attention.	你引起我的注意。
I know what you mean.	我知道你的意思。
That makes sense to me.	我覺得那很合理。
I think it's a good idea.	我覺得這是個好點子。
You have a good plan.	你有很好的計畫。

外國人將身體面向他人時，你可以回：

Thanks for listening.	謝謝你的聆聽。
Thank you for paying attention!	謝謝你專心聽我說。
I'm glad you understand.	我很高興你了解。
That's good.	太好了。
I'm glad it makes sense.	我很高興這合理。
Do you really think so?	你真的這樣想嗎？
Let me know if you disagree.	如果你不同意，請讓我知道。
I appreciate your attention.	感謝你的聆聽。
I appreciate it!	我很感謝。
You're the best!	你最棒了。

情境對話 中文可對照上方的例句

Dialogue 1

Ⓐ That makes sense to me.
Ⓑ Do you really think so?
Ⓐ You have a good plan.
Ⓑ Thanks.

Dialogue 2

Ⓐ I'm listening.
Ⓑ I appreciate it!
Ⓐ I think it's a good idea.
Ⓑ Do you really think so?

情境 從英文來看外國人使用此肢體語言的情境

I coach a baseball team. I was showing the players how to catch a fly ball. I could tell everyone was paying attention because they were facing me and watching what I was doing.

我訓練一支棒球隊，而我那時候在示範給球員們看如何接住飛球。我可以辨認出每個人都有專心看，因為他們都面向我並看我的動作。

Feeling Uncomfortable at some Occasions
在某些場合不自在

☞ **在某些場合不自在時需要用到的動作,用英文要怎麼說呢?**

在某些場合不自在時就會產生各種手勢和肢體動作,下列是在某些場合不自在時會用到的手勢與肢體語言,請看圖片,並對照動作的英文和中文。

情境 1

Force smile 硬擠出的微笑

情境 2

Curving shoulders forward
肩膀向前彎曲

情境 3

Burning ears 耳朵發燙

情境 4

Slowly rubbing palms together
慢慢搓揉手掌

※ 補充說明:咬著下唇也是在某些場合不自在時會使用的肢體語言,可回去 Unit 8 p.73 複習。

情境 1 Forced Smile 硬擠出的微笑

指嘴唇抿成一條線，並且似乎保持直線，甚至還可能稍微向下彎曲，眼睛和臉的其他部位不帶笑意。這種笑容表示人們在約會或工作面試等情況下，感到不舒服和不開心。

外國人硬擠出微笑時，他們會說：

I should go.	我得走了。
I'm going to go.	我要走了。
I'm heading out.	我要走了。
I'll talk to you later.	待會兒再和你聊。
I was just leaving.	我剛離開了。
I'm going to head home.	我要回家了。
I was just on my way out.	我剛要離開。
I'm tired!	我累了。
See you later!	回頭見！
I'd like to leave.	我想離開。

外國人硬擠出微笑時，你可以回：

Why?	為甚麼？
Why are you leaving?	你為甚麼要走？
Have one more drink!	再喝一杯吧！
You can't leave yet.	你還不能走。
You have to stay.	你得留下來。
Goodbye.	再見。
Drive safely!	小心開車！
I'll see you tomorrow.	明天見囉。
Can't you stay a little longer?	你不能再多留一會兒嗎？
See ya!	掰掰！

情境對話 中文可對照上方的例句

Dialogue 1

Ⓐ I should go.
Ⓑ Why are you leaving?
Ⓐ I'm tired.
Ⓑ You can't leave yet.

Dialogue 2

Ⓐ I'm going to head home.
Ⓑ Drive safely!
Ⓐ See you later!
Ⓑ See ya!

情境 從英文來看外國人使用此肢體語言的情境

I can't believe Ryan came with us to the concert. I gave him a forced smile when I first saw him, and then ignored him the rest of the night. I can't stand him!

我無法敢相信 Ryan 會和我們一起去聽音樂會，我看到他時勉強擠出一個微笑，然後整晚都無視他。我真受不了他！

情境 2 Curving Shoulders Forward 肩膀向前彎曲

指肩膀向前彎曲,而整個身體都會向前彎曲,看起來像是在往下看,頭部和眼睛通常面向並看著地板。這個姿勢表示人們感到不舒服或受到威脅,並且嘗試在身體上和精神上保護自己。

外國人把肩膀向前彎取時,他們會說:

I'm uncomfortable.	我不舒服。
I'd like to leave.	我想離開。
I feel out of place.	我感覺格格不入。
This is awkward.	這好尷尬。
I'm not welcome here.	我在這裡不受歡迎。
I don't like it here.	我不喜歡待在這裡。
I'm going to go.	我要走了。
I'll find somewhere else to sit.	我會再找其他地方坐。
I'd prefer to leave.	我想要離開。
I feel weird.	我覺得很奇怪。

外國人把肩膀向前彎曲時,你可以回:

What's wrong?	怎麼了?
Why?	為甚麼?
Why do you feel that way?	你為甚麼會有這種感覺?
Don't leave!	不要離開!
I don't want to leave.	我不想離開。
You just got here.	你才剛到這裡。
You're fine!	你很好!
What's the matter?	怎麼了?
Why are you leaving?	你為甚麼要離開?
Stay with me.	待在我身邊。

情境對話 中文可對照上方的例句

Dialogue 1

Ⓐ I'd like to leave.
Ⓑ You just got here.
Ⓐ I'm not welcome here.
Ⓑ You're fine!

Dialogue 2

Ⓐ I'll find somewhere else to sit.
Ⓑ Why?
Ⓐ I feel out of place.
Ⓑ Stay with me.

情境 從英文來看外國人使用此肢體語言的情境

I took my little sister to a college party. She was young and felt out of place. I could tell that she wasn't having fun because she was standing in a corner with her shoulders slumped forward. I got her a drink and introduced her to a few people. She seemed to feel better after that.

我帶我的小妹妹去參加大學派對。她年紀還小,感覺自己格格不入。我看的出來她沒有玩得很開心,因為她站在角落,肩膀向前傾。我幫她拿了飲料,把她介紹給幾個人。在那之後,她似乎覺得好些了。

情境 3 Burning Ears 耳朵發燙

指耳朵突然發燙、發紅。當人們說「我的耳朵發燙」，這代表他們覺得有人在別處講他們的事情，這可能是在講好的或壞的事情。

外國人的耳朵發燙時，他們會說：

My ears are burning.	我的耳朵好燙。
Someone's talking about me.	有人在說我。
I hope they're saying good things!	我希望他們說好的事情！
Are your ears burning?	你的耳朵在發燙嗎？
Someone must be talking about you!	有人一定在說你的事情！
Your ears are burning.	你的耳朵在發燙。
Are my ears red?	我的耳朵很紅嗎？
Are my ears burning?	我的耳朵在發燙嗎？
I feel like my ears are burning.	我覺得我耳朵在發燙。
Someone must have said my name!	有人一定在說我的名字！

外國人的耳朵發燙時，你可以回：

Why do you say that?	你為甚麼這樣說？
What?	甚麼？
They're not talking about you.	他們不是在說你。
I bet they're not.	我打賭他們沒有。
No, why?	沒有，怎麼了？
Yes, they are.	對，耳朵在發紅。
I think they did.	我覺得它們有發燙。
What are they saying?	他們正在說甚麼？
Of course they are.	當然，它們在發燙。
Don't worry about it.	別擔心。

情境對話 中文可對照上方的例句

Dialogue 1

Ⓐ My ears are burning.

Ⓑ Why do you say that?

Ⓐ Someone's talking about me.

Ⓑ They're not talking about you.

Dialogue 2

Ⓐ Are your ears burning?

Ⓑ No, why?

Ⓐ They were talking about you.

Ⓑ What are they saying?

情境 從英文來看外國人使用此肢體語言的情境

When I got to the dinner party, I could feel my ears starting burning. My friends told me they had been talking about me right before I walked in!

我到晚宴的時候，我覺得我的耳朵開始發燙。我朋友們跟我說，他們在我進門前一直在談論我！

Slowly Rubbing Palms Together 慢慢搓揉手掌

情境 4

將手掌併在一起，並緩慢地揉搓，這個手勢表示人們認為有不好的事情會發生在他人身上。這個舉動意味著他們希望有人受傷、或是運氣不好。

外國人慢慢搓揉手掌時，他們會說：

Watch this!	看這個！
Something bad is about to happen.	壞事要發生了。
He's going to get it!	他會得到報應的！
You'll get what you deserve!	你會得到應得的報應！
He's going to lose.	他要輸了。
He's going to get hurt!	他會受傷的！
I know he'll lose.	我知道他會輸的。
Keep an eye on them!	注意他們！
I'm going to beat them!	我會把他們打敗！
They're in for it!	他們就為此而來！

外國人慢慢搓揉手掌時，你可以回：

What's going to happen?	將會發生甚麼事？
What's this about?	這是在做甚麼？
What are you doing?	你在做甚麼？
What do you mean?	你是甚麼意思？
What's wrong?	怎麼了？
That's not good.	這樣不好。
You can't do that!	你不能那樣做！
Don't do anything stupid.	不要做蠢事。
I'm watching.	我正在看。
What did you do?	你做了甚麼？

情境對話　中文可對照上方的例句

Dialogue 1

Ⓐ Something bad is about to happen.

Ⓑ What do you mean?

Ⓐ I know he'll lose.

Ⓑ That's not good.

Dialogue 2

Ⓐ Watch this!

Ⓑ What's going to happen?

Ⓐ He's going to get it!

Ⓑ That's not good.

情境　從英文來看外國人使用此肢體語言的情境

During the game, my friend leaned over and told me to watch the game closely while rubbing his palms together slowly. I didn't know what he meant, but I was worried he did something stupid. It ended up being a new play that he taught the team. They got a touchdown, and we ended up winning.

在比賽的時候，我的朋友靠了過來，告訴我要密切注意比賽，同時慢慢地搓著手掌。我不知道他是甚麼意思，但我擔心他做了蠢事。原來是他教球隊的新把戲，他們做了一記觸地得分，最後我們贏了。

Telling a Lie 說謊

☞ **說謊時需要用到的動作，用英文要怎麼說呢？**

說謊時就會產生各種手勢和肢體動作，下列是說謊時會用到的手勢與肢體語言，請看圖片，並對照動作的英文和中文。

情境
1

Downward glance 向下瞥

情境
2
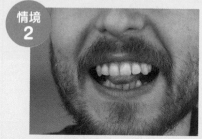

Biting the tongue 咬住舌頭

情境
3

Rubbing the end of nose back and forth 來回摩擦鼻子後端

情境
4

Pulling earlobe downward
把耳垂往下拉

※ 補充說明：嘴唇抽動也是在說謊時會使用的肢體語言，可回去 Unit 24 p.195 複習。

情境 1　Downward Glance 向下瞥

向下瞥是指人們在與他人交談時眼睛往下看。當一個人說話時向下瞥，他們就有可能在撒謊或逃避回答問題。此外，如果某人在談話過程中往下看，他們可能是對交談的對象感到恐懼。

外國人向下瞥時，他們會說：

I don't know!	我不知道！
I can't tell you!	我不能告訴你！
I'm not talking to you.	我不是在和你說話。
I don't know who did it.	我不知道是誰做的。
I'm not sure.	我不確定。
I can't talk to you.	我不能跟你說。
I'm not positive.	我不是太確定。
I feel nervous.	我感到緊張。
I can't talk right now.	我現在不能說。
I'm embarrassed.	我覺得很尷尬。

外國人向下瞥時，你可以回：

Are you lying to me?	你在騙我嗎？
You're lying!	你在說謊！
Tell me the truth.	告訴我真相。
You're not being honest.	你沒有誠實。
Why don't you say what you mean?	你為甚麼不說你是甚麼意思？
What are you embarrassed about?	你在尷尬甚麼？
Why are you nervous?	你為甚麼緊張？
What's bothering you?	你在煩惱甚麼？
Please talk to me.	請和我談談。
Tell me what's wrong.	告訴我怎麼了。

情境對話　中文可對照上方的例句

Dialogue 1
Ⓐ I feel nervous.
Ⓑ What's bothering you?
Ⓐ I can't talk right now.
Ⓑ Tell me what's wrong.

Dialogue 2
Ⓐ I don't know who did it.
Ⓑ Tell me the truth.
Ⓐ I'm not sure.
Ⓑ You're lying!

情境　從英文來看外國人使用此肢體語言的情境

It seems like there is something wrong with my friend. Every time we talk, she avoids looking at me and looks down a lot. I think she may be hiding something from me.

我朋友似乎有點怪怪的。每次我們在講話的時候，她都會避免看著我，並且常常往下看。我想她很可能對我隱瞞了一些事情。

情境 2 Biting the Tongue 咬住舌頭

咬著舌頭時，會看起來好像在嚼東西。人們會在閉著的口中輕輕地咬住舌頭，好將注意力從其他地方移開。咬住舌頭一般表示人們想要說些甚麼，卻說不出口，或是不願意說出他們想要甚麼。通常，人們不想在可能會傷害別人的情況下講真話。

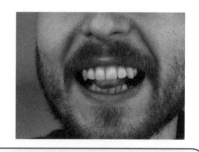

外國人咬住舌頭時，他們會說：

That's pretty.	真漂亮。
You look great.	你真好看。
I love it!	我喜歡它！
This is perfect.	太完美了。
I think you made a great choice.	我認為你做很好的選擇。
I agree with you.	我同意你的看法。
That's awesome!	棒極了！
My opinion doesn't matter.	我的意見不重要。
I don't want to upset you.	我不想讓你不開心。
I think you know what I'm going to say.	我想你知道我要說的話。

外國人咬住舌頭時，你可以回：

Thank you!	謝謝你！
You're so sweet.	你真貼心。
You're too kind.	你太客氣了。
That's nice of you to say.	你這麼說真好。
Are you being honest?	你有說實話嗎？
Are you sure?	你確定嗎？
Really?	真的嗎？
Don't lie to me.	不要騙我。
Give me the truth.	告訴我事實。
I don't believe you.	我不相信你。

情境對話 中文可對照上方的例句

Dialogue 1
Ⓐ I think you made a great choice.
Ⓑ Thank you!
Ⓐ I love it!
Ⓑ I'm glad.

Dialogue 2
Ⓐ You look great.
Ⓑ Are you sure?
Ⓐ I don't want to upset you.
Ⓑ Give me the truth.

情境 從英文來看外國人使用此肢體語言的情境

My best friend asked me to go to wedding dress shopping with her. She tried on one dress that was really ugly. She seemed to really like it, so I told her I liked it too. I didn't want to hurt her feelings, so I bit my tongue.

我最好的朋友找我和她一起去逛婚紗。她試了一件非常醜的禮服，但她似乎真的很喜歡，所以我告訴她我也喜歡。我不想傷害她的感受，所以我忍住沒說。

Rubbing End of Nose Back and Forth 來回摩擦鼻子後端

指用食指的側面來回摩擦鼻尖。這可能是鼻子發癢，但也可能暗示有人在說謊。如果是鼻子發癢，人們會迅速、用力揉鼻子。但如果在說謊，則會快速輕擦。有人正在說話時這樣摸鼻子，他就在說謊。如果人們正在傾聽時這樣做，代表他們懷疑自己聽到的事，並認為那可能是錯誤的。

外國人來回摩擦鼻子後端時，他們會說：

I made it up.	我編出來的。
I don't know if it's true.	我不知道這是不是真的。
It might be a lie.	這可能是謊言。
I'm telling the truth!	我說的是實話！
You look great.	你真好看。
You look skinny in that dress.	你穿那件洋裝看起來很瘦。
Your shirt is fantastic!	你的襯衫真好看！
I think he might be lying.	我想他可能在撒謊。
He's a liar.	他是個騙子。
He made that up!	他編出來的！

外國人來回摩擦鼻子後端時，你可以回：

Why would you do that?	你為甚麼要這麼做？
I don't believe it.	我不相信。
I think it's a lie.	我認為這是個謊言。
I think you're lying.	我認為你在說謊。
Are you being honest?	你有誠實嗎？
I think so, too.	我也這樣認為。
How do you know?	你怎麼知道？
I don't think so.	我不這麼認為。
I think he'd lie.	我覺得他在說謊。
I don't think he'd lie.	我不認為他會撒謊。

情境對話 中文可對照上方的例句

Dialogue 1

Ⓐ You look skinny in that dress.
Ⓑ Are you being honest?
Ⓐ No!
Ⓑ Why would you do that?

Dialogue 2

Ⓐ He made that up!
Ⓑ How do you know?
Ⓐ He's a liar.
Ⓑ I think he'd lie.

情境 從英文來看外國人使用此肢體語言的情境

I went to a New Year's Eve party last night. I wore a fancy dress and thought I looked great. Julia came up to me at the party and told me she thought my dress was nice. She rubbed her nose the whole time, and she didn't seem sincere. I think she was being rude.

昨晚我參加了跨年夜派對，我穿著一套時髦的禮服，以為我看起來很棒。在派對裡，Julia 上前來告訴我，她覺得我的衣服很漂亮。她一直揉著鼻子，看起來好像很不真誠。我覺得她很沒禮貌。

情境 4 **Pulling Earlobe Downward 把耳垂往下拉**

指人們用大拇指和食指握住耳垂並把耳垂往下拉，通常人們做這個舉動是因為他們在說謊。當人們說謊的時候，他們會身體發燙、耳朵發紅，使得他們去摸耳朵和脖子。

外國人把耳垂往下拉時，他們會說：

I'm almost finished with the report.	我快把這份報告完成了。
I'd love to go to dinner.	我想要去吃晚餐。
This is beautiful.	這真美。
I love your dress.	我喜歡你的洋裝。
The report is finished.	這份報告完成了。
I'm not sure.	我不確定。
I don't know what time I'll be there.	我不知道我甚麼時候會到那裡。
I'm running late.	我要遲到了。
I overslept.	我睡過頭了。
I would never cheat on you!	我不曾欺騙你。

外國人把耳垂往下拉時，你可以回：

Are you sure?	你確定嗎？
You don't mind?	你不介意嗎？
Are you lying?	你在說謊嗎？
Don't lie to me!	不要騙我！
Be honest with me.	老實跟我說。
I don't believe you.	我不相信你。
Give it to me straight.	跟我有話直說。
I don't think you're being honest.	我不覺得你有誠實。
I don't agree with that.	我不同意。
I don't think so.	我不這麼認為。

情境對話 中文可對照上方的例句

Dialogue 1

Ⓐ I'm almost finished with the report.
Ⓑ Are you sure?
Ⓐ Yes, I'm sure.
Ⓑ Don't lie to me!

Dialogue 2

Ⓐ I love your dress.
Ⓑ Are you lying?
Ⓐ No.
Ⓑ Be honest with me.

情境 從英文來看外國人使用此肢體語言的情境

I asked Reese if she'd like to go to dinner tonight. She said yes, but she was acting funny. She was pulling on her ear and she got kind of flushed. I couldn't tell if she was being honest or if she was lying.

我問 Reese 今晚要不要去吃晚餐，她答應了，但是她的行為有點古怪。她拉著耳朵而且又有點臉紅，我很難看出她是說實話還是在說謊。

Caring about Someone
關愛他人

☞ **關愛他人時需要用到的動作，用英文要怎麼說呢？**

關愛他人時就會產生各種手勢和肢體動作，下列是關愛他人時會用到的手勢與肢體語言，請看圖片，並對照動作的英文和中文。

情境 1

Soft voice 輕柔的語調

情境 2

Eskimo kiss 愛斯基摩式親吻

情境 3

Holding someone's hand
握住他人的手

情境 4

Wrapping arm around someone's
waist 手臂環在他人的腰上

情境 5

Patting someone on the upper back
輕拍他人的上背

情境 1 Soft Voice 輕柔的語調

指和他人說話時使用輕柔或柔和的語調，讓說出來的話聽起來很輕盈而且正面。這種語調通常用在與兒童或嬰兒說話的時候，或者是人早上醒來時所使用的語調。

外國人用輕柔的聲音說話時，他們會說：

Good morning!	早安！
How are you today?	你今天好嗎？
Hello!	哈囉！
It's good to see you!	很高興見到你！
Welcome to the class.	歡迎來上課。
You're so cute!	你真可愛！
I love your shoes!	我喜歡你的鞋子！
Can I take your coat?	我可以幫你拿外套嗎？
Thanks for coming over!	謝謝你過來拜訪！
Do you want a snack?	你要吃點心嗎？

外國人用輕柔的聲音說話時，你可以回：

Hey!	嘿！
I'm good.	我很好。
How did you sleep?	你睡得好嗎？
Thank you!	謝謝你！
You're so nice.	你人真好。
You're sweet!	你真貼心！
You're too kind.	你太客氣了。
Of course!	當然好啊！
Anytime!	隨時！
I'd love one.	我想來一個。

情境對話 中文可對照上方的例句

Dialogue 1

Ⓐ Good morning!
Ⓑ Hey!
Ⓐ How are you today?
Ⓑ I'm good.

Dialogue 2

Ⓐ Thanks for coming over!
Ⓑ Of course!
Ⓐ Can I take your coat?
Ⓑ Thank you!

情境 從英文來看外國人使用此肢體語言的情境

My daughter talks in a sweet, soft voice when she first gets up in the morning. This morning she came out of her room and asked me for breakfast right away in her sleepy voice. She's so sweet!

我女兒早上起床時，她說話的聲音好悅耳、輕柔。今天早上，她從房間裡出來，馬上用想睡的聲音跟我要早餐。她真的好可愛。

情境 2 | Eskimo Kiss 愛斯基摩式親吻

愛斯基摩式親吻是指兩個人用鼻子來回摩擦。這是一個充滿關愛的吻，通常是父母對孩子做的親吻。

外國人愛斯基摩式的親吻時，他們會說：

You're so special.	你很特別。
You're sweet!	你好可愛！
I love you!	我愛你！
I hope you have a good day!	希望你今天過得好！
Give me a kiss!	親一下！
I'll see you soon!	一會兒見！
Be good!	要乖喔！
Listen to your teacher!	聽老師的話！
Have fun!	玩得開心！
I missed you!	我很想念你！

外國人愛斯基摩式的親吻時，你可以回：

Thank you.	謝謝你。
You are, too.	你也是。
I love you, too!	我也愛你！
Have a good day!	祝你有美好的一天！
Goodbye!	再見！
I'll be good.	我會乖的。
I will!	我會的！
I'll listen!	我會聽話的！
I missed you too!	我也想念你！
I'll have fun!	我會很開心的！

情境對話 | 中文可對照上方的例句

Dialogue 1

Ⓐ You're sweet!
Ⓑ You are, too.
Ⓐ I hope you have a good day!
Ⓑ I will!

Dialogue 2

Ⓐ I love you!
Ⓑ I love you, too!
Ⓐ Listen to your teacher!
Ⓑ I'll listen!

情境 | 從英文來看外國人使用此肢體語言的情境

When I drop my son off at preschool, I give him a quick Eskimo kiss. It's our tradition! He loves going to preschool!

每次我把兒子送到幼兒園時，我都會給他一個快速的愛斯基摩式親吻。這是我們的傳統！他超愛去幼兒園上課！

情境 3　Holding Someone's Hand 握住他人的手

指把他人的手握在手中。這是表達關愛最常見的手勢，夫妻和父母／子女會在公眾場合握住彼此的手，以展現彼此之間的連結。

外國人握住他人的手時，他們會說：

Come with me.	跟我來。
I love you!	我愛你！
Let's go together.	我們一起去吧。
I'll walk with you.	我跟你一起走。
Let's go this way.	我們走這裡吧。
I'll lead the way.	我會帶路的。
You can lead the way.	你可以帶路。
I'll help you.	我會幫你的。
Do you need help?	你需要幫助嗎？
I'm here for you.	我在這裡等你。

外國人握住他人的手時，你可以回：

I'll follow you.	我會跟著你。
Okay!	好的！
Sounds great.	聽起來不錯。
It's a plan!	就這麼決定了！
Perfect.	完美。
That would be nice.	這樣很好。
I'd like that.	好啊！
I needed help.	我需要幫助。
I appreciate the help.	我很感謝你的幫助。
Thanks for the help.	感謝你的幫助。

情境對話　中文可對照上方的例句

Dialogue 1

Ⓐ Let's go together.
Ⓑ I'd like that.
Ⓐ I'll call you.
Ⓑ That would be nice.

Dialogue 2

Ⓐ I'll walk with you.
Ⓑ Sounds great.
Ⓐ Let's go this way.
Ⓑ Okay!

情境　從英文來看外國人使用此肢體語言的情境

When we were walking home, John grabbed my hand and held it in his. He told me he would walk me home. I think he likes me!

我們走回家的時候，John 抓住了我的手，並握在他的手中，他告訴我他會陪我走回家。我想他喜歡我！

情境 4 Wrapping Arm around Someone's Waist 手臂環在他人的腰上

將一條手臂環繞在他人的後腰上,並將手掌放在對方臀部之上的腰部。這是一種深情的表達,通常出現在兩個彼此相愛的人之間,有可能是重要的另一半,或是父母／子女。

外國人把手臂環在他人的腰上時,他們會說:

I love you.	我愛你。
I like sitting by you.	我喜歡坐在你旁邊。
Come here!	過來這裡!
I want to be closer to you!	我想靠近你!
I'll walk with you!	我會陪你走!
I think you're awesome.	我覺得你很棒。
You're the best!	你最棒了!
You're amazing!	你太棒了!
I think you're special.	我認為你很特別。
I'm glad you're here.	我很高興你在這裡。

外國人把手臂環在他人的腰上時,你可以回:

I love you, too!	我也愛你!
You're nice and close.	你人真好、真親密。
Scoot over!	靠過來!
Get closer.	過來一點。
There's enough room.	這裡位子夠了。
Thanks!	謝謝!
I like walking with you.	我喜歡和你一起走。
I like having you here.	我喜歡你在這裡。
You're pretty great, too!	你也很棒!
Me, too!	我也是!

情境對話 中文可對照上方的例句

Dialogue 1
Ⓐ I like sitting by you.
Ⓑ Get closer.
Ⓐ You're the best!
Ⓑ Thanks!

Dialogue 2
Ⓐ I'm glad you're here.
Ⓑ Me too.
Ⓐ I think you're awesome.
Ⓑ You're pretty great, too!

情境 從英文來看外國人使用此肢體語言的情境

My wife and I went for a walk on the beach yesterday. I wrapped my arm around her waist while we were walking, and told her how much I loved her. It was nice to spend time together like that.

昨天我和我太太在沙灘上散步。我們一邊走著,我一邊將手臂環繞在她的腰上,並告訴她我有多愛她。能像這樣花時間在一起,真是太好了。

Patting Someone's Upper Back 輕拍他人的上背

指用手掌輕拍他人的上背，這是表示
幹得好、做得好的手勢。在他人背上輕拍
是正面的，這代表你為他們感到驕傲。

外國人輕拍他人的上背時，他們會說：	
Good job!	做得好！
Great work!	做得好！
I'm proud of you!	我以你為傲！
You did awesome!	你做得很棒！
Nice try!	做得不錯！（沒有成功時講的話）
You'll get it next time!	下次你就會得到了！
You're awesome!	你真棒！
I'm happy for you!	我為你感到開心！
You make me happy.	你讓我快樂。
You make me proud!	你讓我感到驕傲！

外國人輕拍他人的上背時，你可以回：	
Thanks!	謝謝！
Thank you.	謝謝你。
Thanks a bunch!	非常感謝！
It was nothing.	沒甚麼。
It was easy!	那很簡單！
That's nice of you.	你人真好。
I hope so.	我希望如此。
Do you mean that?	你是那個意思嗎？
You're so thoughtful.	你太體貼了。
That's so kind!	你太好了！

情境對話 中文可對照上方的例句

Dialogue 1

Ⓐ Good job!
Ⓑ Thank you.
Ⓐ I'm proud of you!
Ⓑ That's so kind!

Dialogue 2

Ⓐ Nice try!
Ⓑ Thanks!
Ⓐ You'll get it next time!
Ⓑ I hope so.

情境 從英文來看外國人使用此肢體語言的情境

After the meeting, my boss gave me a pat on the back and told me I did a great job during the presentation. I was so nervous about it, so I felt really proud of myself after that.

會議結束後，我老闆拍了拍我的背，對我說我在簡報時做得很好。我之前為了簡報而很緊張，所以在這之後，我為自己感到驕傲。

Comforting someone
安慰他人

👉 **安慰他人時需要用到的動作，用英文要怎麼說呢？**

安慰他人某些事物就會產生各種手勢和肢體動作，下列是安慰他人時會用到的手勢與肢體語言，請看圖片，並對照動作的英文和中文。

Consolation hug 安慰的擁抱

Outstretched arms 張開的雙臂

Patting a butt 輕拍屁股

※ 補充說明：手臂放在他人肩膀上也是在安慰他人時會使用的肢體語言，可回去 Unit 14 p.129 複習。

情境 1 **Consolation Hug 安慰的擁抱**

這是一種安慰傷心的人的擁抱。給予安慰的人或傷心的人都可以擁抱對方，手會放在背部附近。給予安慰的人也會將一隻手放在對方的背部，另一隻手勾住對方的肩膀，並輕拍背部。若安慰的對象在哭，他們通常會把頭靠在對方的肩膀上。

外國人做出安慰的擁抱時，他們會說：

I'm sorry for your loss.	節哀順變。
I wish I could trade places with you.	我希望能和你感同身受。
Everything will be okay.	一切都會沒事的。
It's not the end of the world.	這不是世界末日。
I'm sorry to hear that.	很抱歉聽到這件事。
There are plenty of other fish in the sea.	還有很多機會。
There are some things you can't change.	有些事情無法改變。
Maybe it's for the best.	或許這是最好的情況。
You did your best.	你已經盡力了。
You can try again.	你還可以重來。

外國人做出安慰的擁抱時，你可以回：

Thank you.	謝謝。
I'm so upset.	我好難過。
I feel awful.	我覺得很糟。
I can't stop thinking about it.	我無法不去想這件事。
I'm mad at myself.	我好氣我自己。
I screwed up.	我搞砸了。
I messed everything up!	我搞砸了一切！
I should have tried harder.	我應該要更努力的。
It won't be the same.	不會是一樣的了。
You're right.	你說得對。

情境對話　中文可對照上方的例句

Dialogue 1

Ⓐ I'm sorry for your loss.
Ⓑ Thank you.
Ⓐ Everything will be okay.
Ⓑ You're right.

Dialogue 2

Ⓐ You did your best.
Ⓑ I'm so upset.
Ⓐ It's not the end of the world.
Ⓑ I'm mad at myself.

情境　從英文來看外國人使用此肢體語言的情境

We lost the basketball game today because I missed the last shot. I was mad at myself. My dad gave me a big hug after the game and it made me feel a little bit better.

今天我們輸了籃球比賽，因為我最後一球沒有投進。我很生自己的氣。比賽結束後，我爸給了我一個大大的擁抱，這讓我感覺好一點了。

情境 2 **Outstretched Arms 張開的雙臂**

指在他人的面前將手臂完全伸直，手掌朝上。通常由一個人向另一個人伸出雙臂，向某人如此伸出手臂是支持與關愛的表現，這個手勢告訴對方你想要接觸、擁抱他們。

外國人張開雙臂時，他們會說：	
Give me a hug.	給我一個擁抱。
Hold on to me.	抱緊我。
You're okay.	你會沒事的。
I've got you.	我抓住你了。
I'll carry you.	我會支持你。
I'll make it better.	我會讓事情變得更好。
I'll fix this.	我會解決這個問題的。
Let me help you.	讓我來幫你。
I understand.	我明白。
You seem upset.	你好像很沮喪。

外國人張開雙臂時，你可以回：	
I'll hug you.	我會擁抱你的。
You're going to be fine.	你會沒事的。
I'm sad.	我很傷心。
Let me hold you.	讓我抱著你。
I'll protect you.	我會保護你的。
I'm here for you.	我在這裡陪你。
I'll help you.	我會幫助你的。
I'm scared.	我很害怕。
Are you going to be alright?	你會好起來嗎？
It's okay.	沒事的。

情境對話 中文可對照上方的例句

Dialogue 1
Ⓐ Give me a hug.
Ⓑ I'm here for you.
Ⓐ I'm sad.
Ⓑ It's okay.

Dialogue 2
Ⓐ You seem upset.
Ⓑ I'm scared.
Ⓐ Hold on to me.
Ⓑ It's okay.

情境 從英文來看外國人使用此肢體語言的情境

My daughter had a nightmare last night. I heard her crying for me. I ran to her room and put my arms out for her right away. I held her for a little bit, and she calmed down and went back to sleep.

我女兒昨晚做了噩夢。我聽到她哭著叫我，我跑進她的房間，立刻向她伸出手臂。我抱著她一會兒，她平靜下來，又重新入睡。

情境 3　Patting a Butt 輕拍屁股

指一個人以擁抱的方式扶著另一個人（像擁抱一樣），並用手掌重複輕拍對方的屁股。這個動作幾乎是用在嬰兒或幼兒上，讓他們在哭的時候冷靜下來，或哄他們入睡。大人會將小孩扶在胸前並拍他們的屁股，他們通常還會發出「噓」的聲音讓小孩冷靜。

外國人輕拍屁股時，他們會說：

Shhhhh.	噓！
You're okay.	沒事的！
Hush!	噓！
Don't cry!	別哭！
Mom is here.	媽媽在這。
Dad has you.	爸爸陪你。
Close your eyes.	閉上眼睛。
I'll sing you a lullaby.	我唱搖籃曲給你聽。
I'll hold you.	我會抱著你。
I've got you.	我在你身邊。

外國人輕拍屁股時，你可以回：

I'm sad.	我很傷心。
I'm angry.	我很生氣。
I'm tired.	我好累。
I don't want to leave.	我不想離開。
I don't feel good.	我不舒服。
I'm sick.	我生病了。
I don't want to go to school.	我不想去學校。
I want to stay with you.	我想要跟你在一起。
Hold me.	抱我。
Can I stay here?	我可以待在這裡嗎？

情境對話　中文可對照上方的例句

Dialogue 1

Ⓐ Shhhhhh.

Ⓑ I'm sad.

Ⓐ You're okay.

Ⓑ I want to stay with you.

Dialogue 2

Ⓐ Hush!

Ⓑ I don't feel good.

Ⓐ Mom is here.

Ⓑ Can you hold me?

情境　從英文來看外國人使用此肢體語言的情境

My daughter had her first day of school today. When we got to school, she didn't want to go in. She said she was upset and didn't want me to leave. I told her she'd be okay and gave her a quick pat on the butt. She ended up having a great first day.

我女兒今天第一天上學。我們去學校的時候，她不想進去。她說她很難過、不想要我離開。我跟她說她會沒事的，並在她屁股上快速地拍一下。她最後有個美好的第一天。

UNIT 31

Flirting and Dating
調情、約會

☞ 調情、約會時需要用到的動作，用英文要怎麼說呢？

和喜歡的對象或情人調情、約會時就會產生各種手勢和肢體動作，下列是調情、約會時會用到的手勢與肢體語言，請看圖片，並對照動作的英文和中文。

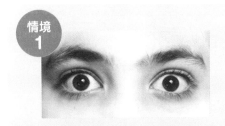

情境 1

Wide eyes 睜大眼睛

情境 2

Puckered lips 噘嘴

情境 3

Tongue between teeth smile
舌頭在牙齒間的微笑

情境 4

Flirtatious smile 調情的微笑

情境 5

Woman playing with an earring
女子擺弄耳環

情境 6

Kissing on the lips 接吻

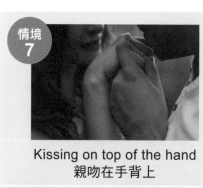

情境 **7**

Kissing on top of the hand
親吻在手背上

情境 **8**

French kiss 法式深吻（舌吻）

情境 **9**

Butterfly kiss 蝴蝶之吻

情境 **10**

Touching someone's cheek
觸摸他人的臉頰

情境 **11**

Leaning body towards someone
身體靠向他人

※ 補充說明：親吻臉頰（p.16）、揮動小指（p.18）、嘴唇微張（p.207）、握住他人的手（p.224）、手臂環住他人的腰（p.225）也是在調情、約會時會使用的肢體語言，可對照頁碼翻回去複習。

情境 1 Wide Eyes 睜大眼睛

人們可以藉著將下巴往下傾斜，並往上看著某人來把眼睛睜大。這種表情常常發生在女性看著感興趣的對象時。有時和喜歡的對象對到眼時低頭，也是強烈的調情表現。睜大眼睛看著他代表你喜歡他們、或對他們感興趣。這也可能表示對其他人感到害羞，或是對自己沒有把握。

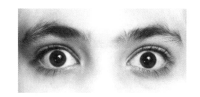

外國人睜大眼睛看你時，他們會說：

I like you.	我喜歡你。
You're cute!	你好可愛！
I think you're hot.	我覺得你很性感。
You're funny.	你好有趣。
I like being with you.	我喜歡和你在一起。
I'm attracted to you.	我被你吸引了。
I'd like to get to know you better.	我想要更了解你。
I feel nervous.	我覺得好緊張。
I'm feeling shy.	我覺得好害羞。
I like spending time with you.	我喜歡和你在一起。

外國人睜大眼睛看你時，你可以回：

I like you, too.	我也喜歡你。
I think you're pretty.	我覺得你好漂亮。
Don't be shy.	不要害羞。
Don't be nervous around me.	在我身旁不要緊張。
I find you attractive.	我覺得你很有魅力。
I want to be with you.	我想和你在一起。
I want to spend time with you.	我想多和你相處。
Can I kiss you?	我可以吻你嗎？
Why do you feel shy?	你為甚麼感到害羞？
I'm falling for you.	我被你迷住了。

情境對話　中文可對照上方的例句

Dialogue 1

Ⓐ I like you.
Ⓑ I like you, too.
Ⓐ I'd like to get to know you better.
Ⓑ I'd like that, too.

Dialogue 2

Ⓐ I'm feeling shy.
Ⓑ Don't be shy.
Ⓐ I think you're hot.
Ⓑ I want to be with you.

情境　從英文來看外國人使用此肢體語言的情境

I met a girl at the bar tonight. I saw her looking at me across the bar with really wide eyes, so I introduced myself to her. We spent the evening talking and getting to know each other.

今晚我在酒吧遇到一個女孩。我看見她從酒吧另一邊，睜大眼睛望著我，所以我向她介紹自己。我們就聊了一整晚，認識彼此。

情境 2 **Puckered Lips 噘嘴**

指嘴唇往內縮並向前推，這是親吻時嘴唇會形成的形狀。這個表情通常表示渴望某樣東西（可能是某件事物或某個人），也可能意味著對某件事感到不確定，尤其是用手指摸嘟起的嘴唇的時候。

外國人對你噘嘴時，他們會說：

He's cute!	他很可愛！
I like her.	我喜歡她。
I want them.	我想要這些東西。
I'm thinking.	我正在思考。
I'm not sure.	我不確定。
Let me think about it.	讓我想想。
Give me a kiss!	給我一個吻！
Come here!	過來這裡！
You're mine!	你是我的！
I like it!	我喜歡！

外國人對你噘嘴時，你可以回：

I think he likes you.	我覺得他喜歡你。
You should talk to her.	你應該去跟她說話。
Go talk to her.	去和她說話吧。
Get them.	把它們買下來吧。
You should buy them.	你應該買它們。
Give him your number.	給他你的電話號碼。
You should give her your number.	你應該給她你的電話號碼。
I'm giving him my number.	我要給他我的電話號碼。
Give me a hug.	給我一個擁抱。
Kiss me.	親我。

情境對話 中文可對照上方的例句

Dialogue 1

Ⓐ He's cute!
Ⓑ I think he likes you.
Ⓐ Really?
Ⓑ Give him your number.

Dialogue 2

Ⓐ I want them.
Ⓑ You should buy them.
Ⓐ They're expensive.
Ⓑ Get them.

情境 從英文來看外國人使用此肢體語言的情境

I saw a cute guy at the bar last night. We made eye contact and I puckered my lips at him. He came over and talked with me, and we ended up giving each other our phone numbers. He kissed me at the end of the night.

昨晚我在酒吧裡看到一個可愛的男生，我們對到眼，然後我向他嘟起嘴，他就走過來跟我說話。最後我們交換了電話號碼，最後他吻了我。

情境 3 Tongue between Lips Smile 舌頭在牙齒間的微笑

這是一種常見的微笑，在上下排牙齒之間可以稍微看到舌頭。人們覺得這樣會使自己看起來更有吸引力。年輕人在嘗試吸引喜歡的對象時，會露出這種微笑。

外國人露出舌頭在牙齒間的微笑時，他們會說：

I think you're cute.	我覺得你很可愛。
You're hot.	你真性感。
I like you!	我喜歡你！
I want to get to know you.	我想多認識你。
I'd like to talk to you.	我想和你說話。
Can I get your number?	可以給我你的號碼嗎？
Take my number!	記下我的電話號碼！
You're adorable.	你很可愛。
Let's hook up!	我們來親熱吧！
I want to kiss you!	我想吻你！

外國人露出舌頭在牙齒間的微笑時，你可以回：

Give me your number!	給我你的電話號碼！
Here's my number.	這是我的電話號碼。
I like you, too!	我也喜歡你！
Give me a call.	打電話給我。
Text me.	傳訊息給我。
I'll call you!	我會打電話給你！
You're pretty cute, too.	你也很可愛。
I'd like to get to know you.	我想要認識你。
Let's get together.	我們交往吧。
What are you doing later?	你等一下要做甚麼？

情境對話　中文可對照上方的例句

Dialogue 1

Ⓐ Can I get your number?

Ⓑ Here's my number.

Ⓐ I want to get to know you.

Ⓑ Give me a call.

Dialogue 2

Ⓐ What are you doing later?

Ⓑ Nothing.

Ⓐ Let's get together.

Ⓑ Let's hook up!

情境　從英文來看外國人使用此肢體語言的情境

I like to send my boyfriend cute pictures of myself. I sent him a selfie yesterday where I was smiling with a little bit of my tongue hanging out. He thought it was adorable.

我喜歡傳我自己可愛的照片給男朋友。昨天我傳了一張自拍照給他，當時我微笑著露出了一點點舌頭。他覺得這樣很可愛。

情境 4 Flirtatious Smile 調情的微笑

這種微笑類似於半個微笑。半邊嘴角上揚，眼睛和臉頰都帶著笑意，下巴通常向下傾斜，眼睛抬頭看著有興趣的對象，咬嘴唇或輕舔嘴唇可以加強這個表情。這種笑容是與他人進行更多互動的邀請，並告訴對方你想要更認識他們。

外國人露出調情的微笑時，他們會說：

You're gorgeous.	你好漂亮。
I think you're attractive.	我覺得你很迷人。
I'd like to get to know you.	我想要多認識你。
Can I have your number?	可以給我你的號碼嗎？
What's your number?	你的電話幾號？
Here's my number.	這是我的電話號碼。
Call me!	打給我！
Let's grab a drink sometime.	我們有時來喝一杯。
Can I take you to dinner?	我可以和你吃晚餐嗎？
May I sit by you?	我可以坐在你旁邊嗎？

外國人露出調情的微笑時，你可以回：

You're too kind.	你人太好了。
That's nice of you to say.	你這樣說真好。
I'd like that, too.	我也想要。
Yes, here you go.	好的，這裡。
My number is 605-5664.	我的電話號碼是605-5664。
Let's go out tomorrow.	我們明天出去吧。
I will!	我會的！
You can sit here.	你可以坐在這裡。
This seat is taken.	這個座位有人坐了。
I'm dating someone else.	我在和別人交往。

情境對話　中文可對照上方的例句

Dialogue 1

Ⓐ I'd like to get to know you.
Ⓑ That's nice of you to say.
Ⓐ Can I have your number?
Ⓑ Yes, here you go.

Dialogue 2

Ⓐ I think you're attractive.
Ⓑ You're too kind.
Ⓐ Can I take you to dinner?
Ⓑ I'm dating someone else.

情境　從英文來看外國人使用此肢體語言的情境

A guy kept hitting on me at the bar tonight. He started by giving me a flirtatious smile and eventually asked for my phone number. I told him I would take his number, but I don't think I'm going to call him.

今晚在酒吧，有個傢伙一直對我調情。一開始，他給我一個調情的微笑，最後跟我要了電話號碼。我告訴他我會記下他的號碼，但我不認為我會打給他。

情境 5 Woman Playing with an Earring 女子擺弄耳環

指女子用食指和拇指扭或拉她耳垂上的耳環，這是緊張的表現，普遍是發生在一個人被另一個人吸引的時候。女生在第一次約會的時候，如果喜歡這個對象可能會這麼做。

外國女子擺弄耳環時，他們會說：

I'm having a good time.	我今天很高興。
I had a great time.	我今天過得很好。
Dinner was good!	晚餐很好吃！
I enjoyed seeing you again.	很高興能再見到你。
We should do this again.	我們應該再約見面。
Can I get your number?	可以給我你的號碼嗎？
Let's do this again.	我們下次再約吧。
I'd love to see you again.	我想要再見到你。
I enjoyed your company.	我喜歡你的陪伴。
It was fun to hang out with you.	跟你出去很好玩。

外國女子擺弄耳環時，你可以回：

Me too.	我也是。
I liked it!	我喜歡！
It looked great.	看起來很好。
I did, too.	我也很高興。
That's nice.	太好了。
I loved seeing you.	我很高興見到你。
Here's my number.	這是我的電話號碼。
I'll call you.	我會打給你。
Let's get together again.	我們再約見面吧！
I had fun, too!	我也很開心！

情境對話 中文可對照上方的例句

Dialogue 1

Ⓐ I'd love to see you again.
Ⓑ Me too.
Ⓐ Can I get your number?
Ⓑ Here's my number.

Dialogue 2

Ⓐ I enjoyed seeing you again.
Ⓑ I had fun, too!
Ⓐ We should do this again.
Ⓑ I'll call you.

情境 從英文來看外國人使用此肢體語言的情境

I had a date with Maria on Saturday. When we finished dinner and were talking, she told me she was having a really good time. I could tell she was nervous because she kept playing with her earring while talking to me.

我和 Maria 星期六去約會。我們吃完晚餐、在聊天的時候，她跟我說，她今天真的很開心。我可以看出來她很緊張，因為她在跟我講話的時候一直在玩耳環。

情境 6 **Kissing on the Lips 接吻**

指兩個人的嘴唇碰觸在一起。對彼此有重要意義的人會以在嘴唇上親吻來打招呼或說再見，而彼此相愛的人也通常會在唇上親吻來展現愛意。

外國人接吻時，他們會說：

Welcome home!	歡迎回家！
How are you?	你好嗎？
How was your day?	你今天過得如何？
It's good to see you.	見到你真好。
I'm glad you're here.	我很高興你在這裡。
You look great.	你看起來很漂亮。
Goodbye!	再見！
Have a good day!	祝你有美好的一天！
Drive safely!	小心駕駛！
I love you!	我愛你！

外國人接吻時，你可以回：

Thanks.	謝謝。
Good to see you.	很高興見到你。
It was good.	很好。
Hey there!	嘿，你好！
I'm so happy you're here.	我很高興你在這裡。
I've missed you.	我很想你。
Take care!	保重！
I'll see you soon.	我們很快會再見面。
Good night!	晚安！
I love you, too.	我也愛你。

情境對話 中文可對照上方的例句

Dialogue 1

Ⓐ Welcome home!
Ⓑ Thanks!
Ⓐ How was your day?
Ⓑ It was good.

Dialogue 2

Ⓐ Have a good day!
Ⓑ I'll see you soon.
Ⓐ I love you!
Ⓑ I love you, too.

情境 從英文來看外國人使用此肢體語言的情境

My husband was traveling for work last month. I didn't see him for almost three weeks. When I picked him up at the airport, I gave him a big kiss on the lips!

我先生上個月出差去了，我已經將近三個星期沒見到他了。當我在機場接他時，我在他的嘴唇上給他一個深吻！

情境 7 Kissing on Top of the Hand 親吻在手背上

把他人的一隻手握在手中,將他人的手舉到自己的嘴唇邊,親吻手背。通常在親吻手背時,會與接受者進行眼神交流。這是一種具有騎士風範的舉動,男性對女子有特別的心意時通常會這麼做,這個手勢表現出對他人的愛慕與熱情。

外國人親吻在手上時,他們會說:

It's nice to meet you.	很高興認識你。
I think you're amazing.	我覺得你很棒。
You're beautiful.	你真漂亮。
You look great.	你看起來很好看。
I'm happy to meet you.	我很高興見到你。
Thanks for coming.	謝謝你來。
I'm glad you're here.	我很高興你在這裡。
I'm happy we're together.	很高興我們在一起。
You look wonderful.	你看起來很棒。
You make me happy.	你讓我快樂。

外國人親吻在手上時,你可以回:

I'm happy to be here.	我很高興來到這裡。
I've missed you!	我很想你!
You look amazing!	你看起來很好!
Thanks for having me.	謝謝你邀請我。
I'm glad we could make it.	很高興我們能趕到。
You're a sight for sore eyes.	非常高興能見到你。
It's been so long!	好久不見了!
You're too kind.	你太客氣了。
You're so sweet!	你真可愛!
Thanks!	謝謝!

情境對話 中文可對照上方的例句

Dialogue 1

Ⓐ It's nice to meet you.
Ⓑ I'm happy to be here.
Ⓐ Thanks for coming.
Ⓑ Thanks for having me.

Dialogue 2

Ⓐ You look wonderful.
Ⓑ Thanks!
Ⓐ I'm glad you're here.
Ⓑ You're so sweet!

情境 從英文來看外國人使用此肢體語言的情境

I went out on a date with Brian last night. When he walked me to the door at the end of the night, he gave me a kiss on the top of my hand. It was so sweet!

昨晚我和 Brian 去約會。在晚上結束時他陪我走到家門口,並在我的手背上親了一下。那真是太甜蜜了!

情境 8 French Kiss 法式深吻（舌吻）

法式深吻是兩個人的嘴唇和舌頭接吻。這種親吻充滿激情與浪漫的氛圍，通常是伴侶在浪漫或性愛的情況下發生的。

外國人在舌吻時，他們會說：

I love you.	我愛你。
You look beautiful.	你看起來好美。
You mean so much to me.	你對我很重要。
I want to take you to bed.	我想帶你去床上。
I never want to leave.	我永遠都不想離開。
Can you stay here?	你可以留下來嗎？
Don't go anywhere!	不要去任何地方！
Kiss me again!	再吻我一次！
I want to be with you.	我想和你在一起。
I think we should go home.	我想我們該回家了。

外國人在舌吻時，你可以回：

I love you, too.	我也愛你。
You're too sweet.	你太可愛了。
Don't ever leave me.	永遠不要離開我。
I'm staying here!	我會待在這裡！
Lead the way.	帶路吧。
Let's go!	我們走吧！
I'll stay overnight.	我會留下過夜。
Come home with me.	和我一起回家。
Let's go to my place.	去我家吧。
You're so kind.	你人真好。

情境對話 中文可對照上方的例句

Dialogue 1

Ⓐ I love you.
Ⓑ I love you, too.
Ⓐ You mean so much to me.
Ⓑ You're so kind.

Dialogue 2

Ⓐ I want to take you to bed.
Ⓑ Lead the way.
Ⓐ I want to be with you.
Ⓑ Let's go!

情境 從英文來看外國人使用此肢體語言的情境

After the movie, Ryan leaned over and gave me a French kiss. He told me that he really liked me and wanted to date me. I told him I'd love to be his girlfriend.

看完電影後，Ryan 靠過來，給了我一個法式深吻。他跟我說他真的很喜歡我，想和我交往。我告訴他我願意當他的女朋友。

Butterfly Kiss 蝴蝶之吻

蝴蝶之吻是親吻某人時，兩人的臉部非常靠近，以至於一個人的睫毛刷在另一個人的臉上，讓對方的臉癢癢的。因為睫毛很輕，刷動時就像是蝴蝶的翅膀。對於彼此相愛的人來說，這是一個非常親暱的動作。

外國人在做蝴蝶之吻時，他們會說：

I love you.	我愛你。
You mean everything to me.	你是我的一切。
You're amazing.	你太美好了。
I think about you all the time.	我隨時都在想你。
I don't want to lose you.	我不想要失去你。
Please don't ever leave me.	永遠不要離開我。
Stay with me forever.	永遠和我在一起。
I'm in love with you.	我愛上你了。
Don't stop kissing me.	不要停止親我。
You're my favorite person.	你是我最喜歡的人。

外國人在做蝴蝶之吻時，你可以回：

I love you, too.	我也愛你。
I love you more!	我更愛你！
I'll never leave you.	我永遠不會離開你。
Will you marry me?	你願意嫁給我嗎？
Move in with me!	搬進來和我住！
Let's get married.	我們結婚吧。
I want to spend my life with you.	我想一生都和你在一起。
I can't stop thinking about you.	我無法停止想你。
I will!	我會的！
You're so sweet.	你真可愛。

情境對話 中文可對照上方的例句

Dialogue 1

Ⓐ You mean everything to me.
Ⓑ You're so sweet.
Ⓐ I'm in love with you.
Ⓑ I love you, too.

Dialogue 2

Ⓐ I want to spend my life with you.
Ⓑ Please don't ever leave me.
Ⓐ Will you marry me?
Ⓑ I will!

情境 從英文來看外國人使用此肢體語言的情境

Sometimes in the morning, my husband and I will give each other butterfly kisses before getting up. It's our way of letting the other person know how much they are loved.

有時候在早晨，我和我先生會在起床前給彼此蝴蝶之吻，這是我們讓對方知道自己有多麼被愛的方式。

情境 10 Touching someone's Cheek 觸摸他人的臉頰

指手臂伸向他人,並用手掌捧住那個人的臉頰。這個手勢表現出對愛人的關愛或愛慕。

外國人觸摸他人的臉頰時,他們會說:

I love you.	我愛你。
You're special.	你很特別。
You mean so much to me.	你對我很重要。
I want to be with you.	我想和你在一起。
I like you.	我喜歡你。
I think you're cute.	我覺得你很可愛。
You're sweet.	你很可愛。
I like being with you.	我喜歡和你在一起。
I'll help you out.	我會幫你的。
You're okay!	你很好啊!

外國人觸摸他人的臉頰時,你可以回:

I love you, too.	我也愛你。
I feel the same way.	我也有同感。
I do, too.	我也是。
I want to be with you, too.	我也想和你在一起。
Let's be together.	讓我們在一起。
I'd like to get to know you better.	我想更認識你。
Can we go out sometime?	我們有空可以出去嗎?
You're adorable.	你真可愛!
I like spending time with you.	我喜歡和你相處。
I feel that way, too.	我也有這種感覺。

情境對話 中文可對照上方的例句

Dialogue 1

Ⓐ I love you.
Ⓑ I love you, too.
Ⓐ You mean so much to me.
Ⓑ I feel the same way.

Dialogue 2

Ⓐ I like being with you.
Ⓑ I feel that way, too.
Ⓐ I think you're cute.
Ⓑ Can we go out sometime?

情境 從英文來看外國人使用此肢體語言的情境

My husband took me out for dinner last night. We talked about how much we still enjoy being with each other. He put his palm on my cheek and told me he loves me more than ever. It was so romantic!

我先生昨晚帶我出去吃晚餐。我們談到我們還是多麼喜愛和彼此在一起,他把手掌放在我的臉頰上,告訴我他比以往任何時候都愛我。真的好浪漫!

情境 11 Leaning Body towards Someone 身體靠向他人

當人們站著或坐著時，他們通常是挺直的姿勢。如果他們把身體靠向他人時，這是他們對那個人感興趣或受到他／她的吸引的一種動作。

外國人把身體靠著他人時，他們會說：

I think you're pretty.	我覺得你好漂亮。
I like you.	我喜歡你。
You smell good.	你真好聞。
I'd like to get to know you better.	我想要更了解你。
I think you're beautiful.	我覺得你很美。
You look nice tonight.	你今晚很好看。
Let me buy you a drink.	讓我請你一杯酒。
Can I get your number?	我可以跟你要電話嗎？
Here's my number.	這是我的電話號碼。
I'll call you.	我會打給你。

外國人把身體靠著他人時，你可以回：

Thanks!	謝謝！
Back up.	後退。
Give me some space.	離我遠一點。
You're too close.	你靠太近了。
That's really nice of you.	你人真好。
I'd love that!	我很樂意！
No, I'm sorry.	抱歉，不方便。
Sure!	好啊！
Let's get a drink sometime.	我們偶爾可以來喝一杯。
That's great!	太好了！

情境對話 中文可對照上方的例句

Dialogue 1

Ⓐ I think you're pretty.
Ⓑ Thanks!
Ⓐ Let me buy you a drink.
Ⓑ I'd love that!

Dialogue 2

Ⓐ Can I get your number?
Ⓑ Sure!
Ⓐ I'll call you.
Ⓑ That's great!

情境 從英文來看外國人使用此肢體語言的情境

I was sitting at the bar having a drink. A woman sat down next to me and started talking. She leaned towards me closely and asked for my number. I told her I wasn't interested.

我坐在吧檯區喝酒，有個女子坐在我旁邊並開始講話，她靠我非常近並跟我要電話，但我跟她說我沒興趣。

UNIT 32 Sexually attracting to someone 對他人有性趣

☞ **對他人有性趣時需要用到的動作，用英文要怎麼說呢？**

對喜歡的對象或情人有性趣時就會產生各種手勢和肢體動作，下列是對他人有性趣時會用到的手勢與肢體語言，請看圖片，並對照動作的英文和中文。

情境 1

Suggestive smile 挑逗的微笑

情境 2

Tongue licking lips 舌頭舔嘴唇

情境 3

Shaking butt back and forth
屁股往前、後扭動

情境 4

Pushing butt towards someone
屁股推向他人

情境 5

Slapping a butt 打屁股

情境 6

Pinching a butt 捏屁股

244

情境 1　Suggestive Smile 挑逗的微笑

這種微笑是嘴唇稍微上揚，下巴往下傾斜，眼睛則往上看著他人。做這個表情時可能會稍微轉頭，這是在對他人感性趣時最常出現的表情。但也可以是會心一笑，這代表人們知道即將發生的事，他們認為其他人都被蒙在鼓裡很好笑。

外國人露出挑逗的微笑時，他們會說：

I think you're handsome.	我覺得你很帥。
You're beautiful.	你好美。
I'd really like to get to know you.	我真的很想更認識你。
I find you funny.	我覺得你好有趣。
You're attractive.	你很迷人。
I like your dress.	我喜歡你的洋裝。
Can I have your number?	可以給我你的電話號碼嗎？
Let's grab a drink.	我們去喝一杯吧。
Would you like to get dinner?	你想去吃晚餐嗎？
I'd love to talk to him.	我很想和他說話。

外國人露出挑逗的微笑時，你可以回：

Thank you!	謝謝！
I think you're pretty cute, too.	我也覺得你很可愛。
I'd like that.	好啊。
Here's my number.	這是我的電話號碼。
I really like you.	我真的很喜歡你。
Text me.	傳訊息給我。
Give me a call sometime.	偶爾打電話給我。
I'd love to!	我很樂意！
Let's go!	我們走吧！
You should talk to him.	你應該和他說話。

情境對話　中文可對照上方的例句

Dialogue 1

Ⓐ I think you're handsome.
Ⓑ I think you're pretty cute, too.
Ⓐ Can I have your number?
Ⓑ Of course!

Dialogue 2

Ⓐ I'd really like to get to know you.
Ⓑ Give me a call sometime.
Ⓐ I will!
Ⓑ Here's my number.

情境　從英文來看外國人使用此肢體語言的情境

I saw a beautiful girl at a party last night. She gave me a suggestive smile, so I introduced myself to her. I asked her to dinner this week and she said yes!

我昨晚在派對上看到一個美麗的女孩，她給我一個挑逗的微笑，所以我向她介紹自己。我邀請她這星期一起吃晚餐，她答應了！

情境 2 Tongue Licking Lips 舌頭舔嘴唇

慢慢舔嘴唇可以表示對某種東西的渴望，通常是針對人們面前的東西（人或食物等）。而快速舔嘴唇則可能是感到壓力的表現，代表人們感到壓力很大，正在進行需要大量注意力的事情，或是處於緊繃的狀態。

外國人用舌頭舔嘴唇時，他們會說：

I want you.	我想要你。
I'd like to kiss you.	我想親你。
I think you're attractive.	我覺得你很迷人。
I want pizza!	我想要吃披薩！
Let's get ice cream.	我們去買冰淇淋。
I'll have the chocolate cake.	我要吃巧克力蛋糕。
That looks yummy!	看起來很好吃！
I'm hungry!	我餓了！
I'm focusing on this.	我正在專心處理這個。
I don't understand.	我不明白這一點。

外國人用舌頭舔嘴唇時，你可以回：

Do it.	來吧。
Kiss me then.	那就吻我吧。
You're cute, too.	你也很可愛。
Let's get some.	我們去買一些吧。
I'm in!	我也要！
Want to try it?	想試試嗎？
I'd like some, too.	我也想要一些。
It's delicious.	好好吃。
I'll leave you alone.	我會讓你獨處。
Let me help you.	讓我幫你吧。

情境對話　中文可對照上方的例句

Dialogue 1

Ⓐ I think you're attractive.
Ⓑ You're cute, too.
Ⓐ I'd like to kiss you.
Ⓑ Do it.

Dialogue 2

Ⓐ That looks yummy!
Ⓑ Want to try it?
Ⓐ No, that's okay.
Ⓑ It's delicious.

情境　從英文來看外國人使用此肢體語言的情境

My wife and I went out for dinner yesterday. We went to a new restaurant and the atmosphere there was really good. My wife looked at the food and licked her lips. I found her sexy when she did that.

我和我老婆昨天去吃晚餐，我們去了一間新開的餐廳，那裡的氣氛非常棒。我老婆看著食物舔著嘴唇，我覺得她那樣做的時候很性感。

情境3 Shaking Butt Back and Forth 屁股往前、後扭動

這個動作是指前後扭動屁股讓屁股搖擺，通常是用在跳舞的時候，並想要讓人把焦點放在屁股上。人們通常會在跳舞的時候加入這個動作吸引他人注意，可能是對他們的情人或是在性方面受到吸引的人。

外國人往前、後扭屁股時，他們會說：

I want you!	我想要你！
Watch me!	看著我！
Want to dance with me?	想要跟我跳舞嗎？
Come dance!	來跳舞吧！
Let's dance together!	我們一起跳舞吧！
I love this song!	我愛這首歌！
Can I get your number?	我可以跟你要電話嗎？
Call me sometime!	有空打給我！
I'll call you!	我會打給你！
Here's my number.	這是我的電話號碼。

外國人往前、後扭屁股時，你可以回：

Come over here.	過來這裡。
Let me touch you!	讓我摸你！
I'd love to!	好啊！
You're teasing me!	你在挑逗我！
Stay with me tonight.	今晚留下來陪我。
Let's get together sometime.	讓我們有些相處的時間。
Here's my number.	這是我的電話號碼。
Come home with me.	跟我回家。
Kiss me!	吻我！
Let's get out of here.	我們離開這裡吧。

情境對話 中文可對照上方的例句

Dialogue 1
Ⓐ I love this song!
Ⓑ It's a good one.
Ⓐ Come dance!
Ⓑ I'd love to!

Dialogue 2
Ⓐ I want you!
Ⓑ Come home with me.
Ⓐ Okay!
Ⓑ Let's get out of here.

情境 從英文來看外國人使用此肢體語言的情境

When we went to the bar on Saturday, there was a girl that kept talking to me. When she danced, she would shake her butt and look at me. I knew she liked me. I finally asked for her number.

我們週六去酒吧的時候，有個女生一直跟我聊天。她跳舞的時候一直扭動屁股、看著我，我知道她喜歡我，所以我最後跟她要了電話號碼。

Pushing Butt towards Someone 屁股推向他人

情境 4

當人們把屁股朝向其他人時,這可能是一種侮辱(像在說「kiss my ass」),或是誘惑喜歡的對象。通常女人會彎腰或翹屁股來吸引男人,這個男人可能是她們感興趣的對象、或是在交往的對象,而她們希望這個人能夠覺得她們很性感。

外國人的屁股推向他人時,他們會說:

What's up?	嗨!
What's your name?	你叫甚麼名字?
I'd like to get to know you better.	我想要更認識你。
Can I get your number?	我可以跟你要電話嗎?
Can I call you sometime?	我有時候可以打給你嗎?
Why don't you call me?	你為甚麼不打給我?
Here's my number.	這是我的電話號碼。
I think you're cute.	我覺得你很可愛。
You look handsome!	你看起來很帥。
You're hot!	你真性感!

外國人的屁股推向他人時,你可以回:

Let's dance!	去跳舞吧!
I think you look great.	我覺得你很好看!
Let's get out of here.	我們離開這裡吧!
Here's my number.	這是我的電話號碼。
I'll call you!	我會打給你!
Why don't we dance?	我們不如去跳舞吧?
Kiss me!	吻我!
Want to come to my place?	要去我家嗎?
You're too sweet.	你太貼心了。
Dance with me.	跟我跳舞吧!

情境對話 中文可對照上方的例句

Dialogue 1

Ⓐ You're hot!
Ⓑ You're too sweet.
Ⓐ Can I get your number?
Ⓑ Here's my number.

Dialogue 2

Ⓐ I'd like to get to know you better.
Ⓑ Want to come to my place?
Ⓐ Yes!
Ⓑ Let's go.

情境 從英文來看外國人使用此肢體語言的情境

There was a girl at the party that kept making eye contact with me. She finally came over by me and leaned in to talk to the bartender. She did it so her butt would stick out right in front of me. She was hot! We ended up leaving together later that night.

派對上有個女孩一直和我對看,她終於走到我旁邊,往前傾跟調酒師講話。她這樣做的時候屁股會剛好面向我,真的很性感!我們當晚最後一起離開了。

情境 5 Slapping a Butt 打屁股

這個動作是指人們用空著的手打另一個人的屁股。當這個動作發生在兩個親近的人之間，代表打屁股的人對另一個人有性趣。運動員之間也會做這個動作，和擊掌很相似，這代表做得好或是好球的意思。

外國人在打屁股時，他們會說：

We should go back to my place.	我們應該要回我家。
I want you.	我想要你。
Let's get out of here.	我們離開這裡吧！
I'm taking you to my place.	我要帶你回我家。
Let's go to bed!	去床上吧！
Nice game!	很不錯的比賽！
Good game!	很棒的比賽！
Nice shot!	好球！
You did great.	你表現得很好。
You played well, too!	你也打得很好！

外國人在打屁股時，你可以回：

Let's go!	走吧！
Let's do it.	我們來做吧！
I'll follow you.	我跟著你走。
You're turning me on!	你讓我慾火焚身！
Take me to bed!	帶我去床上！
You played great.	你打得真好。
Good game!	精采的比賽！
Give me five!	擊掌！
Nice hit!	好球！
Nice job today.	你今天打得真好。

情境對話 中文可對照上方的例句

Dialogue 1

Ⓐ I want you.
Ⓑ You're turning me on!
Ⓐ We should go back to my place.
Ⓑ Let's go!

Dialogue 2

Ⓐ Good game!
Ⓑ You played great.
Ⓐ You played well, too.
Ⓑ Thanks!

情境 從英文來看外國人使用此肢體語言的情境

I was making dinner when my husband got home from work. He slapped my butt and gave me a big kiss. We ended up going to bed instead of finishing dinner.

我在準備晚餐的時候，我先生下班回到家。他打我的屁股並給我熱烈地親吻，我們最後進了臥室而沒有吃晚餐。

情境 6 **Pinching a Butt 捏屁股**

這個動作是指用食指和拇指捏另一個人的屁股，通常用在親密的人之間，這代表捏的人想要性並想讓對方知道。

外國人在捏屁股時，他們會說：

I want you.	我想要你。
I'm going to kiss you.	我要親你。
Take your clothes off.	把你的衣服脫掉。
I want to take you to bed.	我要帶你去床上。
Let's go to bed.	去床上吧。
Let's go back to my place.	去我家吧！
Do you want to leave?	你想離開了嗎？
Let's get out of here.	我們離開這裡吧！
I'm coming home with you.	我要跟你回家。
Let's have sex!	來做愛吧！

外國人在捏屁股時，你可以回：

I want you, too.	我也想要你。
I want you to kiss me.	我想要你親我。
Kiss me!	吻我！
Let's get out of here.	我們離開這裡吧！
Let's go somewhere quiet.	我們去安靜的地方。
I want to leave with you.	我想跟你離開。
Take me home.	帶我回家。
Let's get out of these clothes.	我們把衣服脫了。
I want to touch you.	我想要摸你。
You're so beautiful.	你真美。

情境對話 中文可對照上方的例句

Dialogue 1

Ⓐ I want to take you to bed.
Ⓑ I want you, too.
Ⓐ Take your clothes off.
Ⓑ I want to touch you.

Dialogue 2

Ⓐ I want you.
Ⓑ Let's get out of here.
Ⓐ Let's go back to my place.
Ⓑ Take me home.

情境 從英文來看外國人使用此肢體語言的情境

My wife and I were at a bar. After a few drinks, she got really touchy and pinched my butt. She asked if I wanted to go somewhere private. We ended up having sex in my car!

我老婆和我去了酒吧。喝了幾杯酒之後，她變得很愛毛手毛腳，還捏我的屁股。又問我要不要去隱密的地方，最後我們在車上做了！

Not feeling comfortable
身體不太舒服

☞ **身體不太舒服時需要用到的動作，用英文要怎麼說呢？**

身體不太舒服時就會產生各種手勢和肢體動作，下列是身體不太舒服時會用到的手勢與肢體語言，請看圖片，並對照動作的英文和中文。

情境 1

Watering eyes 眼睛濕潤

情境 2

Cupping the neck with two hands
雙手握住脖子

情境 3

Hand touching someone's forehead
手放在他人的額頭上

情境 4

Fever sweating 發燒出汗

情境 5

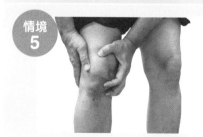

Rubbing knee or ankle 揉膝蓋或腳踝

情境 6

Ringing ears 耳鳴

情境 1 Watering Eyes 眼睛濕潤

眼睛濕潤是指人們的眼睛分泌淚水，卻不是在哭泣。當人的眼中有異物（例如：睫毛）或因過敏而不適時，眼眶就會濕潤。

外國人的眼睛濕潤時，他們會說：

Is it dusty in here?	這裡灰塵很多嗎？
Do I have something in my eye?	我的眼睛裡是不是有東西？
Is there an eyelash in my eye?	我的眼睛裡是不是有根睫毛？
Do you have allergy medicine?	你有過敏藥嗎？
Is my makeup running?	我的妝花了嗎？
Do my eyes look red?	我的眼睛很紅嗎？
My eyes itch.	我的眼睛好癢。
I keep rubbing my eyes.	我一直在揉眼睛。
My eyes are sore.	我的眼睛很痛。
I can't see well.	我看不太清楚。

外國人的眼睛濕潤時，你可以回：

What's wrong?	怎麼了嗎？
Your eyes are red.	你的眼睛好紅。
You have an eyelash in it.	你眼睛裡有根睫毛。
Is there something in your eye?	你的眼睛裡有東西嗎？
Do you have allergies?	你有過敏嗎？
Your makeup is fine.	你沒有脫妝。
Your eyes are watering.	你的眼睛濕濕的。
I don't see anything in your eye.	我沒看到你眼裡有任何東西。
Don't rub them.	不要揉眼睛。
Do you need eye drops?	你需要滴眼藥水嗎？

情境對話　中文可對照上方的例句

Dialogue 1

Ⓐ Do I have something in my eye?
Ⓑ I don't see anything in your eye.
Ⓐ My eyes are sore.
Ⓑ Do you need eye drops?

Dialogue 2

Ⓐ Is my makeup running?
Ⓑ Your makeup is fine.
Ⓐ My eyes itch.
Ⓑ Your eyes are red.

情境　從英文來看外國人使用此肢體語言的情境

My eye was watering really bad in school. Mark looked at it for me and he found an eyelash in it.

在學校的時候，我的眼睛流眼淚流得嚴重，Mark 看了一下我的眼睛，發現裡面有根睫毛。

情境 2 Cupping Neck with two Hands 雙手握住脖子

這個手勢是指雙臂交叉，雙手繞在脖子上，手掌拱起並握住脖子。這在全世界都是指窒息的意思，如果有人做出這個手勢，就表示他無法呼吸，非常緊急，需要立刻急救！

外國人用雙手握住脖子時，他們會說：

Help!	救命！
Call for help!	快去求救！
Call an ambulance!	叫救護車！
He needs help!	他需要幫助！
He's choking!	他噎到了！
She can't breathe!	她不能呼吸！
I need help!	我需要幫助！
Hurry up!	趕快！
They aren't breathing!	他們沒有呼吸了！
They're choking!	他們要窒息了！

外國人用雙手握住脖子時，你可以回：

I called!	我打電話了！
I'll call for help.	我會去求救。
I know CPR!	我會心肺復甦術！
I can help.	我可以幫忙。
I'm a doctor!	我是醫生！
Let me have a look.	讓我看一下。
What can I do?	我要怎麼做？
She's going to be fine.	她會沒事的。
I'll do CPR.	我要做心肺復甦術。
The ambulance is coming.	救護車已經路上了。

情境對話 中文可對照上方的例句

Dialogue 1

Ⓐ Call an ambulance!
Ⓑ I called!
Ⓐ She can't breathe!
Ⓑ The ambulance is coming.

Dialogue 2

Ⓐ I need help!
Ⓑ What's wrong?
Ⓐ They aren't breathing!
Ⓑ I'll do CPR.

情境 從英文來看外國人使用此肢體語言的情境

We were eating dinner at a restaurant last night. A lady at the table next to us coughed and started grabbing her neck with her hands. She was choking on her food. I called an ambulance and my husband kept hitting her on the back to try to help. She eventually coughed up what she was choking on and then she felt better. It was so scary!

昨天晚上我們在一家餐廳吃晚餐，我們隔壁桌的一位女士咳嗽，接著開始用雙手握住自己的脖子，她被食物噎到了。我叫了救護車，我先生不斷打她的背，試著幫助她。最終她把噎住的東西咳了出來，她後來好多了，真是太可怕了！

情境 3
Hand Touching someone's Forehead
手觸摸他人的額頭

這個手勢是把手掌放在另一個人的前額，拱起手讓整個手掌都包覆在對方的額頭上，這是確認發燒的方式。當孩子說自己覺得不舒服，或是看起來像生病時，許多父母就會對孩子這樣做。如果額頭發燙，就可能是發燒了。

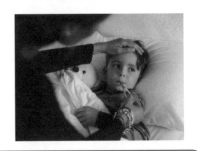

外國人的手摸他人的額頭時，他們會說：

Do you feel okay?	你還好嗎？
You look pale.	你的臉色很蒼白。
Are you sick?	你生病了嗎？
Do you feel sick?	你覺得不舒服嗎？
Do you have a fever?	你發燒了嗎？
Do you feel warm?	你感到悶熱嗎？
What's wrong?	怎麼了？
What's bothering you?	你哪裡不舒服？
Let me check you.	讓我看看你。
You feel hot.	你在發燙。

外國人的手摸他人的額頭時，你可以回：

I'm okay.	我很好。
I feel okay.	我感覺還好。
I'm alright.	我沒事。
I feel hot.	我覺得很熱。
I feel sick.	我覺得不舒服。
I'm going to throw up!	我快要吐了！
I'm really cold!	我真的好冷！
My tummy hurts.	我的肚子好痛。
I have a headache.	我頭痛。
I have the flu.	我得到流感。

情境對話 中文可對照上方的例句

Dialogue 1

Ⓐ Do you feel okay?

Ⓑ I'm okay.

Ⓐ You look pale.

Ⓑ I feel okay.

Dialogue 2

Ⓐ Do you have a fever?

Ⓑ I feel hot.

Ⓐ What's bothering you?

Ⓑ I have a headache.

情境 從英文來看外國人使用此肢體語言的情境

My son looked really pale tonight. I checked his forehead with my hand, and he felt really warm. I'm worried he may be getting sick.

我兒子今晚的臉色看起來很蒼白。我用手檢查了他的額頭，他覺得很悶熱，我擔心他可能要生病了。

情境 4 Fever Sweating 發燒出汗

人在生病發燒的時候，體溫比平常還高，身體在發燒時透過顫抖來做出反應，這會散發更高的身體熱能，而汗水是身體熱能增加的結果。

外國人在發燒時流汗，他們會說：

I have the flu.	我得到流感。
I'm sick.	我病了。
I don't feel good.	我覺得不舒服。
I have a fever.	我發燒了。
I'm running a temperature.	我的體溫在升高。
I feel awful.	我感覺糟透了。
I called in sick.	我打電話請了病假。
I can't work today.	我今天無法工作。
I'm not feeling well.	我覺得不舒服。
I have a virus.	我感染病毒。

外國人在發燒時流汗，你可以回：

Oh no!	哦，不！
That's terrible.	太可怕了。
That's not good.	這不太好。
What's wrong?	怎麼了？
Will you be okay?	你會好點嗎？
Do you need a doctor?	你需要看醫生嗎？
I'll get you some water.	我給你倒杯水。
Go back to bed.	回去床上躺著。
Do you need anything?	你需要甚麼嗎？
I'll get you a blanket.	我給你拿條毯子來。

情境對話　中文可對照上方的例句

Dialogue 1
Ⓐ I'm sick.
Ⓑ What's wrong?
Ⓐ I have the flu.
Ⓑ That's terrible.

Dialogue 2
Ⓐ I don't feel good.
Ⓑ I'm sorry to hear that.
Ⓐ I have a fever.
Ⓑ Go back to bed.

情境　從英文來看外國人使用此肢體語言的情境

I was so sick last week. I think I had the flu. I had a fever for a few days. I would go from being really cold to hot and sweating. It was awful!

上週我病得很重，我想我得了流感。我發燒了幾天，我的身體忽冷忽熱，流了一身汗。那真是太慘了！

情境 5　Rubbing Knee or Ankle 揉膝蓋或腳踝

人們受傷時會快速抓住身體的某個部位（例如膝蓋或腳踝），並一遍又一遍地搓揉，通常他們的臉上有痛苦的表情，甚至在哭泣，這表示他們所觸碰的部位受了傷，搓揉那裡可以減輕疼痛。

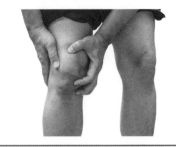

外國人在揉膝蓋或腳踝時，他們會說：

Ouch!	哎喲！
That hurts!	好痛！
I hurt my foot!	我把我的腳弄傷了！
I stubbed my toe!	我踢到腳趾了！
I twisted my ankle!	我扭到腳踝了！
My knee hurts!	我的膝蓋好痛！
I felt it pop!	我覺得它折到了！
I think I broke it.	我想我把它弄斷了。
It hurts bad.	超痛。
I can't stand up!	我站不起來！

外國人在揉膝蓋或腳踝時，你可以回：

Are you alright?	你還好嗎？
Did you get hurt?	你受傷了嗎？
Did you hurt yourself?	你傷到了自己嗎？
What happened?	發生了甚麼事？
Can I help you?	我能幫你嗎？
I'll get you some ice.	我給你拿點冰塊。
I'll get a bandage.	我去拿繃帶。
I'll call for help.	我去找人來幫忙。
I'll take you to the hospital.	我會帶你去醫院。
Let's go see the doctor.	我們去看醫生吧。

情境對話　中文可對照上方的例句

Dialogue 1

Ⓐ Ouch!

Ⓑ What happened?

Ⓐ I stubbed my toe!

Ⓑ That hurts!

Dialogue 2

Ⓐ My knee hurts!

Ⓑ Are you alright?

Ⓐ I can't stand up!

Ⓑ Can I help you?

情境　從英文來看外國人使用此肢體語言的情境

I found John in the backyard. He was rubbing his knee, and it was bruised and swollen. He said he fell when he was mowing the grass. I'm going to take him to the doctor to make sure he's okay.

我在後院找到了 John，他那時在搓揉瘀青、腫脹的膝蓋。他說他在割草的時候摔倒了，我要帶他去看醫生，以確保他沒事。

情境 6　Ringing Ears 耳鳴

耳鳴是指耳朵聽到外在以外的聲音，聲音可能是鈴鈴聲、嗡嗡聲，或卡嗒聲。聽到不真實的聲音代表人們的耳朵可能有問題，必須讓醫生檢查出原因。

外國人在耳鳴時，他們會說：

Did you hear that?	你有聽到嗎？
What was that?	那是甚麼聲音啊？
I hear something.	我聽到一些聲音。
Do you hear anything?	你有聽到甚麼嗎？
My ears are ringing.	我耳朵在耳鳴。
I keep hearing something.	我一直聽到一些聲音。
Did you hear that click?	你有聽到卡嗒聲嗎？
I think my ears are ringing.	我想我的耳朵在耳鳴。
I need to see a doctor for my ears.	我的耳朵需要看醫生。
My ears always ring.	我耳朵一直在耳鳴。

外國人在耳鳴時，你可以回：

What?	甚麼？
Hear what?	聽到甚麼？
I don't hear anything.	我沒有聽到任何聲音。
No, I didn't.	不，我沒有。
Why do they do that?	為甚麼會這樣？
What is it?	那是甚麼？
I hear it, too.	我也聽到了。
Is it loud?	很大聲嗎？
Are you okay?	你還好嗎？
That's annoying!	這樣真的很困擾。

情境對話　中文可對照上方的例句

Dialogue 1
Ⓐ What was that?
Ⓑ What?
Ⓐ Did you hear that.
Ⓑ No, I didn't.

Dialogue 2
Ⓐ I need to see a doctor for my ears.
Ⓑ What's wrong?
Ⓐ My ears always ring.
Ⓑ Why do they do that?

情境　從英文來看外國人使用此肢體語言的情境

My husband has a hard time hearing. He says it's because his ears always ring. I think he just can't hear very well. I told him he needs to see a doctor for it.

我先生很難聽得很清楚，他說這是因為他的耳朵一直在耳鳴。我覺得他只是沒辦法聽得很清楚，所以我告訴他需要為此去看醫生。

Body feeling hot or cold 身體感覺熱或冷

☞ **身體感覺熱或冷時需要用到的動作，用英文要怎麼說呢？**

身體感覺熱或冷時就會產生各種手勢和肢體動作，下列是身體感覺熱或冷時會用到的手勢與肢體語言，請看圖片，並對照動作的英文和中文。

情境 1

Excessive heat sweating 太熱而流汗

情境 2

Sweating from movement 在運動中流汗

情境 3

Runny nose 流鼻涕（水）

情境 4

Shoulders pushed up and arms crossed 肩膀上推、雙臂交叉

情境 5

Shivering body 身體顫抖

情境 6

Chattering teeth 牙齒顫抖

情境 1 Excessive Heat Sweating 太熱而流汗

外面很熱時，我們的身體自然會產出汗水。流汗很重要，因為汗水中的水分會蒸發，並幫助身體降溫。

外國人太熱而流汗時，他們會說：

It's so hot outside.	外面好熱。
It's sweltering outside.	外面好悶熱。
The humidity is awful.	太潮濕了。
The gym is so hot.	體育館太熱了。
I'm really warm.	我真的覺得很悶。
I can't cool off.	我不能平靜下來。
The sun makes it hot.	太陽讓這裡很熱。
It's too hot to be outside.	外面熱到不能出去。
I was mowing.	我當時在割草。
It's 100 degrees Fahrenheit!	華氏 100 度了！

外國人太熱而流汗時，你可以回：

Are you okay?	你還好嗎？
You should sit down.	你應該坐下來。
Take a break.	休息一下。
Let's take a break.	讓我們休息一下。
Find some shade.	找陰影處吧。
Let's go inside.	我們進去裡面吧。
It's cooler inside.	裡面比較涼。
I'll get some water.	我去倒些水。
Don't work so hard.	不要做得太辛苦。
You need to relax.	你需要放輕鬆。

情境對話 中文可對照上方的例句

Dialogue 1
Ⓐ It's so hot outside.
Ⓑ Take a break.
Ⓐ I was mowing.
Ⓑ I'll get some water.

Dialogue 2
Ⓐ I'm really warm.
Ⓑ Let's take a break.
Ⓐ I need to sit down.
Ⓑ Find some shade.

情境 從英文來看外國人使用此肢體語言的情境

When I got home, Andrew was sitting on the porch, covered in sweat. He looked awful! He had just finished mowing the grass. I told him it was too hot to work outside today, but he did it anyway.

我回到家時，Andrew 坐在門廊上，他滿身大汗。他看起來糟透了！他剛割完草。我告訴他今天熱到不能在外面工作，但他還是這麼做了。

情境 2 Sweating from Movement 在運動中流汗

在運動中流汗在運動員和正在運動的人身上很常見，而這在花費大量體力做某事時也很常見。例如，打掃房屋、割草、或洗車，都可能使人們流汗。

外國人在運動中流汗時，他們會說：

I just went for a run.	我剛剛去跑步了。
I was mowing the grass.	我除草了。
I was playing basketball.	我打籃球了。
I'm riding my bike.	我正在騎自行車。
I'm working out.	我在健身。
I was at the gym.	我之前在體育館。
I'm on the treadmill.	我在跑跑步機。
I played tennis.	我打了網球。
I was walking the dog.	我遛了狗。
I was working in the garden.	我在花園裡工作。

外國人在運動中流汗時，你可以回：

You stink!	你好臭！
You're sweaty.	你流好多汗。
You're so gross.	你太噁心了。
Where were you?	你在哪裡？
How was your workout?	你的健身如何呢？
How do you feel?	你感覺如何？
Are you tired?	你累了嗎？
You should drink something.	你應該喝點東西。
Hit the showers.	去淋浴吧。
That sounds fun!	聽起來很有趣！

情境對話 中文可對照上方的例句

Dialogue 1

Ⓐ You stink!

Ⓑ I was playing basketball.

Ⓐ Hit the showers.

Ⓑ Sorry!

Dialogue 2

Ⓐ I was working in the garden.

Ⓑ You're sweaty.

Ⓐ It's hot outside.

Ⓑ You should drink something.

情境 從英文來看外國人使用此肢體語言的情境

I ran into Ryan at the gym. I had just finished my run and was so sweaty and gross. He wanted to give me a hug to say hello, but I told him not to.

我在體育館遇到 Ryan。我才剛跑完步、流很多汗、一身汗味。他想擁抱我來打個招呼，但我叫他不要這樣。

情境 3 Runny Nose 流鼻涕（水）

鼻子和鼻竇有過多的分泌物就會流鼻涕或鼻水。這種分泌物順著鼻子流下，讓人們一直發出吸鼻子的聲音或用紙巾擤鼻子。這可能代表人們得到感冒或是生病了，但也可能代表他們正對某件事感到沮喪。

外國人流鼻水時，他們會說：

I have a cold.	我感冒了。
I need a tissue.	我需要一張面紙。
Do you have a tissue?	你有一張面紙嗎？
I need to blow my nose.	我需要擤鼻涕。
I'm feeling sad.	我很傷心。
I'm upset.	我很失望。
I'm having a bad day.	我今天過得很糟糕。
My boyfriend dumped me.	我男友把我甩了。
I lost my job.	我丟了工作。
I got fired!	我被開除了！

外國人流鼻水時，你可以回：

That's a bummer.	真是令人討厭。
That stinks.	太糟糕了。
Here's a tissue.	這裡有一張面紙。
That's too bad.	這太糟糕了。
What's wrong?	怎麼了？
Don't be sad.	不要難過。
Are you okay?	你還好嗎？
Do you need a tissue?	你需要一張面紙嗎？
Can I get you something?	我能幫你拿點甚麼嗎？
I'm sorry!	我很抱歉！

情境對話　中文可對照上方的例句

Dialogue 1

Ⓐ I'm feeling sad.
Ⓑ What's wrong?
Ⓐ My boyfriend dumped me.
Ⓑ That stinks.

Dialogue 2

Ⓐ I'm having a bad day.
Ⓑ Are you okay?
Ⓐ I lost my job.
Ⓑ I'm sorry!

情境　從英文來看外國人使用此肢體語言的情境

I haven't been feeling well for a few days. I have a runny nose and I keep sneezing. I think I have a cold.

這幾天以來我一直不太舒服，我流鼻涕，又一直打噴嚏。我想我感冒了。

情境 4

Shoulders Pushed up and Arms Closed
肩膀上推、雙臂交叉

這是指將手臂環繞在身體前方,雙手各自握住另一隻手臂的上臂,肩膀聳起後固定住,身體通常會拱著背向前彎。這個姿勢表示這個人覺得很冷,正在嘗試讓身體溫暖。

外國人肩膀上推、雙臂交叉時,他們會說:	
I'm freezing!	我要凍僵了!
Is it cold in here?	這裡很冷嗎?
Are you cold?	你很冷嗎?
I'm chilly.	我很冷。
It's cold outside.	外面很冷。
Start a fire!	生火吧!
Turn the heat up.	調高熱度。
I need a sweater.	我需要一件毛衣。
Get me a blanket.	給我蓋一條毯子。
I'm shivering!	我在發抖!

外國人肩膀上推、雙臂交叉時,你可以回:	
I'm cold, too.	我也很冷。
I can't warm up.	我沒辦法暖起來。
I'll start a fire.	我來升火。
Here's a blanket.	毯子在這裡。
It's not that cold.	沒有那麼冷。
Yes, it's cold.	是的,很冷。
I turned it up.	我把它開大了。
I think it's fine.	我認為很好。
Here you go.	拿去。
You're crazy.	你瘋了。

情境對話 中文可對照上方的例句

Dialogue 1

Ⓐ Is it cold in here?

Ⓑ I'm cold, too.

Ⓐ I'm shivering!

Ⓑ I'll start a fire.

Dialogue 2

Ⓐ It's cold outside.

Ⓑ It's not that cold.

Ⓐ Get me a blanket.

Ⓑ You're crazy.

情境 從英文來看外國人使用此肢體語言的情境

I could tell that Louise was cold. She had her arms crossed and her shoulders were raised. I offered to let her borrow my coat, but she wouldn't.

我看得出來 Louise 很冷。她把雙臂交叉,肩膀高聳。我跟她說她可以先穿我的外套,但她不願意。

情境 5 Shivering Body 身體顫抖

當人們在顫抖時，他們整個身體都在抖動。他們通常會把手臂交叉、身體往前，腿緊緊交纏而肩膀成聳肩的狀態，這代表他們非常冷。

外國人身體顫抖時，他們會說：

I'm freezing!	我快凍死了！
I'm cold!	我好冷！
It's cold in here!	這裡好冷！
Are you cold?	你很冷嗎？
I'm chilly!	我覺得好冷！
I need a coat.	我需要一件大衣。
Let me grab a blanket.	讓我拿一條毯子。
I'm going to start a fire.	我要來生火。
Let me turn the heat up.	讓我把暖氣調高。
I need to warm up!	我需要要暖起來！

外國人身體顫抖時，你可以回：

I'll turn the heat on.	我會把暖氣打開。
I'll get you a blanket.	我幫你拿一條毯子。
Do you need a coat?	你需要一件大衣嗎？
Get a sweater!	去穿毛衣！
I'm okay.	我很好。
I'll start a fire.	我去生火。
Here's a blanket.	這裡有條毯子。
I'm chilly!	我覺得好冷！
Are you cold?	你很冷嗎？
It's really chilly today!	今天真的很冷！

情境對話　中文可對照上方的例句

Dialogue 1

Ⓐ I'm freezing!

Ⓑ I'll turn the heat on.

Ⓐ Are you cold?

Ⓑ I'm okay.

Dialogue 2

Ⓐ It's cold in here!

Ⓑ Do you need a coat?

Ⓐ Let me grab a blanket.

Ⓑ Here's a blanket.

情境　從英文來看外國人使用此肢體語言的情境

We went camping last weekend. One evening, my son was shivering, so I moved his chair closer to the fire. He warmed up right away.

我們上周末去露營，有天晚上我兒子在顫抖，所以我把他的椅子靠近營火，他馬上就覺得溫暖了。

Chattering Teeth 牙齒顫抖

這個動作是下巴快速上下移動，造成牙齒反覆發出喀嗒聲。這稱為牙齒顫抖，通常會伴隨著身體發抖。可能指出這個人感到非常害怕或身體覺得很冷。

外國人牙齒顫抖時，他們會說：

I'm petrified.	我嚇呆了。
I'm so scared.	我好害怕。
The movie was scary.	這部電影很恐怖。
I'm freezing!	我快凍僵了！
It's cold in here!	這裡好冷喔！
Turn the heat on.	把暖氣打開。
Start a fire!	來升火吧！
I need a blanket!	我需要一條毛毯！
I'm so cold.	我好冷喔。
I'm shivering!	我在發抖！

外國人牙齒顫抖時，你可以回：

Don't be scared!	不要害怕。
You'll be fine.	你會沒事的。
Everything will work out.	每件事都能解決的。
What's the matter?	怎麼了？
What's wrong?	發生甚麼事？
Borrow my jacket.	我借你我的外套。
Here's a sweater!	這裡有一件毛衣！
You can share my blanket!	你可以跟我一起蓋毯子！
Sit over here.	過來這裡坐著。
I'll warm you up.	我會讓你暖起來。

情境對話　中文可對照上方的例句

Dialogue 1

Ⓐ I'm so scared.
Ⓑ What's the matter?
Ⓐ The movie was scary.
Ⓑ You'll be fine.

Dialogue 2

Ⓐ I'm so cold.
Ⓑ You can share my blanket!
Ⓐ I'm shivering!
Ⓑ I'll warm you up.

情境　從英文來看外國人使用此肢體語言的情境

I went to a wedding over the weekend. It was outside, and the weather was bad. It was really chilly and cloudy. I was so cold in my dress! Even my teeth were chattering. Ryan let me borrow his suit jacket to warm up.

這周末我參加一場婚禮，是辦在戶外的婚禮，而且天氣不好，非常冷又烏雲密布。我只穿著禮服，感覺非常冷！我的牙齒甚至在顫抖。Ryan 讓我借穿他的西裝外套取暖。

Other gestures
其他手勢 / 肢體

UNIT 35

☞ **在其他情境下需要用到的動作，用英文要怎麼說呢？**

在慶祝、祝福及吃美食時就會產生各種手勢和肢體動作，下列是慶祝、祝福、吃美食時會用到的手勢與肢體語言，請看圖片，並對照動作的英文和中文。

情境 1

Congratulatory hug 祝賀的擁抱

情境 2

High five hands 擊掌

情境 3

Raised eyebrows 眉毛上揚

情境 4

Index and middle fingers crossed
食指和中指交叉

情境 5

Kissing fingertips 親吻手指頭

情境 6

Pointing nose in the air and sniffing
鼻子指向空氣、聞一下

情境 1 Congratulatory Hug 祝賀的擁抱

祝賀的擁抱是對於親友生命中的大事、成功或努力（例如：婚禮、生子、畢業、升遷、中大獎）所給予的讚美。這是兩人之間熱切而愉快的擁抱，伸出的雙臂做出擁抱的邀請，接著雙方用手臂環繞彼此，高度約在上背部，並用力收緊手臂，經常加上在背部多次充滿活力的拍打。

外國人在慶祝時擁抱，他們會說：

I'm so happy for you!	我真為你高興！
Congratulations!	恭喜！
You did it!	你做到了！
Way to go!	太棒了！
We're so proud of you!	我們為你驕傲！
What an achievement!	真棒的成就！
How fantastic for you!	你真是太棒了！
You deserve it!	這是你應得的！
What a great day!	真棒的一天！
I knew you could do it!	我就知道你可以！

外國人在慶祝時擁抱，你可以回：

Thank you!	謝謝！
Thank you so much.	非常感謝。
I'm so excited.	我很興奮。
I'm so proud of myself.	我為自己感到驕傲。
I feel really proud.	我感到非常自豪。
I'm thrilled.	我好激動。
I feel amazing.	我感覺很驚喜。
I'm pumped up!	我超開心的！
I feel good about it.	我覺得這樣好棒。
You're so kind.	你人真好。

情境對話　中文可對照上方的例句

Dialogue 1

Ⓐ Congratulations!

Ⓑ Thank you!

Ⓐ You deserve it!

Ⓑ I'm so proud of myself.

Dialogue 2

Ⓐ I knew you could do it!

Ⓑ Thank you so much!

Ⓐ We're so proud of you!

Ⓑ I feel amazing.

情境　從英文來看外國人使用此肢體語言的情境

I got a new job today. My husband was so happy for me. He gave me a big hug and told me he was proud of me.

今天我找到新工作了，我先生很為我高興，他給了我一個大大的擁抱，並告訴我他為我感到驕傲。

情境 2 High Five Hands 擊掌

擊掌是用於慶祝的手勢，由兩人將手臂抬高，並以張開的手掌互相拍擊，可能只用單手，或是雙手都用上。擊掌也可以用來問候，而運動員會用擊掌來慶祝比賽的勝利、或表現很好的比賽。其他人也會用擊掌來慶祝某件事，例如：喜歡的球隊贏得比賽、通過艱難的測驗、或是找到新工作等。

外國人在擊掌時，他們會說：

Good job!	做得好！
Nice work!	幹得好！
You did great.	你做得很棒。
You did it!	你做到了！
Good shot!	好球！
Nice hit!	漂亮！
You rock!	你超棒！
I'm proud of you!	我以你為榮！
You're doing good!	你做得很好！
Keep it up!	繼續保持！

外國人在擊掌時，你可以回：

Thanks!	謝謝！
Thank you!	謝謝你！
I gave it my all.	我全力以赴了。
I tried my best.	我盡力了。
I was so happy.	我很開心。
We all did great.	我們都做得很好。
I'm proud of myself.	我為自己感到驕傲。
You did great, too.	你也做得很好。
You too!	你也是！
I'll keep trying.	我會繼續努力。

情境對話　中文可對照上方的例句

Dialogue 1

Ⓐ Good job!

Ⓑ Thanks!

Ⓐ I'm proud of you.

Ⓑ You did great, too.

Dialogue 2

Ⓐ Good shot!

Ⓑ I tried my best.

Ⓐ Keep it up.

Ⓑ Thank you!

情境　從英文來看外國人使用此肢體語言的情境

We won our baseball game tonight. I had a really good hit and felt really proud of myself for how I played. After the game, everyone gave each other high-five's and hugs.

今晚我們贏得了棒球比賽，我打出一個超棒的安打，我為自己的表現感到自豪。比賽結束後，每個人都互相擊掌、擁抱。

情境 3 **Raised Eyebrows 眉毛上揚**

眉毛上揚是指抬起眉毛、皺起額頭、並且誇張地睜大眼睛，這表示人們感到很驚訝。眉毛抬得越高，就表示越驚訝。驚訝有可能是因為好事，例如：收到生日禮物或好消息，但也可能是因為壞事，例如：失去工作，或被重要的人拋棄。

外國人的眉毛上揚時，他們會說：

I'm so surprised!	我好驚訝！
I can't believe it!	我無法相信！
Is this for real?	這是真的嗎？
I'm shocked!	我感到震驚！
I don't believe my eyes!	我不相信我的眼睛！
No way!	不可能！
I don't know what to say!	我不知道該說甚麼！
I'm at a loss for words.	我說不出話了。
This can't be happening!	這不可能發生！
How can this be?	怎麼會這樣？

外國人的眉毛上揚時，你可以回：

We're serious.	我們是認真的。
This is really happening!	這真的發生了！
This is for you.	這是給你的。
Surprise!	驚喜！
You deserve it.	這是你應得的。
You earned this.	這是你得到的。
We got you!	我們嚇到你了！
You didn't know?	你不知道嗎？
Did we surprise you?	我們有讓你驚喜嗎？
Congratulations!	恭喜！

情境對話 中文可對照上方的例句

Dialogue 1

Ⓐ Is this for real?

Ⓑ This is really happening!

Ⓐ I'm shocked!

Ⓑ You earned this.

Dialogue 2

Ⓐ I'm so surprised!

Ⓑ You deserve it.

Ⓐ I don't know what to say.

Ⓑ Congratulations!

情境 從英文來看外國人使用此肢體語言的情境

We got my grandma a new car for her birthday. She couldn't believe it. Her mouth fell open and her eyes got so wide. She was so surprised!

為了慶祝奶奶的生日，我們給她買了一台新車，她簡直不敢相信。她的嘴巴大張，眼睛睜得好大，她感到非常驚喜！

情境 4 Index and Middle Fingers Crossed 食指和中指交叉

這個手勢是指在人們面前伸出手臂,將手舉起,並把食指和中指交叉,形成「X」形,其他的手指通常會輕輕握成拳頭,手掌可以朝外或朝內。這是祝福人們好運的手勢,祈求的時候會使用。如果人們盼望某件事實現(例如:求職順利),他們就可能說 "Keep your fingers crossed for me."。

外國人的食指和中指交叉時,他們會說:

Cross your fingers!	祈求好運吧!
Keep your fingers crossed.	持續祈求好運吧。
My fingers are crossed!	我在祈求好運!
I'll cross my fingers.	我會祈求好運的。
Make a wish!	許個願!
I hope it comes true.	我希望這會成真。
I'll keep them crossed.	我會一直祈禱的。
I'm crossing them for you.	我為你祈求好運。
I have my fingers crossed.	我為你祈求好運。
Keep 'em crossed!	祝我好運!

外國人的食指和中指交叉時,你可以回:

I'll do it for you.	我會為你這麼做的。
I got them crossed!	我為你祈禱了!
They're crossed for you.	我為你祈禱著。
Good luck!	祝你好運!
You got this.	你沒問題的。
Thank you!	謝謝你!
I need all the luck I can get.	我需要所有我能得到的好運。
I'm hoping for a miracle.	我希望能有奇蹟出現。
I think it'll happen.	我認為這將會發生。
You're the best!	你是最棒的!

情境對話 中文可對照上方的例句

Dialogue 1

Ⓐ Keep your fingers crossed.
Ⓑ I got them crossed!
Ⓐ I need all the luck I can get.
Ⓑ You got this!

Dialogue 2

Ⓐ Make a wish!
Ⓑ I'm hoping for a miracle.
Ⓐ My fingers are crossed.
Ⓑ I need all the luck I can get.

情境 從英文來看外國人使用此肢體語言的情境

My brother applied for a new job in Arizona. He really hopes he gets it. I told him I'd keep my fingers crossed for him.

我弟弟在亞利桑那州應徵了一份新工作,他非常希望能得到那個工作,我告訴他,我會持續為他祈求好運的。

Kissing Fingertips 親吻手指頭

這個手勢是將食指按住拇指，親吻其他三個手指尖，或是拇指和食指，然後迅速將手指由嘴邊拉開。這是人們在跟別人談論美味佳餚時會用的一種手勢，如果他們在描述食物時用了這個手勢，就表示他們認為非常好吃。

外國人親吻手指頭時，他們會說：

It's amazing!	太好吃了！
I loved it!	我喜歡！
It tasted so good.	這真好吃。
It was the best.	那是最棒的。
I'll get that again.	我會再來吃一次。
I'll make that again.	我會再做一次。
I thought it was good.	我覺得它很好。
It was the best!	那是最棒的！
I loved the pasta!	我喜歡這盤義大利麵！
The cheesecake was amazing!	這個起司蛋糕超棒！

外國人親吻手指頭時，你可以回：

I'm glad you liked it!	我很高興你喜歡它！
I'm so happy.	我很高興。
I'm thrilled.	我很開心！
Good!	太好了！
Thanks.	謝謝。
You're so nice!	你人真好！
That's nice of you to say.	你這麼說真好。
You're thoughtful!	你真體貼！
I enjoyed it, too!	我也喜歡它！
You can say that again!	一點也沒錯！

情境對話 中文可對照上方的例句

Dialogue 1

Ⓐ How is it?
Ⓑ It's amazing!
Ⓐ I'm glad you liked it!
Ⓑ I loved it!

Dialogue 2

Ⓐ The cheesecake was amazing!
Ⓑ I enjoyed it, too!
Ⓐ I'll make that again.
Ⓑ Good!

情境 從英文來看外國人使用此肢體語言的情境

I made dinner for my friends last week. Everyone loved my lasagna! Sara even kissed her fingertips and said it was the best she's ever had.

上週我為朋友們做了晚餐。大家都愛上了我的千層麵！Sara 甚至吻了她的指尖，說這是她所吃過最好吃的千層麵。

情境 6

Pointing Nose in the Air and Sniffing
鼻子指向空氣、聞一下

這個動作是指頭向後仰,將鼻子指向天空。這麼做的人會深呼吸,表示他聞到了很棒的味道。很多人在外面聞到一些很香的食物時,就會做出這個動作。

外國人把鼻子指向空氣、聞一下時,他們會說:

Do you smell that?	你聞到了嗎?
What is that?	那是甚麼?
Is someone grilling?	有人在烤東西嗎?
Do I smell cookies?	我聞到的是餅乾嗎?
That smells amazing!	聞起來好香啊!
It smells like roses.	聞起來像是玫瑰。
I love this smell.	我喜歡這種味道。
What perfume is that?	那是甚麼香水?
Are you wearing cologne?	你有噴古龍水嗎?
Dinner smells great!	晚餐聞起來很香!

外國人把鼻子指向空氣、聞一下時,你可以回:

What is that?	那是甚麼?
That smells good!	聞起來好香!
Is that a steak?	那是牛排嗎?
I smell it, too.	我也聞到了。
I can almost taste it.	我幾乎都吃到這個味道了。
Thanks!	謝謝!
I think so.	我也這麼認為。
I don't know!	我不知道!
I hope you like it.	希望你喜歡。
I can't smell it.	我聞不到。

情境對話 中文可對照上方的例句

Dialogue 1

Ⓐ Do you smell that?
Ⓑ That smells good!
Ⓐ What is that?
Ⓑ Is that a steak?

Dialogue 2

Ⓐ What perfume is that?
Ⓑ I don't know!
Ⓐ It smells like roses.
Ⓑ I hope you like it.

情境 從英文來看外國人使用此肢體語言的情境

When we got to the festival, my dad put his nose in the air and breathed in deep. He said he could smell something grilling. One of the booths was grilling cheeseburgers and selling them. We each got one. They were delicious!

我們參加慶典時,我爸爸把鼻子朝向空氣、深吸了一口氣。他說他可以聞到燒烤的味道,其中有個攤位在賣現烤的起司漢堡,我們每個人都來了一個,真是好吃!

台灣廣廈 國際出版集團
Taiwan Mansion International Group

國家圖書館出版品預行編目（CIP）資料

秒懂老外，一句簡單英文就能通：200多種生活情境對話，一個
手勢、一句英文，英文溝通馬上完成！／白善燁著；談采薇譯.
-- 初版. -- 新北市：語研學院，2023.06
面；　公分
ISBN 978-626-97244-2-0
1.CST: 英語　2.CST: 會話　3.CST: 讀本

805.188   112005920

LA PRESS 語研學院
Language Academy Press

秒懂老外，一句簡單英文就能通
200多種生活情境對話，一個手勢、一句英文，英文溝通馬上完成！

作　者／白善燁　　　　　　　　　編輯中心編輯長／伍峻宏‧執行編輯／陳怡樺
譯　者／談采薇　　　　　　　　　封面設計／曾詩涵‧內頁排版／菩薩蠻數位文化有限公司
　　　　　　　　　　　　　　　　製版‧印刷‧裝訂／東豪‧弘億‧秉成

行企研發中心總監／陳冠蒨　　　線上學習中心總監／陳冠蒨
媒體公關組／陳柔彣　　　　　　數位營運組／顏佑婷
綜合業務組／何欣穎　　　　　　企製開發組／江季珊

發　行　人／江媛珍
法律顧問／第一國際法律事務所 余淑杏律師‧北辰著作權事務所 蕭雄淋律師
出　　　版／語研學院
發　　　行／台灣廣廈有聲圖書有限公司
　　　　　　地址：新北市235中和區中山路二段359巷7號2樓
　　　　　　電話：（886）2-2225-5777‧傳真：（886）2-2225-8052
讀者服務信箱／cs@booknews.com.tw

代理印務‧全球總經銷／知遠文化事業有限公司
　　　　　　地址：新北市222深坑區北深路三段155巷25號5樓
　　　　　　電話：（886）2-2664-8800‧傳真：（886）2-2664-8801
郵政劃撥／劃撥帳號：18836722
　　　　　　劃撥戶名：知遠文化事業有限公司（※單次購書金額未達1000元，請另付70元郵資。）

■ 出版日期：2023年06月
ISBN：978-626-97244-2-0　　　　版權所有，未經同意不得重製、轉載、翻印。